ABOMINATION

SECOND EDITION

KIMBRA SWAIN

CRIMSON SUN PRESS

Abomination: Path to Redemption Book 1, Second Edition©2018, Kimbra Swain / Crimson Sun Press, LLC

kimbraswain@gmail.com

Cover art by Jay Villalobos at Covers by Juan

Formatting by Crimson Sun Graphics

ISBN (paperback): 9781675608227

CHAPTER 1

ABIGAIL

I hid from the world for twenty years. Evil had found a way to destroy those I loved, in turn, destroying my determination. For almost all of my life, I'd fought evil with my supernatural abilities. Just when I thought I'd won; it reared its ugly head and demolished any happiness or hope I had.

Tucking myself away on my private island, I continued my work from a distance, thinking it was enough. It wasn't. That evil took my absence and turned it into opportunity to grow. Now, I had to make up for lost time, which as we all know, was impossible to do. But I had to try. The fate of the entire world depended upon it.

As I stood in the underground bunker that belonged to the Agency, I felt the power to strike back at that evil. My confidence grew as I watched the scene before me. Above my hand, four floating orbs twirled in a delicate dance. An orb of cold iron to strike at the heart of fairy and human alike. A ball of hollow steel to shape into whatever weapon I chose. A solid sphere of quartz to amplify any spell. A molten sun to represent the core of my power from a long line of magic wielders tied to the sun gods.

The bunker near Boulder, Colorado, housed the training facilities and main offices of Kenward, Blake, and Shanahan, Inc. Otherwise known as the Agency.

Standing behind a two-way glass, I watched the latest group of recruits training in our facility. The students stood in a large gymnasium lined with floor mats, performing the steps of a martial arts form or kata. Their instructor paced between the rows of students, calling out each step.

He was the reason I'd made the trip to the lower floors of the facility. He was my only hope of doing this right.

Tadeas Nahuel Duarte could correct a limp hand or false move by the students with the intensity of his eyes. The recruits strove for excellence out of fear and respect of their instructor. His dark green eyes were keen to each precise movement of the kata. Rarely did Mr. Duarte have a student that washed out of his classes. Most of his students proved to be the best Canvas Crew members that we had in the field. Once they passed his training, they would be thrust out into the real world where a kata might calm your mind, but it wouldn't save your life.

Standing next to my boss and mentor, I watched intently each move that he made. His strength hid behind his lean, muscular form. I knew what kind of power he harnessed within that frame. The Agency had adopted Mr. Duarte as a teenager and raised him within our facilities. He was born in Guatemala and was the best natural fighter I had ever seen. Since I'd lived for over one hundred years, the compliment wasn't bestowed lightly. I found him most interesting because of his instincts. I had studied him over the past two years. At first, it was a general curiosity of his teaching methods. As I watched him, my goals changed for myself and for Mr. Duarte.

He wore a black moisture-wick t-shirt, black cargo fatigues, and heavy combat boots. Each of the students was dressed in the same manner, but with a varying color scheme. His dark skin and black hair glistened with sweat from this class session. As a teacher, he believed in being as, or more active, in class than his students. It inspired the trainees to push harder for him. His natural leadership skills drew the students to him in a solid loyalty and trust. His treatment of his students and fellow instructors garnered him the highest respect. Occasionally, he came across a student who was more hard-headed than usual, but eventually, the stubborn teenager would find some inspiration in Mr. Duarte. He could tame even the wildest of recruits.

Training to be part of a Canvas Crew was a painful process, but absolutely necessary. Most of the students were orphans or teens we picked up off the streets. They came from all walks of life but had one thing in common, no future. We tried to give them one by giving them a purpose for the greater good of the world.

However, overall, the system that the Agency had built was failing. I had to admit my own failure in it because I had built it from scratch. The world was changing more rapidly than the Agency could handle. The world had become increasingly deadly and violent. Technology spurred forward intelligence and infiltrated all of our lives. You could not walk the sidewalk these days without bumping into someone texting or taking some self-absorbed picture to post on social media. We, as a company, needed to adapt to the times. I decided to take it upon myself to start making changes in our organization, as I had in the past. But lately, we were lagging behind and many changes still needed to be made.

Recently, I had started a whole new recruitment force for the Agency which focused solely on intelligence and technological warfare. The next world war wouldn't be fought on battlegrounds but through our ever-increasing digitalized world. I needed to make personal changes as well. I sat on the sidelines for close to twenty years, still doing my job but pretending that the way I did it was enough. Sadly, it wasn't, and it had taken me too long to realize that my involvement had to be more than mere observation. If I didn't make a personal change outside of my carefully crafted comfort zone, the Agency would suffer for it. In fact, it might even cease to exist.

Kenward, Blake, and Shanahan, Inc. was a multi-tiered global network established by Gregory Theodoard to monitor world financial, political, and social events focusing on the supernatural elements that may be involved. Theodoard, who was the Greek Titan Hyperion, started the network to complete his divine duties which included ensuring that the sun rose and set each day. In essence, his job was to keep the world turning. The Agency morphed with the ages, and its latest restructuring started in 1918 when I set out to revamp it to modern times. I took the responsibility for adapting the network as society and technology became more advanced.

The orbs continued to swirl above my palm as Mr. Duarte made his final remarks to the students, then released them for the day. Even though most of them left to shower and rest, several approached him requesting further instruction on fighting techniques. The program demanded the students' physical and mental acuity. Along with the physical training, we put them through rigorous weapons and computer training. Mr. Duarte spoke to each of them sternly but remained open to their inquiries to better themselves. I noticed a woman entering the classroom. Mr. Duarte didn't acknowledge her, but I knew he sensed her presence in the way he changed his posture. She waited silently beside the outer door.

At this point, the grey-haired man standing next to me asked, "Are you sure about this, Abby?"

"No. But at this point, I can no longer stand on this side of the glass simply watching him. I need to interact to get a feel for who he really is. I cannot take this lightly," I replied to Gregory Theodoard, President, and CEO of KBS, Inc.

"It's been twenty years. Why now?" he asked. It was not an authoritative question, but a question of concern. Mainly because he was my grandfather. Well, not my grandfather immediate, but more like great, great, great, and so on, grandfather. He's existed from the beginning of time. He's gone by many names, but his task has always been the same. He watches the world and makes sure in some existential way that it keeps turning. There have been threats to the world beyond the human wars and pestilence that have broken out over the centuries. It's our job to prevent those things from happening. Recently he confided in me that he could feel the tension escalating again. We haven't had a global threat since the vampire uprising in 1964.

"You gave me this task and I...."

"You volunteered. Don't put this on me," he cut me off.

"Yes, I volunteered. I even brought the whole thing up, but you know as well as I do that it needs to be done. And this is how I've chosen to proceed," I stated, yet still unsure that this was the right approach.

His brow furrowed because he knew I was just as stubborn as he was. I had very little family in this world, and he was one of them. He had plenty of offspring floating around the globe. Most of them didn't even realize their bloodline would trace back to a Greek Titan, but nonetheless, he and his fellow gods had seeded the earth with their offspring in order to fill it not only with the plain human population, but also to create those exceptional beings. Great artists, scientists, charismatic leaders, religious inspirations, great warriors not just on battlefields but on fields of play, each of them given a bit of that special something.

He turned to face me. Ignoring him, I continued to face toward the two-sided glass. Mr. Duarte talked to the final student while the woman waited for him on the back wall. I sighed seeing her there. If

I was going to do this, she was going to cause me problems. I felt it in my bones. Then I turned to meet my grandfather's bright blue eyes. He had waited for my full attention, well, as much of it as he could get at any given moment. I tilted my head waiting for his response.

"Abigail, I trust your judgment, as I always have. But I won't lie to you that I'm not concerned about your approach. There has to be an easier, more truthful, way." I started to retort, but the look in his eye and a slight raise of his hand at his waist caused me to clamp my mouth shut and just listen. It was rare that he showed any sort of emotion. Especially concern or even love. "You are my greatest child."

Those words struck me. In recent years, he hadn't shown that much pride or love in me. I knew he loved me, but it was never a spoken thing. He always pushed me harder and harder. To be better, to see more, to discern between the light and the darkness. He made me who I was.

"I never want to see harm come to you, but this world is changing. I need you more than ever to help keep it safe, but I will admit some selfishness in that for the past twenty years you have been by my side here. You have been safely hidden from our enemies. I don't like the idea of you going back out into the fray. However, I know it is necessary. Do this as you will, but remember, that I warned you that this was the wrong approach." And with that, he turned and left the room.

Somewhere in the middle of his admission, I had crossed one of my arms in front of my body, an involuntary reaction to his outpouring of concern, but maintained the balance of the orbs in the other hand. His admission made me uncomfortable and peaceful all at the same time. I was Abigail Davenport, a daughter of Hyperion, a descendant of Helios, and a wielder of magic. It was time I got off my ass and used my talents as they were meant to be used.

Turning back to the window, I watched Mr. Duarte walking to the door of the training room with the woman. They spoke, and she smiled at him. He reached to flip out all the lights in the room and held the door open for her to exit. And as the door shut and the room went completely dark, I resolved myself at that moment to continue with my plan. The time had arrived for me to step out from behind the mirror and act. I closed my palm, and the orbs disappeared.

CHAPTER 2

VANESSA

Somewhere in the backwoods of Mississippi, a group of businessmen and women gathered to watch a demonstration. A demonstration of power like they had never seen. I was willing to bet they didn't know such power existed. Eighteen of the most influential money movers in the world who had shared interests joined together to watch an experiment that was intended to change the world. Our group, Geo-Enhancement Alliance, needed funding. Lots of it. We brought these people out here to demonstrate our abilities.

As an assistant to John Mwenye, his apprentice actually, I'd seen the world from east to west. But more importantly, I'd seen it from light to darkness. Mr. Mwenye and I were some of the darkest beings on the planet.

"Miss Vaughn, are we ready for the test?" Mr. Mwenye asked. I looked up from my monitors and instruments and nodded to him. Standing in the midst of the potential investors, he began his welcoming speech. We were in the middle of nowhere as we intended. We desired no attention from the authorities, human or otherwise. Since a light rain fell, the investors had small black umbrellas to hide under, except for one man who stood as if the sun were shining. They all watched Mwenye closely as he talked, the forest muted around us.

Together, Mwenye and I had worked on this project and found that even with our resources we would need more people to get the project kick-started. Through our mutual friends in the alliance, we had come up with twenty names of potential investors. Two of those declined our offer to view the experiment. A group of four scientists stood behind me. They were the top in the world in geological studies. Most of them focused their research on mining and fracking.

We stood in the center of a clearing in the dense pine forest. The clearing was about 50 yards wide at its largest point. It would be the safest place to be for this particular demonstration. After Mr. Mwenye greeted all of them, he nodded to me. I picked up an insulated silver case at my feet. Slowly walking toward him, I was sure not to jostle the case. He gently took it from me, placing it on the ground at his feet. He was over 6 feet tall and slender. His jawline drew a sharp edge from ear to chin with dark midnight brown eyes. His ice- cold gaze met mine, so I bent down next to him as he opened the case. Muttering a few words, he lifted the silver orb out of the case using a levitation spell. The orb hung in the air in front of him, as the rain splashed all around it making the magical field around it visible. I picked up the empty case, then walked back to my position outside the ring of investors. Mr. John Mwenye, the world's most renowned Necromancer, was the most powerful magic wielder I had ever met. It was my honor to be his student and lover. For almost 50 years, I had followed him around the world. He gave me the gift of eternal youth, which he had discovered the secret of many years ago. He blessed me by sharing it with me. He looked to be in his mid-thirties, however, I knew he was well over 200 years old.

As he explained the element to those around him, I conjured a small spell of protection around our little gathering. It was a basic thin ring around the entire group stretching about ten feet off the ground like an invisible barrier to outside forces. The rain still poured down from above, but I had no need to block it. The danger would not come from above. What we were about to attempt would be large enough to impress our guests, but not large enough to draw any outside attention. This would be the fourth and final test of our theory, as well as a demonstration to show those here the product of 45 years of research and planning. As I locked eyes with him again, he nodded giving the go ahead.

"Now, my friends," he spoke in the disjointed yat dialect of a man who grew up in New Orleans, "Please steady yourselves for the test." He put his hands in the air, calling skyward in Mobilian, an ancient dead language spoken by the Native American inhabitants of this area of the United States. Its last known usage was around the time the French settled in New Orleans. I wasn't sure where he had learned it, but he cast most of his spells in the language. For whatever reason, he refused to teach me the forgotten language. There were many things he refused to teach me despite my devotion and dedication to our cause and craft.

Below his feet, a small hole opened up by his command. Throwing his hands down like slamming a shovel into the ground, the orb dashed down into the hole as the earth closed above it. The crowd stood in silence for a few moments. Holding my protection spell in place, they looked around waiting for something to happen. Mwenye stood staring at the ground, ignoring their doubts. The potential investors mumbled to each other as nothing happened. I knew it would take longer than their patience would allow, but the payoff would be worth it in the end. The less they believed now, the more the impact of the demonstration would make when concluded. A couple of them gathered, speaking in low tones. I concentrated on hearing them even though they whispered.

"Looks like Mwenye has finally gone crackpot on us," one of them said to the other.

"I can't believe they dragged us out here to the middle of Podunkville, for nothing," the other said. Turning away from the circle of people, they walked back to where we had parked their cars. It wasn't my fault they were walking outside my protection spell. I made no effort to move the spell to protect them. We gave clear instructions at the beginning for everyone to stay within our circle.

Then I felt it, a small rumble, intensifying. One of the women gasped. The man next to her tried not to fall as the ground started to shake. Holding my spell in place, I watched as panic took over the faces of those inside the circle. Mwenye still focused on the ground below him, moving his lips in a silent rhythm. The two men outside my protective area stopped in their tracks, turning back to look at the group. Across the clearing, I saw half dozen trees fall inward to the field.

I continued to hold my spell in anticipation of the finale which was quickly approaching. The ground shook harder. They tried to steady themselves by bracing one another. My computer was locked to its table, but the whole table shook. The four scientists behind me supported each other. To the east of us, a large crack started to form in the earth, racing its way toward us. The crack headed straight for the two men outside the protective barrier. As the earth opened beneath them, they knew they were doomed. They could not even scream before it swallowed them into the earth.

The crack raced toward the group, and some started screaming. Mwenye looked up to all of them and said in Latin, "*Pacem. Sile.*" The group calmed as the crack reached the edge of the barrier. I would have loved to release the spell, and let the earth swallow them all, but we, unfortunately, needed them. Mostly, we needed their money. The element we used was highly volatile and extremely expensive. Once we obtained enough of it, we could enact a larger plan that would, in turn, provide these jerks the opportunity to make more money. As the crack reached the edge of the barrier, the earth ceased to shake. The fissure stopped about 3 inches short of the barrier. I released the spell and sagged a bit from the effort. When Mwenye nodded to me, I thought for a moment it was approval of my protection spell, however, I quickly realized he was only looking for the Richter reading of the earthquake.

"3.7," I said, looking down at my computer.

And in his smarmy manner, Mwenye waved his hand in front of him and said, "And that my friends, is how you awaken a dead fault line."

THE GEOLOGIST AND I GATHERED OUR EQUIPMENT, THEN WALKED back to the cars. Mr. Mwenye had given the investors a week to decide whether they were in or out. Since he spoke to several of them individually, I hoped that we had some that wanted in immediately. It would ease the pressure on him which would ease it on me as well. Overall, the demonstration seemed to be a success. Only time would tell. As we pulled away in the black Chrysler, I looked back to see two other black cars parked on the old dirt road. Their occupants would not be returning, which made me smile. How dare they question Mr. Mwenye's power?

"You should have adjusted your protections," he said quietly.

"They should not have called you crazy," I said.

"My dear, lest you forget, I am crazy," he replied.

"No, Sir, you are brilliant and a genius. Besides, I think it added to the demonstration," I smirked, yet hoped he appreciated my efforts to exonerate him.

Turning to look at me, his eyes from the pupil to the sclera turned black. "Dead men have no money to give to our research, and they were there at my request. I'll have you remember, Miss Vaughn, that I have a reputation to keep. You keep your petty ideals out of my life's work. If you ever do that again, I will make you *mine*."

I shivered, moving away from him. To be a man that I admired, he knew how to scare me. Looking up to the front of the car, I saw the driver's eye cut back to us. The driver was *his*. Mwenye had found a way to pull the life out of a human just to the point where they would still live, but all of their life force would be consumed by him. They were no better than zombie slaves. I'm not even sure what you'd call them. Thralls didn't quite cover it. He owned them by commanding their bodies through their souls inside him. It corrupted him more with each life he took, but it also made him extremely powerful.

He idly twisted the snake ring on his finger. The ring was an exquisitely carved black metal. The eyes of the snake were blood red and sparkling. With just a few words, he could rip my soul out of me, the beginning of a whole new torture the likes of which I had never known.

"Yes Sir, of course," I said submitting to his authority over me, "I apologize. It will never happen again."

"See that it doesn't," he said coolly. "Now come over here and make me a happy man."

I cringed at his request. There were days I loved him. However, there were days when he had exerted power that he hungered for more. Using power like the protection spell sucked the energy out of me. I could not feed off the power of other people as he did, or at least I hadn't tried yet. Whenever he used it like he did today, he thrived. Right now, the power consumed him radiating darkness around us in a black quagmire. His soul was the darkest I knew, and I loved and revered it. Crawling over to him, I pulled my skirt up around my waist. He smiled with his obsidian eyes, knowing that no matter how he treated me, that I would always serve his needs. His dark brown hands slid up my legs, pushing the skirt up further. I felt the coolness of the ring slide along my skin. I straddled him and did my best to make him happy.

CHAPTER 3

ABIGAIL

*M*y ribs exploded in pain like they were on fire. The burning sensation exclaimed loud and clear what a monumentally bad idea this had turned out to be. Feeling the copper taste rise in my mouth, I spat blood onto the mat, then realized my mistake too late.

"I know you did not just spit blood on my mat!" Mr. Duarte yelled. I felt his imposing form hovering over me. Leaning down over me, his breath brushed hotly against my cheek. "Get up and go again."

Wearily, I rose to my feet, taking the defensive first stance he had just shown me. I leaned forward on my toes waiting for my opponent's next move. My opponent, a beefy man, was much larger than me. The fight was a mismatch, but that was the purpose of the exercise. I was above average height at 5'9 but this joker was 6'3 at least and had a good 100 lbs. on me. He was fast, skilled, and showed no emotion. He had beat the crap out a woman, yet he showed no remorse.

It was the way we at the Agency taught all men. And women for that matter. No emotion. No remorse. If a confrontation on the streets escalated to a physical fight, one could not afford to have a heart or compassion. Mr. Duarte remained close to the fight, hovering in his intimidating manner. I had to dismiss that if I wanted to at least make it look like I was competent which was essential to staying in the program.

If I were being completely honest, I could squash this over-sized bug in a moment, but that wasn't the game I was playing. I had taken a spot in the Agency's new class of trainees pretending to be a street orphan who had no clue how to fight or protect herself. I don't know whose brilliant idea it was to get beat to hell on a daily basis. Oh, yes, that was my brilliant, stupid, idiotic idea. Just as grandfather had said so many weeks ago.

My opponent took several offensive strikes at me as I defended each one of them in turn. But he sped up his steps as Duarte urged him on, and I let myself get tangled up in my own footwork only to catch another cross against my chin, hitting the mat hard with a pronounced thud. The room spun, fading to black. I faintly heard him yell, "Get up, Rachel!" before completely passing out.

I WOKE UP ALONE ON THE MAT IN THE DARK, REALIZING THEY didn't even help me to the infirmary this time. Usually, I woke up there. I hoisted myself up, trying to play the part of the poor, injured girl even though my bruises had already started to heal. As my head cleared, I wobbled toward the door.

Scanning the room in the darkness, a shadow leaning against the far wall caught my eye.

"Don't leave until you've cleaned your blood off my mat," he said. I could hear the disappointment in his voice. It wasn't just the blood that irritated him. It was my performance as well.

I bowed my head in respect to him as he approached me. "Yes, Sir. I'm sorry."

"Don't be sorry, Rachel. Get better. Your life depends upon it," he said, walking up to me as if he had more to say. His presence loomed over me for a moment, then he brushed past me moving toward the door. The slight touch sent a shiver down my body.

I walked over to the light switches to turn on the lights. There were several splats of blood where I had lain. One of them was smeared. I realized my cheek was covered in blood from where my face had rested on the mat. I grabbed some supplies from the closet and began to clean the mess.

Before entering the program, I had my grandfather bind my magic, so I would not be tempted to use it. I didn't want to give myself a way out. He would be close by watching if I ever needed it released. I wanted to be on equal footing with the students to get the full experience of being under the instruction of Tadeas Durate. Even in the mundane task of cleaning a floor, I couldn't use my magic. The lights flicked on behind the two-sided glass revealing my grandfather with a grave look on his face. I nodded to him in reassurance. He flicked the light back off, but I could feel his disapproval radiating toward me even without my magic.

Magic was like blood to me. It's been a part of me since birth. It flowed through me, influencing every move and decision I made. I struggled without it now. Thankfully, a long life of experience helped me through this experiment. Most wielders don't come into their talents until puberty, but mine had been there from the first moment I could remember. I was different from most wielders because of that early manifestation of power. Perhaps caused by some diluted form of grandfather's blood flowing through my bloodline. Perhaps one of my unknown parents had bestowed the gift upon me. None of those things I knew for sure. All I knew is that it filled me, consuming my very being. Plus, I was extremely good at wielding it. A natural.

Wielders go by all sorts of names. Mages, witches, wizards, and druids were of the light variety. The darker wielders usually went with warlocks, sorcerers and various -mancers. I never seemed to identify with any of them. They were all governed by a group of stuck up pricks who called themselves The Conjurer's Association. And for the most part, if you had any sort of magic, they knew you, making sure that you knew them. Within this elite group, there was an even more elusive entity called the Fraternity of Magic. The FOMs were Master Wizards. Most had been around for ages, and in none of that time did they ever feel the need to lower themselves to humanity's standards save one, Jasper Samara, who taught me to harness the inherent power in me. They had their own set of laws and expected the rest of the magic world to follow them.

However, I fell under my grandfather's authority which made me virtually untouchable by them. My activities with The Agency were noble, and although I didn't give a second thought to the TCA or the FOMs, I tried to work within their expectations as to not cause any friction between them and The Agency. In fact, The Agency employed a great number of wielders of different sorts. All of us followed the rules that they established to keep the attention away from ourselves and our activities, and the TCA out of our daily operations.

I finished cleaning the floor, making sure I left no blood behind. Leaving blood with open access could cause problems for me if it fell into the wrong hands, but here in the training center, everything was greatly controlled by the magical entities that controlled the Agency. I didn't worry too much about that sort of thing here. After returning all the cleaning supplies to their storage, I turned off the lights to slowly make my way back to the sleeping quarters.

The trainee quarters were a typical barrack style. Bunk beds to sleep in with trunks to hold personal items. The rooms were not segregated by gender. So, most of the time I saw far more of my fellow students than I wanted to, but generally, I kept to myself, keeping my eyes down. I didn't want to make friends. That would cause problems for my real reason for being in the training center in the first place. Grabbing a clean set of clothes from my trunk, I headed toward the showers.

Each shower head had its own stall, but it didn't have a curtain or privacy from the traffic in the shared restrooms. I hated this part more than anything. Undressing quickly, I turned the water on. I tuned out all the surrounding sounds and focused on getting cleaned up as quickly as possible. My thoughts drifted back to my shower at home with its massive space and multiple shower heads. I missed home badly. Home. My safe haven. My thoughts drifted to the island with its caretaker.

"Hey, you are alive." A female voice behind me interrupted my solitude. I only grunted in response. "Aw, come on Rachel. At least he didn't kick you out of the program."

"He probably will soon enough. By the way, thanks for leaving me out there knocked out and bleeding," I replied. I hated the way we did things, especially in regard to getting kicked out of the program. When you were kicked out, The Agency dropped you back out on the streets to fend for yourself. It motivated the students, but over the years, I'd seen so many people wash out, only to read their obituaries later. There would be some small blurb about the homeless teenager that overdosed on drugs or got killed in a gang fight. I wanted to change that—among other things—about our program. Ultimately, that was my goal here. It was the beginning of big changes in the way we did things.

Turning off the water, I turned to face Samantha Taylor, my bunkmate. She slept on the top bunk, except when she shared a bunk with one of the guys, which was pretty often. I found that the trainees found comfort or worked out aggression with each other in a sexual manner. She was a wiry 5'7. Her dark hair was cut to her chin and straight. The Agency had picked her up in Seattle from a homeless shelter. She'd been in trouble for prostitution and theft. I know that, like many of our recruits, she had done what she had needed to do to survive on the streets after running away from her home. The best I could tell her parents weren't bad people. No abuse or any such thing. She was just a rebellious teen. Once she had decided to go back home, it was too late. Her parents were killed in a car accident. Tragedy filled the stories of my classmates. I had my own stories, but they seemed far removed from the fresh hell most of these kids were living in, in this ever-changing world.

"He wouldn't let us help you." She handed me the towel as a look of concern crossed her face, "You are really bruised up this time. Rachel, I hate seeing you go through this. Maybe if you talk to him, he can find a way to get you out of the program and do something else around here. Surely they need kitchen help or cleaning people."

I waved my hands at her assertion. She had no way of knowing who I was or why I was here. I said, "No, no. I either do this or I wash out. I will get it. I promise. I think I did better today." I knew that I hadn't on purpose.

"Rach, you got knocked out. That's not better."

"He was ten times bigger than me," I protested.

"Yeah, well on the streets you will find guys bigger than Travis, and they won't go easy on you."

"You think he went easy on me?" I said.

"Yes. Well, he tried, but Mr. Duarte kept urging him on. Finally, instead of getting his own ass kicked, I suppose he decided it was better to finish you off."

"It was a mercy knockout?" I said, realizing it was true.

"Something like that." She looked at her feet with the admission.

I frowned. Perhaps I'd played this weakling deal up too much. I'd have to start slowly showing that I was somewhat competent just to finish my mission here which became more and more complicated by the day. My purpose entering the program was to observe first-hand how Tadeas Duarte taught our recruits. Even though I could be his star pupil, I wanted to be the one that would wash out. Because he rarely had a washout, I wanted to see how he would react to my failure. As my time in the class passed, I could tell he became progressively frustrated with me. As his student, I showed him all the proper respect. However, my intentional lack of performance gave him no hope that I would progress beyond his class. He had handled it very well so far. Sometimes he even instructed me one on one, trying to inspire my performance. His instruction was spot on every time, but I failed to apply it. He had tried threats, searching for a way to make me competent enough to pass the course. Because at The Agency, we gave our instructors not only the praise for producing the canvas crews that we put on the streets, but we also held them responsible for taking the washouts back out to the streets. We expected it to be an agonizing ride to drop someone back out on the streets with nothing.

Rather than placing blame for a failing student, the expulsion was a test of the instructor's fortitude and emotional state. If an instructor started to exhibit no remorse for losing students, we removed him from the training center. We wanted our instructors to be brutal and forceful. However, a lack of emotions indicated that the instructor had grown immune and disconnected from the very lives that we were trying to save. Those who became detached were found other positions within the Agency.

Duarte hadn't had a washout in years until me. Every time he looked at me I knew that it bothered him greatly. Yet today was the first time as he yelled in my ear that I had heard a bit of desperation in his voice. It pained me to put him through it, but I needed to know if he was exactly what I looked for going forward with my plan for the future of The Agency. I had come to the conclusion that he was exactly what we needed.

I wrapped the towel around me and walked into the cold concrete barracks toward our bunk, "Look, Sam," I turned to face her as she followed me, "I will do better tomorrow. You will see. I know I can do this."

"Yeah sure, Rach," she replied with the utmost lack of confidence, "You should eat, but I warn you, those bruises aren't pretty."

"Hoodie it is," I replied.

"Good idea," she said as she turned to follow Travis and some of the others from our class out the door. They were heading to the cafeteria to eat. Our sessions were over for the day. After dinner, most of the students would use the downtime to sleep. The training was physically demanding. Some watched television or played video games in the social room while others found more *nocturnal* activities to pass the time.

I planned to go eat, then head back to one of the dark training rooms to gather my thoughts and go through my forms. I took that private time to center myself, focusing on my goals for this endeavor and working through potential issues.

Slipping the navy hoodie over my head, I tied my blonde hair up in a ponytail. My stomach rumbled loudly. I hadn't eaten much since I started this farce 3 months ago. The typical class was 6 months, depending on the needs of the canvas crews. The food here wasn't that great. Cafeteria style offerings. I usually hit the salad bar, but occasionally went for some pasta for the carbs. Today I needed protein. I had to heal up all the bruises I had accrued during the last session. Normally I did this magically, but now I relied solely on the healing qualities of my not completely human body. By the time I got to the cafeteria, it bustled with many students. The clamor gave me a pounding headache. It was my goal to eat quickly, then get out.

The Agency would have 4 to 6 classes going at any time, and

most at different stages of the process. Each class had anywhere from 12 to 20 students depending on who and how many recruits we could gather up. We didn't rank them or try to put them in certain groups. We never told them where they stood until they got their assignments or got their ride back out to the streets.

I grabbed a burger with bacon and cheese and a plate of fries. My starving stomach growled with pleasure at the smells. The beating had taken more out of me than I realized. This whole mundane living was ridiculous. I chuckled at my conceited self as I sat down alone at a table close to the side door. There were several entrances to the cafeteria, but I always instinctively positioned myself close to a door. Fights were known to break out, and I wanted no part of that sort of thing. If you started a fight anywhere except on the mats, you automatically washed out. Therefore, the Agency required all the instructors to eat with the students to enforce the rules. Well, not eat with them per se, we were all in the same room. The instructors all ate at one table, and we all knew the unwritten rule not to sit at that table. I kept my head down and methodically ate my burger and fries. I tried not to go too fast, but I was anxious to get out of the room. I needed to start planning my next moves.

Suddenly, a dark shadow covered my plate, and someone sat down with a tray across from me. I looked up to meet the dark green eyes of Tadeas Duarte. I stopped chewing the mouthful of burger I had just bitten off, staring back at him. A million things ran through my mind as to why he was seated with me. Most of all, it would draw attention that I certainly did not want. I must have looked displeased because he immediately started explaining himself.

"Miss Bennett, I don't mean to disturb you outside of class, but I feel compelled to talk to you about today's session."

I finished chewing my burger, picked up a fry, and started twirling it in ketchup. I didn't want to appear too interested in what he was saying. But I was *very interested*. The instructors hardly ever spoke to the students outside the training rooms. It was outside his comfort zone as well as everyone else's in the room. More than a few people took notice of him sitting across from me. Ignoring the murmurs, I pretended not to care.

"Would you please stop that and look at me for a minute? Let me have my say, then I will be on my way," he pushed. There was an urgency in his voice, but also care and concern. The same desperation I'd heard from him in the fight with Troy.

"Okay," I responded. Dropping the fry, I folded my hands under my chin and looked him in the eye, giving him my full attention. However, I made clear to him I couldn't care less. Or perhaps I didn't. He watched me trying to figure out my expressions. I had confused him completely to the point that I was confused myself. Something in his caring stare unsettled me by tugging at my heart.

"I have tried every way I know how to keep you from washing out. I've tried all sorts of approaches and none of it works. You do understand what happens when someone washes out right?" he paused and looked at me. I didn't respond, continuing to watch him while forcing a blank expression. He pushed his tray of food to the side and put his elbows on the table to use his hands while he talked. It was one of his more endearing characteristics. I don't think he could carry on any sentence without hand movement. Someone must have chided him on it because he fought the urge to use his hands to speak when he was in class with us. Realizing it now, he clasped his hands in front of his forehead leaning toward me in frustration. "I want everyone to succeed, but it seems like you, for whatever reason, have no desire to complete the program. Please tell me why that is, and if that's the case, I will stop wasting my time trying to help you."

Ashamed of myself, I broke eye contact with him. While he invested his time and emotions into training me, I was here playing games with him. He genuinely wanted me to succeed, and I mocked his efforts. As a general rule, my admiration and respect for an instructor who excelled in his field drove me not to fail him or lose his regard. This time, though, it was part of my charade. I remember my own magical training. I excelled mostly in part because I never wanted to let my master down. "I do want to complete the program," I muttered, hoping to provide him with some clarity.

He growled slightly in frustration and caught himself. "Then perhaps you can tell me why you are holding back?" he said flatly.

My eyes shot up to his dark green stare. How in the world had he known that I held back my skills? It was impossible. I had played this to the hilt. His instincts were phenomenal, but I didn't think they were that good.

"I don't know what you mean," I denied as truthfully as I could. But I felt like a fly caught in a web as the spider closed in on me for the kill.

"I've watched your every move, and I know you are holding back, Rachel!" He stopped, waiting for me to explain myself. Crap. I hadn't planned for this. Especially at this stage of the process. While impressed with his observation of me, it frustrated me, because I couldn't understand how he had picked up on it. I made sure I only used the most basic of fight sequences and mostly defensive ones at that. But he *knew* I was a far better fighter than I led him and everyone else to believe. I could see it in his eyes. He knew that I was pretending, but he didn't understand why.

Panic set in my body, and I reacted quickly. "I'm sorry, Mr. Duarte. I know I'm failing, but I really am trying my best. Please excuse me." Stammering through the lie, I hadn't convinced him. Jumping up from my seat, I grabbed my tray then dropped it off at the wash station. Slipping out the side door, I heard the door close behind me with a click. I rushed to the nearest corridor, ducking around a corner to see if he would follow me. I waited for a second with my back against the wall breathing heavily.

Laughing at myself because my anxiety and adrenaline reached a peak when I had been caught in my lie, I took a deep breath to compose myself, closing my eyes. When I opened them, he stood before me with his arms crossed.

"Oh, bloody hell," I spouted as his sudden appearance startled me. I almost lost grip on the British accent that I concealed so that I could play the part of a wayward American teenager. I hadn't heard him when he approached which was part of his skills and why I was interested in him in the first place. The sneaky bastard.

A male student rounded the other end of the hallway from the barracks and saw us standing there. I don't know what he thought, but he turned on his heel, scurrying back the way he came. Duarte stepped closer to me. He wasn't going to let me bolt again. His dark eyes flicked to an almost yellow color. The change caught me off guard. I knew about his abilities, but he didn't know I knew about them. Reading my expression, he gritted his teeth and closed his eyes. When he opened them again, they were the dark green color I expected them to be.

Tadeas Nahuel Duarte was a shifter. Stories of were-beings had existed for years, but very few of the stories were factual. While some of the details were just myth, the truth was that these shifting baddies did exist in our world. Duarte descended from a long line of Mayan Jaguar Guardian shifters. He was born in a village in Guatemala to a mother with no husband. The village people beat her to death for her sins, throwing him as an infant into the jungle. Fortunately, some passing missionaries found him and took him back to the nearest Catholic Church, where a Guatemalan family adopted him. They returned him to the church just after his sixth birthday for no reason that the Agency could discover. In Duarte's file, he simply stated that he didn't remember why his family returned him. The priests kept him at that point, raising him to one day take orders as a priest in the church. There are years in his past where I have no definite information on what exactly happened to him. But instead of taking orders, he fell in love with a local girl and proposed to her. Before they were married, he shifted for the first time and tragically replaced his source of hope. At the time, he was in his late teens. It was very late in life to face that initial shift. Most shifters change for the first-time during puberty, much like when wielders manifest magic. He should have shifted before that time, but I had no records indicating that he had prior to killing his fiancée. Eventually, he came to The Agency via my former partner, Lincoln. Duarte had thrived here as an instructor of canvas crews for many years.

In the past in Guatemala, a village would welcome the arrival of a guardian shifter. The teen would be paired up with the local magic wielder, in this case, a shaman. The pair protected the village from all sorts of entities that might seek to harm its inhabitants. I never found the true story of why they cast him out as an infant, but he was born in a time when missionaries were starting to infiltrate some of the outlying villages in the Central Americas. I had to think the two things were related. Perhaps the village felt like their newfound faith didn't support the tradition of a guardian. Perhaps because of the influence of the Catholic religion, there was no longer a shaman in the village to train him. Either way, it started a long, sad story for the beginning of Duarte's life. He had overcome it here in the training center. He had made something of himself, passing his knowledge and skills on to each new generation of Agency fighters. I knew by watching him over the past two years that he wanted that same victory for every single student that came into his training.

I didn't have a lot of time to decide how to handle this. I started asking the questions to deflect, "Why do you think I'm holding back?"

"I don't know why. Please enlighten me," his frustration edged his voice. This was not going well for me. He could have me removed from the program immediately if I didn't handle this correctly, and all the work I'd done up until this point would have been for nothing. I may have ruined any chance to recruit him to my cause simply by lying to him. He stepped closer, leaving no room between us. I shivered at how close he was to me.

Get your head on straight, Abigail Davenport, I told myself.

I closed my eyes tightly because I couldn't look at him. I think I might have instinctively flinched like I intended to run, but he slammed his hand against the concrete wall not allowing me to move to my left. I hadn't planned on running, but I couldn't now if I wanted. "I'm sorry," I stammered.

"Stop fucking apologizing and answer me, Rachel." He had used my first name outside of class. Instructors never used first names. Plus, he cussed, which I'd never heard him do in front of students. His patience with me had evaporated.

"I meant; not why, but how do you know I'm holding back?" I stammered through the sentence because he intimidated me.

"Rachel, I've been here in Boulder for over 20 years teaching students. I've seen a lot of washouts, especially in those early days. But I have never once seen someone like you who purposefully let herself get beat to a pulp on a daily basis. Is it some sort of weird kinky thing? Or some sort of self-loathing? I don't know, but I know you are capable of a lot more than you are letting on. A whole lot more."

This little speech made me think he was grasping at straws. One last ditch effort to figure it out. That he really didn't know I was holding back. I admired him for caring enough to push me this hard. That he would step out of the norm to confront a failing student in the effort to better their lives. I had no doubt his intentions were of the truest nature. He wanted me to succeed. It wasn't simply because he had such a flawless record that could be broken. Duarte didn't want to see any of us thrust out on the streets again. The tension between us couldn't have gotten any thicker. I didn't know how to respond. I think he took my indecision as fear and stepped away from me. Opening my eyes to meet his emerald anticipation, his stare pleaded with me to give him some explanation.

I took the opportunity to get away to think things over, "I promise," I said, "tomorrow will be different." I turned as fast as I could, hurrying toward the bunk room. I shot a glance back at him as I turned the corner, and he had put his hand back on the wall almost as if he held himself up.

It was quiet, but I heard him mutter, "It's your last chance, Rachel." My steps faltered for a moment, but I picked my pace back up. Tears welled up in my eyes. I was just playing the part, right? The poor helpless runaway who couldn't fight and was about to be kicked back on the streets. Rachel cried. Not Abigail. Oh hell, I hated this. What in the world was I thinking getting myself in this position? Perhaps grandfather was right. No, I knew the answer to that one. Grandfather was right, and I'd lose Duarte in the process.

I RUSHED TO THE NEAREST TRAINING ROOM, SLIPPING INSIDE AS quietly as possible. I tried to compose myself. Occasionally, I'd find a couple making out or having sex, but training rooms were unlike the other areas since they were restricted to training only. The Agency didn't care what you did in the dorms or the closets or the bathrooms as long as it was consensual and not in a training area. Thankfully, the room was empty. I didn't bother to turn on the lights. Even with my magic bound up, I could still feel the room by memory. All the training rooms were the same. Large empty spaces with a central training mat and hardwood floors on the outside. Stepping three paces forward, I felt my footing change to the mat. Taking off my shoes, I sat down on the mat with my legs crossed. I took deep breaths to calm myself from the confrontation with Duarte. Meditation was never a comfort for me because my brain never stopped. However, I needed to organize my thoughts and decide if he truly had some instinct that I held back or if he was just grasping at straws. It would make a difference in how I responded tomorrow in order to stay in the class and reach my ultimate goal in recruiting Duarte for my purposes. I came to the conclusion based on his frustration and his attempt to corral me in the hallway, it was desperation. In the next few days if I showed a little improvement each day then maybe he would settle down and not get worked up enough to kick me out.

Standing up, I took a position in the center of the mat. In the darkness, I repeated all the forms I had learned in my lifetime, mixing them together to create whole new patterns to reflect my thoughts, conforming then realigning to a new goal. Concentrating on the kata would clear my head in order to prepare myself for tomorrow, and finally decide how to approach what I'd do.

CHAPTER 4

TADEAS

*A*s I returned to the cafeteria, I picked my tray up from where Miss Bennett had sat and approached the instructor's table. Several of them gave me incredulous looks. Meredith didn't though. She looked slightly pained. After a few minutes of trying to eat in the silence, I gave up and headed back to my small apartment on the second floor. Halfway up the stairs, Meredith entered below, calling out to me, "Tadeas, wait up."

Slowing my pace, I allowed her to catch up. Meredith was a friend. Most of the instructors and I didn't get along, but she was different. We had tried some years ago to have a relationship beyond friends, but I feared ever having that kind of connection with anyone. Consequently, I broke it off. It hurt her feelings, but we agreed to remain friends, because frankly, this life gets rather tedious. Seeing these kids come through here year after year gets to be tough for anyone to handle alone. She and I had been here longer than any of the other instructors. Both of us had been offered other positions in the Agency, but I could never see myself sitting at a desk or out in the field considering my shifting abilities.

"What is it with you and this one?" she asked. She knew that it bothered me when someone washed out under my teaching.

"I don't know, Mere. I keep trying to put my finger on it, but she's holding back. She's hiding something. She's *very good* at hiding it, but I watch her every single day. The ability is there. She's just not using it, and I just don't understand," I explained as I opened the door to the 2nd floor, allowing her to pass through ahead of me into the empty hallway.

"Just let her wash out. You know if you put her on the streets she will be killed or worse the moment she's put out there. It's our jobs to make sure we send the best students we can to the proxies. You shouldn't send one that's going to cause problems for a proxy."

I waved my hands at her as if I could push her logic away like swatting at a fly. She grinned at me waving my hands around.

"Stop, Meredith. This is serious."

"I know it is. And I know I don't have to tell you what your job is. Hell, it's my job too. Granted you are much better at it than I."

She fished for a compliment. I obliged, "Don't say that. You have your own way Meredith, and it is very effective. Your students are great."

She twisted her face slightly, and I knew that telltale sign. "What are you hiding from me? What is it with you women?" I teased using the word that would poke her feminist sensibilities.

"Whoa there, buddy, don't suppose because we are friends that I'm gonna let you pull that chauvinist bullshit on me," she teased me unabashedly now.

I couldn't help but laugh at her, but like Rachel, she was hiding something. I waited for her to spill it—which it hadn't worked with Rachel—but I knew it would with Meredith. If a man wanted a woman to tell him something, all he had to do was

34

wait silently. Eventually, the woman would reveal her hidden information. Although Rachel had proven me wrong on that count, I knew Meredith would spill what she knew given a moment of silence.

"Fine. There is no sense in holding back because you won't let it go. Speaking of which, I'm surprised you let her off the hook so easily tonight."

"I didn't let her off the hook. I followed her into the hallway. She could report me for misconduct."

"But she won't."

"But she won't," I affirmed, "and I told her tomorrow was her last chance or she's out."

All the humor left her eyes. "You didn't?" she questioned.

I could only hang my head because I had never threatened a student with a washout. Especially this early in the process. We had many weeks to go, but I was tired of being bamboozled by whatever game this girl played. "I did," I replied.

"Well, I'll be damned," Meredith said with a full-on southern drawl this time. She was from one of those hot, humid states in the south of the U.S. "Tadeas Duarte finally grew a pair of balls."

"Shut up, Meredith." I was done with her too, for mocking me. Rachel's fate weighed on me, while Meredith chose to make fun of my sensibilities. As I reached for the door to my apartment, she placed her hand on mine.

In a very feminine tone, she said, "Hey, look. I know you are tired and frustrated. I'm just trying to get you to loosen up a bit. Can I come in for a minute?"

I hated to let her in my room. Every time, she came in things would get tense between us which eventually resulted in her leaving the room hurt. There was some unwritten expectation about letting a girl in your room that led her to believe that there was more there than friendship. One of the guys tried to explain it to me. "Duarte, if a girl asks you to come into her room, don't you expect certain things to happen with that kind of invitation?"

"Hell, no. I don't expect anything," I told him. He laughed at me and replied that it was the reason I wasn't getting laid anytime this century. That wasn't the reason, but at least he had the timing right. I had a few short meaningless relationships in the past couple of years. Well, like two, but it just wasn't for me. I couldn't be serious with anyone. I feared that I would hurt her, or maybe I was too afraid of living with a reminder of the past. I relented, "Yes, you can come in, but only for a minute."

She knew I was timid about it but had asked anyway so maybe she really had something to tell me. She walked over to my couch, plopping down like she lived here. I immediately regretted my decision to let her in. "Now tell me exactly what she has done or said to make you think she's holding back."

I stood in the center of the small room thinking over the last few weeks of training with Rachel Bennett. Our apartments weren't huge, but they were nice. We spent most of our time here in the basement of the Boulder facility. The room featured neutral soft carpets, and I had added a large recliner with the couch. Both were a comfy worn leather. A flat screen tv recently replaced the old tube model I had previously, but I didn't have time to watch much of it. When classes were in, I taught, ate and slept. When I didn't have classes, I tried to get out of the compound to get good food and drinks. I had visited new places within a day's drive. I also did a little hiking and fishing from time to time. Something my adopted father liked to do when I was very small. I never fully understood its value as a child, but as an adult, getting outside where there were no sounds except those of the surrounding forest was comforting and refreshing. The beast inside me appreciated the wildness of it.

"When she is sparring, it is like she purposefully does all defensive moves."

"That's not all bad. Maybe she thinks it's her best chance to survive," Meredith offered, but her answer wasn't genuine. She was definitely hiding something.

"No. That's not all. I see her movements. She has these slight reactions to strikes that should develop into counterstrikes, but she doesn't complete them. She forces the defensive move or even worse takes the hit. She's taken so many hits she could have countered or defended. Her bruises get worse every day." I ran my hands through my hair. It was starting to get too long and curl on the ends. I hated it, and I needed a trim as soon as possible. "I can see her muscle reaction. I can see the move about to play out, but she doesn't do it. She knows what to do and isn't doing it."

"Maybe she's afraid of hurting someone or perhaps she likes being hit," Meredith offered.

"I don't think so." I sat down on the couch next to her, with my elbows on my knees and my face in my hands. Rachel Bennett's case was maddening. I couldn't figure for the life of me what she was doing. Because I was a shifter, a predator cat, reading muscle reactions was where I saw the opponent's moves before they started. And where I would finish my opponent off. I could almost read every single move they would make just by watching the muscles shift under their skin by pure instinct. It was crazy, but I swore at times that I could smell the move before my foe made it. I could see Rachel coiling her muscles to strike only to shift to defense or drop the strike altogether, then get her lights punched out. Every time she hit the mat, something inside of me hurt for her. I remembered the moment she walked into the room for training. She was built perfectly for fighting. Her muscle structure indicated that she had trained, but when she stepped onto the mat for the first time, it was evident that she was incompetent until I watched her more closely. Perhaps I had watched too closely. Maybe there was something more to my concern for her, but I dismissed that thought. It wasn't possible.

"Well, you are right. She is hiding something." Meredith said flatly, "And if you really want to know what it is, we have to go spy on her."

I shouldn't have been stunned that she had been hiding something from me. However, her admission bewildered me. "Spy on her? I don't want to spy on her, Meredith. I probably scared the crap out of her, and she's somewhere crying." I knew she cried. The smell of her salty tears filled my nostrils as she ran away from me in the hallway.

"I doubt that," she smirked, as she stood up offering her hand to me. Taking it, she pulled me to my feet and led me back out into the hall. We went down the opposite flight of stairs back to the backside of the training rooms. Putting her hand on each observation room door as we passed, Meredith felt for occupants through the doors using magic. At the door to the observation room for my main classroom, she held her finger up to her lips telling me to be silent, then stepped into the dark room. Observers from the Agency would come down to see new recruits or critique our teaching methods. It had a double-sided glass that looked like a mirror on the other side. Everyone knew it was a window. We weren't hiding anything, but it provided a barrier from distraction. The curriculum would change slightly from time to time, but generally, we taught kids to survive on the streets, and a lot of those survival skills were spent in hand to hand combat training. The staff upstairs would come to view our methods to make suggestions.

Looking into the darkness of my training room, I saw Rachel's outline pacing through forms in the darkness. She wore the same clothes from the cafeteria minus her shoes. I had seen her do forms before in class. She was awkward and her movements were not precise. Most of the time she just looked like she was drowning. But not now, in the darkness, I could see her muscular frame move with ease and precision. The precision of a highly trained martial artist and fighter.

"What the hell?" I murmured. Her fluid movements were

mesmerizing. I'd never seen the combinations before, but they were beautiful, elegant variations on the kata that I knew.

"She does this every night. I saw her come in here last week. I knew you were having trouble with her, so I slipped in here to watch. I actually thought she might be hooking up with some guy. But every single night she's in one of these rooms, doing forms. Sometimes she just sits on the floor not moving for hours at a time."

"Meditation," I whispered.

"Um-hmm," Meredith confirmed. Stepping closer to the glass, I watched her movements. The beauty amazed me. Whoever she was, she had extensive martial arts training. "That's not all, Tadeas. I know you don't look in the magical spectrum like the rest of us, but look at her your way."

Meredith had a slight magical talent. Like putting her hands on the doors, she knew which room Rachel occupied by touching the door and reaching out with her senses to feel Rachel's presence. Wielders could switch their sight into the magical spectrum and see things no normal human could. For me as a shifter it was different. Especially as a Jaguar Guardian, I didn't shift-sight. I shifted planes of existence. Our world was layers upon layers of different planes. There was a whole other world that overlaps ours called the spirit world. It was where ghosts, demons, and angels tread, including guardians like myself. There was also a separate plane where the Fae lived in what they called the Underworld. Beneath that was what most of the world called hell or Hades, but it all existed in the same location, just layered on top of each other. I couldn't shift into any plane, just the spirit world. I wouldn't dare do it outside the compound without a magical partner. I had never had one as I should have been paired with as a new shifter, but my life took a different path. I avoided traveling to the spirit world at all costs. But here it would be okay for only a moment to take a look.

Closing my eyes, I concentrated on the cool feeling of the

spirit world. Its temperature was always much cooler than what we feel in the real world. I reached out with my senses, pulling on the edge of the plane. In an instant, I felt Meredith and the world around me melt away. Opening my eyes, I found myself in the monochrome bleakness of the spirit world. It was chilly and motionless. In this realm, there were no walls.

The wall between Rachel and I faded away. Stepping closer to her, I could tell something was very wrong. Around her entire body, an intricate black rope was woven around her. It bound and covered her head to foot. I couldn't even see her face or her blonde hair, but I knew it was her by her scent. She always smelled like honeysuckle and cinnamon. A contradiction of smells, for sure, but it was how I identified her. Each and every person had their own unique scent and sometimes it changed based on their mood, but there was always that underlying smell.

Circling her as she followed the steps of each form, I realized she was improvising through several disciplines at once. She was highly trained, but she was bound. I had never seen a binding on someone like this in the spirit realm. My enhanced sense of smell picked up on her sweat from the exertion plus the smell of salt from her continued tears. A part of me wanted to slam back into reality and do whatever I could to remove the binding. Surely someone upstairs in the Agency could help her. I slowly moved back through the wall to the observation room to ensure that I didn't reveal myself to her in any way. I did not want to frighten her.

When I shifted back to the real world, Meredith stood there leaning against the wall with her arms folded. I grabbed her by the arm and pulled her out of the room and down the hallway to the doorway to the stairwell. "What the fuck is that, Meredith?"

"What did you see?" she asked trying to get my perspective since our sight was different.

"She's covered in black ropes. Like a binding of some sort," I said. It had upset me enough that my voice cracked.

"Hmmm," she said.

"What? For god's sake Meredith, tell me what that is?"

"Don't go all white knight on me, Duarte, but I'm pretty sure it's a magical binding. She obviously is a powerful wielder. Whether she knows that or not, or whether she did this to herself or someone did it to her, I cannot tell. I hoped you could see something that I couldn't."

"How long have you known about this?" I asked.

"Since," she hesitated, and I grabbed her arm and pulled her toward me. She was going to lie to me. I could see it in her eyes. I refused to let her do it.

"How long, Meredith?"

"Since the first time I saw her go in the room a week ago," she replied, "And let go of me before I bust you in the face."

In my frustration, I had grabbed her too tightly. "I'm sorry. I'm just afraid she's in pain or danger even. If someone did this to her, and she doesn't know, Meredith, think of all the things that could happen." I thought back to my first time shifting. The memory or lack of it plagued me. If she had a magical ability that she didn't know about and the binding failed, it could be disastrous.

Meredith knew those thoughts going through my mind. She put her hand on my cheek. "I said, don't go all white knight on me, Tadeas. This isn't like your story. This isn't what happened to you. I think *she* did this on purpose. The guys upstairs are very diligent to make sure none of our recruits have magical abilities. Or any abilities for that matter. No shifters. No vamps. Nothing. Just plain humans. She did this to get in here, and they probably know. Now we need to figure out why."

My anger flared, but this time it had an altered focus. If Meredith was right, someone was meddling in my class. I might not be much in this world, but my class was mine. "I take pride in my training and instruction. And I'll be damned if I'm going to let some pretty wizard meddle in my affairs. She is so done, but not before I make an example of her." Fuck. I had admitted to Meredith what I thought of her physical appearance. It had slipped in my frustration.

However, Meredith stepped back and grinned not mentioning the slip. "Yep, you did grow balls."

CHAPTER 5

VANESSA

ollowing Mr. Mwenye into the conference room, I noticed that the men and women sitting around the table gave him looks of respect, but when their eyes turned to me, all I saw was aversion and contempt. They hated me for whatever reason, but Mr. Mwenye insisted that I be by his side. They would all just have to accept me. At the head of the table, the Director sat facing the city beyond the wall of windows. We were on the twentieth floor of a high rise in Philadelphia, PA. A temporary office and headquarters that we set up for the Geo-Enhancement Alliance until we received the proper funding. Then, we would move the offices inland. We were looking at locations in San Antonio, Texas and Colorado Springs, Colorado. Too bad the place in Boulder was taken.

Around the table sat the major players and board members of the GEA. All were magically endowed or a supernatural entity that was extremely respected in some circles. The GEA had a vision for the future. One that I was proud to share whether they liked me or not. John Mwenye, my mentor, grew up from a small child in British East Africa which became known as Kenya. He migrated to the city of New Orleans in 1852 where a free African-American community developed a thirst for dark religion and magic.

A tall, lanky man lounged back in one of the chairs twirling a pen just above his hand. He had a three-day ever present mostly grey stubble on his slender face. He had pale blue piercing eyes. Today his hair looked like it hadn't been cut, so a grey curly mop sat on his head. His face was weathered with time. I will admit though that when Edgar Donovan smiled, it would light up a room. Not something you'd expect from an old guy like him, but of course age was relative in this room. Mr. Donovan was a Master Wizard, and a member of the Fraternity of Magic, an elite group of wizards in the official governing body of The Conjurer's Association. I was sure Mr. Donovan's activities with us would be frowned upon by his fellow frat brothers, but the FOMs and the TCA did little these days beyond fluff their own feathers. Mr. Donovan said to me many times that I was lucky to be under the care of Mr. Mwenye, that way I didn't have to deal with the pompous idiots in the TCA. I trusted him about as far as I could throw him. However, he had extreme powers that anyone could feel by being near him, but he rarely used it. I would clearly define him as being old school. Some say that Mr. Donovan possessed a wealth of knowledge about magic that could not be matched by any wizard. Today he could pass for homeless with his unkempt facial hair, yet the designer suit would be a dead giveaway of his actual wealth, power, and influence in the world.

Across from him, leaning over a very old bible, sat the man we called The Priest. I did not know his real name and apparently, it wasn't important for he had so many names over the years that I'm not sure *he* even knew his real name. He had become our main contact for information in the religious world.

He made connections over the years from Europe to South America and also here in the United States. He believed himself to be the conscience of the group. He believed in our goals and endeavors, but I was sure his goal was to see that as few people lost their lives as possible. Which I supposed was admirable to some, but frankly, I didn't care how many worthless humans died. We intended to bring change upon this world to better the lives for all. The Priest had kind eyes and heartfelt facial expressions. He was actively protected by the Director. No matter how many times he directly contradicted our plans, the Director would not dismiss him or punish him for his defiance.

Also seated at the table, a beautiful young Japanese maiden named Botan Doro. Miss Doro was probably best described as a succubus of Japanese origin. She was thin, petite and beautiful. Her almond eyes looked upon those around her with a coy allure. She had spent ages seducing men, amassing wealth and obtaining the respect of numerous corporations in the Asian markets. Most of her acquisitions came from her dead lovers. She had many known husbands, many aliases and had over time morphed to whatever the culture and times dictated for her to complete her work. Even if she didn't seduce men, she could hold her own in any boardroom of any business in the world. I liked her.

Another woman on the board, a beautiful half-Native American woman who didn't look native at all, was out on a special assignment, and we probably wouldn't see her for quite some time. It's a shame. She was nice to look at and clever. I missed her very much. Her mentor, Nalusa Chito was also not here. He was a dark-haired, dark-skinned former chief of the Choctaw Nation. He had joined our effort to reclaim some of the lands that once belonged to his people leading them into a new era of dominance over the white man. Whatever served our purpose, I couldn't care less about his lofty and unachievable goals.

I finished out the crew in the room, Vanessa Vaughn, wielder, conjurer, and mistress of the black arts of magic. I was definitely the shortest in the room standing at about 5ft 5in. My long black hair and porcelain skin rivaled the beauty of any woman I'd ever seen. I looked at Mr. Mwenye, and by his face, I could tell he wanted me to keep quiet during this meeting. Several members of our group were missing, but I was sure they were all out on business pertaining to GEA. I had not seen Milton Trujillo in quite some time. Perhaps he had finally kicked the bucket. The nasty old man had a taste for young girls and went to great lengths to entertain as many of them as possible, which for a man his age, relied on an act of God in itself or a lifetime supply of a little blue pill. He had propositioned me once. I almost took him up on it just to make sure I stayed in his good graces. I may look 25, but I certainly was not born yesterday. I didn't tell Mwenye about it though. Never know when you might need that sort of information.

"How did the demonstration go?" the Director asked, never turning to look at us.

"It went splendidly," Mr. Mwenye responded. "I have a couple of prepayment checks for you, as well as four other promises for investment. We need to have the paperwork sent to their offices as soon as it may be possible." He laid a folder behind the Director's chair on the glass top conference table.

"And the two gentlemen that died?" the Director asked. Damn. I had hoped that information hadn't made it back to the group.

"An unfortunate accident, however, they doubted our abilities and, in the end, probably would have compromised our endeavors. It was best that they were dealt with immediately," Mwenye responded, protecting me before the director. Or perhaps he was just protecting himself. If the director pushed the issue, Mwenye would throw me under the bus.

"Either you control her, or I will," the Director responded. And there it was.

"Yes, of course," he said, turning to me. He slapped me hard

46

across the face. I hit the floor. "I told you," he hissed, then turned back to the Director. "It will not happen again. I assure you."

He told me before we entered that he might have to show brute force to make an example of me to save his reputation. I rather enjoyed being slapped around by him, so I said that I didn't mind a bit. Of course, he hit me hard enough that a trickle of blood ran out the edge of my mouth. The Priest handed me a white handkerchief and helped me off the floor. The handkerchief had a cross embroidered on the corner with the initials JCS. I handed the bloodied rag back to him, knowing that I was handing him a gift of my blood. I did it to gauge his reaction to my gift.

"No child, you keep it," he said quietly.

Holding it up in my right hand, I spoke, "*Uro*." The handkerchief combusted into flame burning in an instant. All eyes in the room shot to me with the use of magic, except the Director who just chuckled lightly. "I'm not letting any of you bastards get your hands on my blood," I stated firmly, then took a chair at the opposite end of the conference table away from all of them. Mwenye's eyes flashed completely black, and I knew I'd pay for that one later.

"Enough of the childishness," Donovan said. "There were eighteen investors. You got checks from two and promises from four others. We need not concern ourselves with the two unfortunate souls, but that leaves ten loose ends."

"Yes, your math is correct Edgar, but be assured, I will obtain their allegiance to this plan or they will be dealt with accordingly," Mwenye said condescendingly.

"John, I don't doubt your abilities to kill someone, however, we can't just off ten of the most influential businessmen in the world. I do think that would draw attention that we don't want or need," Donovan said.

"Please trust me when I say, they will join our efforts," Mwenye responded. My mentor would use his unique necromancy to control those who refused to aid us. He was an asset to this rabble. They should respect him for his talents. Edgar Donovan—with his fine suit—looked at us both with derision in his eyes. Yet, with all the darkness that resided in Edgar Donovan, even he cringed at Mwenye's assertion. He knew as well as I did, that if Mwenye wanted, he could make the business partners agree to anything. He was not above going well beyond the rules to accomplish his goals. I found that to be sexy as hell. He was ruthless.

"Donovan is right, Mwenye. We should do whatever we can to engage these partners in an open discussion and persuade them to our cause. I want as little blood on our hands as possible at this point," the Director said.

"Amen to that," the Priest echoed.

"I have Milton out on assignment. He will return to us when he has accomplished his tasks in Boulder," the Director said.

We all looked at each other. I suppose none of us knew that old man Trujillo was in Boulder. The stronghold of Gregory Theodoard's Agency was based just outside of Boulder.

"What are we doing in Boulder?" Donovan asked boldly.

"I have a side plan in action that will assure that Mr. Theodoard's network will be crippled to fight us when the time comes. Without him in our hair, I would say that our goals will be accomplished unhindered," the Director revealed. This was a side plan that interested me greatly. I made mental notes to investigate this revelation further.

"The headquarters for Kenward, Blake, and Shanahan only compromise an extremely small part of the vast network of proxies and regents in the world. They have alternate headquarters and layer upon layer of backup facilities and safe houses," Donovan said.

"You speak as if I do not know our enemy, Mr. Donovan. I assure you, I am well aware of the capabilities of Mr. Theodoard and his Agency. They will bow to us in the end," the Director said.

"If she is still alive as they say, we may have bigger problems than we thought," Mwenye said.

"She is alive, and she will be dealt with finality this time," the Director said firmly.

"Who is she?" I asked after listening to the whole conversation and watching their faces as they spoke about this woman.

"She is our biggest obstacle. She is Abigail Davenport," the Director said.

"I heard she retired," I said. I knew the name. Miss Davenport had established the proxy system that held all darkness in check. I'd even seen Mr. Mwenye avoid her rather than deal with her face to face on several occasions. But I knew that those in this room had dealt her a blow by killing her partner and lover Lincoln. They followed that with the gut punch of turning her fiancé and best friend in the world, Lukas Castille, into an incubus. We had that poor woman wrapped up, and I doubted she would ever be a part of the big game as a whole ever again. Saying she was our biggest obstacle made me scoff inside. I knew I could put her down if needed. No doubt she was extremely powerful. But after years in seclusion and hiding, she was off her game. If I came across her in the near future, I would do us all a favor and end her once and for all. Especially since none of the men in this room seemed to be able to accomplish the task. I leaned back in my chair and smiled deviously. Yes, Abigail Davenport would beg me for her life before it was over.

"She is not retired," Miss Doro said. "In fact, from watching the markets, I believe someone is making large moves with cash and the distribution of assets known to be tied to the Agency through shell companies and offshore accounts. My people and I are having a hard time tracking the moves. The only one I know of inside the Agency who is capable of moving enormous amounts of money around virtually undetected is Abigail Davenport. And if she's moving some we *can* see, I'm sure there is more we don't know about or can't detect. I assure you she is not retired."

"Be sure that we nail this information down, and track as many of those accounts as possible," the Director instructed. "If she is back in the game, and moving assets, then more than likely she knows something is going on. Miss Davenport has always played the long game. She probably started making moves far before any of us knew about it. She's always been a step ahead. I think taking her out at this point would be unwise, however, if anyone gets a shot at her, I demand you take it. I will not have her foiling this plan."

This would be my chance. If I could make sure that I put myself in Miss Davenport's path, I would end her long life, offering her head to the Director and board as proof of my enhanced skills. Perhaps then, I could get a little respect from this group.

The Director continued to watch the sun sink in the sky through the windows. The shadows rapidly shifted in the room, and all were silent for some time.

"Is there anything else today?" No one spoke. "Then, please leave me. I have some calls to make," the Director said, and we all got up and filed out of the room. I left first and headed to the Director's office right across the hall. The Director's secretary sat at the desk just outside the main office.

"Hello, Cassidy," I beamed at her.

Her pert lips and upturned nose featured in the sweetest face I'd ever seen. "Hey Nessa, how are you, dear?" Her red curls cascaded around her face, and her green eyes glittered with life and youth. She looked so innocent. A ripe fruit ready for plucking.

"I'm well. I had hoped you might be done for the day," I responded as I leaned over the desk giving her full view of my cleavage. Her green eyes turned excessively alluring, but she blushed and looked away.

"Why do you ask?" she asked knowing all too well what I wanted. You see, my lover Mwenye adored Miss Cassidy MacSeain, and he had tried to seduce her multiple times. I asked him for permission to allow me to do it for him. He had gladly obliged. I got what I wanted, and if I wanted a happy man, then I would have to get him Miss MacSeain. This wasn't the first time I'd thrown myself at her, but she had always backed out on any plans we had made.

"Well, I thought I'd go get some drinks tonight down at one of the local pubs. Mr. Mwenye has so much going on with this new business venture that he has very little time for me. Perhaps we could have a girl's night out," I suggested as I traced my finger down the side of her face.

"Back off, Witch," Donovan's voice interrupted me from behind. Turning to look at him, I moved quickly to meet him toe to toe. I was not afraid of him, and I wanted him to know it. I slid beside him grinding my hips against his thigh. He reached up and grabbed my throat. As he squeezed, I choked, but it turned me on. I felt the wetness grow between my legs. I was willing to bet that Edgar Donovan was vicious in bed.

"Oh baby, you know how I like it," I purred. He threw me backward, causing me to stumble. I laughed at him despite his aggressive manner. "You do beat all, Donovan. Why don't you come around one day and show me a good time?"

He lowered his eyes to me, then growled, "I would no more touch a whore like you than touch a dog in heat."

"Tell me more, you dirty boy," I cooed at him. Usually, by this time, my overt sexuality made a man cringe, but not Donovan.

"Stay away from her," he said pointing his finger at my face. For an old guy, he still had plenty of power. I could feel it humming around him like the low bass from a subwoofer.

"Oh, I see. Daddy loves his baby girl. You know, Donovan,

even in our circles, incest is frowned upon," I said as I looked over to Cassidy. She had turned her face and body away from both of us. Rage consumed Donovan with my overt display. I felt him pulling in power. A dark shadow coalesced in front of me, I smiled because Donovan would lose this fight.

"Enough Edgar, you know she is only trying to provoke you," the tall Native American man said and turned to me, "And you, I suggest you go use your vast talents somewhere else."

"As you wish, Nalusa Chito. Sorry, you missed the meeting. It was excessively diverting," I said as I walked toward the door. I looked back at Cassidy, winked at her and held up my fingers like a phone. I mouthed the words, "Call me." She frowned and shook her head no. I slipped out the door to see Mwenye waiting on me. I listened to the conversation beyond the door.

"Are you alright, Cassidy?" Donovan asked his daughter.

"Yes, father, I'm fine."

"Filthy whore. I don't know why we have to put up with her," he said.

"Each one of us serves our purpose," Chito replied.

I heard Donovan growl as I approached Mr. Mwenye.

"You struck out again," he commented.

"Well, I managed to provoke Donovan which is always delightful, but as for Cassidy, I don't think she will be joining us tonight," I said disappointedly.

"That's unfortunate. Perhaps next time."

"Perhaps," I leaned into him and ground my hips against him. His lips locked with mine. We were alone in the hallway for just that moment. I pulled away from him and said, "Just means there's more for me."

He smiled, possessively taking my hand. We left the building to return to our condo here in Philly. We would plan our next move and build our powers feeding on each other. Yes, it would be a good night despite Miss MacSeain not joining us. I would have her soul eventually. I wanted hers to be the first I ever consumed. It was pure and wholesome. Qualities I did not possess. I was ready for that move into the darkness. It was just a matter of time now, even though Mwenye doubted that I would ever make that move. One day very soon, I would show them all how dark I could be.

CHAPTER 6

ABIGAIL

The room was dark when I opened my eyes, but I could see Sam sitting on the edge of my bed lightly shaking me. "Hey, sorry to wake you, but I wanted to check on you."

"I'm fine," I muttered and rolled over, putting my back to her. I wasn't happy about being awakened because it took me forever just to drift off. My mind raced after the confrontation with Mr. Duarte.

"You wanna go practice a little?"

"You heard?" Word traveled fast. I'm sure Duarte confronting me was the story of the night.

"Yeah, everyone knows."

"Fucking secondary school."

"It's not high school, Rach. It's real and your ass is going to be out on the pavement if you don't do something. I could teach you a couple of quick moves that might score you a point or two tomorrow in matches. Maybe he will let you stay."

I rolled half over to look at her. She was just trying to help, but I wanted to scream that I didn't need any instruction from her. Instead, I simply replied, "I'm not going to learn anything overnight that would keep him from putting me out." I rolled back over. She placed her hand on my shoulder like she intended to say something else, but she climbed up in her bunk, settling in for the night.

Through my meditation and repeating forms, I had come to the conclusion that Duarte was done with me completely. I don't know how I came to that conclusion, but it seemed right in every way. My entire presence was a complete lie, and he knew it. Studying him over the past two years, reluctant to meet him as myself, I learned about his abilities, and I should have known he would see right through me. I deserved whatever he had to dish out.

It was too late to start over and do it the right way, but I had no other choice at this point. I hated the fact that I had botched the prospect of a partnership with him. He was perfect in every single way for the task.

I had entered this whole endeavor to find a new partner. I hadn't had one in 25 years. My last partner died in the field with me, and the loss devastated me to the point that I couldn't bring myself to connect with another person. Tadeas Duarte was perfect. Someone very important told me about Duarte and his abilities, but I had dismissed it because I never expected Lincoln to die. I needed someone who could fight and hold their own. My last partner was a very deadly hunter of the dark monsters of the earth. Duarte was a shifter of a different flavor, and I wasn't sure exactly what his capabilities were in his shifted form, but I couldn't wait to see what he could do.

I had been out of the game for a while. Sitting on the side-lines, I'd lost my touch. This whole thing was a bad fucking idea. I groaned, trying to sleep. But it evaded me. My mind raced again going through all the scenarios. I even thought about giving up and just walking out now. I could do it. I knew the codes to take me to the upper levels of the compound. There was always that part of me that had hope. Hope is what kept me going after Lincoln died. We were more than just business partners. He had slowly won me over, and I fell in love with him. We were a dynamic pair. Nothing could stop us. Except for a dark master wizard who may or may not have been my father.

My heart started to ache again thinking of him. I wasn't the same since he died. The fire and drive I had lasted past his death because I had promised him to continue on, but it didn't pass the ordeal with Lukas Castille, which was another story I didn't want to think about right now.

My brain delved into dark territory, and I couldn't seem to stop it. I needed to focus. I needed focus and a stiff drink. Preferably bourbon. I needed bourbon.

Eventually, the rest of the room began to bustle with activity. I laid in bed staring at absolutely nothing as the room became quiet again. I considered waiting for him to physically drag me out of here to kick me out. However, like the idiot that I was, I rolled out to take my punishment.

Taking out several pieces of paper from my trunk, I scribbled out a couple of notes in desperation. Perhaps I could start a possible path to redemption for myself to Mr. Duarte. Then, I got dressed for class, running down the hallway to avoid being late.

After a quick stop, I slipped in the doorway to my spot on the mat. The class was overly full. Meredith Spence's class was here too. She stood on the mat next to Duarte with a smug smile on her face. I got an uneasy feeling in the pit of my stomach. Her gaze was damning. My last sliver of hope evaporated under her fiery stare.

"Let's get started," Duarte began, "Instructor Spence has brought her class to ours today for a bit of an object lesson. Several of you are looking more and more like washouts. Therefore, we are bringing the reality of the situation to your full attention. Today is the last chance for one of my own." His eyes locked on me. I cringed, and I swear something broke inside me. I was broken and beaten up enough, but apparently, there was more in there that could break. I involuntarily started to shake. *Good grief, get a grip,* I told myself. "The world that you all will enter is relentless. We have to know before we release you out into that world that you can hold your own. It's our responsibility because the alternative isn't any better. You can get put out now with no support system. With nothing. With no hope. In a desperate attempt to save more than one of you, we are here to see what it's like when someone gets their last chance. Rachel Bennett, please step into the ring."

I started to step, but it was like I couldn't make myself move. I was frozen in place while his green eyes flared with pain. "Now, please," he insisted. I slowly walked to the fighting area. It was an octagon. A few years back we switched from the old circles to the octagon shape to mimic the style of the rising popularity of mixed martial arts. Most of these kids think of martial arts in that context, not Jackie Chan and Bruce Lee.

I took the spot waiting to see who he would choose as my opponent. He grimaced at me as I stood there before him. My act faded away as real fear gripped my heart. I felt this elaborate ruse falling apart around me and was helpless to stop it. My hope evaporated with my lack of ideas to get out of the situation. Even if he picked Travis again to go against me, I'm not sure with all my years of training I could accidentally score a point on him. Waiting to see who Duarte had chosen to go against me, I got the crazy feeling he expected me to fight Meredith because she continued to stare at me. I had done my research on her as well. She possessed a light magical talent. Mostly easy cantrip spells and wards. She was best classified with the magically derogatory term, a sensitive. She was highly sensitive, but not wizard material.

It was how she ended up working for the Agency. We had

numerous talents who worked for us that specialized in one area or the other, and we hauled them out into the field as needed or used them here in the training facilities. She was pretty, plus well-liked by her students. Her turnout rate wasn't as good as Duarte's, but it was good enough to consider her one of the best. I researched her past and came up with dead ends for her parentage, but she clearly had some Native American blood. We pulled her out of a children's home in 1987 in rural Alabama where she was already a teenager. Our masters trained her in various forms of martial arts, and she went through the full orientation of the Agency. She was a star student, and the administration chose her to train students. I talked to her instructors, and those who dealt with her in the administrative wing, and they all said she had a heavy crush on Duarte from the moment she met him. I only came across rumors that at one point they had a relationship. I had observed myself that they were both still close and outwardly appeared to be friends. Duarte, from what I could, tell kept everyone at arm's length, except Meredith. It was part of my reasoning to join his class as a student. I wanted to know him better from a different perspective. I needed a partner, and I couldn't trust someone who kept me at a distance. Our lives would depend on each other's skills and abilities, plus a strong bond of trust. Heaven only knew why I decided to build that trust with a lie. The idiocy of it sank into me as I waited.

Our bond didn't have to be romantic. In fact, it was much better if it wasn't. Romance tended to refocus attention in personal ways and not the mission or objective. My heart needed mending from the past, so I wasn't fit to connect to anyone in that capacity. Even the handsome jaguar.

Meredith continued to stare at me when I realized Duarte took off his utility belt and boots. He handed them to her, as she lightly touched his shoulder. A light touch of reassurance that this was the right thing. She obviously cared about him, knowing that my situation bothered him.

He turned to face me. "Since I can trust none of you to give Miss Bennett a fair fight, I'm going to fight her myself," he glanced toward Travis, and Travis averted his gaze from the fight area. I wanted to fall to my knees and surrender. I could not fight him. I would not. It was beyond my sight to foresee that he would take this route, punishing himself for my failure. Taking it as his own.

Taking the traditional cross stance from me, he bowed. Mechanically I bowed toward him, and as I reached a full stance, he crossed the distance between us in an instant. Before I could make any blocking motion, he struck me across the jaw, and I hit the floor with a thud. I was still conscious, but the pain erupted through my face and jaw compounded by the knockout punch Travis had graced upon me the day before. Before I could push myself up, he went to a knee next to me. He leaned down to my ear and whispered, "I know what you are. The question is, are you binding your own magic or is someone binding you? Why don't you enlighten me?"

He grabbed my shirt and hauled me to my feet. "Again!" he demanded. He took a basic Aikido Hanmi stance, and I instinctively matched his stance. Something clicked inside me, then my training kicked in from years of practice. This was why the best fighters trained the same techniques repeatedly. You can't just master the moves; it has to become an involuntary instinct especially when you've had a major trauma or distraction.

My brain blurred with the revelation that he knew about my magical binding. How in the world had he figured that out? Just last night I was confident that he didn't have a clue about that part of all of this.

He again made his first move to get into my blind spot. His hands bladed outward has he took a sweeping step to my back, using the te-gatana or the hand sword technique. The strike came in hard, and I did not resist his attack. I just gracefully moved out of his range. Aikido, even in its very basic techniques is about avoiding the attack, not blocking or defending against it. I shifted my stance once again to match his as he turned to me. Everything moved in slow motion. Aikido isn't about speed. Somehow, he knew I trained in Aikido extensively. He started performing basic attack techniques and quickly picked up the pace. I countered him by continually avoiding his attacks with my footwork. I was on autopilot. For a moment, I stole a look at Samantha, as shock registered on her face. I hadn't really done anything impressive, but I guess after months of defending and taking hits, just the mere avoidance of an attack shocked her. I lost my attention on my attacker and with a simple wrist hold technique, he had me on my knees with my hand caught in his folding right arm back. The tension caused pain to shoot through my arm. I was at his mercy. His posture put him to my side, and he grunted, "Pay attention, Rachel, and answer my fucking question." I relaxed. Straining against his hold only made the pain worse.

The realization that it was over hit me, and I was done with the ruse. I had considered a humble exit to this whole farce, but I didn't take that way out. Reverting to some of my more immature impulses, I looked him in the eye and smiled, "I don't need magic to whip your ass."

It was enough of a flirtation, challenge, and surprise to distract him. I switched techniques to Ju-jitsu and moved to sweep his kneeling leg out from under him. I rolled behind him, hooking my legs into and around his thighs in a sitting position. While he staggered, off-guard, trying to regain stability, I slipped my left arm under his left armpit and my right arm over his right shoulder like a seatbelt. Grabbing my left wrist with my right hand, I wrenched him back across the chest. The pressure caused him to gasp for a moment, and I slipped my right arm up to his neck to cut off his air. Shooting a look at Meredith I felt the wrath flowing off of her in waves. And it felt good. I leaned up to his ear and whispered, "You want me to let go before or after you pass out?"

He grunted, trying to get position on me. He had missed his opportunity to avoid the hold and now had the more difficult task of getting out of it as I cut off his air. He lurched back from the sitting position to knock me back onto my back, driving me forcefully into the mat with his shoulders plus pressing his heels deep in the mat for leverage. Perhaps I had gotten a little cocky if that's possible for a girl. It was enough for him to tuck his chin and get under my locked hold. He forced his right arm up between my lock breaking it. He twisted out of my hold then rolled away from me on the mat grasping his neck. I was a little jarred from the smash on the mat, but I quickly rolled over to my feet and took a defensive stance. It took him longer to get to his feet.

"Again!" I spouted back at him. Pure anger erupted across his face, and he came at me with a series of closed fist punches, I blocked each one in rhythm. He started peppering in kicks, but I countered each one. I realized I was having fun. More than I'd had in years. I even laughed a couple of times. We were both getting tired as our skills were evenly matched. We had been sparring for a good 10 minutes while the entire class stood mesmerized. Murder flashed across Meredith's face. I was making a fool of Duarte which was not my intention. I had decided it was time to shut up after the last comment and just fight. I had no desire to harm him physically, and I realized as we fought, he didn't either. He never pulled a kill or subdue move on me.

Finally, I calculated his punches in order to take one that would hurt the least. And after a short parry, I straightened, standing completely still. Before he could draw back, I took a right cross on my jaw. I'm surprised it wasn't broken by this point. I hit the mat again, tasting copper.

I laughed again, "Okay, okay, I tap. You win." He reached his hand out to me. His knuckles were split and bleeding. Taking it, he hoisted me up. He stood looking at me in awe. I bowed to him in reverence of his skill and tolerance of my charade to this point.

"I'm sorry for everything," I said, then turned on my heel to walk to the door. It was a pitiful excuse for an apology, but I had caused too many problems for him. The urge to retreat came fast and furious. I wanted to get away from him, not because of anything he had done. Solely because I was ashamed of myself. I didn't deserve to share the mat with him.

"Stop!" he demanded.

"I should go. I've disrupted your process too much. I really am sorry," I explained.

"Who are you?" he asked.

Regret and sadness hit me like a truck as he searched my face for answers. For the first time, I saw him as lost. He had not enjoyed the fight like I had. My mission here had failed. I nodded slightly and said dropping the Americanized speech for my native British accent, "I am Abigail Davenport. I truly am sorry, Mr. Tadeas Duarte."

He would recognize my name. I was sure of it, so I slipped out the door while he stood in shock. Quickly I walked down the hall to the elevator before my emotions caught up with me. Pressing the button to call the elevator, I nervously waited for it. As the elevator doors opened, I heard the training room doors swing open. He rounded the corner in a dead sprint. Not giving up on me until the very end. I admired him. I adored him for it.

"You need to explain this to me," he yelled as he ran toward me. The doors shut between us as a tear rolled down my cheek.

CHAPTER 7

TADEAS

*a*s I opened the door to the training room, both classes stood stunned.

"We are done. Enjoy the long weekend. See you all on Monday." I spouted, and they quickly dispersed before I changed my mind. The moment they all hit the hallway sound erupted in conversations about what had just happened. I wasn't sure what actually happened other than I uncovered a mole in my training class. We fought, and I enjoyed most of it. She was good. Extremely good. The best I've ever seen. I looked up to Meredith to find her scowl sat firmly in place. "What?"

"Did you have fun? Seems like you did by the smirk on your face. Did you forget that she's been in your class all this time doing a form of sadomasochist slug fest? Do you even know who she is?!" she spouted. I hate it when she spouted. Mouth vomit was what one of the other guys called it. Pretty appropriate. It's not just a woman thing though, I've seen plenty of guys do it especially when they get caught in a lie.

"I know exactly who she is. She's Gregory Theodoard's granddaughter."

"She's a fucking badass wizard."

"And she never once used a drop of magic in this room, even against me just now," I pointed out.

"Are you forgetting the fact that she's a big fat liar?" she asked, huffing for breath.

"No, Meredith. I'm not. She's gone. It's done. It's over. Whatever it was." Part of me didn't want it to be over. I wanted to fight her again. She matched my techniques and skill set. It was hard to concentrate on fighting her because I was too mesmerized by her abilities. I shouldn't be surprised now that I knew who she was. Abigail Davenport practically built the Agency. She led our field teams into fights across the globe, but I had heard that she had retired which didn't explain why she was in my training class.

"Maybe they are trying to get rid of you."

"What? Why? You are completely off base." I sat down to put on my shoes. I desperately wanted out of this room and away from Meredith. If I could get back to my apartment alone, perhaps I could make some sense of all of it.

"You want some company?" Meredith asked as if on cue.

"No, Mere, I need to process this. Thanks though. I always know I can count on you." I could not believe that line just came out of my mouth. It was either pure evil or pure genius.

She blushed and said, "Okay, you know where to find me if you need anything."

Leaving me in the room alone, I stood and looked at the mat. I had reviewed the moves over and over. And then it hit me. She left it open for me to get out of the naked choke hold. I hate it when someone lets me win. "Bitch."

I stalked up the stairs to my apartment. Upon entering my room, I immediately went on my guard. I could smell her in there, honeysuckle and cinnamon. Mostly cinnamon. I looked around the small living area and into the open kitchen. Then I searched my bedroom and bathroom. No one there. Walking back into the living room, I noticed an envelope on the table. Staring at it, I sat down across from it. My full name was scribed in a beautiful steady script on the front. Well, if I really wanted to know the truth, it would be in that envelope. I opened it, pulling out a heavy stock single card. The same handwritten script was on the card.

"I cannot express my deepest apologies for the disruption to your process, as well as, any personal harm I may have caused you. I owe you more than an apology. I owe you a full explanation for my deception. If you would, please join me tonight for dinner at The Table in Boulder. The reservation is at 7 p.m. under Davenport. If you choose not to come, please know that I meant no harm, and you are truly the best instructor The Agency has training our crews. I am honored to have been a part of your instruction, watching first-hand the skill and care you endow to each of your students. Sincerely, Abigail Davenport."

I flicked the card back on the table hard enough that it slid off the other side onto the floor. She wanted to kick my butt and go on a date all in the same day. This woman is either completely delusional or the most intriguing woman in the world. She could be on one of those alcohol commercials. Of course, I wasn't going to meet her. Why would I go? I didn't need an explanation from a liar. However, I got up and went to my bedroom closet, anyway. I wouldn't have anything to wear to a restaurant that took reservations. Maybe a pair of my newer khaki fatigues would pass. Opening the closet door, I found a garment bag on the inside hook.

"You've got to be fucking kidding me."

The tag hanging from the zipper featured the same script.

"Just in case you don't have anything to wear."

I ZIPPED IT OPEN TO FIND A DARK GREY SUIT WITH A WHITE DRESS shirt. Both emblazoned with a Calvin Klein logo. "What the hell!" No, this is ridiculous. I'll find a way to return the suit to her, and then I noticed another card in the pocket. Pulling it out in astonishment, I read it.

"*Even if you don't come, keep the suit. It was made for you.*"

I took a few steps back and sat down on the bed staring at the suit hanging in my closet. Calvin Klein meant big money. Of course, she was wealthy; her grandfather basically ran the world. It also meant high maintenance, but this wasn't a date. It actually felt like a weird job interview to which I was absolutely not going.

I laid back, stared at the ceiling, and started to close my eyes. I hadn't slept much the night before trying to figure out the best way to handle the situation. Perhaps a nap would clear my head. I couldn't have predicted any of this. I drifted off to sleep unsure of what I would do about Miss Abigail Davenport.

The nightmare started immediately. I smelled blood. Looking down at my hands, I saw that they were blood-covered claws. I looked across the bed to my beautiful fiancée, but she was covered in blood. Her jet-black hair glistened with thick blood. I jumped to her side on the bed and tried to talk to her, but she sat there staring into space. Her body had been ripped and shredded by a savage animal. Dear God, no please don't let this be happening. I started to cry. Muffled whines escaped my lips, and I turned my back to her body. I couldn't look at it anymore. I looked across the room to a shattered mirror on the far wall and blinked. A large black jaguar stared back at me. I turned quickly thinking it was behind me. I looked back at the mirror as the predator turned to me in unison. No, this is impossible. I tried to wail. I looked down at myself. I felt human, but what I saw was an animal. It was a beast. Just as Father Sergio had told me. There was a beast there. I heard a noise and turned toward the door. A tall dark-skinned, dark-haired man stood there. He had his hands up in defense. Like he was trying to calm me down, then he said the same word I'd heard a demon once use during an exorcism, *hodéezyéél.*

I bolted up in the bed from the nightmare, hurrying to the bathroom to splash water on my face. I had the nightmare whenever I got too emotional. These last 24 hours had been an emotional roller coaster. I took several deep breaths and resolved myself to lay back down. I would ignore Abigail Davenport's invitation. I couldn't let the nightmare stop me or cause me to relent my resolve. I didn't care that I saw her shed a tear as the elevator doors closed between us.

Except, I did care.

CHAPTER 8

ABIGAIL

*I*t was 7 p.m. As I sat at the table alone, I didn't think he'd come. I took the chance anyway, hoping to have the chance to explain myself to him. He deserved that much from me. Perhaps I should have chosen a different venue. Something that wouldn't make him uncomfortable like this formal setting. This kind of interaction fell into my forte, but I was sure it didn't fall into his. I was protecting myself instead of thinking of him. I had so much to learn. No, I had so much to remember about partnership. It was as if Lincoln's death had erased everything I knew about trust.

The waiter who earlier introduced himself as Walt, approached me, "Ms. Davenport, may I get you a drink?"

"Yes please, bourbon on the rocks, please." It would be nice to have a bit of alcohol after the prohibition I placed on myself while in the training classes.

"Any preference, ma'am?"

"Just the good stuff, Walt, something small batch," I replied. Might as well have a good meal. I picked up the menu, looking at the fine offerings. My Aunt Lianne had suggested the place. Boulder was the closest city to the compound. I didn't spend much time in Boulder because my own home was in Europe. The atmosphere was comforting, and they had given me a table away from those being seated in the front of the restaurant for a little privacy. It didn't look like I'd need it since he wasn't coming. A waiter seated a large group of family members on the long communal table in the center of the restaurant. The family members all greeted each other warmly, sharing hugs and handshakes. I smiled watching them all interact.

Then he stepped through the crowd, catching me off guard. Not only was he here, he wore the suit which fit him perfectly. He looked damn good in it. As he approached me, I stood to greet him. I could tell he was as nervous as I was. Hopefully, we could get past that, and perhaps I could make amends to him by explaining everything.

"Hello, Mr. Duarte, I'm very pleased you came." I gestured toward the seat. He looked at it and sat down.

"Miss Davenport, thank you for the invitation."

"I would appreciate it if you called me Abigail. Or Abby."

"Um, okay. Abigail."

Walt appeared with my drink and sat it before me. "Mr. Duarte, would you like a beverage?" I had told Walt earlier that I expected a guest to join me, and Walt, being thorough, asked his name.

Without looking up from the menu, he said, "Just a water, please."

Walt hustled away. "I apologize. Do you not drink alcohol? I ordered a bottle of wine for dinner, but I can cancel."

"No. It's fine. I drink occasionally. I'm just trying to keep a clear head," he stated flatly. I got the feeling this meeting was going to be completely awkward.

"The suit looks very nice," I said. "I made the reservation, and it didn't occur to me that you might not have anything at the compound to wear. I had something brought in for you."

"Eliminating excuses," he said, looking up to meet my eyes. I caught myself holding his gaze for longer than I expected. The same intensity from his classes, but without the determination.

"I don't catch your meaning."

"You eliminated the excuse that I'd have nothing to wear. In fact, I couldn't come up with one single reason not to come, except, that I had classes scheduled for this evening, but in my frustration after the fight, I canceled everything for the rest of the day."

"That wasn't my intention, I assure you, Mr. Duarte." He had to think the worst of me. I deserved it. I'd have to take my medicine. I botched this, and I'd let him get any dig in he wanted.

"If I call you Abigail, you have to call me Tadeas. Otherwise, it will get even more awkward, and I'm not sure I can handle any more awkward today."

I laughed. I couldn't tell if he was joking, but I found it humorous. "Okay, Tadeas."

"And what's with the British accent?" he asked.

I took a sip of my drink. I wanted to chug the whole thing. Awkward indeed. "I'm British. Well, sort of. I was raised around people with a British accent."

"You weren't British in my class."

"No, to fit the part, I Americanized my speech as much as possible. I was out of practice. I was afraid I'd give myself away with it, especially in the hallway last night." I couldn't look him in the eye after I brought up last night's confrontation.

"Perhaps you shouldn't have been hiding in my class in the first place."

A warning shot across the bow. I held steady. "You are absolutely correct. I completely botched this whole ordeal."

Walt chose this moment to return with Tadeas' water, two wine glasses, and the bottle I'd ordered earlier. He deftly opened it for us, describing the features of the wine while pouring us each a taste in our glass. More awkward. I had the feeling that Tadeas hadn't ever had a proper sommelier present wine. I lifted it to my nose and took a whiff. I then swirled it to check the color. He watched the ritual intently and took in each of my movements. I took a sip, then complemented it. Walt filled both glasses completely and excused himself promising to return shortly to take our dinner order. Tadeas picked up the glass taking a tentative a sip. He lifted his eyebrows in surprise. I suppose he approved because he took another sip.

"You were saying," he prompted.

"Just that I know that you have a lot of questions, and I promise to answer them all. I am an open book." It was hard to convey my remorse. Perhaps as the night went on, I could help him understand my motivations. I doubted he would ever forgive me. The night hadn't started out well, but that was to be expected. I would continue to try. He deserved it. He took the time to come. Even if it was just pure curiosity, he was here, and I needed to take advantage of the opportunity.

Walt returned to take our orders. I ordered the Niman pork chop. Tadeas ordered a dry-aged steak which was my second choice. Walt excused himself, as I finished the last of my bourbon. Tadeas nodded at the empty glass, "What kind of alcohol?"

"Bourbon on the rocks. Four Roses Small Batch, I believe." He lifted his eyebrows somewhat surprised at my choice of heavy liquor. "Bourbon is my weakness," I confessed. "And despite what my grandfather and his Irish Scotch says, I think it's best when they age it here in the United States. I think it makes me a traitor to him." I smiled hoping the anecdote would ease his mood. For a moment, I saw a smile creep into the edges of his eyes. I had seen him smile while watching him teach over the last few months, but his smiles were rare. He didn't grace me with one now. Strike one, Abby.

The crowd in the center of the restaurant had a raucous moment drawing both of our attention to the family gathering. "Is your grandfather important to you?" he asked.

"Yes, he is. He's not my grandfather though. More like my great, great, great, and so far, removed great grandfather."

"You aren't like him?" he asked.

"Like him in what way?" I countered.

"He's a god," he said in a low tone so that no one but me heard him.

"Oh, heavens no. I'm just a wielder. I have never known my mother, and all I know about my father is that he's a master wizard. My mother is from my grandfather's family line, but he's so far removed that I don't have any of that 'god' blood in me. Just the genetic signature that connects me to Mr. Theodoard."

He took this in while he sipped his wine. I could tell he had many questions. He just didn't know where to start.

"Tadeas, you have earned my complete honesty. I owe you that after the nonsense that I've pulled. There is nothing you can ask that will offend me. Please ask whatever you wish. Tonight is yours to direct as you choose." This pure promise of truth and openness would give him the authority over the evening and how the conversation went for the rest of the night. I had hoped it would be a gesture that would open the conversation up for both of us.

"I'd say I'd earned at least that," he shot back. Strike two.

I bowed my head. "Yes, at the very least," I softly replied.

And for a good ten minutes, we sat in silence.

Walt appeared with our food. It all looked delicious. I thanked Walt, as he excused himself. I looked at Tadeas' beef and knew I should have ordered that instead. Mine looked good, but I loved a good steak.

"You want some?" he offered.

"Um, no thank you. It just looks wonderful."

He took a bite and said, "It's pretty damn good."

We sat and ate. When I emptied my wine glass, and I knew I had several times, he refilled it. I think he only refilled his once. Walt brought a second bottle when the first emptied, asking if we would be having dessert. I looked at Tadeas prompting him to reply if he wanted, "No thank you, Walt, the dinner was great. My compliments."

"Thank you, Sir. And for you, Ms. Davenport?"

"No, thank you, Walt. Thank you for your attention tonight."

"I will be close by if you decide you need anything else."

"Thank you." He pulled my credit card out of his apron, sliding it across the table to me, then stalked away. I had already given him my credit card to pay for the meal before Tadeas arrived giving him instructions on the percentage of the tip to include on the check. Waiting tables was a thankless job, and I always wanted to make sure that my server was heavily compensated. I liked to do it before the meal. It insured that our service would be great and would be great every time I returned to an establishment. I would have to return here at some point and sample that dried-aged steak. Walt would want to wait on my table when I returned.

"Is there a bill?" Tadeas asked.

"No. I took care of it," I replied. They would send the receipt to my phone, and I could sign it, then submit it back to them. Ah, the age of modern technology.

"Where should I return this suit?" he asked. That one hurt because the suit was his. Just one of many others I had made for him, anticipating him taking the job as my partner. They were all at my home in hopes that this would work out in the end, and I could return to establishing proxies in the United States with a new partner.

"The suit is yours. I ordered it to be specifically tailored for you. You may do with it as you wish," I answered his question in hopes that perhaps he would keep it. He did look fantastic in it. "You clean up good. Maybe you would consider keeping it." I tried to smile at him but had pretty much given up hope.

He blushed. "I don't understand why you would have a custom suit made for me."

"Because my infiltration of your class was with the intent of recruiting you to help me with some upcoming projects. You are uniquely qualified to help me with these projects, and I tried a method of reverse recruiting. I wanted to be under your authority to get a first-hand experience of how you operated, and how you reacted to a difficult situation. My method was flawed, and I failed miserably. I caused an upheaval in your instruction, distracting you from the task at hand. I can apologize infinitely, and it wouldn't cover how I've wronged you." I waited for strike three.

Instead, he leaned back in the seat, stretching his legs out. "I've sat for too long. I need to get up." He stood, buttoned his suit coat, and turned to me. His dark green eyes met mine. This time he held my gaze. "Come on, let's walk," he said as he offered me his hand.

CHAPTER 9

ABIGAIL

*W*hen I took his hand, he steadied me while standing. I think he thought I'd drank too much. I was feeling the alcohol some, but more than anything, his touch made me falter. My heel actually just caught on the carpet, causing me to wobble. I'm not always graceful. We walked to the front door, and I spoke to the valet. "Gerald, would you please get my car."

"No, wait. We just need the key, Gerald," Tadeas said.

Gerald handed the key to me, but Tadeas took it from him before it hit my hand. I couldn't help but laugh at the surprised look on Gerald's face, but Tadeas pulled out a $100 bill and handed it to him. Gerald thanked him, and we exited the restaurant.

Tadeas looked down at the key. "Mercedes, huh?"

"Yes, the Germans know how to build an automobile," I replied.

"You okay to walk?" he asked.

"I'm not drunk, Tadeas."

"I didn't imply that you were. You are wearing 4-inch heels, and I didn't know if you would be up for it," he explained in a way that made me feel like an idiot for defending my current state.

"Oh, well, they are 3-inch heels, because I didn't want to seem taller than you," I replied.

"Why? What does that matter?" he finally laughed.

"Male psychology," I smirked.

"Please, give me a break," he laughed again. He never let go of my hand. "They are nice shoes."

"Why, thank you! I was beginning to think you didn't notice." I felt myself getting way too comfortable with him, considering the friendly banter. I had made sure that all my bruises were healed up right after I had grandfather remove the binding from me. Before that, I had looked like a semi ran over me.

"I noticed," he said, "and I apologize, I should have told you earlier that you look lovely."

"I clean up good," I replied, and he laughed again. "Thank you, Tadeas."

We walked up a block, turning right. We headed a few blocks to Central Park in Boulder, walking in an uneasy silence. He took my hand, placing it in the crook of his arm. Taking a position between me and the street, he blocked me from any traffic on the side of the road. I had debated over my entire wardrobe that I keep in Colorado at the compound which existed in a very small closet in my office but I'd opted to make a call to my home. I'd opened the door to the closet portal in my office, then I'd waited. Within a few minutes, a hanging dress bag had slid through the portal.

I had picked out this white eyelet lace Zimmerman dress.

Now, not *everything* I owned was designer, but this was a special occasion. I had matched it with a nude pair of strappy Jimmy Choo heels. I thought it looked good. Perhaps to convey the innocence which I didn't have.

We walked along the Boulder Creek in the darkness. Being outside after dark always made me nervous. The bad things of the world chose the night as their playground, and I wasn't really dressed for a fight.

"Why are you nervous? Surely you don't think I'd hurt you." Tadeas broke the silence.

"Ok, first of all, the fact that you know I'm nervous is a little strange. But no, I'm not afraid of you at all. I'm afraid of all the monsters in the dark," I replied.

"You know what I am," he half-questioned, half-stated.

"Yes, I do."

"Then you should know I'd never let anything hurt you while you are in my care."

"I thought this was my gig," I responded. He played the guardian role here with me as he did with his students. It made me feel warm and safe. Probably inherent to his kind and abilities.

"You gave me authority over tonight back at the restaurant when you said you were an open book."

"I suppose you could see it that way," I responded with a smile. He walked over to a bench next to the water and sat down. I followed him over and sat next to him. He watched the shadows. I saw his eyes flick to the yellow I'd seen once before. "See anything?"

"No. Seems pretty quiet." The park was well lit and there were a good number of people out walking and jogging. Several couples walked by laughing and chatting.

"So, it was a job interview." He delved back into the situation.

"Yes, of sorts. The job is already yours. The deception was unnecessary. I see that now."

"What is the job exactly?"

"For years I worked with a man named Lincoln, and we established the proxy system in the Western Hemisphere," I explained.

The foundation of our agency was built on the human proxy system. In each large city, a prominent citizen established by the Agency kept an ear to the ground in the government as well as the social scene. Each proxy was assigned canvas leaders and crews based on the population of the city that they represented. These canvas crews were not much more than street gangs. Frequenting the hot spots for criminal activity, they were trained to look for rising supernatural threats in the city.

We established a process of reporting these instances back to the proxy who would report back to the Agency, and the Agency would send out investigators to handle any threat they deemed to be large enough to be handled by the proxy or crews on their own. The Proxies reported to a Regent. There were 2 Regents in the US: East Coast and West Coast. Canada, Central America, and South America each had their own Regent. The West Coast Regent covered the Pacific islands as well. Most of the proxies in place today, I had recruited or vetted in some way.

The human proxy was generally a man, but we did have a few women like Maria Espinoza in Miami. They were wealthy and well-known businesspersons in the community. Sometimes they were a spiritual leader. In many cases, we would have to spend several years establishing the proxies in a city. Getting their name out to the city at large and the powers that be by attending art functions and contributing to local charities. We also had a large network of law enforcement officers who were aware of the monsters in our world who would aid us with info to help eliminate threats that arose.

"Twenty-five years ago, Lincoln was murdered, and I haven't

been able to bring myself to continue that work until now. The proxy system is failing, and I've volunteered to revamp it. Along with how we train canvas crews. Technology is spinning forward so quickly we can barely keep up. We've got to become more adaptable and stop losing too many crew members on the streets," I said, knowing this would be an issue he would appreciate.

"You want to change how I train, how we train crews?"

"Yes, that's one part of it. Your expertise is the training of the crews, and I knew that you could help me with that process better than anyone else. I had hoped that you would have ideas on the best ways to approach it. Ways we can keep these kids alive longer."

"I have always followed the protocol set forth by the Agency, but I have a ton of ideas how we could make it better. It does need to be changed. I may put out full classes, but I know once they hit the streets their life expectancy is very low. That's why it bothered me so much with you, with Rachel." He stopped mid-thought.

"I really hate that name." I offered a half smile.

He looked down into his upturned palms. "Yeah, me too."

"I'd rather not hear it again," I said.

He looked at me and put his hand on mine. "Me, too." He paused for a minute and continued. "I knew with your situation I would be putting you out on the street untrained and vulnerable, but honestly we don't do much more for those who complete the program. The support system isn't strong enough. They fall through the cracks. We may teach them to fight all the monsters to the best of their abilities, but they need more than fighting skills. We are failing them."

He was passionate about this. I had hoped for as much. After watching him push through several classes, I knew that he spent far more individual time with recruits than any other instructor. From being in his class, I had discovered just how much he put into each class and each student. "What else would be required of me?"

"Well, I don't like going into situations alone. Part of why our training is bad. It's always better to have a partner. It's even better to have a whole team to confront issues. We need to be teaching these kids in pairs or teams. Teach them to use each other's strengths and cover each other's weaknesses. But outside of the combat training, my team and I respond to the high threats that the proxies and regents run-up to the Agency. Sometimes they come across a powerful black magic wielder and need us to come in and neutralize the threat. These guys never work alone either. Most of them operate in a hierarchy system, a boss with minions. It's what makes what we do better and more effective. We work together as equals, and I prefer to have a partner, plus my team. And finally, I have to establish new proxies. Normally, we chose regular humans with no abilities because they are in the public eye in these positions, plus they age eventually tiring of their responsibilities. We have a long list of proxies who are ready to retire. I've got to start choosing and establishing new proxies again. I'm sure those methods need to be revamped as well. Frankly, I'm way behind on what needs to be done." I watched him process all the information. He looked down at his watch. It was past 10 p.m. "I'm sorry. Do you need to get back? I didn't mean to keep you out for so long."

"No. No, it's fine, Abigail. I have nothing to do until Monday morning classes. It is getting late here though. We are pushing our luck sitting out here in the night."

"I'm pretty sure the two of us could handle anything that came along."

He smiled. "Yes, I'm sure we could if you weren't wearing those heels. We shouldn't tempt the forces that be. I want to continue the discussion though. I feel like we've barely touched the surface of this topic."

I stood and looked at him. "If you trust me, I have somewhere we can go."

"Where?" he asked, looking up to me.

"Can't tell you. It's a secret," I said and winked at him. He laughed and stood up.

"Okay, but I'm driving."

WE WALKED BACK TO THE RESTAURANT, CROSSING THE STREET TO the valet lot. In the midst of the empty lot sat a beautiful metallic black Mercedes S63 AMG Coupe.

"You've got to be kidding me?" he scoffed.

"What? It's a great car," I said.

"It's a two hundred thousand-dollar car!"

"Yep, you should see my other car though. I think you would like it better than this one."

"What else do you have?"

"A fully restored steel grey 1967 Mustang Shelby GT."

"An Eleanor? Can I drive it too?"

"Sure, if you agree to be my partner," I smiled.

"That's my kind of bribery," he said.

"It's a done deal?" I asked.

"Don't get ahead of yourself, Abby. Get in." He opened the passenger side door for me. I really didn't like anyone driving my car, but I indulged him as much as I could. He waited until I was inside, then lightly shut the door. Crossing in front of the car, he kept his eyes alert, searching for any threats. He slid down into the car and sat for a moment admiring the dash's burl walnut wood accents. I giggled at him in awe of the car.

"Push button start. Let's go," I said, bringing him back from his daydream.

"Where to?"

"Let's take this thing back to the compound, and I've got somewhere we can go from there."

"Can I take the scenic route back?" he asked with a youthful excitement in his voice.

I giggled like a girl at him. "Sure." With that, he shifted into gear, then headed in the complete opposite direction from our destination. Grinning from ear to ear, he cut his eyes to me to see if I disapproved. If I had known all it would have taken was to let him drive my car, I could have saved myself a lot of bruises. I mused over this thought and several others while he took his joy ride. Hell, I could have just bought him one. But looking back, being in his class did help me to understand him better, perhaps the whole thing wasn't a complete fuck up. Just mostly a fuck up.

"I know what you are thinking," he said as he drove.

"What am I thinking?"

"You could have just bribed me with a fancy car."

"Ludicrous! I would never consider you to be such a simpleton, Tadeas Duarte." His statement puzzled me, but I supposed it was just a good guess. Or perhaps his jaguar sensibilities allowed him to pick up on the thoughts of other people. To be honest, I wasn't sure exactly what Tadeas' jaguar could do. I wanted to know though. Jaguar shifters were very rare.

He shrugged and kept driving. The last turn we made directed us back to the main road toward the compound. He drove the car into the underground parking garage, and I showed him where I normally parked it. When we got out, he handed me the key.

"I keep the key in the top drawer of my desk. You are welcome to it anytime."

"Still trying to bribe me?" he asked.

"No, I don't think that will work, but the offer is there just the same."

"Thanks, Abby."

We entered the sparse building that was the cover for the

underground compound. As we approached the elevators, I noticed that he started to tense up again. Something about being here made him feel the need to be professional. This wasn't a bad thing, but I couldn't imagine all the time he spent in the compound working with classes. Besides what he did with his spare time, the rest had to be very boring. The doors opened, and we stepped inside the car. I hit the #4 which would take us down to the level housing my office with the Agency. The compound rested deep below the surface. It had been an old military installation at one time. The Agency has many offices and training facilities all over the world. This was just the main one for the Western Hemisphere. When the doors opened, I directed him toward my office. Standing just outside the door waiting for us was Meredith Spence.

"Meredith, what are you doing here? Is something wrong?" Tadeas asked as he picked up his pace to reach her before me.

"I've tried to call you multiple times tonight, and you didn't answer. I was worried." He glanced down at his phone.

"No missed calls, Mere. I don't know what happened. Why were you worried?"

"Because I haven't talked to you since the beginning of the day, and I didn't know how you were feeling after this morning," she said, looking over his shoulder at me. She had that whole disdain thing going on again. She looked at me head to toe, then back to him and his suit. "But I see that everything is just fine after she lied to your face for months. You went out on a date with her?! What the hell, Tadeas?"

"Um, right here," I said, waving at her. Honestly, I was just trying to lighten the mood a little, but she didn't take it that way. Okay, maybe I was provoking her for coming after him. But only a little.

"You shut up. I'm not here to talk to a lying bitch!" she exclaimed. No kid gloves for me. Tadeas put his hands up between us like we were on the verge of a fight. I just laughed, opening the door to my office. After stepping inside, I shut the door behind me. I didn't need to be in the hallway to hear what she said to him. I listened from the inside with just a hint of a magical listening spell.

"Meredith, really? That wasn't very nice," I heard him say scolding her. "We went out to dinner to talk about why she was in the class and what happened. It wasn't a date. It was business." He spoke kindly to her in soft tones to try to calm her down. He obviously had feelings for her. I wasn't sure why that bothered me, but it did.

"I can't believe that you were distracted by a pretty face and a deep wallet. Besides she's probably set a spell down upon you. She's a powerful wizard. She has been heartless and doesn't give a second thought to you and what you are trying to accomplish. She came into *your* class and made a mess of things," she practically shouted. No need for the eavesdrop spell. She wanted me to hear.

"Meredith, please calm down. Let's go downstairs and talk about this. You are right on all of those counts, and it's why we went out to talk about it. As a matter of fact, it isn't resolved, but I do understand it a little more now. Please, Meredith. I'm fine. I appreciate your concern, but Abigail Davenport isn't the first wizard I've ever met. I doubt there is a spell she could put on me that I wouldn't feel. I'll tell her that I'll talk to her tomorrow, and we can go downstairs and have a drink."

"She doesn't deserve you to have to explain yourself to her, Tadeas. You are an idiot. I can't believe you've done this." I wasn't sure what she thought we had done, but I could assure her that other than some protective hand holding, Tadeas was a gentleman.

"I haven't done anything, Meredith. Just please wait here," he said. He knocked lightly on the door.

"It's not locked, Tadeas," I said. He stepped into the room. His eyes and face were filled with pain. I rose from my desk and spoke. "Look, she's right. You don't have to explain yourself to me. Just go see if you can get her calmed down. I'm sorry to have caused any friction between the two of you. I hadn't realized that the two of you were together." He waved his hand in the air and shook his head. The hand wave made me smile briefly after watching him fight the hand motions in class. He approached the desk, standing across from me.

Lowering his voice, he said, "No, it's not like that between us. She is just upset because this morning rattled me. She's pretty *sensitive* to those kinds of things. Can we meet up sometime tomorrow to finish our discussion?"

"Sure. You name the time, and I'll be here. I wanted to take you out to my home. If we have time, maybe I can show you tomorrow." I walked around the desk to him, taking his hand. His brown skin contrasted against my pale hands. His hand felt warm, but rough and used. "I'm so sorry, Tadeas." He squeezed my hand back.

"How about 10 a.m.? Want me to meet you here?"

"Yes, I'll be here." He released my hand, then turned toward the door. "You really do look great in that suit," I added.

He turned his head back to me, and I could see the light of a smile in his eyes. He just chuckled a bit, waving a dismissive hand at me. I watched him open the door and walk out.

I could hear his voice turn to a stern cadence as they walked down the hallway back to the elevator bank.

I heard her say as they got in the elevator, "I didn't know you had a suit like that. You look great in it." I laughed out loud to the empty room as everything seemed to stand still and quiet. It was past midnight, and early into Saturday morning. I turned to the closet door, opening it. The closet concealed the portal to my home. I stepped through regretting that he wasn't coming with me. We still had many things to discuss. I just hoped we could pick back up where we left off tomorrow morning. I hoped more than ever that Tadeas Duarte would be my new partner.

CHAPTER 10

VANESSA

*W*hen I awoke, I heard voices at the end of the hallway in the apartment I shared with John Mwenye. Waking up alone sucked especially when you knew you went to bed with someone beside you.

Recognizing the other voice, I realized that Nalusa Chito was here. I heard his deep baritone along with Mwenye discussing matters that I assumed they did not want me to hear. I listened anyway, tuning out everything around me and focusing on their voices.

"Do you think the old man would join us?" Chito asked.

"I would think it would be in his best interests," Mwenye replied. "And if it isn't, we will bring his long life to an end."

"He finds a way to survive things. Even Lincoln couldn't put him down although all the legends said he did."

"Legends and stories always favor the heroes. But we all know the true endings, and we also know the heroes aren't always who they claim to be," Mwenye said. "For example, I know for a fact that Miss Davenport is quite well versed in the dark arts. She would put Miss Vaughn to shame. I would give anything to see her walk on the edge of darkness and slip off into my bed." His dark chuckle joined with Chito's.

I burned with the anger rising in me, but I dismissed it for now. I'd let it simmer. I needed to know their plans. My only advantage would be to know things they didn't know I that I knew. Besides his comment about Miss Davenport, I hated that he was leaving me out of his plans. I had earned my place beside him, following his every order without question.

"I doubt that would ever happen, my dark friend. However, the extra materials are being stored in Boulder. We will have access to them whenever we choose to take them out," Chito said. "In the meantime, I'm going to cause a little trouble for some of the individuals there. Hopefully, I can get my hands on that jaguar. As you know, I do not have a jaguar in my collection. The rumor is that he is melanistic. I am willing to bet he is gorgeous."

"You are repulsive, Nalusa. There are shifters who are great allies to us. You should not stuff them or cut off their heads to display on your wall," Mwenye said. I knew he never liked Chito's hunting practices, but he also knew it was handy in certain situations.

"My concerns lie only in that if we ever split from the GEA that those within it might come after us," Chito said.

"Nonsense. Doro loves her money. She would not dare risk it. Donovan has his own agenda, as you know. The Priest has no function in the grand scheme, at all. That leaves us and the Director. With no one to direct, the position becomes impotent. No one will come after us. I'm tired of trying to justify our actions. We are doing this for the betterment of all humanity and to create a power base that will set us up for ages to come."

"I believe in you, Mwenye. I do have concerns about your loose cannon," Chito said.

"Miss Vaughn, I know you are listening. Please come here," Mwenye said. I hated it when he did this to me. I could feel the humiliation that was coming even before he spoke. I hadn't interrupted him. I hated that he knew that I was listening. My freedom was non-existent as long as I lived with him. I slipped into a silk robe, then sauntered down the hallway slowly. Chito looked shocked that Mwenye knew I listened. "Chito, there is one thing you need to understand about Miss Vaughn and me. She does as I tell her to do when I tell her to do it with no exceptions. Isn't that right, my dear?"

"Yes, my love," I responded. I wanted to strangle him. How dare he parade me out in front of Chito?

"Vanessa, were you listening to our conversation?" he asked me.

"Yes, I was," I admitted.

"Why were you doing that?" Mwenye said.

"To see what you were talking about behind my back," I admitted.

"This isn't necessary," Chito interjected.

"It most certainly is necessary. While I agree Miss Vaughn can be a loose cannon, she has infinite talents that make up for it. She is excellent at apologizing for things. Aren't you my love?" he said coolly.

"I am," I said. I looked at him as I pleaded with my eyes. It wouldn't work. He had no heart.

"I would like you to apologize to Mr. Chito for your rude behavior," he said, motioning to Chito.

"I am very sorry for eavesdropping on your conversation, Sir," I said.

"That isn't good enough Vanessa. Please get on your knees and beg him for forgiveness," Mwenye insisted.

"John, that's enough, really. This isn't necessary," Chito said, looking at me horrified. I bent to my knees and bowed my head.

"Nalusa, you questioned my authority over her. This is your answer," he said. "Beg him, Vanessa."

"Please, Mr. Chito, forgive me for being rude," I said. The day quickly approached that I would find a way, no matter what to kill John Mwenye. It didn't matter that I loved him. These were the moments that took every part of who I was away. He might as well have me as one of his zombie minions. I didn't care how many bodies he would jump into with his creepy necromancy skills. I wanted to cut his dick off, then shove it into his mouth.

"You are forgiven, child. That is enough of this," Nalusa said.

"Now, I'm going to get a shower for a meeting later. Vanessa, please sit there on your knees until I tell you to move. Nalusa, it was good to see you. I am glad that we are on the same page regarding the split from the GEA. We will start making preparations immediately. I'm going to start siphoning money off these investors for our own interests even if I have to make them do it because I can make anyone do what I want them to do, can't I Miss Vaughn?"

"You most certainly can, my love," I said almost gagging. A long time ago I had given him power and dominion over me without knowing exactly what I was doing. We made a deal. He would teach me necromancy, and I would do as he commanded. We sealed the deal with a kiss and dark, twisted sex. Ever since then, he asserted his will over me as he wanted. Sometimes I loved it. Sometimes I hated it. Lately, all I wanted to do was kill him.

Nalusa looked pained. I knew his relationship with his apprentice was not like this. Mwenye was far darker than even Nalusa Chito. "I am very sorry my dear," he said, as he got up to leave.

"I made the choice, Sir. I made it a long time ago. There are times when the rent is due," I explained.

"Still, just because you can exert your will on another, does not mean you should," Chito said. "Good day, Vanessa."

"Good day, Sir," I said. Chito left. Mwenye showered, and I heard him moving around in the bedroom.

"I could have made you fuck him," he said.

"Thank you for not doing that to me," I replied. He entered the room dressed for a meeting.

"You kneel there as punishment until I get back," he commanded. The force of it rippled over my skin in goosebumps.

"As you wish, my love," I said reluctantly, and he left. I sat on my knees waiting for him to return. He was gone for 6 hours and 32 agonizing minutes. When he returned, he released me from the position with a simple word.

He smelled like sex. I knew he had gone to meet another partner. Over the years, we had many partners in our bed but never had he gone to someone without me. Not that I knew about. I went to bed knowing that my life was about to change. I contemplated all the ways I could kill him because that is what it would take to free me from his servitude. Making the right moves would be essential to keeping my life while taking his.

CHAPTER 11

TADEAS

"If I had known that all I had to do to get a date was to lie to you, I would have done it a long time ago," Meredith pouted, as she sat on my couch. I didn't want her to come in again, but I didn't want her shouting my business in the hallway either. I had slipped into the bedroom to remove the suit. Putting on a navy t-shirt and a pair of jeans, I tried to reason with her. Frankly, any time I spent with Abigail was none of her business.

"Petty much, Meredith? I don't think you've laid it on quite thick enough," I said. She was starting to get on my nerves with this lingering hope that there was something more between us. She'd gone from attacking Abigail to berating me from the moment we entered the elevator until I rushed her into my room because she knew how to make a scene. My patience wore thin with every word out of her mouth. Our friendship hung by a thread. "We tried that a long time ago. It didn't work. If you want something more, I'm telling you right now that I'm not interested."

"I didn't mean it, for real, but thanks for that reminder of how I'm not the right one for you."

I sat down beside her, looking her in the face. "I'm tired. It's been a long emotional day. I don't handle emotional very well. You know that. Can we please save the rest of this argument for tomorrow?"

"You won't have time tomorrow. You are meeting her again in the morning."

"Wait, you were listening in on our conversation?"

"I'm sorry, was it private?"

"It was behind a closed door, Meredith. That's pretty damn private. I've tolerated you tonight because we *are* friends, but I've had enough. You need to go." She stood, stomping to the door. She looked back at me just before she passed through it.

"She will be the death of you, Tadeas. I wouldn't be able to stand it," she said as she walked out the door, slamming it on the way.

"Holy hell! Enough freaking drama!" I said to the empty room. I stood up, switched off all the lights in the apartment, and made my way to the bedroom. I wondered what I would have been doing had Meredith not shown up. I hadn't decided that I was going with Abigail to her home. I needed to process every-thing we had talked about. Dinner was tense, but once we left the restaurant things were better. Mostly because I decided that if I didn't calm my anger with her, I wouldn't know what the hell had been going on with her in my classroom.

At first, my interest wasn't genuine. I was curious though. I just needed to relax, and I could tell she did, too. But the longer we talked the more I actually liked her. She had a quick wit and a way to explain things that made her likable. She was beautiful which I had noticed in class but didn't allow myself to entertain the thought. She was almost too pretty like she was part Fae which meant trouble. She would make every man in the vicinity look at her if we were together. I'm not sure I could handle that in a relationship. Not that I considered having a relationship with her, just speculation inside a worn and tired mind.

Between her lying to me, because Meredith was right about that part, and her beauty, plus the way she flaunted her money, I didn't think I'd ever be able to trust her in a working relationship, much less a personal one. Stripping out of my clothes, I crawled into my bed.

The bed felt great because sleep was exactly what I needed. I relaxed but my mind still wandered through the events of the night. From the point when I decided to go meet her until now trying to let the day's troubles pass, so I could sleep without nightmares. I went through a ritual of assessing the day and calming myself before falling asleep. I thought about every moment. It would be easier to hate her had I not enjoyed myself. It would also be easier to decline the job offer if she wasn't absolutely right about how we needed to approach training and changing it up to keep these kids alive longer. I needed more time to decide. She didn't say she was on a deadline.

When I had entered the restaurant, my nerves were making my head pound, and I hadn't noticed how nice she looked until we went on the walk together. My initial admiration of her proved to be spot on as she gracefully walked in those heels. I liked her hand in mine like she belonged to me. All of that didn't matter. Abigail Davenport was a liar. No fuck-me heels could change that.

She obviously knew a lot about me before ever coming into my class. I got the impression that she was the type of person to be thorough. She probably knew everything about my past. About the first time, I shifted. The pain of that memory struck me fresh. It had been almost a century since it happened, but it was a bleeding wound in my soul every time I thought about it.

I hadn't really aged since I had reached adulthood. I hadn't learned much about my abilities, because I had no shaman to guide me. But I knew I wouldn't age. I got the distinct feeling that Abigail didn't age either. That she was much older than she looked. It was something in her eyes. Bright green inquisitive eyes. She had spoken of setting up proxies, and I knew that process went back to the early 1900s when the Agency's head-quarters was in Lisbon, Portugal. Age was not something I would dare ask any woman. She looked to be between 25 and 30. I wouldn't even dare to guess.

I thought about Meredith and how angry she was at me. I didn't tell her that I was going to meet Abigail on purpose, because it wasn't her business. Plus, part of me knew she'd blow a gasket, which was exactly what she did. I didn't realize, however, that she still harbored such deep feelings for me even after all this time. I thought that had passed between us. It had been several years ago that we both agreed that we were just friends and that's all we would ever be. Perhaps I had known that she felt that way but dismissed it thinking if we didn't discuss it, that it would go away. Her final words to me about Abigail being the death of me were the last thing I thought about as my brain settled to rest.

Ugh, so much drama. I was exhausted just thinking about all of it again. I drifted off to sleep thinking about driving a sweet Mercedes around Boulder, CO.

I HAD FORGOTTEN TO SET AN ALARM. WHEN I WOKE UP, I HAD that panicky moment when you realize you are supposed to be somewhere but you forgot to plan ahead. I grabbed my phone, almost lost my balance, and fell off the bed. It was only 9 a.m. I still had time to get up and get a shower before meeting Abigail at her office. While showering I decided it might be best if we finished our discussion in her office instead of going back to her home. I would be uncomfortable wherever she lived, and I wouldn't be able to make a sound decision because I was distracted or nervous. I slipped back on the pair of jeans from last night and a clean t-shirt. This one was black. Slipping on my boots, I took a look at myself in the mirror before I left. It didn't matter what I looked like anyway. This was a business deal.

I wondered if Meredith was waiting out in the hall to prevent me from going to see Abigail. I really wanted to avoid another confrontation. Pausing for a moment, I cleared my mind. My feline senses took over, feeling for a presence out into the hallway. I couldn't hear or smell anyone out there. I could smell Meredith's lingering scent from last night, but I knew she was long gone. Her scent was a combination of lavender and sage. I accused myself of being a coward and stepped out into the hallway. Taking the elevator to the fourth floor, I prepared myself mentally not to fall for the charming ways of Miss Davenport. Her green eyes and pretty lips weren't going to distract me from the purpose of our meeting.

As I approached Abigail's office, I could hear the squeak of her chair and the rustling of papers. Then I heard it. The soft steady rhythm of her heartbeat. As a predator, I used my ability to sense heartbeats in every situation to gauge the mood of anyone that I encountered. Abigail's heartbeat seemed different to me. It was definitely different from when she was in my classroom. She was always a bundle of nerves, bordering on exasperation. But as I thought about what she has put herself through by binding her magic, the irregular heartbeat was explainable. I lightly knocked on the door.

"Come in," I heard her call with a muffled voice.

Opening the door, I smiled at her working at her desk. She sat there with a doughnut in one hand and using her other hand to peck out something on a laptop on the desk. She glanced over, grinning at me. She pointed at the box of doughnuts on the desk. The top of the box had a logo for a bakeshop in Boulder. Surely, she hadn't gone all the way back into Boulder for doughnuts this morning.

She wore a light turquoise shirt that dipped in the front, but not low enough to show anything. I could see the edge of her jeans just above the desk line. She wore a pendant shaped like a sun around her neck with a red-orange glittering jewel in the center. I couldn't name the stone, but it was pretty.

"Help yourself, Tadeas, I've got a couple of emails I need to respond to and I'll be ready to go."

I reached for a glazed doughnut, and said, "Yeah, about that." She immediately stopped typing, turning to me with questions in her eyes. "I thought it might be better if we talk here rather than going back to your place. Just to keep it neutral territory." Her eyes darkened a bit with disappointment.

"We will do whatever you wish. I didn't mean to make you feel uncomfortable by inviting you into my home. I will call George and tell him to cancel the lunch preparations."

"Oh, I'm sorry. I didn't realize you would go to the trouble."

"If there is one thing I know about this supernatural world that we live in, it's that you don't skip hospitality." She was right. Hospitality was an old-world tradition. If you invited someone to your home, you should swear to not to harm them while in your home and offer them food and drink. It was a bond that if broken could start a war.

"Well, maybe since you went to the trouble, we could discuss things here, and we could have lunch there. If you would like," I offered not wanting to upset her. I didn't know why, because I had every right to request that we not go to her house. Quickly her disappointment cleared, and my offer seemed to be acceptable to her. I had already given into her.

"Like I said, whatever you wish." Once again, she gave me authority in the conversation and for whatever the duration of the day we spent together. I watched her as she typed emails, then shuffled papers around on the desk. The doughnuts were exceptionally good. At one point, she pointed out the coffee in the corner. The pot was full.

"Would you like me to fix you a cup?" I asked her since she seemed too busy to do it herself.

"Um, no thanks. I don't drink coffee."

"Then why is there a whole pot of it here?" I asked.

"It's there for you if you wanted. There's also sodas, milk and bottled water in the mini-fridge," she pointed out.

There was a mini fridge under the counter that held the coffee pot. There was an assortment of creamers and sweeteners. I drank coffee black, but she had all the bases covered. I got the feeling that's how she did everything. Covered all her bases and impressed the hell out of whoever she negotiated or spoke with.

"Will you do me a favor?" she asked.

"Yeah, sure."

"Please put these doughnuts over there on the counter. I need to quit eating them! The food at the training center isn't bad, but it isn't good either," she laughed.

I picked them up and placed them on the counter but grabbed one more as I headed back to the chair across from her desk. Most people had two chairs adjacent to a desk, but she only had one. I guess she had been away from the office since she came into my class. I couldn't imagine being behind for 3 months on emails and work. Methodically, she went through each of the papers she had on the desk and clicking deftly through emails on the computer. Half of her blonde hair was pulled back in a clip behind her head but there were several strands that weren't quite long enough, and they fell down around her face, framing her green eyes and the light freckles on her cheeks. She smiled as I admired her. Surely, she smiled at an email. I didn't think that I stared enough for her to pick up on it.

Diverting my attention to the rest of the room, I looked at the well-furnished small office. The walls were lined with a rich dark wood, but the whole room seemed light despite the aged-wood look. There was a small 4 tier bookshelf lined with old and new books alike. A wooden file cabinet stood behind the desk. On it sat 3 shining spheres in a stainless-steel dish. One looked to be solid iron. Another looked to be stainless steel. The last one appeared to be a milky glass. There were a few plants spread about the room, mostly succulents that didn't require sunlight. There were no pictures on the walls. None on her desk. In fact, besides the papers she was currently working on, the desk was empty.

She reached inside a drawer to pull out a pen. She scribbled something on one of the papers, then placed the pen back in the desk. Once she finished, she gathered the papers up. Rearranging the order of a couple of them, she placed them in the top drawer of her desk. With a couple of clicks, her screen popped up a picture of a beautiful Spanish style stucco mansion on a hill covered in grapevines. A winery. It looked like a peaceful place. She saw me looking at it. Her lips turned up in a beautiful smile. She had to have Fae blood in her.

"Looks like a nice place," I said, feeling awkward because I had gotten caught staring at her computer screen. She lifted a mug to her lips, one I hadn't seen before this moment, and I saw the steam lift out of it as she took a sip. She set the mug on the desk.

"Wait. I thought you didn't drink coffee."

"It's tea. Chai. It is a pretty picture. There was nothing on my screen that I would have minded you reading over my shoulder. Had my work been private, I would have shut it down before you entered. But since I would like you to be my partner, I thought it might be a gesture of goodwill to show you that I wasn't afraid to do my work in front of you. I don't want to hide anything anymore, Tadeas," she replied. "Before we start into our conversation from last night, I would like your permission to cast a bubble of privacy around us. It will keep anyone outside the walls of this room from hearing what we are saying. Is that okay?"

"Yeah, sure," I said, remembering that Meredith had over-heard us last night. I was willing to bet that Abigail knew it.

I hadn't seen Abigail cast any spells, but I found myself eager to see her in action. She simply took a deep breath and spoke one word.

"*Bulla.*"

A warm sensation built up around me, flooding over me like walking into the sun from a dark place. I felt the pressure of the magic wave pass over me. Suddenly it felt like I was in a cage. I had to calm the beast inside me because no animal wanted to be caged.

"You okay?" she asked.

"Yeah. Just got a little claustrophobic for a moment."

"That's a normal feeling. It will pass in a moment and you won't be able to feel the magic anymore. It's just a small, subtle spell. If you continue to be uncomfortable, just let me know and I can remove it."

"Okay. I'll let you know."

"So, what new questions do you have for me, Tadeas Duarte?"

All the questions from the night before suddenly slipped my mind, and I felt like an idiot. I should have written them down. She looked at me with concern, but offered, "Why don't I ask a couple of questions to get us started? Is that okay?" She tried to ease me deeper into the conversation. She was probably good at everything, and I hated people like that.

"Sounds good. And I should have said it yesterday, too. You are welcome to ask me anything. I have nothing to hide from you."

"Excellent. I'm curious. Are you okay after last night? You did seem to have a little fun driving my car. But the end of the night didn't go as either of us had planned. Is Meredith okay?"

"I'm fine. I still have a lot going through my mind about all of it. I wish I had written my questions down, but I was too tired after going out, then dealing with Meredith. As for her, I haven't spoken to her this morning, but as of last night, she was not happy at all. I'm not sure why she has such hatred for you. Maybe it's just me, but nothing I could say would persuade her that you hadn't influenced me by a spell or something more heinous."

Her brow furrowed as she tensed up. "Is there anything I can do to make it better? She really hates me?"

"I can't think of anything. She's been super emotional lately, and we aren't dating. We are just friends. There is only so much I can do to assure her that you aren't corrupting me or putting a spell on me." I kept repeating myself on the dating thing, not that it mattered to Abigail. Probably only mattered to me, but it was something I wanted Abigail to be clear on. I wouldn't put it past Meredith to claim that we were together.

"I can. I can swear to her that I'm not doing those things. I can swear on my power to make it binding." This was a generous offer on her part. If a wielder swore by her power, it became an oath to keep her word. It meant that if Abigail's motivations ever changed, and she did decide to influence me down a dark path that she would lose some of her power.

"No, that isn't necessary. I think given a couple of days she will calm down, and maybe I can get to the bottom of why she's upset." This seemed to satisfy her, but I could tell it bothered her that Meredith didn't like her. But she seemed to understand it better from Meredith's perspective than I did.

"Okay. Perhaps if we start out talking about the training changes we need to make, then we can progress to the job offer," she said, easing the conversation to a more comfortable topic for both of us.

We spent close to two hours talking about different scenarios and curriculums to start challenging our recruits more and teaching them to work together more rather than to fight on their own. We both agreed that they needed to be able to hold their own in a fight but learning to fight together was more beneficial. Finally, I felt like what I was doing at The Agency was less saving the world and more like saving lives. Abigail Davenport had opened those possibilities for me and for every student that would pass through these walls. I had the smallest bit of hope again. Perhaps a bit of forgiveness, too. I understood that her intentions were honorable even if her methods were not.

As a teen, I had faced a similar situation where I believe the people involved had good intentions, however, their methods scarred me for life.

CHAPTER 12

TADEAS
16 Years Old

The priest stood over me chanting in Latin. I didn't know what I had done, but it was bad. They had me tied to a chair. I felt confused and scared. Tears rolled freely down my cheeks as my awkward maturing body shook in fear. They had repeatedly splashed me with holy water. A cloth covered my mouth preventing me from speaking or screaming. I wasn't wearing a shirt. Just my pants.

There were several priests in the room and a large fireplace blazing with flame. I couldn't see the door because it was behind me. I tried to scream, but only muffles came out. I struggled against the bonds, but the priest continued to chant the prayer of exorcism. I tried the best way I knew how to explain that I was just me, and not some demon.

They spent hours questioning me after one of the priests reported to the archbishop that my eyes had shifted colors. I'd seen my eyes do it before. I had always discounted it as a trick of light. I was me.

At first, I refused to believe it, but I knew exactly what the priests were doing. I'd seen them do it to others. They were trying to exorcise a demon from me. But I wasn't possessed. They wouldn't believe me. I struggled and screamed. The priests leading the chant would switch out when one got tired. And eventually, I gave up as well.

I was very tired. So very tired. I passed out in the chair.

When I awoke, the room was quiet. Father Sergio stood before me with his prayer book. He had always been the kindest to me. He taught me to read. He taught me the Bible. He taught me everything I knew. His eyes were shadowed by pain and regret.

"Tadeas, son, can you hear me?"

"Yes, Father," I replied weakly. I was starving. My cracked lips smacked as my dry throat searched for refreshment. I wasn't sure how long I had been in the chair. Hours? Days?

"Son, please tell me what happened. Did you invite this creature into you? Did you accidentally summon this demon to you? If you did, it's okay. I just need to you explain it to me. We can get it out of you."

"Father," I cried, "there is no demon."

"There is no need to lie, my son. I love you like my own. I want to help. Whatever it was you can tell me. I won't love you any less," he pleaded with me.

"No, Sir. I didn't do anything. There is nothing inside of me," I said.

He squatted down before me, "Tadeas, I see the creature in your eyes. I've seen it before in young men. There is a beast inside you. An unholy beast."

I shook my head and tears ran down my face. "No, Sir, there isn't. I swear on the Bible."

He slapped me across the face. "You do not use God's word to swear upon, Tadeas. You know better, my son."

My cheek tingled from the strike with his palm, and I felt the heat of anger rush to my face. I strained against the bonds on the chair. My body wanted to surge out of them, but something held me in place. I looked up to see my mentor holding his prayer book between us. His lips moved in a silent cadence. He too had joined the chant of the other priests. My blood pounded through my head, and all I could hear was its heavy modulation. I smelled the sweat that rolled down his face. I smelled his fear of what he thought I was. I heard his heart pounding as if it were my own. The embers from the fire behind me drifted around the room. A whole world of smell and sound rushed in on me at once. I strained, trying to scream, but my voice was silent.

Glancing down at my arms, my hands seemed to fade in and out like a flickering candle. A wind shifted through the window-less room moving the flying embers around the room in a different direction. I heard rushing footsteps behind me followed by more murmured prayers. Several of those behind me said, "El Aborrecimiento." I felt a white-hot burning sensation on my shoulder as the smell of burning flesh filled the room.

My body surged again against the restraints. I screamed, but still, no sound came out of my mouth. Then my vocal cords rumbled releasing a deep frightening roar. My mentor's eyes shot open in fear. He fell to his knees, but never stopped his chant. The world around me darkened with a black haze. Father Sergio looked like a ghost to me with a thin white light silhouetting him. Faint lights illuminated behind me casting shadows across the priest. But then I saw him. Behind the priest, a dark figure stood in a black cloak. I could not see his face because he tilted it down-ward, and all I could make out was shifting shadows. I tried to warn the Father, but his eyes were locked on mine. I could not produce any sound other than whines and growls. Tears streamed down his face, watching my body as it convulsed. His voice crescendoed steadily and forcefully. He held a golden crucifix on a chain up to me. I wanted to grasp it. Hold it. I had faith that God would save me from whatever this was. They had taught me to believe. I felt God had a purpose for my life, but then the figure approached Sergio, lifting his hands. I couldn't breathe because every muscle in my body constricted as I dug my nails into the arms of the wooden chair. Long boney fingers protruded out of the demon's black cloak. Finally, I could see his eyes which were burning like tiny fires in the shroud. He said a singular word and I blacked out.

"*Hodéezyééel.*"

I AWOKE IN MY OWN BED AT THE MONASTERY. FATHER SERGIO slept in a chair next to me. My head pounded, and I had a terrible burning sensation on the back of my right shoulder. They had branded me during the exorcism. I knew I would have a cross-shaped scar on my shoulder for the rest of my life. I'd seen them do it before to other wayward-possessed people. I tried to rise up out of the bed, but I had no strength.

Father Sergio woke up and put a firm hand on my chest, "No son, rest. It's over now. I will get you some food and water."

"What happened?" I asked.

"I'm not sure," he replied, "but the demon is gone." He got up, heading toward the door.

"I saw him," I said.

He stopped, then turned back to me. "Who did you see?"

"I saw the demon behind you. Right after they branded me."

Grief wrinkled the edges of his eyes. "I'm sorry that had to be done, but you are a son of the most high God. We marked you for Him. Right after that, the demon left you."

"That's just it, he wasn't in me. He stood behind you. I thought he was going to kill you."

"No, my son, that was you. Had you broken your bonds; you would have more than likely killed me. I'm sorry this happened to you. We need to find out how the demon got in you in the first place. You've always been a good boy. We will have to pray and hope that He gives us the answers we seek. I want you to wear my crucifix for protection." He returned to the bed laying the golden necklace in my hand.

Father Sergio's complete belief in His God had always strengthened me. I had seen the other priests and very few of them truly lived the lives that you would expect them to live. But Father Sergio did. In this case, in my gut, I knew he was wrong. That *thing* wasn't in me. The fight inside of me wanted to kill it. Whatever it was. I wanted it dead. I would find it, and I would kill it before it hurt my mentor or anyone else.

CHAPTER 13

ABIGAIL

For a moment, I watched Tadeas Duarte drift into a memory. I wasn't sure what I had said triggered it or what the memory was. However, he soon shook his head, returning his dark green eyes to me.

"Hungry?" I asked him.

"Yeah, I am."

"Look, you don't have to go to my house, but I swear to you all rights of hospitality. You will not be harmed in any way. In fact, I think you will like the place. I'd really like to show it to you. It's been awhile since I've had a guest." I hoped to lay it on thick to convince him. "If not, we can take a ride back up to Boulder and find something to eat. But seriously, I'm done with cafeteria food."

He laughed. "It's not so bad once you get used to it."

"I'd never get used to it. I'm a stuck-up rich girl."

He shot a look at me as if he was astonished I'd admit to such a thing. Well, at least I knew somewhere inside of him that's what he thought of me. I had no time to let it bother me. We had more important things going on in the world for him to get hung up on my money or for me to worry about what he thought of me personally. "I'm joking," I added.

"Hmph," he grunted. "Where's the portal?"

I pointed to the closet. His instincts surprised me. He'd figured out there was a portal. I got up and walked that direction. He remained seated. "Oh, good grief, decide what you are going to do." I had hoped that came out playful and not tedious. He got up and walked over to the door. Before he could touch the doorknob, I grabbed his hand. "Wait. I have to program it to accept you."

"What?"

"Yeah, the zap it would have given you isn't much harder than static electricity. It's just a warning, but it wouldn't be surviv-able if you tried to go through the portal without my permission."

"A taser doorknob," he stated, "How nice."

"I'm going to cast a spell on the knob, it will glow for a moment then you can put your hand on it. It will code your DNA to the knob allowing you to use the portal as you wish."

"I'm going to put my hand on your glowing knob," he said in a serious tone. I had to look up to him to see if he was joking, then I caught his eye glint with a smile.

"Men," I muttered, rolling my eyes for emphasis. I took a breath and muttered the word, "*Clavem*." The knob began to glow. Timidly he reached for it. "Oh, don't be a baby," I said. He wrapped his hand around it as it pulsed for a moment then winked out.

"Why would you give me access to your home?" he asked. "Who else can use this door?"

"Second answer first, you and me. And first answer last,

because I hope that once you decide to work with me, you will consider it home, too." That sounded like a proposal the way it came out. "I mean, um, well, uh, never mind." I put my hand on top of his turning the knob, then stepped through the glittering portal to my home. I had embarrassed myself trying to be cute. He stepped through the portal in a full roar of laughter which died off the moment he took a look around. I composed myself and said in a formal tone, "Welcome to Casa del Sol, my home. You are always welcome here anytime you wish. Any needs that may arise will be afforded to you. Please consider my home to be your home as well, by my power, I swear it. May your troubles be less, and your happiness be more each time you pass through this door."

"That is the strangest offer of hospitality I've ever heard. Worst marriage proposal as well," and he erupted in laughter again.

"Laugh it up," I said then walked down the hall toward the formally dressed older gentleman waiting for us. He kept laughing but followed me down the hall. George raised his eyebrows at me in question. I just shook my head, and he smiled and turned to Tadeas, "Master Duarte, welcome to Casa del Sol. I am George, the Watcher of this estate. I am at your service." George bowed to him formally. This caused Tadeas to cut back his laughter.

"Thank you, Mr. George," he looked over at me, snickering again.

"Don't even look at me," I said, even though I was grinning too. By this point, seeing him genuinely laugh, even at my expense, made me happy. I had never seen him laugh like that before. I just preferred to share the laughter, not be the subject of it.

"Miss Davenport, lunch is laid out in the dining room," George said turning to lead us there. I turned to follow him and felt Tadeas get close behind me. He lightly touched my arm.

While he was still trying to hold back a laugh, he offered an apology, "Sorry. It just struck me as funny."

I bit the edge of my lip, a bad habit when I was nervous. "It's okay. I'm sure it sounded weird to you. It's a traditional Irish blessing," I turned away from him to follow George. "You have a nice laugh. You should use it more often."

He quickened his steps to walk next to me. As we strolled through the huge house, I cut my eyes to him, watching him as he admired the classic Spanish decor and features. The chateau looked Spanish on the outside too even if we were technically part of France.

"Where are we exactly?" he asked.

"On an island in the Mediterranean. It's completely warded. You can't see it from the sea, and ship captains avoid the area out of instinct. The wards we constructed around the place are only for keeping supernatural beings and monsters out. The portal and a ferry are the only ways to reach the island. The workers who tend the vineyard take the ferry back to Italy each night."

"Vineyard?"

"Yeah, I'll give you the grand tour after lunch, but you saw the picture of it on my laptop." The realization hit him that the elaborate house picture on my laptop was my actual home. We turned into a large gathering room with windowed doors that opened up to an outdoor tiled patio with inviting seats and a view of the courtyard and fountain. Across the courtyard, the entrance to the stables stood detached from the main house. Through a corridor beside the stables, the path opened up to the vineyard. He walked toward the courtyard, staring out the one opened door. Sheer curtains flowed inward as a breeze caught them, blowing a fresh breeze through the room. He stood frozen taking it all in. I walked up beside him, "Everything okay?"

He snapped out of his stare, and said, "Um, yeah. It's nice."

Nice was something, I supposed. He must not have been impressed. "Come. Let's eat, then I'll give you the grand tour."

"Yeah, sure," he shrugged it off. I paced away toward the adjoining dining room. I had instructed George to make sure the dishes were light, but I could tell that he went all out. I reached the table and two settings were laid out. They weren't big dinner settings with all the various silverware, but it was close enough. Both plates were covered with a rounded lid. The spread before us had several offerings besides whatever was under the domes. Tadeas walked up to the head of the table and pulled out the chair. He motioned for me to sit.

"No that's fine, you can sit there," I said.

"This is your home, and I'm just a guest. Please sit."

I obliged him, as he took the place to my right. Lifting the cloches, we found pan-seared scallops covered in a light lemony angel hair pasta. There was a basket of warm breadsticks and small salads.

"Do you eat seafood?" I asked. I had come across far too many people who just didn't have the taste for it.

"Yes, this looks great," he replied. I couldn't tell if he was being polite. I looked across the room as George entered holding a pitcher of lemonade. He poured each of us a glass.

"Master Duarte, is the meal to your liking?" George asked. Tadeas only nodded because he had a mouth full of pasta. "Very good. Miss Davenport, is there anything else I can do for you at the moment?"

"No, George, thank you." George exited the room. I hadn't taken a bite yet. I tried to gauge Tadeas' opinion of the meal. I didn't know his tastes very well. It's hard to observe what people eat sometimes. Especially when 90% of their meals are what they are served from a cafeteria.

"Why does he call me that?"

"Call you what? Master?" I asked. He nodded as he continued to eat. I guessed he was enjoying the meal. "Well, he's technically employed by me, but I couldn't fire him even if I wanted to. He's been here longer than I have. He prides himself on the service of those who enter this home. He watches and knows things. And for whatever reason, which he hasn't explained to me, he has called you Master Duarte since the first time I told him about you. If I had to guess, he considers you already a part of this household and holds you not in the esteem as a guest, but as the master of the house."

"When you say Watcher, you mean with a capital W, right?"

"Yes, he is a Watcher. He does not interfere or meddle in affairs, but he does offer advice. Considering he is a being who has been around longer than my grandfather, I can guarantee it is the best advice you'll ever get," I said. "He is very important to me, and I am blessed to have him in this house."

"How do you get your own Watcher?"

"I'm not sure. He came with the house. It belonged to my grandfather. He gave it to me after…" I trailed off. We were about to enter territory I wasn't comfortable talking about. He looked up from his food. When his eyes met mine, he looked concerned. "I needed somewhere safe to be, and this was the place. He never lived here. He just owned it. I love this place. It's peaceful."

"Somewhere safe," he repeated my words. "Why did one of the most powerful wizards on the earth need a haven? Or is that something you aren't ready to talk about?"

"I haven't always been what I am today. We all grow and learn throughout our lives. And the safe part isn't something I'm ready to discuss." So much for the open book. I added, "But I will if you want me to talk about it further. I did promise to answer all of your questions."

"It's not necessary. I wouldn't have you discuss something that caused you pain and would cause you pain to speak of it again." Outside of losing Lincoln, it was my greatest failure and pain. And I didn't want to talk about it. "You have horses?" he asked changing the subject.

I gathered myself, and replied, "Yes, do you ride?"

"It's been a while, but I used to ride a lot. There was a rancher near Boulder that would house my horse and let me ride on his land. But once the horse passed away, I didn't get another one."

"We can take the riding tour if you would like," I smiled.

"Yes, I'd like that." I knew that George would be within earshot and arrange for it if he hadn't already. As Tadeas cleaned his plate, George entered as if on cue setting a small flan custard before Tadeas. His eyes lit up. "Flan!" he exclaimed. "How did you know it was my favorite from back home?"

I shook my head and said, "I didn't." I looked up at George and smiled.

"Well, it is. I mean the scallop dish was a pleasant surprise. I haven't had them in years, and I really enjoy them. Hard to get them fresh in the middle of Colorado you know, but flan! This is great," he exclaimed as he devoured the little custard covered in caramel.

"Would you like another, Sir?" George asked.

"Oh yes please, if you have another," he replied. It was very childlike, his delight in the simple dessert.

"Would you like one as well, Miss Davenport?"

"Yes, if we have enough after Master Duarte has devoured his share of them. If not, please give him mine."

"No, no you have to have one, too. Do you like them?"

"I do like flan, but clearly you enjoy it far more than I do."

"There is more for each of you, Miss Davenport," George said. Of course, there was. George had handled everything. He knew exactly what Tadeas would like and arranged for it. I'd have to give him a raise. Only, I didn't pay him. His reason for being on this island was something that very few people knew. But, It was his story to tell. I had never asked, but it seemed as though it was the type of question he wouldn't have answered. I just accepted it. Watchers were retired angels. After eons, occasionally an angel would grow weary of his duties and he would

121

be afforded the option of spending his days in heaven or as a Watcher here on earth. I wasn't sure exactly what his duties were, but occasionally one of the archangels would come by to speak to him privately.

The only ones I ever had the pleasure of talking to personally were Uriel and Gabriel. And they were vaguer than George in answering questions. The conversations were never too in depth. I only knew of a half-dozen Watchers in the world. It was strange to me that one would be bound to this island. It was warded before I came here. I just added my own wards to it. Lincoln had added wards as well. When I shifted to magical sight, I could see them surrounding the outside of the island, the outside of the house and the inside of the house. Something about the ley line beneath the place powered the wards far past the lives of its makers. It was the one last remaining remnant I had of Lincoln. I would never leave this place. It was home.

I had gotten lost in my thoughts when George arrived with two more flans, one more for Tadeas and my first one. "You sure you don't want mine?" I asked him.

"You don't take someone else's flan, Abby. It's just not right," he laughed. I smiled at him and began to eat it. It was good. I hadn't had one in a while. It wasn't my go-to dessert for sure, but this one was particularly good. When we finished, he stood up and patted his belly like he was fat. There wasn't an ounce of fat on him. He had to stay in shape for all the fighting he did in his instruction. "May I go back into the other room?"

"Of course, you can go anywhere you'd like here. All the doors are unlocked, except for two and I'll show you those myself. But you are welcome to explore as you would like. I'm going to clean up these dishes, and I'll join you shortly," I said, standing to collect the dirty plates.

"Oh, I thought you had someone to do that for you," he said turning to pick up plates, too.

"No, it's my house. George might be a great butler, but he's not a kitchen maid. I'll just get these washed up really quick."

"I'll help," he offered.

"No, you are a guest. I can't allow you to do your own dishes," I replied as I took the couple he had in his hands, stacking them on top of mine. He reached over pulling the whole stack from me. He walked toward the door George had came out of with the flan earlier. "I said, you aren't going to do your own dishes."

I could hear him walking down the short hallway that led to the kitchen. "I'm sorry I can't hear you. Would you mind bringing the rest of those dishes with you when you come this way?" he said.

I shook my head. Stubborn man. Which I supposed that I deserved after many, many years of being the most stubborn woman on the planet. Dear God, I missed Lincoln. Every little thing reminded me of him.

Gathering the rest of the plates, I placed them on a cart that was stowed just across the room. I pushed the cart down to the kitchen where he was already running water in the sink.

He shook his head at me. "Oh, how convenient, a cart. You should have pointed it out before I walked all the way down here with that handful of dishes." I threw my hands up in surrender and walked over to him.

"Wash or rinse and dry?"

"Wash."

"Okay," I conceded, grabbing a towel to dry as he washed.

CHAPTER 14

ABIGAIL

*A*fter we had finished the last plate, I waved at the kitchen with my arms wide. "This is the beginning of the tour. Welcome to the kitchen," I smirked.

"Yeah, I got that one," he said.

"Come on, I'll show you the rest. Inside or outside first?"

"Outside," he said.

We walked back to the room opening up to the courtyard. Waiting on the cobblestone patio were two saddled horses. A deep chestnut brown horse with black hair and a golden-brown horse with blonde hair stood tied to a hitching post just outside the doorway. I walked up to the dark one and stroked his nose. "This is Claudius or Claude. He will be yours today. And this," I said walking over to the lighter horse, "is Caprica, my horse. I mean, they are all mine, but she is my favorite." Walking back over to Claude, I held the reins while Tadeas climbed on his back. He mounted the horse without an issue. I slipped a wedge of apple I had picked up in the kitchen to Claude. "Now Claude, you be nice. No more bucking friends off your back."

Tadeas' eyes widened, at my statement. "Wait, what?"

I winked at him before climbing atop Caprica. I lead her to the edge of the open patio past the fountain and through an arched corridor to the rear of the house. It opened to a wide expanse of fields covered with rows of grape vines. They were all green and thriving. It took my breath away every time I saw it. I looked over at Tadeas, and he still had a worried look on his face.

"Don't be a baby. He's harmless."

He shot me a look and said, "I've been thrown from a horse, and it's not harmless."

"One day you'll learn when I'm joking," I returned.

He took a deep breath and finally looked out to the field. "It really is beautiful. What's the building just over the hill there?"

From this viewpoint, we could see the rooftop of the actual winery. "That's where the wine is made, fermented, bottled and aged. The path between here and there is very stable. No danger in taking it full speed. Go ahead. Claude would love the exercise. I'll follow."

"I'll race you," he said daring me.

"You want to lose?" I asked.

"I just want a fair match. No throwing like yesterday."

"I did not throw the match until the end."

"You left yourself open. It gave me a way to get out of the choke hold," he shifted on his saddle and looked at me.

"Well, I couldn't put you down in front of your students. We weren't really playing fair, you know. You had something on me. It caught me off guard. I had to counter that and yet, I felt bad all the same. So yeah, I left myself open."

"Don't ever do that again. If we fight, we fight fair. Agreed?"

"I won't let you win. But it doesn't mean I won't cheat. Heeyah!" I slammed my heels into the side of Caprica, and she took off in a blaze. I heard him curse behind me while frantically urging Claude ahead. He gained on me because I had given him the faster horse. I supposed I was throwing again. I leaned into the saddle, prompting Caprica again. She found her next gear. I turned my head slightly to the back. I still had 5 lengths on him. I reached the crest of the hill that hid the bulk of the winery building from sight, then eased a little on Caprica because I knew the backside of the hill was moderately steep at about 35 degrees from the crest to the bottom. He saw me slow and took the same cue before reaching the top. The path stopped in front of the winery building where there was a small cobbled patio and a hitching post with a water trough. I had beaten him. But, I cheated. And it was hilarious. I laughed most of the way and had finally caught myself by the time we both stopped in front of the winery. I waited for him to berate me, but he just looked me in the eye giving me that stern instructor look that he gave his students, "Next time you're mine," he teased.

"Don't make promises you can't keep," I returned. "Come in and taste a bit."

We tied up the horses, and I showed him the process we had there to make the wine. We made several variations on red and two whites. The process of making wine was not something I wanted to clutter my mind with. Thankfully, the people that work on the island and George were professionals. I just got to drink the benefits and enjoy the scenery. I knew a little about the process, but there was way too much chemistry involved. I preferred physics. Tadeas took it all in as we walked through the various processes. There were quite a few workers on the island today. All of them tipped their hats to us and said hello as we passed through.

I took him into the bottle storage room where they did packing in crates to ship back to the mainland and distribute. You can't get Casa del Sol wine in any store. It was all privately shipped out to various patrons and partners of my grandfather's business. I opened a couple of bottles, then pulled sampling glasses out of a small cabinet. We tasted them and chatted about wine, our preferences, and experiences with it. A good wine could bring people together, celebrate a victory, or cap the end of an excellent day. Of course, it was good for drowning sorrows, as well, which is why I grabbed the open bottles that we had and placed them in Caprica's saddle bag for later. If Tadeas refused to be my partner, at least I'd have wine.

"What's next?" he asked.

"Well, the only other buildings on the property are a small chapel," which I pointed to just to our east, "and the boathouse about two miles from the front door of the house back to our west. It's not much to see though. The chapel is nice though. Want to see?" I asked.

"Um, yeah sure."

We both got on the horses again, and I asked, "I meant to ask you if you had plans for this evening. If you need to be back by a certain time or anything."

"No. No plans today," he said.

"Excellent," I smiled as I walked Caprica toward the chapel.

"No race this time?" he asked.

"Nah, I'd hate to have to humiliate you twice in one day," I said.

This time he laughed. I found myself admiring his laugh. He had let go of himself enough for a couple of moments for me to hear it. Somewhere inside of me, I got the impression that Tadeas hadn't laughed much in his life. Despite all the sorrow I had faced, Tadeas' life, from my perspective, had been much darker.

"You wish," he said.

"You are learning, Tadeas. Who said you can't teach an old dog new tricks? Um, I mean cat. Do cats do tricks?" I teased.

He shifted in his saddle a bit, but returned my jab with, "No, but wizards do."

"They do, indeed," I agreed. During our banter, we had

made our way to the small chapel. I dismounted the horse and went into my history lesson.

"It was built in the 17th century in the Spanish style to match the house. The doors are hand carved Spanish oak with iron accents. It only has 4 pews and a modest pulpit. The stained-glass window in the back above the altar though is quite beautiful." I opened the doors and the mandala style glass window shone brightly in the dark little room. The sun hit it just right, and it cast yellow and orange hues all over the room. "The sun represents the home here and the cross before it represents the Most High God and the sacrifice of his Son."

"I didn't know you were religious," he said.

"I was raised a good little Catholic girl when I was very young. But I believe in God, just not in the religions of this world."

"Your grandfather..." he started to say but stopped himself.

I sat down on one of the pews and thought of the best way to explain it to him. "Yes, my grandfather is a construct of an ancient belief system. His power comes from those who believe in him and through the years that power comes through those who believe in The Agency and what we do there. However, I believe we all came from somewhere. A Master Creator who made all of this. That there is a purpose greater than ourselves, and that purpose is the continuance of mankind, His greatest creation. There, of course, is more to it than that. Just a summary of my basic beliefs."

He slowly walked to the front of the room. "I don't like the church. Not this one, but the Catholic Church." I knew why he didn't, and I didn't want to bring that subject up to him. I knew it was not a happy story. He turned and looked at me. "You believe in God and Jesus and all that stuff?"

"Well, Jesus was real. I know someone who met him."

He looked at me confused. "Who?"

"Jasper Samara."

"Jasper Samara, the magi. Like one of the three that visited the baby like the story from the Bible?" he asked doubtfully.

"One and the same," I said. "He was my master. He trained me to use my magic. I feel most days that I'm quite old, but Jasper is extremely old. He's the only Master Wizard that I know personally. I've met a few briefly over the years, but Jasper and I traveled the world together. Especially through Asia. His skill, knowledge and experience are unmatched." Tadeas looked shocked but took it all in. "My grandfather arranged my training, of course. Jasper doesn't speak of those days much, but I have heard him tell the story."

"That's amazing."

"Yea, it is. I was honored to learn from him. Humbled actually."

"And he's still around?"

"Yes, but sometimes when I occasionally speak to him, I know he is getting weary of this world. I'm not sure he will be around much longer." These thoughts brought a wave of sadness over me. It felt like all of those I counted on the most had left or were leaving me. I looked up at Tadeas as he contemplated all that I had told him. I needed him to join me in this. I needed a new someone to depend on. If he refused me after all of this, I'm not sure I'd bother trying to recruit someone else.

He looked up at me and caught me looking at him, "What is it?"

"I was just thinking about business," I replied.

"I suppose we should talk about that more," he said.

"Yes, but not right now. Let me show you the house and perhaps you'll stay for dinner, and then we can talk more. Is that okay?"

I thought he might try to get out of it, but instead, he said, "Sure. It's been a long time since I've had three non-cafeteria meals in one day."

"I don't count doughnuts as a meal."

"I do! They were great."

"They were good."

"Did you go all the way into Boulder this morning and get them?"

"I cannot reveal to you all of my secrets in one day," I teased as I got up to leave the little chapel. "But just this once, I'll admit, that I had them delivered and just picked them up on the surface side of the compound at the main gate."

"Who delivers doughnuts? That's a brilliant business strategy. Wish I had thought of it."

"Well actually, the brilliance is in an independent contract company who is like a food delivery Uber. I just call the company, tell them what I want, pay over the phone and they pick up and deliver it," I said shutting the chapel door behind me.

"I'm going to need their phone number," he said.

"Goodbye, cafeteria food!"

"Yes, at least sometimes," he said, "I can't afford to eat out all the time."

"You have money," I said.

"Not like you," he said. I hated this subject. I already knew that he held my wealth in low regard.

"Money is money. You signed up for the company salary investment, didn't you?" I knew that he had. I managed all the instructional staff's accounts, just part of my regular job with the Agency when I wasn't moonlighting as a vagabond orphan.

"Yea, but I haven't looked at any of it since I signed up. There can't be much there," he said.

"You've never looked at your account?"

"No. Why?"

"Tadeas, the Agency monitors all the financial markets across the world in an attempt to catch any anomalies that might lead to disaster or a global catastrophe. Those are the people managing your account. I highly suggest you look at it," I said as I climbed back on Caprica.

He got back on Claude and eased up close next to me. "Abby, look at me." I turned to face him. "You know exactly how much money is in that account, don't you?"

He started to see the full picture of who I was and what I do. Of course, I knew exactly how much money was in it.

"Not exactly right this moment. The market is constantly changing, and the investments go up and down with the markets. The total fluctuates daily, and I couldn't give you an exact amount right this minute. I mean it's Saturday, no one is trading today. And I haven't looked closely in the past three months because…."

"How much, Abby?" he cut me off.

"Seven point four million," I said. He gasped and about fell off the horse. I instinctively reached to him with my magic, uttering the word, "*Stabilis*." He steadied on the saddle, but instead of being thankful that he didn't fall off, he scowled at me.

"I'm sorry. I just didn't want you to fall off. I…." As I stammered out the apology, he clicked his heel into Claude, trotting off toward the main house.

We reached the corridor archway and there was another hitching post just outside it, and he dismounted and stomped off down the corridor.

"Tadeas wait, please, I'm sorry."

He stopped and spun on his heel to face me, and I stopped short.

"I don't care about the magic, Abby."

"Then what is it?"

"What else do you know about me? How much digging have you done into my life? It's my life, Abby. It's not yours to go poking around in. There are things I'd rather no one in this whole world know, and you've spent two years digging around in things I'd rather not share. I'd rather no one know," he yelled.

I closed my eyes to force back tears. He was right again. I had dug around in his life. The money was something I would normally know just because I was in charge of all those accounts. That was not the explanation he wanted or needed to hear right now. I just assumed he knew how much money that he had and chose not to use it.

"I may know the things connected to you like your background, your shifting gift, your money, but for all of that, I didn't know *you*. Who *you* are and what makes *you* tick. That's why I started this whole thing. I wanted to know you without you knowing me. Without who I am getting in the way. I have said and will repeat that I was wrong. It was stupid of me to do all of this when in the end the one thing that would ultimately determine our partnership, would be trust. I violated that from the beginning. I know that it will take time. And I don't expect you to ever forgive me, but I keep hoping there is a chance." I slowly walked toward him. I didn't want him to run any further. I held back the tears because I knew men who complain that a woman crying is the ultimate weapon she could use in an argument. I didn't want to use any weapons against him. I tried to steady myself and look him in the eye. His jaw tensed as he gritted his teeth.

"I don't think it's going to work, Abby," he said. "You are right. I'd need to trust you, and I just don't. I don't know that I ever could."

I couldn't stop them anymore. Once the first tear fell, I turned my back to him and walked back to the opening of the corridor. The sun started to set, and the sky turned a deep orange. I leaned on the wall and didn't turn back to face him. I could feel his presence still there. I could hear him breathing. He took several deep breaths. At least he wasn't walking away. We stood there for what seemed about an hour but actually was only a minute. Wiping my tears with the back of my hands which were dusty from the ride, I smudged dirt all over my face. Grabbing the edge of my t-shirt, I brought it up to my cheek to wipe it away. I could hear him walking slowly toward me. He stopped just short of me. With my magic surging through me while I was emotional, I could feel his eyes on me. Maybe he was just watching the sun sink in the sky, dipping closer to the rooftop of the winery. Shadows shifted and the world around us grew darker.

He finally spoke. "I know that you put a lot into this, and the work you want to do is very important for all of us, for the whole world. I know I don't fully understand the job you are offering me, but I do know that we would be in situations where my life would be in your hands, and yours in mine. And if there is no trust between us, we both die. You should probably start recruiting someone else as soon as possible."

"There is no one else."

"There are several good instructors in the Agency and plenty of other agents out there running this whole operation. I'm not sure why you picked me in the first place. There are better options," he said.

"No, there aren't. You are right. I did my homework. I found no one like you. No one I would trust with my life completely, but you." I had desperately looked for someone other than him. Through my time at the Agency, Tadeas' name had come up in many conversations. I hadn't paid it any attention until Lincoln told me about him.

"Why me? It doesn't make sense, Abby."

I tensed at the sound of my name on his lips. "Lincoln said it had to be you." He had moved to stand next to me still facing the sunset but turned to look at me astonished when I said it. "He knew you. He told me once, that if something ever happened to him, that you would be the best and only replacement."

"I didn't know Lincoln, Abby. You are mistaken. He certainly knew you."

"No, I'm not mistaken," I said softly. He was completely confused. Lincoln was everything to me. It was almost like he knew that in the future we wouldn't be together. He told me of

Tadeas, but I ignored him the first couple of times. He told me he was a good man, and that our talents and skills would make for the successful partnership. I dismissed it for the time. Lincoln was immune to injury. He was given skin like flint rock from his father. He was the Navajo Monster Hunter. He would live forever, but he didn't. And it took me 25 years to realize that he was right. I needed another partner. I needed Tadeas Duarte.

He stepped closer to me and said, "No more secrets. Tell me."

"Lincoln was the man that brought you to the Agency the night Isabel died." The air grew stale. Tension like electricity flowed between us. Suddenly I felt like I was in immediate danger.

CHAPTER 15

TADEAS

*H*earing Abigail utter her name propelled me into a rage. I was angry already, but not she or anyone who knew about Isabel had any right to even speak her name. Especially me. I stepped back from her astonished. Anger, sadness, and despair started to overwhelm me. I felt the beast inside of me growling, clawing to get out. I tried to suppress it like I had taught myself to do. I had already forced it down once in the corridor, by taking deep breaths. I continued to step back away from her. Her heart rate picked up to a level that I knew she felt like she was in danger. She knew what I was, and what I could do.

No matter my anger at her, I didn't want to hurt her. Not like this. I felt my eyes shifting back and forth from yellow to green. "No," I muttered. A wall of sound rushed over me as I turned my back on her. The rush of my animal instincts forced their way past my human ones. I tried to shut out all the noise, but I realized there was no noise except in my head. Concentrating on the world around me, I realized the night sounds had ceased. Even the horses stood like statues. Their instincts kicked in as mine did, sensing a nearby predator.

It wasn't just the amplified sounds. The smells of the evening swelled up around me. I could smell the grapes, the horses, and the blood pumping through her body. Abigail had stopped breathing. I felt fear coming off of her. I could smell it. Good. She needed to be afraid of me. Then she would understand that I was dangerous. If I shifted right now on her, I would kill her, and they would hunt me down. They would kill me. It would serve me right for all I had done to Isabel. I was a murderer after all. I was about to have a repeat performance. Then I heard her softly chanting behind me in Latin. I slowly turned, releasing the anger to flow through me. I did not hold back.

"*Angele Dei, qui custos es mei,*
Me tibi commissum pietate superna;
Hodie, Hac nocte illumina, custodi, rege, et guberna."

I froze in place. A child's prayer calling for a guardian angel. A bright light erupted between us, and I turned from it. I blocked my face with my hands. When I looked at her, she stood there just like she did before, but her green eyes illuminated with a golden light around them. She held her right hand out with the palm up, and four orbs hovered, rotating just above it. The three spheres I saw in her office, plus one that looked like a miniature sun. Watching her, I felt myself begin to back down. She looked like an angel glowing in the darkness.

I didn't know if what she was doing calmed me but looking at her using her magic in full form eased my anger. I slowly backed away from her just to be sure I was safe. There was no fear in her eyes. Only compassion.

And power.

She thrummed with power. Her heartbeat had settled into a

steady and strong thump. The animal inside me didn't know whether to strike or run. She slowly walked toward me, speaking in a gentle voice, "Tadeas Nahuel Duarte, guardian jaguar, you have nothing to fear from me. You have nothing to fear from yourself. What happened all those years ago to Isabel was not your fault. The church failed you. The wielders of the world failed you. The angels failed you." She continued to walk toward me, closed her palm and the orbs vanished. I felt the wall at my back. I was cornered and afraid that I might still strike at her, but she stood toe to toe with me. She started to raise her arm, to do what I'm not sure, but I latched onto her forearm and dug my claws into her skin. Blood welled up around the wounds, then dripping to the ground. She didn't flinch or withdraw.

"I can't hold it back. Please, Abby," I begged. I didn't want to kill her. She was bleeding because of me.

"You can. Hear my voice, *Eximo*." she breathed the word lightly and my claws retracted. I released my grip on her arm. "You have no desire to hurt me, do you?"

"No," I choked out.

She looked down to her arm and said, "*Consano. Ignis.*"

The wound closed, healing itself. The droplets of blood on her arm, my hand, and the ground sparked with a quick white fire, burning away. There was no heat or pain to the fire. She continued to raise her hand to my face, and she spoke one last word. "*Quies.*"

My heart rate slowed. The animal inside of me stood still. I closed my eyes and felt at peace.

"What did you just do?"

She swallowed, closing her eyes. Then I felt the rush of it. She released all the power that she had gathered to herself. I felt it fly past me like a swift, strong breeze. She slumped a little. I reached up to steady her because her skin suddenly paled. Her eyes darkened, and her face was ashen.

"Are you okay?"

"Yes," she whispered. "I was just holding a lot of power in there. It's been a while since I'd pulled that much to myself."

I knew that magic wielders of the light variety drew power from within themselves, and the earth around them. But they only used the power from the earth when it would not harm any living plant or animal. I also knew that once the magic was spent, the wielder became weakened. I had felt power before with the wielders at the Agency. I even met a wizard out in Boulder one day by chance.

Abigail's power felt different somehow. She stepped away out of my reach. She was still pale, and it looked like she might faint. However, she straightened herself and said, "Let's go inside, please. I need to sit down."

Turning toward the patio with the big fountain, I noticed for the first time that George stood there staring at both of us. I followed behind her, dipping my head not to look at the Watcher who might call in his brothers to strike me down for hurting her. When she reached him, she put her hand on his shoulder, whispering something I couldn't hear. He nodded his head, then rushed back into the house. Once I caught up to her, she continued into the large sitting room. I realized I was shaky, too.

There was a fire in the fireplace, and the room felt warm and safe. She sat down on one of the couches. George returned to her carrying a glass of water.

"Do you need anything else?" he asked, his face twisted with concern.

"No. Please get Tadeas something."

"I, I don't need anything," I stammered.

"Are you sure, Sir? It was a good ride and back. Surely something cold to drink. Maybe water or lemonade?" I was sure he had seen the whole thing. He was a Watcher. She had called for an angel with her prayer.

"Water is fine," I said, realizing I wanted him to leave the room. I walked over to where she sat on the couch. The color returned to her face, and I knelt before her. "What was that? Please tell me." I had never felt such peace before in my life. I didn't think it was possible to control the shift once it reached that point. She had spoken Isabel's name again, and instead of angering me it only drove me to seek answers. I could tell she still tried to gather herself. Giving her whatever time she needed to recover, I took a few steps back to a chair that turned toward the couch at an angle. Sitting on the edge of the seat, I watched her closely. She took small sips of the water, and with each sip, she looked more like herself. George returned, handing me my water.

"What else, ma'am?"

"Nothing, George, thank you. Give us a few moments, and I think Mr. Duarte will be leaving."

"Yes, ma'am." He seemed sad to hear that I was leaving.

When she finally looked at me again, her eyes were the normal bright green again. "I am okay. It just takes a minute sometimes to recover from drawing in that much power. I wasn't sure how much I would need to help you, and I pulled far more than I needed. Are you okay? Any aftereffects of the spells?" she asked worried about me. I had clawed her. I made her bleed, and she was concerned about me.

"I only feel at peace."

"Yes, the last one was peace. It should calm you and the animal, but I shouldn't speak of it separate from you. It is you. Without it, you do not live. Without you, it does not live. Such as it is for all shifters; werewolves, weredragons, skinwalkers..." her voice trailed off.

"It does things I would never do."

"Yes, because no one ever helped you control it. No one taught you how."

"I can't control it."

"*Yes, you can*, but only if a shaman shows you how. You should have been helped a long time ago. I wasn't aware that you were never trained by anyone. Not even in the Agency."

"A shaman? You mean a wielder like you?"

"Yes."

I HAD ONLY LEARNED THE STORIES OF THE JAGUAR GUARDIANS IN the Mayan tradition after I arrived at the Agency. They told me what I truly was. The early priests in Mayan culture taught of the sacrificial heart, the act of giving unconditional love, and loyalty to your fellow mankind. Through the years this belief was perverted and became more literal, thus the stories of human sacrifice by Mayan priests. The Jaguar spirit was the enforcer in a way to ensure mankind followed selfless practices and integrity, the most important virtue of the belief system.

The jaguar in spirit form stalked those without a pure heart until they found their way, and conversely, those who ignored the urging of the spirit met the full vengeance of the guardian. Mayan people were often honored to have a jaguar guardian born into their village. He became a protector of all the people within the village. A shaman would guide the newly- born jaguar to accept their power and magic. To embrace their calling and thus control their talents. They healed and advised the jaguar. They worked together to spiritually lead the village to practice the virtues of integrity and selflessness. It was not an easy journey for the jaguar to accept the dual life of walking the day as a human and walking the spirit world as an animal.

When the Europeans came into the main continent, they brought their religion. The human sacrifices spurred fear into these new conquerors. They burned villages to the ground for these practices in the name of their God. And soon villages converted to Catholicism to avoid being laid to ash. The shamans and priests were run out of the villages or hunted down and killed. If a jaguar spirit child was born into a converted village, they would kill it or leave it for dead in the jungle. That's what happened to me. They tossed me in the jungle and left me for dead. I don't remember it since I was an infant, but the story was told by the Catholic missionaries that found me in the jungle. My adoptive parents told me the story when I was young, but none of them knew about the jaguar.

My life with those parents didn't last long. I knew the innocent reason they told me, but I suspected that somehow, they found out about my beast, and returned me to the church. That's when Father Sergio took me under his wing, and I worked in the church and monastery. He taught me the Word of God. He wanted me to be a priest, too. He was an honorable man.

But for all the knowledge of what I was, no one had ever come forward to teach me how to control it. Even with all the wielders at the Agency, not a single one attempted to instruct me. I set it upon myself to learn to control it. I found that if I avoided emotional situations and followed a strict routine, the animal within me would sleep. The physical exertion and outlet of instructing the recruits to fight was the best medicine.

As so, I lived that way for over a hundred years. I stopped aging around 30 and never developed a grey hair or a wrinkle. I spoke to a werewolf once in the Agency who stopped aging at 20, the lucky bastard. Not aging had plenty of drawbacks though. Those around you that were purely human, lived, aged and died. Yet you were always the same. I was afraid to do anything other than the routine I had set up to control it. I had many offers to do other things within the Agency, but I just stayed where I was until Abigail came into my life.

Even now, I knew she had just changed everything for me.

CHAPTER 16

ABIGAIL

*A*fter recovering from the surge of power within me, I looked down to assess the damage to my arm. I didn't expect him to claw me, but I knew it was a possibility for him to strike out as I moved closer to him. I had to show Tadeas that I wasn't afraid of his beast and that it could be controlled. It also pained me to have to do it. He should have been taught many years ago. Sometimes I think that the Agency, for all the good we do, was way too big. The things that had been slipping through the cracks may have seemed small but were actually so very important. We didn't finish what we started with Tadeas.

Rubbing my arm in remembrance of the pain, I felt no true ache because the power I had drawn in blurred out all of it when it happened. Tadeas watched me with terror in his eyes. He alternated between fear and shame. I hated that look in his eyes. He had done nothing wrong.

Since Lincoln knew about him, I would have thought that someone would have taught him. Lincoln should have taught him or made sure that he was paired with a wielder. My heart broke for Tadeas. He was noble and strong, but once the animal started to take over, he became almost childlike and afraid. Inspecting my arm, I saw that there was no visible scar on my arm.

He saw me rubbing my arm. "Are you hurt?"

"No, it's healed completely. Just a nagging memory there now." I had no idea where to go from here. Things were threatening to fall apart in the corridor, and now all was calm again. The day had been an emotional rollercoaster. I had resigned myself that he wouldn't work with me, but maybe, just maybe he would agree to let me help him control the animal. At the very least I could empower a token for him to carry to suppress it. But even that didn't feel right to me, it was part of him. A beautiful, terrifying part of him, but suppressing it would only cause problems in the future. Controlling it would be very easy once he understood the full capabilities of it and most of all, embraced it. These things should have happened before Isabel had died. "I feel like I am constantly apologizing, but I spoke her name again. For bringing back the memory and causing you pain, I am sorry."

He turned his face to the fire. The flames created shadows across his features and reflected in his eyes. "I would appreciate it if you didn't mention it again."

"I won't. If you want to leave, I understand. Today has not gone how I planned. My ultimate goal today was to invite you into my home, let you relax and enjoy the beauty and peace here. I have failed as a host." Those words triggered something in him, and he rose and moved to the couch beside me.

"You said that the church failed me, and I get that. You said the wielders of the world failed me, and I understand that too, but you said the angels failed me. What did you mean?" He noticed from this perspective of the room that we could see George hovering just around the corner.

"A jaguar spirit is a guardian. Much like an angel. The angels know of every child that is born on this earth and can be called on to protect the child if needed. But the angels are not perfect. Only God is perfect. Sometimes they fail in their duties. They failed to help you. At the very least to guide you to someone that could help you. I don't know if it was the church in Guatemala that influenced that because you should have been helped there as well. Perhaps they thought you were safe already."

He nodded in George's direction. "Wouldn't he be able to tell me what happened?"

"Unfortunately, no, George was not that kind of angel. Not that he could tell us, anyway. Once an angel retires, he cannot interfere with the world anymore."

"You prayed for a guardian angel. I know that prayer from being raised a Catholic. Why did one not come?"

I smiled at his knowledge of the prayer, and the shock that would come when I told him why I used it instead of a spell. "Because silly man, I prayed to the guardian inside of *you*. The part of you that would not harm me. I prayed to what *you* are really supposed to be because *I* believe in *you*."

He shuddered as the reality of my actions in the corridor became fully realized in his mind. I recited the words in English, "Angel of God, my guardian dear, to whom His love commits me here, ever tonight be at my side, to light and to guard, to rule and to guide."

He stood up to pace the room in front of the fireplace. I can only imagine the torrent of thoughts running through his mind. "You controlled it by believing in me?" He looked back to me, and even with the fire behind him and his face shadowed I could see the doubt in his eyes.

"Yes, that's all it takes. I called upon what you are supposed to be, and it responded. It's not how a Mayan shaman would do it. But it's how Abigail Davenport would do it. Magic isn't about doing things a certain way. Following a cosmic or scientific formula. Magic is about what you believe and what you know to be true. Sometimes it's just a matter of self-fulfilling destiny," I explained. "It responded not only because it's what I believe you are, but because somewhere inside of you, you know it's what you believe you are. What you were meant to be."

"No, I know what I am. I'm dangerous. I could have killed you back there" His words were frustrated, but his tone was steady.

"No, Tadeas, you cannot hurt me."

"Just because you believe something is true, doesn't mean it is," he contradicted.

"The act of believing it wholly and completely makes it true."

"It's not that simple," he argued.

"You are right. There is nothing simple about utterly trusting someone. I spent two years learning who you are and learning to trust you even before you knew me." I knew I was bringing the subject back up about me virtually spying on him for two years, but this was a slightly different perspective so maybe it would help ease the whole conflict a bit.

"It saved your life," he muttered, still pacing the floor.

"From a certain viewpoint, I suppose it did." I stood and walked over to him, faced him and put my hand firmly on his arm just below his shoulder. He lifted his eyes to me, and I said, "And I would do it all over again, exactly the same way, even with you angry at me, just to get to know what a wonderful, noble person you are."

Without warning, he wrapped me up in his arms and hugged me. He was strong. Almost squeezed the life out of me. He held on for a minute because he didn't want me to see him cry, but I knew. He whispered in my ear, "Thank you."

We stood there for a moment before I felt his arms start to relax. It was wonderful. I remembered that hugs are awesome especially when they aren't from your grandfather or your butler. It had been a very long time since anyone had embraced me that wasn't an old man. He pulled back, but still kept his hands touching my arms. I missed his warm embrace immediately. As if something very special had been jerked away from me. I swallowed pushing back my own psychological problems to focus on him.

"I don't know about you, but I need a serious drink," I said.

"I'm actually starving," he responded. Which was all George needed to appear from his not so concealed spot and announce that dinner was ready and waiting in the dining room. Tadeas reached up to my cheek and rubbed it a little.

"Crap. There's still dirt there," I said.

"Yeah, there is."

"Give me a few minutes to clean up, and we can have dinner if you dare stay any longer," I said, genuinely hoping he would stay.

"I think I've committed myself for the entire day, haven't I?" he said.

"As a matter of fact, you have. George, keep it warm for us. I need a few minutes to clean up from the dust," I said as I headed toward the hallway to my bedroom.

"Yes, ma'am."

Just before I rounded the corner out of sight Tadeas asked, "Hey Abby, if it's not a bother, can I wash up somewhere, too?"

"Oh, I'm sorry. I'm a terrible host. Of course, George will you show Tadeas his room?"

"*My* room?" he asked, heavy on the 'my' part.

"I told you. I had hoped you would consider this your home, too."

"There you go proposing again."

I smirked at him, looked toward George and pointed back at Tadeas, "Please George, do something with him before he starts thinking he's a comedian again." George smiled and slightly bowed to me, and the last thing I saw was George motioning Tadeas to follow him. I rushed to the flight of stairs leading up to a set of double doors. I slipped in the doors to my bedroom quickly without looking back. I just needed a little room to breathe for a minute. I felt the lock click shut behind me. My ward kept the door locked at all times. I took a deep breath and leaned into the door. I felt exhausted. I couldn't decide if I felt more tired or hungry. Probably more tired. Not to mention, I was astonished that he was still here. Each little conflict throughout the day managed to resolve itself. But the whole thing had not been a walk in the park or even through a vineyard.

I walked into the large tile-covered bathroom and clicked on the lights. The bathroom was spacious with a claw-footed tub along the back-center wall, plus a giant walk-in shower. An alcove led to a huge walk-in closet full of clothes I rarely wore.

I looked at myself in the mirror above the double vanity. My pale face was covered in dirt. *Good grief.* I walked over, turning the water on in the shower. No amount of wiping was going to get this dirt off. I hadn't noticed the road was extremely dusty, but it had been several days since it rained. I ducked into the closet, removed my rings and necklace, and slipped out of the dusty shirt and jeans.

By the stains on my body, you would have thought I wallowed in the dirt somewhere along the way because even my socks and underwear were all full of grime. I jumped in the shower, washing off quickly. To be honest, I wanted to stay under the warm water and let it wash all the dirt and emotion from the day off of me. But I was the host, I had to get out of the shower and get dressed. I debated on what to wear. I chose a simple pale green sundress and a pair of flat sandals. I put my rings and sun necklace back on, and with a flick of my hand and one word, *Assicco,* my blonde hair dried and fell loose around my head. I looked at myself in the mirror. At least I was clean.

I hurried back down the hall to the sitting room where

George dusted the mantle. "It was awfully dusty today. He still in his room?" I asked.

"Yes, he is. I think he was impressed."

"You *think* he was, or he *was* impressed?" I questioned him.

"He was. I think he is taking a shower, too."

"It couldn't be helped. Dirt and dust covered me head to toe. Everything okay, George?" He paused his dusting and looked back at me.

"It was close in the corridor, wasn't it?" he asked.

"No, it wasn't. I believe in him."

"Yes, but you still doubt yourself," he pointed out. He went back to dusting. Before I could rebuke him, I heard footsteps coming down the hallway. Tadeas walked in with his hair still slightly wet. He wore a white button-down shirt and khaki slacks. A buzz of attraction zipped through me, but I quickly dismissed it. No need to complicate things further.

"Sorry I had to shower. I hope you weren't waiting long," he explained.

"No, I showered too. I didn't realize all the dust that had accumulated all over me," I said. He shook his head smirking at me. I heard George grunt behind me. "George's grunt means dinner's getting cold."

He walked down the steps into the room, nodded toward the dining room then waited for me to pass him before following me. The table could seat up to 20 guests. Once again, like at lunch, it had two cloches sitting at the end. However, this evening, there were two large silver candelabras spaced evenly on the table. They each had twelve white candles which were lit. George had broken out the silver candelabras. I scowled. George and his damn atmosphere. I turned back to give him a look, but Tadeas was right behind me. I slammed into him not realizing how close he was to me.

"Whoa, what's wrong?" he asked.

"Oh, I was just going to have a quick word with my butler,

but never mind." I heard the old man chuckle from the other room. "I better not find any dust in that room," I shouted.

It was by sheer luck that Tadeas was even still here, much less George trying to make it romantic. Tadeas laughed as he walked over to pull out my chair. I sat down without a word. I was all out of witty comebacks. He sat down, and we removed the domes above our plates. George once again did not disappoint. It was my favorite meal. Herb crusted lamb chops and new potatoes, glazed and roasted carrots, a fresh tomato and cucumber salad and rolls. I saw Tadeas eyes open wide, but he was unsure of the plate before him.

"If you don't eat it all, you can't have any pudding." Maybe I wasn't out of witty comments just yet.

"Ok Floyd, I gotcha. It's lamb, right?"

"Yep, my favorite," I said, cutting into the chop.

"I've never had it."

"What? How in 125 years have you never had lamb?" I asked.

"They don't serve it at the cafeteria," he said still looking skeptical. He stabbed a potato with his fork and ate it.

"Touché. Which reminds me. I need to get you that number for the restaurant delivery service."

"Yes, you do."

"You can still have pudding if you don't eat it, but at least give it a try," I said. "I won't be offended if you don't like it, but George might." Just then George showed up with a bottle of our own red wine, a Cabernet Sauvignon. He poured us both a glass, grinning like an old fool before leaving the room. "I don't know what I'd do without that man." I hadn't meant to say it out loud, but there it was.

"He certainly knows how to serve a good meal," Tadeas said with a chunk of lamb in his mouth.

"Well?"

"It's good. I like it."

"Sounds like it hurt you to admit it."

"Bah. Shut up, and eat, woman." At that, I had to laugh. I would never let anyone tell me to shut up or call me 'woman'. But apparently, he had earned that one. While we ate, we chatted a little about the horses and the stable which we didn't go into this afternoon. I talked about the house, and how long it had been here. About how the workers go back and forth to the mainland every evening, and only a very few of them are here on weekends except for the rare occasion when the winemaking process is in full production like it was today. Tadeas talked about work and fighting techniques and more ideas for changing the training. If anything, I had him hooked on that part. We kept the conversation light, avoiding the heavier topics that had plagued our day.

As we finished dinner—which included amaretto cheesecake for dessert—George gathered the dishes. I eyed him, and he shrugged. I let him do it. Perhaps it was penance for the candelabras.

Tadeas got up and walked back into the sitting room. George had opened all three sets of double doors, allowing the sounds of the night to drift into the room. The fire had died down and wasn't blazing like before. The room was cool and relaxing. Instead of sitting down, Tadeas continued out the doors to the covered part of the patio, taking a seat on one of the cushioned iron benches. I sat down on the same one only on the other end. I pulled one leg up underneath me and leaned back into the cushion.

"Is it too cool out here for you?" he asked.

"No, this is great," I said. George appeared and asked if we needed anything else. I told him, no, and he wished us both a good night.

"He going to bed?"

"Yeah probably, or whatever he does in his room late at night." We sat and listened to the sounds of the night. Mostly crickets and occasionally a frog. "You are welcome to stay here tonight. The room is open to you whenever you need it," I said.

"You weren't kidding about the clothes and the room. The closet is full. The drawers are full. The bathroom is fully stocked. Not to mention it's all the brands of shampoo and soap that I generally use. It's just a bit creepy, Abby."

I looked down, nervously fiddling with my fingernails. I was tired of fighting with him. "I'm thorough," I said softly. Hoping that was an indication that I was resigned not to argue with him.

"I'm not mad. It's actually kinda flattering. I don't think anyone on this earth knows me as well as you do. I mean look at these clothes. They fit perfectly. There are at least three formal tuxedos in there, all custom made. I admit I'm a little impressed." That made me smile, but I tried not to smile too much. Good thing I didn't because that's when he dropped the whammy. "I have to say no to joining your team, Abby. Maybe it's because I'm not ready for a change. Maybe I'm afraid. I'm not sure exactly. But I do know my instincts are telling me no."

I was glad I didn't look up. I was tired. Craving the comfort of my bed, I was ready to hang up my efforts to make amends with him. I was done.

He continued because I didn't respond to him. "I know you put a lot of time and effort into this, and I do want to work with you on changing the training at the Agency."

"You don't need me for that," I said. My voice was dead and thready as I choked on my disappointment and failure.

"True, but I want you to be there just the same. I hope that maybe Monday morning you could go to class with me, and we could start changing it all around." I started shaking my head no, but he kept talking, "They all know who you are now. I think they might have questions for you. They might like to have you there and know what the whole purpose was, to know that somebody upstairs cares about what happens to them."

"No, I don't want to do that," I said barely above a whisper.

He slid closer to me on the bench. I still wouldn't look at him. None of it mattered now.

"I know you don't want to, but you need to. At least once, go in there and be a part of the change. It would complete at least part of your plan that you've worked on for the past two years. It wasn't all just about me. It was about them, too." His closeness made me uncomfortable because I was slowly losing grip on my emotions. I pushed back anger and sadness. I wanted to get up and move away. But he grabbed my hands. "Please say yes, that you will come, at least just once," he pleaded with me. It was only pity because he had rejected me. I was willing to bet this was exactly what continued to give Meredith hope. He would shoot her down, then feel bad trying to offer some sort of consolation prize. I didn't need a consolation prize. I needed my bed, silence, and away from Tadeas Duarte.

I continued to shake my head, trying to pull my hands away from him, but he held tight. "Maybe, I don't know. Just let me sleep on it. Okay?"

"Okay," he said, releasing my hands. Swinging my legs off the bench, I pushed up away from him. Leaning on the post holding up the overhang, I realized that I wasn't just tired, I was completely exhausted. I nervously rearranged my hair, pulling it away from my shoulders and over to one side and twirled the end of a clasp of strands when I heard him swear behind me.

"What the fuck!" I felt him move quickly toward me, and I tensed up. It was like he had seen or sensed a danger that I didn't see. He stepped behind me so quickly that I couldn't move. One hand moved to my waist, while his thumb swept down across the back of my right shoulder. Moving my hair around had revealed my exorcism scar. I shuddered as he rubbed over it again. I knew that he had one too even though I'd never seen it.

"How did you get this?" he asked. His voice cracked. I felt the tension in his voice and his fingers digging into my waist.

"The same way you got yours."

CHAPTER 17

ABIGAIL

16 Years Old

The priest stood over me chanting in Latin. I didn't know what I had done, but it had to be bad. They had tied me to a chair. In my confusion and fear, I cried. The priests in the room had repeatedly splashed me with holy water. My mouth was covered with a black cloth. I wore the simple black dress required by the orphanage for girls who weren't becoming nuns. My bare feet brushed the cold stone floor.

A fire in the fireplace blazed illuminating the gathering of priests in the room. I couldn't see the door because it was behind me. I tried to scream, but only muffles came out. I struggled against the bonds, but the priest continued to chant the prayer of exorcism. I tried the best way I knew how to explain that I was me, and not some demon.

They spent hours questioning me after one of the nuns saw me move a box in my room around with magic. I had always tried to be careful to hide it, and I didn't realize that she had entered the room. She ran out of the room, grabbing one of the priests to tattle on me.

I knew what these priests were doing. I'd seen them do it to others. They were trying to exorcise a demon, but I wasn't possessed. They wouldn't believe me no matter what I tried to say. I struggled and screamed so they covered my mouth again with the gag. The priests would switch out when one got tired. And eventually, I gave up as well.

I was very tired. So very tired. I passed out in the chair.

WHEN I AWOKE, THE ROOM WAS QUIET. FATHER FRANCIS STOOD before me with his prayer book. He glared at me with disdain and hatred. His eyes were dark. I was only sixteen years old, but I knew evil. I could feel it radiating off of him. I had been put in the orphanage as a very young child. I didn't know either of my parents, but I did know magic. I also knew the church hated magic. They would call me a witch, or worse they might think I was possessed and try to drive the "demon" out of me just as they were doing now. I just couldn't stop using it though. Just for little things like moving boxes or lighting a candle in my room. It felt like a part of me just as much as my heart beating in my chest.

Father Francis began the exorcism chant again. I strained against the bonds, trying to scream again. His voice continued to get louder. Feeling a force bearing down on my chest, I heaved out breaths through my nose. Even with my magical instincts, I didn't know how to get myself out of this situation. If they didn't cast out the demon, they might execute me. I continued to strain, trying to get loose. My anger grew inside me. A thrumming in my body grew as the voice of the priest grew louder.

Behind me I could hear more priests praying and chanting, saying prayers in Latin that normally I could understand, but my fear blocked them out. Occasionally, one would lay his hand on my shoulder, sending a cold surge through my body. I cried until my tear ducts were dry. The priests continued to chant. I'm not sure how long it lasted. I would black out occasionally from straining on the bonds.

Suddenly, the room grew darker. The Father before me looked down at my hands. Taking a step backward, his prayer faltered, but he quickly resumed it. My hands glowed with a white light which progressively illuminated the dark room. Turning my palms upward, soft glowing orbs formed above them with wisps of miniature lightning flashing around them. I wasn't trying to do this, it was just happening. I couldn't control it. Part of me wanted to fling them at every person in the room, striking them all down for this, but I fought it. Then I heard the word behind me.

"Abomination."

Several of the priests behind me repeated the word. "Abomination." Their robes shifted as they crossed themselves.

At that point, I knew that I was going to die. Father Francis nodded to one of them behind me. I tried to brace myself for it, and the flashing orbs above my hands grew brighter. Someone grabbed the back of my dress to rip the fabric exposing my right shoulder. A white-hot pain shot through my body, throwing my fear into overdrive. I could smell flesh burning. My flesh.

I screamed in agony causing the magic to surge through my body evaporating the bonds, and I leaped up out of the chair toward Father Francis to strangle him. Then the room went completely black.

I woke to rain dripping down on my face. I jostled back and forth with movement like being in a carriage. I heard a kind, strong voice say, "Steady, Girl. You are safe now. Just rest."

I couldn't open my eyes, but I did feel safe with those calm words. The voice wasn't of one of the priests who had just tried to kill me. I felt a warm hand on my arm. My shoulder felt like it was on fire. I drifted off back to sleep listening to the shuffling of the vehicle, and the pattern of the rain.

I OPENED MY EYES SLOWLY UNSURE OF WHERE I WAS. I LAID IN A soft bed covered by several blankets in an undecorated room. My torn black dress wrapped awkwardly around my body. Someone had put socks on my bare feet. Next to me in a wooden chair, a dark-skinned man, with long black hair pulled back and braided, slept.

Or at least I thought he was until he said, "Go back to sleep, girl. All is well now." I reached to my shoulder and felt a bandage there. The man reached over, pulled my arm back and his kind, dark eyes met mine. "Don't mess with that now. You'll get it to bleeding again. It needs a little time to heal."

"Where am I?"

"That doesn't matter right now. You are safe. You rest."

"Who are you?" I asked.

"A friend," he replied.

"Well, I figured that much," I said.

He lifted his dark eyebrows and chuckled at me. "I am Lincoln. I am a friend of your grandfather's. He will be here soon."

"I don't have a grandfather," I said.

"Yes, girl, you do. Now rest," he said. I shifted to my side to take pressure off my right shoulder, then drifted off to sleep. Perhaps due to the trauma of the exorcism, my mind didn't register what he had said. I fell into a deep, dreamless sleep.

CHAPTER 18

TADEAS

The moonlight highlighted the patio, but Abigail's face turned dark. She put her hand on my chest, lightly pushing me away. I had invaded her personal space. Seeing the brand on the back of her shoulder threw me for a loop. Abigail Davenport was a rich, talented, beautiful wizard. She lived under her grandfather's care as far as I knew. I didn't understand how she had gotten the same exorcism brand that I had? Her eyes darted to the doorway then back to me. At that moment, I knew, it was over. She didn't want to talk about the brand, and she didn't want to talk to me. I understood that completely because I didn't want to talk about mine. I did not press the issue. Backing away, I raised my hands up in surrender. She grimaced, then said, "Goodnight, Tadeas."

Bolting through the doors, her footsteps echoed across the hardwood floor to the tiled area in the hallway. I didn't dare follow her. Sitting down on the bench I stared at the moon, but it gave me no answers. I made up my mind while in *my room* that I couldn't work with her. Trust should have been an issue, but it really wasn't when I really thought about it. Her manner and presence demanded a level of trust. The fact that she knew everything about me down to the shaving cream I liked was downright creepy. But that wasn't it either. I couldn't put my finger on it exactly, but something just didn't seem right. Maybe if I took a little more time, away from this place to think about it I would come to a different conclusion.

Her eyes were full of hurt and disappointment. I tried to tell myself that I'd done the right thing considering all the things she had put me through. However, no self-coaching could lock away the nagging intuition in my head that said I would regret turning her down.

Realizing it was well past midnight, I decided to stay in my room for the night and leave early in the morning. Perhaps before she even woke up, then I could sneak out. In fact, I could tell George to thank her for everything.

There was no doubt that this place was special. I could feel it with the calmness of my soul. I needed more of that in my life. Perhaps I could come and stay occasionally. Take Claude out and keep him exercised. I should really get out of the compound more, but she would always be here. Probably wishful thinking on my part. She could lock me out of that closet as quickly as she allowed me in it.

I opened the door to my room, and the moon's light was bright enough that I didn't need lights. I took off the pants and shirt, folding them neatly on the chair for in the morning. Digging through the drawers, I found a pair of black sweatpants and a plain white t-shirt.

Climbing into the bed, I noticed that even it felt like the same mattress I had back at the compound. Dismissing my paranoia, I refused to pull the sheets off just to see it was just like the one at home. Home. Never once in my life, had I called somewhere home. This could be home for me, but not now. Home had always been a part of my life that was always missing. Abigail and George would be my family. We could work together and keep the world safe. Too many adolescent wishes that didn't match the reality of the situation.

As I drifted off to sleep, I remembered the golden glow around her green eyes as she calmed the jaguar inside me. It frightened me that she had that kind of power over me. Maybe that was it, she could control me. I wanted no part of that. Learning to control the jaguar would be fine, but her controlling me. No, thank you.

A SCREAM TORE THROUGH THE SILENCE, AND I BOLTED UP IN BED. Then another blood-curdling shriek of panic. I threw off the covers, rushing to the door. When I walked out into the hallway, I heard it a third time. It was Abigail. As I turned to run to her door, a voice spoke from behind me.

"You best leave that be, Master Duarte," George said. He looked haggard. He sat in a large chair next to a table. Leaning forward, he put his head in his hands as she screamed again.

I wanted to tear through the doors and kill whatever was in there hurting her. "Someone is in there. She's in pain. We have to help, George."

"No, son. She's dreaming. It will stop in a minute."

I started walking toward the double doors, anyway. She whimpered inside the room. I felt that rush of sound hit me as my jaguar sense kicked in. Her heart pounded. She took heavy breaths. She shifted back and forth in the bed. I looked back at George and pleaded with him, "Please George, let me help her."

"Master Tadeas, if you open that door, the wards on it will blow you to bits. The dream will pass, and she will rest again soon." His voice sounded pained. He clearly cared deeply for her.

Shifting back and forth on my feet helplessly, I heard her heartbeat slowing to normal. Before long she was resting again.

I sat down in the chair next to George and asked, "What is she dreaming about?"

"A nightmare. A memory," he said.

"How often does it happen?" I asked.

He looked at me with a steady gaze. He wanted to tell me something, but he hesitated.

"Please, George. That sounded awful. She seems fine now, but something awful must have happened to her," I pleaded with him.

"Did you tell her, no?" he asked changing the subject.

"I did, but I'm still not sure," I said.

"You answered her, but you admit that you aren't sure?" He raised his eyebrows at me.

"I need to think on it more," I said.

"Then that is what you should have told her," he gruffed. Clearly, he was upset with me. Looking down at me as he stood, he said, "I know that it is a big decision, and it isn't one to be made in one day even though the both of you seem to want to make it quick and be done. The decision is far bigger than either of you could understand at this point. I've said too much. Good-night, Master Duarte."

The Watcher had spoken.

Reaching out with my senses on purpose, I knew she continued to rest with a steady heartbeat and breath. George was right. I should have waited to tell her I needed more time. When I told her no, I saw her face, and I felt like a huge idiot. But I couldn't tell her yes, either. I should have just asked for more time. I thought about George's words, and how he changed the subject on me. Maybe he hadn't changed the subject at all. Somehow because I had declined the offer, it triggered the nightmare.

"*Madre de Dios, los siento*, Abby." I crossed myself, pulling out the gold crucifix on a chain that I still wore from my teen years in the church and kissed it. The necklace reminded of where I came from and that even a good man can do harm to another like Father Sergio did to me. Like they did to Abigail, too. When they tried to exorcise her demon, it traumatized her bad enough that she still had nightmares.

Back in my room, I laid on the bed staring at the ceiling. I couldn't sleep solidly after that, but I tried to calm my mind and rest. Eventually, I got up as dawn began to touch the sky with her rosy fingers. I went into the closet where there were more shoes than any man on the face of this earth owns and picked out a pair of running shoes. They were better than any pair I had back at the compound. I put them on and quietly went into the hallway. As I passed the sitting room, I looked in to see George sweeping the floor.

"George, which way is the boathouse? Abby said it was about a mile and a half to it. I want to go for a jog before I leave," I asked him.

"If you go out this way on to the patio, the boathouse is in the complete opposite direction from where the two of you rode horses yesterday. It's closer to 2 miles to the dock. Just be aware that the protective wards end at the island's edge. If you go on the dock, it is unprotected," he said.

"Should I be worried?" I asked.

"No Sir, I just felt like it was valuable information to have," he replied. "Would you like breakfast when you return?"

"No, George. I'm gonna run, get back, and get out of your hair. I have overstayed my welcome, I think."

"That's not possible, Master Duarte. But as you wish. Have a good run," he said, returning to his sweeping.

The fountain splashed water lively out on the patio, and the sun just started to peek above the horizon. I turned opposite of the arched corridor from yesterday and took off in a sprint through a green field with a small well-worn path. After a moment, the path turned into a cobblestone road large enough for a vehicle. I followed it toward the sunrise. After about 7 minutes, the sun was up over the horizon, and I could see the boathouse and dock not far away. I didn't see a boat, but after the way Abby explained it, there wouldn't be a boat today. It was Sunday, and the workers were probably getting ready to attend various worship services or mass. Perhaps preparing a meal for the whole family around lunch time. I knew the things that families did, and for a short time, I had a family. A traditional one.

FROM INFANCY UNTIL SIX YEARS OLD, I LIVED WITH THE GARCIA family in Antigua, Guatemala. They were devout Catholics, and we attended mass every Sunday. As an infant, I was christened by Father Sergio. My parents loved me. They were unable to have children. We did not have much. I could use the cliché about how we had plenty of love, but it would seem trite. However, it was the truth. Just after my sixth birthday, they took me to the church on a Monday. I asked why we were there. My father shushed me, and my mother cried. Father Sergio came out to meet us in the entry to the large Cathedral.

"Well, hello Tadeas. It is good to see you, son," he said. "Good morning Mr. and Mrs. Garcia."

My parents greeted him, and my mother bent down and hugged me. "Tadeas, my beautiful boy, I love you," she said through tears.

"I love you, Mama. Why are you crying?" I asked. My father put his arm around her as she stood up.

"You be a good boy, Tadeas," my father said.

I started to cry. I didn't know what was happening. Father Sergio put his arm on my shoulder. "Don't worry. I promise to take very good care of him." I looked up to him with tears in my eyes. My parents turned and left me there.

I screamed, "Mama!" I could hear her crying outside the door, but Father Sergio held my shoulder tight.

"Come with me, Tadeas. You are going to be staying with me for a while now. I'll show you to your new room," he spoke kindly.

"I don't want a new room. I want my momma!" I cried, straining against him and reaching for the door.

"Son, please sit here with me for a minute." He gently guided me to one of the wooden pews and sat me down. "Your mother and father love you very much, but your heavenly Father needs you to stay here and help me for a bit. Do you think you can help me? I am going to teach you about God. One day you can be a priest like me."

I cried, not understanding any of this. I didn't think I had done anything wrong, and I was sure they loved me. I just wanted my mother, and as a young boy, I couldn't comprehend what could have caused them to leave me behind.

After a few years, when I was old enough to understand, Father Sergio told me that my parents were struggling to get by. They were afraid I would starve if I stayed with them. They brought me back to the church. Father Sergio kept his promise. We had school every day, and I learned to read. I learned about science and art. All from the Catholic Church's perspective, but it was a good education. At some point in my teen years, I had learned that the Garcia's moved closer to the coast in hopes of finding more work. They both died in 1902 when an earthquake struck the country, and many people were left homeless and died.

As I reached the dock, I stood at the island's edge taking in the beautiful sea vista. Some of us from the compound took a vacation to the beach in south Texas a couple of years ago. The water of the Mediterranean seemed much bluer than the Gulf of

Mexico. Light waves splashed along the dock and seawall. A small boathouse sat on the shore. The house, weathered by the wind and sea, looked sturdy. I closed my eyes and listened to the ocean. Then I noticed it, a thrum of power just ahead of me. I could feel the ward protecting the island. It was extremely powerful. I wondered what it was like to step through it. George had mentioned its presence, but that I had nothing to worry about. Stepping out onto the dock, the smell of salt air assaulted my nose. The ward not only protected the island but kept the smell of saltwater out which I thought was pretty cool. I wasn't aware that wards could work as filters.

Stepping back onto the island to feel the change again, I laughed, then stepped back onto the dock. It was a good thing no one was around, or they would have reported me as a lunatic. Or been horrified by my lack of dance skills.

The pier was quite large, so the boat must be huge. I could just imagine Abigail having some expensive yacht that ferried vineyard workers back and forth to the mainland. I'm not sure how long I stood there enjoying the sun and the water. What I really wanted to do was take a swim. Maybe next time. If there was a next time. Looking down at my watch, I had been gone longer than I intended. It was almost 7 a.m. here.

"Wait a minute," I said out loud to no one in particular. When we left Colorado yesterday at lunchtime, we arrived here off the coast of France… at lunchtime. The portal must be more than just a locational portal. It must have a temporal shift on it as well. Manipulating time lined up close to the top of the TCAs restrictions of magic. No wonder no one could come through the portal except whomever Abigail allowed to go through. I had a few questions about that portal. I had a lot more questions about everything, but something told me I might not ever get the answers I wanted.

I didn't know how long Abigail would sleep, but I wanted to get back and leave before she was up. I couldn't do that though.

It would be rude. Not only rude but cowardly. At the very least I should thank her for her hospitality. The rules of hospitality required me to do it. I was going to be a sweaty mess by the time I got back. As I ran, the sweat plastered my hair to my forehead reminding me that I needed a haircut.

Planning what I would say to her, I ran back to the house. Maybe ask to have more time to think it all over. I didn't want her to get her hopes up, but George was right. Go figure. I should have asked for more time. Maybe a little space, too. I pushed her to come to class with me tomorrow, so much for space, eh? I didn't think I'd ever been so indecisive in all of my life. As I approached the house, I saw no evidence of anyone moving around. However, when I entered through the patio doors, I smelled bacon, and I loved bacon. I decided a quick shower was in order, followed by bacon and goodbye. I could do this.

AFTER A LUXURIOUS SHOWER, IN PROBABLY THE BIGGEST monstrosity of a shower that I've ever seen, I felt clean and relaxed. I admit that I turned every knob and pushed every button in that shower. It had 5 shower heads. Definitely, a man shower. While toweling off, I looked for the clothes I had left in the chair. They were gone along with the sweaty ones I just took off. Dammit, George. Going back into the closet that even a celebrity would envy, I picked out a really cool looking pair of jeans and a black t-shirt. Leaning over to put on my old tactical boots, I saw brand-new Belleville tactical boots on the shelf. Without hesitation, I slipped them on my feet.

I looked at my old boots, and said, "Sorry boys, there are some new kids in town." Fancying myself a comedian, I went on the pursuit of bacon.

Following my nose, I found only one plate in the dining room. A mound of scrambled eggs sat beside 4 or 5 pieces of perfectly cooked bacon along with toast and a cup of coffee. George watched me from the other end of the room. I looked up at him. "Abby doesn't drink coffee."

"No Sir, she doesn't," he smiled, then walked out of the room. I devoured it all. George refilled my coffee and brought a second helping of bacon.

"Thanks, George," I said.

"You are most welcome, Master Duarte," he replied with a slight bow. "Will you be leaving this morning?"

"Yes, Sir. I was going to wait for Abby to get up and say good-bye, but if she is sleeping in, she deserves it," I said, smiling at him. But then I realized that look. "Out with it, George."

"She is downstairs, Sir."

"What's downstairs? I didn't get the full tour of the house yesterday." He hesitated to tell me. I couldn't blame him. I hadn't been a very good guest. I did try to kill her yesterday. "Never mind George. I get it. She doesn't want to see me."

"I don't think she knows you are still here," he said.

"Oh? How's that possible?"

"You were outside the wards when she looked for you this morning. She didn't sense you here, and she went downstairs. I thought you were going to leave anyway without saying goodbye. I didn't tell her otherwise."

"George, you lying to her?" I asked astonished.

"Hmph. I do not lie. I am bound to non-interference," he grunted. "She has an office downstairs and a vault. She's in the office. I'll show you the way if you'd like."

"Um, I dunno. I don't want to interrupt her."

"Master Duarte, I would never let you interrupt her unless I thought she needed to be interrupted," he stated flatly then walked to the sitting room. I took the cloth napkin, wiped my face quickly, and followed him. He passed down the hallway to the staircase that led up to the bedrooms, but instead of going up, he went around to the side. He put his hand on the wall and a door formed. A warded door. He reached down and opened the door. There was a staircase going down. It made a 90-degree turn. I couldn't see the bottom. He waved toward the steps. "She's down there. Good luck," he smirked as he walked away.

Staring down the steps, I looked back down the hallway to the door that opened to the portal. *"Oh, don't be a chicken-shit,"* I told myself and headed down the steps. When I got to the bottom, a massive room opened up with various monitors and multiple computers. Some of the monitors showed newscasts, others showed various trading market numbers. One, in particular, had the name of everyone who worked in the training area at the Agency from custodian to instructors with a monetary amount next to the name. I saw my name there with the 7.4 million next to it. I closed my eyes and grimaced. She must manage the accounts of the whole training area, not just mine. I thought to myself, *"Check the asshole box for me. It's right under potential partner, infinitely single Hispanic male, and jaguar guardian."*

Right in the midst of this underground lair, a blonde woman in a bathrobe sat with both of her legs propped up in the chair sipping a cup of tea. When she set the mug on the desk, I saw in large letters, I Love Dogs, on the side. I had only seen her in more formal settings, not as casual as this. Dismissing the thought of her long bare legs, I cleared my throat because the last thing I needed was a fireball to the face. Or one of those floating orb thingies which I noticed also sat in a silver dish on the desk. She spun in the chair and looked surprised.

"Hey um, I just didn't want to sneak up on you," I said, waving at her like a newb.

She cocked her head sideways and said, "Damn, George," and rolled back around to watch the screens.

"Yeah, he's the damnedest," I said, trying to find the right words, but still stumbling over myself.

"You heading out?" she asked.

"Yeah, I guess so." I started to continue, but she cut me off.

"Be careful on the portal back, it's a bad jump. Time zone effect," she said.

"Um, yeah I wondered about that because yesterday when we got here it was the same time it was in Colorado."

She chuckled still not looking at me, "And how long did it take you to figure that out?"

"It hit me on my run this morning."

"Hmm. Run. Where did you run to?"

"To the boat dock. The sea is nice."

"Ah! You went *on* the dock," she said, realizing why she couldn't feel me on the island. Her eyes lit up with understanding.

"Yeah, I even dipped my feet in the water."

"You are welcome to come back and swim if you want. As long as it isn't storming, the water is nice. It's safe here. Oh, this is yours. I forgot I had it," she said, handing me a plain black credit card with the initials KBS on it. Across the bottom, it had my full name.

"What's this?" I asked, looking at the card.

"You didn't pick it up 6 months ago when we issued cards to those who had the investment accounts. I had it in my desk here. It's tied to your account. You can use it at any time."

Ignoring the card, because it reminded me of the discussion yesterday that started our downward spiral, I asked, "What should I know about the portal?"

"Well, when you go back, you will gain a bunch of time back via the time zone change. It's what 8 a.m. here?" She clicked the mouse on the desk and the monitor to her right showed the time 12 a.m., "See you can go back and get some sleep before getting up again in the morning."

I was utterly confused. "What? It's the same time when you come here, but not when you leave?"

She laughed again. "No, that's because it was Saturday."

"What the hell does Saturday have to do with it?"

"Everything," she said flatly, picking up the offensive mug to sip her tea. She finally turned around to look at me and put her feet on the floor. I could tell she was wearing cotton shorts and a tee shirt underneath the robe. She looked so good this way that I had to talk down my male hormones. Until I met her eyes, they were red and bloodshot. "It's a funny story, really. I'd like to tell you sometime, but not today. Are you leaving right now?" she asked.

I shuffled my feet and looked down at the boots. They were such nice boots. "These boots are great." I managed to newb it up again.

"Yes, they look good on you." She barely smiled at me. Like she tried to force it. I got the feeling I was torturing her.

"Grrrr," I let out a manly frustrated noise, sitting down on the bottom step of the stairs.

"What's wrong, Tadeas?"

"I am going to sound like an idiot, just so you know." She squished her face up not understanding where I was going with such a statement, but I rambled on. "And after thinking about last night, and yesterday, and the last three months, I think maybe I need to alter some of the things I said last night."

"Huh?" she uttered.

I ran my hands through my hair, making that man noise again. My frustration got to me, and I stood to pace the room. She sat about 5 feet away from me watching silently. "I need a haircut."

"I like it long," she said, finishing off her tea but continuing to hold the mug.

"Really?" I asked, stopping to look at her.

"Yeah, but not too much longer than it is now."

"Huh," I muttered shrugging my shoulders. "Look, I know I'm not making any sense. And that's the problem. I can't think straight here with you. I keep thinking I've made the decision once and for all. But honestly, I need more time to think it over without rushing to a decision. As it stands, I'm not comfortable with the way it is now. I don't know if my answer will change, but I rushed it last night. I'm not proud of my actions yesterday afternoon or last night."

She simply looked at me and said, "Sure. Take whatever time you need." As if none of it bothered her. I knew what this was. She had hidden her emotions away about it. That bad thing about hiding emotions was they were bound to bubble up to the surface at some point.

Standing to walk toward me, she said, "I'll show you out." I could hear her heartbeat very clearly. It remained steady meaning she was in complete control. She went up the stairs with that damned empty mug in her hand, and I followed like a lost dog. Or a cat. Or a boy. Just lost.

CHAPTER 19

ABIGAIL

"*Hold it together, girl,*" I told myself. My mistake was thinking he had left. When I felt for his presence on the island, I didn't feel it. What were the chances that the moment I was looking for him, was the very moment he was on the dock? The same chances that a non-interfering angel had interfered.

I was resigned that I had failed, and I would sit in my office on my safe island, forgetting about the Agency and the world for that matter. Well, not completely. Hard to ignore the world when there are 20 screens of it in front of you. I was wearing my bathrobe for heaven's sake. George could have told me he was still here. I'm going to have to have a talk with him. Non-interference, in this case, was inexcusable. Ugh, George. I heard his footsteps behind me as we climbed the stairs. I don't even have shoes on. I sighed.

"Something wrong?" he asked.

"Yes. No. Not really," I sputtered. If I tried to talk, I'd sound more ridiculous and rambling than he did downstairs. I just had to get him to the portal door, then say goodbye. After that, I could wash Tadeas Duarte from my mind and rest. Whatever happened would happen. Picking up the pace to the portal, I hoped this wouldn't take long.

"George didn't tell you I was still here," he muttered behind me.

Spinning around on him, he stopped in his tracks. I must have looked positively wild. Disheveled hair, barefoot, bathrobe, shorts, and a t-shirt. It hit me then I didn't have a bra on. Self-consciously I wrapped the robe up, tying it so quickly that the ends of the belt flung around as I let go of them. The mug almost slipped out of my hand in the process. George had brought my tea in the damned thing. Which means he knew that Tadeas was still here when he gave me the stupid mug. My anger was building, and I wasn't sure I could hold back. "As a matter of fact, he didn't. Is there anything I need to know?" I asked. He didn't know what to say.

"Um, I don't think so," he said with his eyebrows raised.

"Good," I said. I turned on my heel and started walking again. However, before my good sense, manners, and several life-times of experience could kick in, I tore him a new one. I spun around this time so fast that he almost ran into me. I swear he almost squeaked. Taking a step back, his eyes widened at my fury. "What you are telling me, Mr. Duarte, is that you spent the night in my warm, peaceful house. You used my property for your self-improvement. You are taking a $300-dollar pair of boots. You ate my *fucking bacon*, and you think you have the gall to come to me and ask for an extension on a job offer you already turned down?" My voice was several octaves higher and much louder by the end of the rant. The control I had on my demeanor evaporated. My heart pounded in my chest.

"Um, um, well, if I can't..."

"No. Don't you dare start stammering at me again, Tadeas

Duarte! I've had about enough mindless chatter in the last 24 hours to last me another lifetime!" I said, swinging my finger in his face. It felt good to yell at him. I had tried to be humble because I did make the initial mistake, but I was sick of trying to placate him. No more.

"I apologize if I've offended you, Abby. You won't have to worry about my mindless drivel anymore," he huffed, passing me to open the door to the portal closet. I thought that was it, then he turned on me returning the favor by sticking his finger in my face. "But for your information, you are the one that stalked me for two freaking years, and you think I was just going to be okay with that? Did you think that I'd fall at your feet and thank you for offering me a job? Honey, you are pretty, but you ain't that pretty."

"I don't want your compliments. I don't care what you think I look like or about how much money I have. I have spent so much time worrying about what you thought of me, but you made it abundantly clear that you think I'm just some rich, blonde bimbo trying to pick up her next good lay. You couldn't be more wrong." My voice cracked. It did matter what he thought of me. *"Don't you fucking cry now, Abigail,"* I told myself.

"I should go," he muttered, then walked through the shimmering portal without looking back.

"Yes, you should," I snarled, throwing the damn mug at the wall next to the door. It shattered into a million pieces along with my heart.

George was right behind me, and I turned around into his chest. He wrapped his arms around me, letting me cry. "You needed to let it out," he said softly.

"No, not like that," I sobbed, already regretting my words. "He wanted more time. And instead of me getting exactly what I hoped for, his indecision ignited anger in me. And now I'm being a blubbering baby. Some badass wizard, I am."

"You both are confused right now. Just give it a little time," he comforted me. "Besides he didn't eat all the fucking bacon."

I smiled a little at that. George used the "f" word. A wise man once told me that you can use the "f" word in a business or formal setting once per day, but only for emphasis. There isn't anything more important than bacon.

Lifting my eyes to him, I said, "I went about this the wrong way. It can't be fixed."

"It doesn't matter the way you did it, child. The people involved are the right people, and eventually you both will come to an understanding," he said with full confidence.

"Can you see the future, George?" I asked because I didn't know all the capabilities of a Watcher.

"No, Miss Abby, I can't."

"Then you need a trip on the reality bus," I replied.

He cocked his head and laughed. "Maybe I do. But you will find that I have just a little more experience watching this world over eons, and you learn a few things along the way. I watched both of you. It will work out."

Well, I suppose if the retired angel had faith in it, then I could, too. But at this point, I just wanted to go back to bed. I did. I kissed him on the cheek before walking back to my bedroom. I dropped the bathrobe on the floor and got back in bed.

I DON'T KNOW HOW LONG I SLEPT WHEN THE NIGHTMARE returned. Darkness swirled around me. A tunnel leading to an apartment in New York City. Four mob thugs. A sorcerer. And my death. I screamed hoping that this time I could make it stop. I didn't want to live it over and over again. Then the black swirled again, and I slept.

When I woke up, I knew I had the nightmare again. It had been so long since that darkness stirred inside of me. My body shivered even though I was under the blankets. It was the middle of July, but I was cold. Taking deep breaths, I reminded myself it was a memory. A long-gone memory.

Stumbling to the bathroom, I started running hot water in the bathtub. I went down to the room across from the sitting room. I fondly called it the bourbon room because I love bourbon and this room had a beautiful wooden two-seater bar. Two large leather recliners that flanked a rich Spanish wood carved mantel and fireplace. Two sets of double doors led out to the courtyard patio. Pouring a shot of Buffalo Trace, I downed it quickly. I poured two more in one glass, added a couple of cubes of ice, and headed back to the bath.

George watched me from the sitting room. He was dusting again. I shrugged wondering how much dusting this house really needed. Once back to the bedroom, I pulled a small table into the bathroom next to the tub. I really needed a small side table for this very purpose. Bourbon and a bath.

I decided that I'd go shopping when I get back to Colorado. If I went back to Colorado. I lounged in the tub, drinking my bourbon. Once the water started to chill, I got out and dried off. I felt much better with a tiny buzz. Grabbing a long, comfortable maxi dress from the closet and a pair of sandals, I dressed myself to go for a walk. As I passed Tadeas' room, George came out.

"Would you like something to eat?" he asked.

"No thanks. Everything okay in there?"

"Yes, just straightening up just in case he returns."

"Just in case he returns! I love you, George. Infallible optimism."

"Comes with the territory. Besides your contact with Master Duarte isn't finished, yet."

"Hmph," I grunted. "Fat chance old man. I'm going for a walk."

"Okay then. You *will* eat when you get back," he stated, not asking.

I walked up and patted his cheek. "Yes, I will. When I get back."

He smiled, satisfied with my answer, and I headed out along the path to the dock. As the wind blew around me, I could feel a storm building over the water in the distance. It would be several hours before it got here. Figuring that I had plenty of time to avoid the storm, I continued to walk.

As I approached the water, I realized that I was following the same path Tadeas had today. It was time to make my own way. Perhaps I could find another way to operate without having a partner to depend on. It certainly would avoid any complications as my past partnerships had. I needed to control my own life and stop obsessing with this futile endeavor.

Turning back toward the house, I chose a new direction. Instead of walking through the patio, I took the path around the back side of the stables that overlooked the field of grapes. Perhaps it was time for me to retire. I could choose a successor as opposed to a partner. The whole reason I went into seclusion was that I doubted my ability to continue to do my job with the Agency. My mental stability wasn't the best at the time, plus I had things to hide. While hiding, the world changed. Developing technology moved so rapidly, that I knew I was way behind the times. It was probably best that I just hang it up. If I ended up with another dead partner… The thought of it wrenched through me. I had lost Lincoln. It would kill me to lose Tadeas even if we weren't connected the way Lincoln and I were. Tadeas made the right choice to move on. He may have made it in haste, but I was sure that he would come to the same conclusion after thinking it over again.

As I continued to walk, I rather enjoyed my romp through

self-pity. I reminded myself that I was a formidable woman. A powerful one. Someone who caused the darkness of this world to cringe and hide. That part of me was still there. I just had to believe in it. I came to a rotunda built in the midst of the vines and sat down on one of the stone benches which reminded me of that very fact.

The rotunda had 12 Greek columns. One for each month of the year. Stone benches crossed between every other set of columns, six of them. The sixth month of the year, June, was my birth month. A large silver inlaid circle for conjuring rested in the granite floor. The circle framed with a repeating pattern of Celtic shield knots was carved into the granite. The shield knot represented protection. The Celtic traditions were part of my heritage, my grandfather had explained. After leaving Tartarus, he found a home amongst the deities of the Tuatha De Dannan, and thus my maternal family had ties to those old myths. The center of the circle had a Christian cross. The head of the cross pointed north, and each side pointed to a navigational direction. Dark blue and grey marble made up the sections of the cross. The whole thing opened to nature with no walls, but the dome ceiling was supported by the columns.

The inside of the dome had a beautiful painting representing Helios, Eos, and Selene. A giant golden sun flanked by a silver moon and thorny vines with large pink roses stretched all around it. The children of my grandfather, Hyperion. He took a modern name once the time came for him to be in the public eye as the leader of KBS, Gregory Theodoard. He always said names were important. That we should have noble names. Names that represented who we were. That was a joke in my case. My first name had always been Abigail meaning "father's joy." The irony. I didn't even know my father, and I highly suspected that he had me killed many years ago. When my mother had someone drop me off at a girl's home in Bristol, England, they were told my name, Abigail. I was no more of a joy to my father than I was to my mother who dumped me off at the age of 3.

Over the years, I had many aliases, but as an orphan child, I made up Davenport. I liked the sound of it. Sounded very British. It became who I was, Abigail Davenport.

Looking around the majestic structure I realized that I hadn't conjured or cast anything in this circle since before Lincoln died. I really had no need to do so. The wards that my grandfather and Manannan Mac Lir established protected the island. Along the way, Lincoln added to them, and eventually, I did as well. Therefore, I never needed to protect myself on the island. The whole rotunda was something I spent money on because I could. It was beautiful without a doubt. But an indulgence. Lincoln had me practice maneuvers for the field inside it. We used circles in combat as a sneak attack to trap a foe. Beyond that, it was just a pretty little porch.

Deciding this wasn't the place I needed to be, I looked up across the vineyards. The tower of the small chapel reached above the trees pointing upward to the darkening sky. Following my instincts, I walked to the chapel.

As I approached the church, I felt the winds shift. I thought perhaps the storm would pass me now. I entered the quiet little church. It was dark. Not much light outside with the clouds to illuminate the stained glass.

"*Incendio,*" I muttered and the candles and torches around the room kindled to life. The flames flickered with drafts from the wind outside. I sat down on one of the benches, focusing on the altar ahead.

"I could pray, I suppose," I said to the empty room.

"Praying is always a good idea," said a strong male voice I recognized behind me.

"You know it isn't a good idea to sneak up on a wizard," I told him. He was six-foot tall, with boyish features, shoulder length sandy blonde hair that curled a bit on the ends and pale blue eyes. Today he wore a white t-shirt, black leather jacket, and blue jeans.

"I think I could handle anything you threw at me," he said smiling.

"You going all 'rebel without a cause' on me?" I asked.

"What's that?"

I giggled. "Never mind. I thought you guys kept up with things in the world."

"We keep up with the people in the world, not the trivial things, Abigail." He walked up and sat beside me a few feet away. He looked up to the stained glass. "You know a storm is coming?"

"Yes," I replied. When an archangel talks to you, he rarely says what he means. I could only guess that he wasn't referring to the one blowing in outside, but the one my grandfather had felt coming for a while now. "Prophet, did you come to warn me?"

"No, we were concerned."

"We?"

"My brothers and I," he said. He meant the angels, but more specifically the seven archangels.

I turned to him. Gabriel's beauty astounded me every time that I saw him. All confidence and grace. Of the seven, I've only met Gabriel and Uriel. Since my grandfather had Lincoln pull me out of the Catholic children's home, the two of them had visited me before something large and supernatural would happen. Gabriel always brought warnings. Uriel bestowed knowledge. "Gabriel, I know you can't tell me everything, but please tell me as much as you can," I said, knowing the reason for his visit.

"Actually, my brothers and I are concerned about you. It seems you are in a great turmoil now. I personally have never seen you unsure about yourself."

I hung my head down. He had better things to do than be here comforting me because my *not* partner "broke-up" with me.

"It's not just about the jaguar, although he is part of the bigger picture," he said, reading my thoughts.

"Stop that. It's creepy."

He smiled at me again. He couldn't half smile. Every smile was always a radiant one that lit the whole room. It was so powerful that I had to look away again. I blinked, and he sat right next to me. The aura around him surged with power. I found it hard to concentrate. Slowly I could feel him toning it down for me again, reading my thoughts.

"You have sat on the sidelines for far too long. Your work in this world is important. The things that used to tremble at your name and cower in deep caves of the earth are emerging again. We need you to do what you were born to do." Well, that blew my retirement out of the water.

"What is that exactly, Gabriel? Give me something to go on, because right now, I feel like my time has come to an end." I wasn't trying to be trite with him. I didn't want to be struck down in my own chapel, but it was a valid question.

He lifted my face with his hand gently but forced me to look into his pale blue eyes. The world around us blurred, and in the depths of his eyes, I saw the continents crumbling at the edges, falling into the sea, thousands of voices crying out in the waters, and sinking into the deep ocean. A single crystalline tear flowed down his face, hanging on the edge of his blade-edge jawline. Then the wind blew the chapel doors open, and all the flames went out. He no longer sat next to me but stood at the door with his back to me. I could hear his voice over the wind.

"The darkness is growing. The storm is close now, Abigail. Fight for the world as you once did. I believe in you. We are always here if you need us," he said. With a loud crack of lightning, he was gone. The room grew lighter, and the torches flickered to life again. I sat stunned. Had he shown me the future? I shivered at the images I saw. Many lives crying out for help. I closed my eyes, and I could hear their voices. "Abigail, help us!"

Shaking my head, I felt my heart cringe as tears flowed down my face. No matter what happened between Tadeas Duarte and myself, I had to do my job. I had to find myself again and be the force I once was in the world. The angels were counting on me. The Archangel Gabriel believed in me.

"*Praefoco*," I muttered. The flames extinguished washing me in darkness. Closing the doors behind me, I saw the storm passing the island on the west. The wind still wrapped my skirt around my legs, whipping my hair into a frenzy. I tried holding it down watching the lightning striking in the distance. The storm would not hit here, but it was beautiful to watch.

Transfixed by the storm, I pondered its power. Storms were magic. Violent elemental magic with lightning, wind, and water passing through the world. No force could stop an oncoming storm.

That was my problem. I stood by watching the storm grow, moving around my safe haven. It moved over people with no regard. The evil in this world did not care for the humans within it. For twenty years, I was no better than the storm. I sat in my comfortable chair, drank tea, and watched the world on my monitors. Lincoln, most of all, would be disappointed in me. He had begged me to continue on despite his impending doom.

The time had arrived that I could no longer watch the storm affect those around me and do nothing about it. I needed to act because a natural storm couldn't. However, a magical one could, and I had the means to calm the storm. *Quies*.

CHAPTER 20

VANESSA

The phone rang on the table beside the bed. I had to untangle myself from Mwenye and the poor girl that had joined us last night. As I rolled over, the girl fell to the floor with a thud. Great, another dead body to make disappear. Mwenye had the bad habit of consuming the life of those we picked up on the streets. He didn't care whether or not they had a family. He served his own purposes.

"What?" I said into the phone.

"Hey, it's me," a lovely voice said on the other end.

"Yeah, give me a minute," I said happy to hear her voice, and slid out of bed. I hurried down the hallway to the kitchen in the condo. "Okay go ahead. I didn't want to wake him."

"Have you done it yet?" she asked.

"No, I told you. I am waiting on someone special."

"If you kill Donovan's daughter, he will have your head on a platter," she said. "Please don't do that."

"Look, if I do, it will be because we are leaving these

187

pompous idiots behind. Did you call to scold me, or do you have information?" I asked her.

"I do. And you don't have to be harsh with me. I know who you really are," she said. She was right. She knew that most of my seductive talk was a front to complete the tasks we needed to complete.

"I know," I said simply, waiting for her to continue.

"She was here in the recruiting classes. She pretended to be a student," she said.

"You are saying that she isn't retired?"

"No, and she's recruiting a new partner from what I understand."

"Very interesting. Who is it?" I asked. Abigail Davenport had not had a partner in 25 years. Ever since Lincoln died, or was murdered, I should say.

"It's Duarte," she said. I could hear the hurt in her voice.

"Oh, Meredith, I know you liked him. You know what that means though," I said, trying to prepare her for the worst.

I know. He has to die too."

"The Director ordered the hit on her a few days ago. I'll get this information through the proper channels. Just keep tabs on them. Be my good girl," I coaxed her.

"You don't have to persuade me, Nessa. I know the greater purpose. I did hope I'd get a chance to fuck him, though. He's handsome." She truly sounded hurt over losing a potential lover.

"Don't worry. There are lots of handsome men in this world. I'll introduce you to a lot of them," I consoled her.

"Like Mwenye?" she asked. She knew I loved Mwenye, but to be honest he didn't classify as a pretty man.

"He has an abundance of attractive qualities," I replied. I could hear him stirring in the back. He would be up soon. Hopefully, he would dispose of the girl and not make me do it.

"Yes, eating souls is hella sexy," she smirked.

"Whatever, you take care of your fine ass, and I'll see you soon. Keep quiet, and be my good little spy, okay?"

"Yes, dear," she said, hanging up the phone. I smell the faint smell of burnt flesh. Well, at least, Mwenye cleaned up the mess. His incineration spell left behind a smell, but not even a single piece of ash.

He walked into the room in a black silk robe which matched his ebony skin. "Phone call?" he asked.

He probably knew who was on the phone. In fact, he probably knew every word that she had said to me, but yet he tested me still.

"Yep, good info from Boulder," I said. "I knew this plant would work."

"What's the info and I'll decide how valuable she is," he stated. I told him about Duarte, and that Abigail had gone undercover into the recruiting classes to recruit him.

"What is he?" he asked.

"Hmm? What do you mean?" I said.

"She would not recruit some mundane human. What sort of monster is he?" he demanded.

"Oh, he's a shifter." He walked across the room to me so fast I barely had time to flinch. He had me pressed against the wall. His hands pinned my forearms down, and I couldn't move as he put magical pressure on me. I cried out in pain as his finger dug into my arms.

"Do not toy with me, Vanessa Vaughn."

"He's a jaguar," I choked out. Tears rolled down my face as he squeezed my arms tighter.

"I want to know everything about him and do not return to my sight until you can tell me what I want to know. Are we clear?" he demanded.

"Yes," I said softly.

"Yes, what?" he lowered his tone.

"Yes, my love," I whispered. He leaned down still holding my arms and kissed me. Then he slung my body across the room. I bounced off the back of the couch and crumpled on the floor. Gathering my robe, I hurried off to my bedroom. Dressing quickly, I grabbed my phone before scurrying out the door. He stood at the window, stoic and unmovable. Little by little, John was losing his compassion. It wouldn't be long before the souls inside his body consumed him in return.

Our relationship had always been rough sex. He had always taken the dominant position with me, but day by day, it was more violent and hateful. I dismissed the current issue, focusing on going to meet a sweet little redhead named Cassidy.

"Hey Cass," I purred as I entered the room. Sometimes I wished I were Fae. It didn't matter which way you choose to go, when one of the Fae walked into the room, you wanted her or him. They oozed sex. Cassidy did, but she blushed when I spoke to her.

"Hi, Vanessa, how may I help you?" she said formally.

"Look I need some info on a shifter. Don't we have a data-base of known shifters?" I asked.

"Yes, we do. You need some help looking through it?" she offered to help.

"That would be lovely." I pulled up a chair beside her behind the desk as she opened the computer software. Now I know my way around a computer, however, I am not allowed access to these systems. She did not need to know that. I stroked my hand up her arm. "You are so sweet."

"Ok. Do you what type of shifter?" she asked, ignoring my touch.

"Yes, he's a jaguar and his last name is Duarte." She tapped a few keys pulling up a full profile on Tadeas Nahuel Duarte. He originated from Guatemala. Deceased biological parents.

Deceased adoptive parents. Raised by Catholic Church. Exorcism attempt in 1908. (The Church was stupid. They probably saw him change and thought he was possessed. Idiots.) Ran away from the church. Engaged to an Isabel. Killed fiancée on first change. Taken by Agency. Employed there since 1910.

"Sad story," Cassidy said.

"Um hmm. That's what happens when shifters aren't taken in by those of us who know what they are. I'd like to help this guy. He's handsome," I said.

"Yes, he is. Very," she agreed. "But how would you help him?"

"Well, he's been stuck in the Agency since he was 18 years old. He doesn't know any life other than the Agency. I doubt they are respecting him as the beautiful creature that he is. I'd like to catch him one day outside the compound and have a few drinks with him. Maybe convince him to help us better the whole world," I explained. Bless her heart, she was so naïve. I could not wait for the day I could consume her.

"Yes, he might like to change his perspective," she added sweetly.

"You are just the most darling thing," I said, leaning over and kissing her on the cheek. I heard the Director and someone coming out of the main office. "I got to run, Cass. Thank you very much. You've got to let me buy you a drink sometime." I grabbed my jacket and hit the door running as soon as the Director came into the room.

I stood at the door and listened.

"Who was that?" the Director asked.

"It was Vanessa. She was looking for a shifter." I grimaced. I should have told her not to tell.

"What shifter?" the male asked. It was The Priest.

"This guy. His name is Tadeas Duarte," I heard her say and heard her computer monitor swing around. "His story is so sad. Vanessa wants to recruit him."

"What is it, Sergio?" the Director asked.

"*Madre de Dios*, I thought he died," he said.

"You know him?" both Cassidy and the Director asked at the same time.

"I do. He was under my care in Guatemala. I tried to keep him from shifting. He was a good boy, but he murdered a woman. I tried hunting him down, but never found him," he said.

"Interesting. Why did Vanessa say she was interested in the shifter?" the Director asked Cassidy.

"She didn't say specifically, but that she wanted to help him. Try to get him out of the Agency. Maybe come here with us." The director growled.

"Vanessa Vaughn is not allowed in these systems for a reason, Cassidy. If she approaches you for any more information, you ask me first. Are we clear?" the Director spouted at the poor girl. I could hear her sniffing as if the Director made her cry. I wanted to rush in there and beat the Director's face in which I didn't think was possible considering what he was.

"Easy, child." I heard The Priest comforting her. Then a door slammed inside the office. I took this as a good time to exit. I had already spent too much time here. I took off toward the stairwell to try to sneak out. I rounded the corner and almost plowed over Milton Trujillo.

"Good god, Milt, old man, get the fuck out of the way."

He chuckled, "Miss Vaughn, what evil are you about today?"

"No evil. Just getting information for our endeavor," I explained.

"Ah yes, anything you'd like to share with me?" he asked.

"No, not really."

"You haven't told Mwenye yet have you?" he surmised. "Well, that's fine. I don't want you to lose that pretty little head. Best not tell me now."

"Thanks, old bastard," I spouted at him as I ran toward the stairs.

"Anytime, dearie," I heard him say as the door shut behind me. He wasn't so bad. He was just old, and he liked really young women. And they loved him. I could not figure it out.

EVENING HAD JUST SETTLED IN WHEN I RETURNED TO THE CONDO. I stopped by a bar on the way back to slam back a few shots. I needed the liquor badly. I'd probably have to pay more for this morning. I slipped in the door, and he stood exactly as he did when I left. Still in his bathrobe, but he held a glass of dark liquid. I approached him quietly with my head down, stopping about two feet behind him.

"Tell me," he said.

I gave him the name and the details that I read in the profile. He stood there thinking. I did not dare move. I could feel his power building. He fed on souls more often these days. His skin and eyes grew darker. The sex was rougher. The dead piled up. I would never say it out loud, but it felt like he was losing control. I knew I needed to plan my exit soon, or I would be a victim. I just had to play this game for a bit longer.

"Very good information, Vanessa," he complimented me. I raised my head slightly. I wasn't sure I heard him correctly. He opened his robe and said, "Now come over here and get on your knees and show me that you are sorry for this morning."

"My pleasure, Sir," I obeyed. There once was a day that I loved to service him. My days of being his slut were coming to an end. Soon, I would make him wish he'd treated me better. No one else in this world would put up with his deranged bullshit like I did. Yes, one day the nasty vile man would miss me.

CHAPTER 21

TADEAS

I swore that I heard something break behind me as I exited the portal. Ducking to the side a bit, I waited before shutting the door. But nothing else came through the portal. I teetered for a moment and caught myself on the wall. The office was dark and silent. Closing the door on the closet, I moved closer to the door to the hallway. I listened. I smelled. I needed to get to my room as fast as I could and avoid Meredith at all costs. The anger at Abigail still churned inside me. I needed quiet. My security blanket of routine was ripped off of me, and I wanted it back as soon as I could.

Opening the door, I ran down the hall to the stairwell. I wasn't taking chances of meeting up with anyone on the elevator. Running down the two flights of stairs, I paused at the door again to listen and feel. Nothing. Just 20 more feet down the hall and I would be home free. Dropping my keys before I opened the door, I swiped them up and jammed them into the doorknob hoping no one heard me.

In my haste, the door slipped out of my hand, banging hard to the open position then swung back at me in a fury. I needed to calm down. Grabbing it on the backswing, I tried to coax it closed without making noise.

Finally, I was back and alone. I leaned with my forehead against the door, letting out a painful sigh. Nothing about this morning went to plan. I wanted to leave her with an understanding. Not to give her hope or straws to grasp, but to be able to work together in the future. I should just give up on all of it, forget it ever happened, and go back to teaching. She had given her blessing on changing the classes. My focus could be to make sure we made the right changes for the canvas crews. I could get a few hours of sleep and then start making a plan to change the way I taught.

I tried to sleep. I tossed and turned. I'm pretty sure the bed at Casa del Sol was actually more comfortable than this one. I gave up and went to my desk in the alcove off the kitchen. I switched on the computer and went to the fridge to grab a drink. The fridge was pretty much empty. I started a pot of coffee. The phone rang, and I swiped it up fast because it was still early in the morning here in Colorado.

"Hello," I whispered, hoping whoever it was would think I was sleeping.

"Mr. Duarte?" a female voice asked.

"Yes, is that you, Miss Taylor?"

"Yes, Sir. I'm sorry to call you this early, but I wondered if you had a way for me to reach Rachel? I mean, Abigail." Of all the people in the class, she seemed to be the only one that Abigail connected with during the whole undercover operation.

"Um, not at present, but the next time I see her I can deliver a message for you if you would like," I answered her, completely confused as to why she would want to talk to Abigail this early in the morning. Did she think Abigail was in my room?

"Yes, please, if you would tell her I need to speak to her soon. I mean, if that's possible."

"Sure. She might come back to class and teach us a few new things. Are you okay? Is there something wrong that I could help you with perhaps?" Maybe she reached out to me for a whole different reason that she couldn't say.

"Nothing is wrong. I just need to talk to her sometime before I leave here. I'm sorry to bother you," she said, hanging up the phone. Her call seemed extremely out of the ordinary. I would go back up to the offices tomorrow and see if I could find someone who had a phone number for Abigail to deliver the message.

I leaned back in my chair smelling the coffee brewing. How could one woman be so utterly frustrating? I had a buddy once here in the training center that used to talk about his wife. They were trainers in the facility. A few years ago, they went out into the streets to do more, but he told me that they got along great. Perfect harmony 99% of the time. Except when it came to deciding where to go eat on the weekends. Their relationship depended on being able to get out of the compound for date night and other activities. He said the only thing they ever fought about was where to eat. He would name a couple of places. She would say no. He would ask her to suggest. She would say that anywhere was fine. He would want to choke her because she just said no to two places. Therefore, anywhere obviously wasn't fine. "I'll never understand it!" he exclaimed, frustrated even talking about it. One of the other guys overheard us talking about it. He confirmed the frustration. Apparently, his girlfriend had this same choke-hold on their date time. It sounded like misery to me. I felt some of that now. Not that Abby and I were even attracted to each other or anything like that. She was just frustrating and extremely good looking, so it was kind of the same.

"You pig," I said out loud as I got up to fix a cup of coffee. I pulled a plain black mug out of the cabinet, smirking at the mug she had today. I was willing to bet George gave her that mug on purpose. I poured a cup and sat back down at the computer. Surfing through a ton of websites, I looked up the price of the boots I wore that I got out of the closet on the island. Abby didn't lie. They were $300 boots. I whistled when I saw the price, but then I looked again. There were several other styles I really liked. I pulled the credit card she had given me out. It was my money. I might as well give it a try. I ordered 2 more pairs.

The floodgates opened. I ordered the series Blu-ray discs of MacGyver because that dude was awesome. I ordered a Blu-ray player because I didn't have one. Then, to put a hole in it all, I discovered Amazon. The internet and a credit card proved to be a dangerous combination. I probably spent over a couple of thousand dollars with just a few clicks, and apparently, I was good for it.

The card sat on my desk next to my keyboard. Looking down at it, I remembered the moment Abigail handed it to me. Shorts and a t-shirt. Sex in a bathrobe. The logic center in my brain flashed with the word: Liar. Opening the desk drawer, I took out a pair of scissors, then cut the card into a billion pieces. My only regret was not buying alcohol before I cut it up because that was exactly what I needed. My logic center pinged again at me. Maybe not.

Instead of dwelling on it, I went to the couch, turned on the tv with the volume on mute, and watched the flickering of the lights until about 10 a.m. I wondered what she did after I left. I didn't regret what I said. Harsh as it was, she came at me. I merely defended myself from the onslaught of an angry woman. Abigail didn't strike me as an angry woman though. When she approached me in the corridor, preventing my shift, she glowed with confidence and power. If anything, I wanted to remember her like that. I believed that is who she truly was in this world. Perhaps the combination of both of us created volatility. I've had recruits who were excellent in the program, but our personalities just clashed.

We didn't clash in the classroom though. I hadn't let her in. I blocked her off like I did everyone else. She was smart enough to know it, got frustrated, and told me exactly how she was feeling. I wanted the truth from her. She simply gave it to me.

AS THE DAY PASSED, I SUMMONED UP THE COURAGE TO VENTURE out of my room. Of course, I looked both ways going down the hallway before rushing to the stairwell. I found it was better than waiting on the elevator and possibly running into Meredith. Her room was around a corner from mine. I had to pass that hallway to get to the stairwell door. When I passed by she stood in the hallway, but she wasn't alone. Travis, my recruit, pressed up against her, and they were making out. Tongues lashing and soft moans. I stopped in my tracks. Stunned. That kind of contact with a recruit was against the rules. She saw me and pushed him away.

"What the hell is going on here?" I asked which was the wrong question, by the way. I was about to have a second woman berate me today.

"None of your god damned business, that's what!" Meredith yelled. Travis just turned away from both of us. He tried to go back into the room, but the door was locked. So, he skulked around the corner.

"Meredith, do you want him kicked out of the program? Because that is what is going to happen now. Geez Louise, if you had just stayed in the room, I would have never seen it."

"I wanted you to see it," she smirked. I felt a slew of anger rising to her mouth, and I just watched her let it go. "You have made it clear that I am nothing to you. I went and got what I wanted. You aren't going to kick him out. It's not your call. You have to take it upstairs, and they are not going to allow you to do it. You will look like the jilted man."

She sounded pretty confident. Unless she had a relative up there, I highly doubted they would side with her on this issue, despite what she tried to imply about me. It was strictly forbidden. The recruits could have as many relationships among each other as they wanted, but not recruits and instructors. I began to wonder what I ever saw in Meredith in the first place.

"Mere, the rules are pretty clear on this one. You will be lucky if they don't reprimand you," I said. I did feel bad for her. Technically, we had always been friends. She clearly wanted more than that from me, but I didn't lead her on. If this was a desperate attempt to gain my attention, she had failed. This repulsed me. We were leaders and mentors to these kids who already had rough lives.

"Good. I hope they do. And then I'm going to tell them about you and Abigail traipsing around Boulder, having fancy dinners. Where were you all day yesterday? In her bed? She's a fucking whore and she has you wrapped up." Meredith knew all the things to say to make me angry. She didn't believe them. She just knew it would make me mad. I held my composure the best I could.

"I visited her home. It was very nice, but I returned home early this morning around 1 a.m. And not that it is any of your business, I did not sleep with her, nor do I intend to sleep with her. I will probably never see her again," I calmly explained.

"Go to hell, Duarte," she said as she stomped back off to her door, went in, and slammed it.

"Two for two, Duarte. At least you are 100% at this point," I said to no one in particular.

As I hit the stairs going up to her office, my words hit me in the pit of my stomach. I would probably never see her again. It shouldn't bother me. That's what I wanted, right?

After a short climb up the stairs, I went to the door of her office. I reached in with my senses. No one was there, but I could smell the lingering aroma of honeysuckle.

Opening the door to the empty office, I found it just as we had left it yesterday. Her laptop sat closed on the desk with nothing else. She did say I was welcome to use her car whenever I wanted, and the keys were in the top drawer. Perhaps a trip out of the compound was what I needed.

Amongst the neatly organized pens, pencils, paperclips, and other office supplies in the top drawer of her desk, the key to the Mercedes sat near the front in a plastic desk organizer. I hadn't come here for the key, but I picked it up. Staring at it, I remembered the night in Boulder.

Her hand in my arm, joking and laughing. I liked her laugh. Taking her car would just prolong our relationship which I considered to be a dead end. As I started to lay the key back into the desk, the door to the office swung open, and a tall red-headed beauty stepped in. She wore one of those office dress things that women wear that are supposed to make them look professional and feminine at the same time. It was light green and complimented her eyes. There was no doubt the woman was one of the Fae. I knew exactly who she was.

"Oh, Mrs. Theodoard," I said.

"It's Miss, and you may call me Lianne. How are you, Mr. Duarte?"

"Please, it's Tadeas. I'm well. I was looking for a number here in the desk. I need to call Abigail and deliver a message," I replied, trying to cover the fact that I sat at her desk, in her chair with the drawer to the desk open.

"I came here hoping she would be here today. I've emailed her several times about signing this important paperwork. We seem to keep missing each other. Will you do me a favor?" she asked. Her dark brown eyes sparkled when she talked. She was one of Gregory's many offspring. She had Celtic deity ties, but I wasn't sure which one exactly. She was a goddess for sure.

"Of course, ma'am," I said.

"Aren't you a sweet thing? I'll tell you what. We will do a

mutual trade. I'd hate to have to owe you a favor in the future," she said. I'm not exactly sure what she meant by that, but my mind went the wrong direction.

"Um okay, what are the terms?" I knew to try to play it safe with these types. You never know what kind of binding you'd put on yourself with just a simple favor or what seemed to be a benign gift. I knew a Goddess or Fae could get you in a quick fix, and the next thing you know you'd find yourself turned into an Ogre or another foul beast, or be a slave to their every desire. I thought maybe that part wouldn't be very bad.

"Terms. You are a silly man, but a wise one as well. Very nice. I will give you her phone number on the island, in exchange, you will emphasize to her that she has to sign these papers as soon as that may be possible. Very simple, no loopholes. I have no desire to own your soul. Or your body for that matter. I don't even know what I'd do with a man like you."

My eyes widened, and I choked up. I squeaked out, "Okay, so I tell her about the papers, and you give me her number. That's it?"

"Unless you want more," she added.

"Um, no, thank you, ma'am, but I agree to the stated terms," I answered. She smiled, producing a blank white business card out of thin air. She handed it to me but didn't let go. I gulped. She spoke one word as she looked deeply into my eyes. I squeezed mine shut.

"Abigail." And with her name, I could feel a warm sensation in my hands. She pulled her hand away and chuckled at me. "You are adorable, Mr. Tadeas. If there is anything I can do for you in the future, please feel free to ask. My days of making side-ways deals are long over. This world is a different place. It was fun to tease you though. I had no idea a Hispanic man could blush like that." She turned on her very high heels, clicking out of the room. I could hear her giggling down the hallway.

"Holy crap," I said out loud. The blood in my face started to

ABOMINATION

drain, and the heat subsided. At least one woman today wasn't mad at me. I looked down at the card, and instead of being blank it simply said in burned out letters, Abigail. Under her name, the charred international number provided the way to open the lines of communication back up to her. I didn't hesitate despite all my misgivings. Dialing the number quickly before I lost my nerve, a familiar male voice answered. It was not the voice I wanted to hear.

"Hello, this is George speaking," he said formally.

"Hey George, it's Tadeas. I know she doesn't want to talk to me, but I've got two messages to deliver, and I made a deal on one. Therefore, I'm required to deliver it," I tried to explain.

"Master Duarte, you are correct. She does not want to speak to you. However, I would give her the phone anyway, except for she went back to bed after you left, and has not awakened. I will not disturb her," he said flatly. It was clear the old man was not happy with me, either. To be honest, hearing his kind steady voice made me pretty much loathe myself. I tried to tell myself that I meant the things I said to her, but I didn't mean any of them. Surely, George knew that, but even then, I couldn't take them back now.

"George, I'm sorry you saw all of that, and I promise one day I will find a way to make it all right again. Please tell her when you talk to her that I have two messages for her, one from Samantha. She's one of the girls in my class. The other is from Lianne Theodoard. I'm not sure how I became Abby's answering service, but I guess I am for the moment." The line was silent, and I thought I had lost him.

"I will deliver the message that you have messages for her. Best you don't make deals with Lady Lianne though," he said.

"You are right about that one. She has a way with words, but the deal was only that I deliver the message in exchange for a number to reach Abigail to give her the message from Samantha. Nothing else," I explained. Not that I needed to explain to

George. For one, he probably already knew about all of it. Or something anyway. And secondly, it was no one's business, but mine.

"Very good, Sir. Have a good day," he hung up before I could say anything else. I guess George hated me too now. I could see that he was more than just a housekeeper and butler to her. He loved her like he would his own child. As far as I knew, Abigail didn't know her real father. Neither did I. Something else we had in common. However, she had one that loved her like a father and that made all the difference. I knew that kind of love once, too.

As I mused the desk phone rang. I started to reach for it but then realized this was not my desk and not my office. I got up to leave the phone to ring thinking that she probably had an answering machine, but I heard a voice echo in my head.

"*Tadeas Duarte, answer the phone.*"

"What the ever-loving hell. Could this day get any stranger?" I said before picking up the receiver, "Um, hello?"

"Ah yes, Mr. Duarte, this is Gregory Theodoard. Would you please come up to the fifth floor and meet me in my office? We have a few things to discuss," he said. I gulped.

"Yes, Sir. I'm on my way." Much like George, he simply hung up. "My day just got stranger, don't question it again. One of the archangels might pay me a visit and blow strange out of the water," I said to the empty office. I closed the drawer and sat the phone receiver down. I stood up and mindlessly stuck the key to the Mercedes in my pocket. I rushed up the stairs to the 5th-floor stairway door.

Just inside the door, the room was decorated like a plush office with a large frosted double glass door at the opposite end. Trying to gain my composure, I pushed into the next room.

The assistant at the desk looked up at me and said, "Ah yes, Mr. Duarte, please follow me. He is waiting for you." She rose from the desk, and I followed her to the right down a long hallway with another glass wall at the end. On the frosted glass door there, a relief in clear lettering read, "Gregory Theodoard." The assistant waved at the door.

Taking a deep breath, I walked through his door to meet with the Titan. The office was surrounded by windows, which was odd since the whole place was underground. The scenery to my right depicted a large rising mountain. Its top covered in snow. I recognized it as Mount Olympus in Greece. To my left was a lush forest with small winged creatures flying around like fireflies, the sky was dark and looked like dirt. It must be the Underworld where the high sidhe lived.

Suddenly, I realized Mr. Theodoard wasn't the only person in the room. Miss Lianne Theodoard stood next to him. He sat at a large wooden, hand-carved desk. I looked down after my encounter with her from a minute ago. I blushed again.

"See," she said.

He laughed a deep, full laugh. I had spoken to him several times over the years, but mostly in passing. I had never been in this office, and we certainly had never been alone. Miss Lianne walked to the door of the room smiling. I nodded at her as she passed, diverting my eyes from her, "Lady Lianne." I greeted her politely using the moniker George used. She got to the door, and I heard her stop.

"Did you reach her?" she asked.

"No ma'am, but I will. It was a deal," I said trying to sound confident. "If I do not speak to her in the next few hours, I will travel through the portal and tell her face to face."

"That would be unwise. The portal should not be used twice in a 24-hour period. I know you aren't completely human, Mr. Tadeas, but it would upset your internal clock. You might be awake for days. It shouldn't be used lightly." She waited for me to respond before she left the room.

"Thank you, ma'am. Abigail, I mean, Miss Davenport, did not mention that to me."

"You are most welcome," and she turned and left the room.

I lifted my eyes to Mr. Theodoard, and he chuckled. "Son, please come in and sit down. May I offer you food or drink?"

"No, Sir. I thank you for the offer," I said thinking to myself hospitality had been invoked.

"I apologize for my daughter Lianne. I think sometimes she forgets the effect that she can have on a man." His deep blue eyes were watching me as he spoke. His grey hair laid perfectly on his head. He had plenty of wrinkles and wear on his face, but he was not frightening except for knowing who he was and what he could do to me. If anything, he seemed very grandfatherly. A lot like George in a way.

"Um, yes she is a beautiful woman," I said complimenting her and trying my best not to make it sound lewd.

"She propositioned you, did she?" he asked.

This whole discussion began to make me uncomfortable, and I shifted my weight in the chair as if I had sat on a thumbtack. I knew I should not lie to him, but also, I did not want it to seem like I had enjoyed her banter at me. It was nothing more than flirting. "She was very kind earlier to me, and while I appreciate her attention, I did not accept them, Sir."

He roared with laughter, slapping his knee. I was bewildered. "Son, I sent her down there to find Abigail and instructed her to proposition you. Had you accepted her offer, you wouldn't be sitting here."

Gulp. Well, at least I had passed someone's test today. "May I ask why, Sir?"

"Of course, you may, in fact, you may ask anything you wish of me as long as I am allowed the same to you," he stated.

"Yes, Sir, I agree," I said, making another deal for the day, thus digging my hole a little deeper.

"Fantastic. This one is a simple answer though," he said turning serious. "You mean a great deal to my granddaughter and her plans for the future. Sleeping with her Aunt probably is not the way to fix things between the two of you."

"How do you know that we are currently not, um, talking?"

"I am who I am, Son. She means the world to me. I watch her every move and the moves of those around her."

"Well, I see where she gets it from," I blurted becoming entirely too comfortable with this conversation. My eyes widened when I realized what I had said.

He roared again. "Yes, I suppose she got some of that from me. At least I hope she picked up a few of my better qualities. I can't say much for her taste in alcohol, but otherwise, she is a magnificent woman."

"That she is," I said unable to stop myself. I shifted again in the seat. It felt weird.

"I must confess something to you, Tadeas. May I call you Tadeas?"

"Yes, Sir, of course."

"Ah yes, Gregory for me please, too. I confess the chair you are seated in is called the Chair of Truth. You cannot lie while sitting in it. I normally do not tell anyone who enters this room about the power of that chair. It has saved me and this company many times. I cannot have that secret getting out. However, if my Abby trusts you, then so do I."

"I will tell no one of it Sir, but I'm not so sure *your* Abby trusts me."

"Nonsense. You have been to the island correct?"

"Yes."

"And she made it possible for you to go through the portal whenever you wish?"

"Yes."

"Did you know that now only two people in this world can pass through that portal with no escort?"

"She did mention something to that effect, but she also proposed with the following sentence so, it didn't sink in. She hasn't told me everything. I don't mean that negatively at all. There really hasn't been time, actually. I'm not sure that there ever will be." Mouth vomit. I hated mouth vomit, and I hated this chair.

"The chair was made by my brother's daughter, Veritas. She made it specifically for me to keep in this office. It cannot be moved from that spot. And unfortunately, until I allow you to leave, you cannot get out of it. I apologize for the ruse, but I needed to look you in the eye myself. Abigail has complete confidence in your abilities. She believes you are an honorable man. I admit that a lot of her opinion of you started with her former partner, and my best hunter, Lincoln. His death was a great loss to all of us. I can tell you that even now she struggles with it. I disagreed with her method of infiltrating your class, but she insisted upon it. She is not one to go completely on the word of another, not even Lincoln's word. She had to know you for herself. We discussed other ways of doing it, but she was sure she'd never get you to see the real her, in turn, preventing her from truly knowing you. She is stubborn. She gets that from me too, I suppose. The quick tongue though, she got that all on her own."

"Don't I know it." Stupid chair.

"Got a taste of that did you?" he laughed, but his face turned solemn again. "She cannot work alone. She has a full team that she works alongside, but she needs a partner. A protector. A guardian." He turned to look at the scene behind him, and it shifted to a beautiful Spanish style home sitting among a vineyard.

"It's a beautiful place," I said.

"It is. I used to love being there, but she needed a haven to be safe from time to time. A place to rest. A peaceful place. I gave it to her, and George was there to manage the grounds and be there for her. She needed him, too." I still didn't understand why one of the most powerful wielders in the world needed a safe place. Not to mention her own Watcher.

"He's like a father to her."

"Yes, the father she never had. She has one, mind you, but he's one of the reasons she needs a haven. I would like to keep her away from him at all costs." I saw a fire in his eyes reflecting on the glass window to Casa del Sol. "If you take the job, you must know that there are a great number of evil things in this world that want her dead. She has very few friends. She doesn't trust many because she can't afford to trust. It could cost her life. I lost her once. I will never do that again."

"You lost her, Sir? I don't understand." I tried not to pry, but apparently this chair makes you say the things you don't even mean to say.

He turned back to me, but his eyes were dark and distant. "She died once, and it was the very worst pain of my long existence. After that, I put Lincoln with her to guard her. I did not intend for them to fall in love, but they did. It wasn't ideal, but I approved of the match. He was the only man on this earth I trusted. You see Mr. Duarte, I can't trust anyone either. Every offspring I have on this earth wants this desk, this room, and *that* chair. Even the red-headed beauty, Lianne. Now she's never made any overt try for my position in this world, but one day she will. Just like they all do. But I know one person who will never seek it out."

"Abby."

"Yes, she is my hope for the future. I trust her when I can trust no one else. And if she trusts you, then so do I."

I looked into his eyes and he meant it. He wasn't patronizing me or trying to get me to agree to the job. He meant he trusted me. "I am humbled and honored, Sir."

He waved his hand in the air, dismissing my statement. "I suppose it was a heavy thought. Do forgive me as I have one more, then you are free to ask anything you wish of me. You must know this, even though the two of you may never work this out, but I suspect you will. You may never become her partner. However, I know you probably will. However, whatever contact you have with her, please be mindful, I will not interfere with her methods or her desires. I will not meddle in small quarrels or disagreements. But if you ever hurt her, I will tear your entrails out by your nostrils and hang you by them in the desert. And though every creeping thing on this earth will feast on you, it still won't be enough to cover my anger toward you. Are we clear, Tadeas Nahuel Duarte?" The room shook with his statement.

"*Madre de Dios*," I exclaimed, crossing myself as I had when I was younger. I reached for my crucifix. I felt it warm under my shirt. I wanted out of the damn chair. The room had grown dark. The displays blackened and swirled with ominous grey smoke. He loomed over me even though he still sat in the chair. I seriously almost pissed myself. Then the darkness receded and every screen in the room turned to a beautiful blue sky with fluffy clouds floating by. I am a formidable guy, but Gregory Theodoard was a Titan. He was Hyperion. He could incinerate me with a thought. I cowered and tried to straighten myself in the chair. He sat there looking at me waiting for me to compose myself.

"I, um, Sir, well, I." My voice shook. I have never in my entire life been that afraid.

"I'm sorry, Tadeas. But it needed to be done. I did the same to Lincoln so long ago. Welcome to the club," he said with a smile. His demeanor had changed within seconds.

"Thank you, I think."

"I'm impressed you didn't lose your faculties."

"Just barely, Sir." Motherfucking chair.

He roared with laughter again. "Ask whatever you want, Son. You earned it."

"How did she die?"

"I apologize, but I am bound by oath. If she wants you to

know that story, she will tell you herself, but I warn you, it is not an easy story for her. And if she tells you, honor that trust and respect her for it. I have a feeling she will tell you."

"I'm not so sure. I have plenty of amends to make."

"As does she," he stated. "Does that shock you? She has a quick tongue. It's her greatest fault in fact. She controls it much more now than she used to, but sometimes it still gets the better of her. I imagine she instantly regretted it."

"May I ask how she is alive now?"

"Yes, that one I can answer. The All-father, Odin, owed me a favor. I called it in. He brought his Valkyries and resurrected her."

"Wait. She's a Valkyrie?"

"In spirit yes, but not in practice. I would never let her be under the thumb of the Aesir. But it was the only way I could bring her back. Her death was not part of the larger plan for the world. Someone cheated. They broke the rules of the universe. Once she revived, in turn, her mother gave her the gift of eternal youth and beauty. It healed her body from the devastation of the murder. I believe her mother regretted abandoning her to a girl's home in England when she was only 3 years old. As atonement, she made her in her own image, an eternal beauty."

"There is no doubt, she is beautiful. Who is her mother?" I asked.

"Another oath binds me. Even Abigail does not know her name, but she will tell you what she knows of her if you ask," he said.

"You seem confident that she will forgive me and give me a second chance."

"No, she has already forgiven you and seeks your forgiveness. I know this for truth."

I sat still and thought long about the things I could ask him.

"Tadeas, you are welcome to come back any time to sit in my chair, and I will answer any question you have. Knowing the price to pay by sitting in the chair, grants you the privilege to be able to ask what you want. You are free to go. Please do not wait too long to talk to her. After the 24 hours is up, please try to contact her. I do hate to see her this upset and unsure of herself. She has yet to regain her confidence after multiple heartaches," he said.

"I will, Sir. I promise." I stood up, and he came out from behind the desk to escort me to the door. He offered me his hand. I shook it. He almost crushed my fingers.

"I'm sorry. I forget my strength."

"Sure, you did," I blurted and looked back at the chair. He died laughing and opened the door.

"After effects of the chair, I believe."

"Indeed, Sir." I smiled at him and walked down the long hallway as he shut the door, returning to his office. Outside of the whole entrails part, he seemed like a nice guy. He loved Abigail. I couldn't blame him too much for the threat. Perhaps a little over-board, but he was a deity. And generally, you don't piss them off and live to tell about it.

On the other hand, I thought about Abigail and the few things he had told me about her. Her life had not been easy. I was wrong in many ways. I wasn't sure that I wanted to be her part-ner, but sitting in the chair did help me see one thing for sure, I wanted her to forgive me. The animal inside of me stirred. "I'd tear someone's entrails out if they hurt her, too," I said as I walked into the room with the assistant. Her head shot up and her eyes grew wide. "Um, sorry. It's been a strange day. Excuse me," and I bolted for the door. I really needed to stop talking to myself out loud.

CHAPTER 22

TADEAS

*W*hen I entered the room with the elevator, the doors opened and someone came out. I didn't even notice who, but I ducked inside and jammed the #2 button. The elevator descended. My stomach growled in protest. The plan was to grab something to eat in Boulder, then a short work-out before bed. Along the way, I'd try to call Abigail to deliver the messages. I was happy to avoid the cafeteria food for another day. The funny thing was, I never thought it was that bad until Abby pointed it out. It wasn't bad, per se, just mundane. Repetitive. I supposed you didn't know what you were missing until you tried something new. My routine had kept me locked in the basement for so long that I never realized the possibilities.

As the door started to open on the 2nd floor, I hit the button for 4 and the doors closed again. I was glad no one else was riding. I exited the elevator, then headed to Abby's office. Maybe I could find the number for that delivery service. I needed to try to call her again. It was Sunday evening. I had classes all day tomorrow, but Tuesday was a full range day for the class. They would be in firearms training all day. And while I usually went with them, I wasn't required to. If necessary, I could hope through the portal on Tuesday to deliver the messages. Slowly I opened the door to her office. It was empty again.

I sat down behind the desk, pulling out the top drawer. I remembered I had placed the Mercedes key in my pocket. Inside the draw, I found a small planner. I flipped through it quickly, but it only listed meetings and such, no phone numbers. I reached in my pocket and took out the key. I pulled out my cell phone and hit the retry on the last number called.

"Hello, this is George. How may I help you?"

"Hey, George, it's me again."

"Master Duarte, how has your day been?"

"George, I didn't think my life could get any stranger, but today it has. Is she available?"

"No, Sir, she is still resting. I think the weekend took a lot out of her. I suspect she didn't sleep much when she lived in Boulder for the last three months, either," he said.

"No, probably not. Well, I really need to speak to her. I wanted to ask to borrow the car."

"It's my understanding Sir, that she intended for you to use the car whenever you wished."

"Yes, she said that, but I still felt like I should ask," I explained. I certainly wasn't looking for another reason to talk to her.

"I give you permission, Sir."

"Can you do that?" I asked.

"Technically no, but I'll take the blame if she says anything. She won't though, Sir. To my knowledge, she hasn't rescinded any of her offers to you," he said, reminding me that she still wanted to be my partner despite my terrible attitude. I laughed at him. He seemed to enjoy pulling rank on her occasionally.

However, I wondered if something more was wrong with her. It wasn't like George had any obligation to tell me.

"Thanks, George. Is she okay, Sir? I mean, she isn't sick or anything is she?"

"No, Sir. I don't believe it is anything like that at all," he said.

"Thanks again, George. I'll try again in the morning."

"Very well, Sir," he said and hung up the phone.

Taking the elevator to the surface, I was almost giddy to get to drive that sleek Mercedes again. It sat right where we left it on Friday evening. As I approached the driver's side door, it automatically unlocked. Once settled into the soft leather seats, I hit the push button start and sped away into the evening. The clock on the dash shone in a bright blue, 7:30 pm. I entered the bustling part of downtown Boulder near The Table restaurant and found a tavern just down the street. It didn't seem too busy.

Ducking into the tavern, the smell of good food filled the place. The bar seemed to be very busy, but I found a stool to wait for the bartender. He was a young man with reddish-brown hair and a trim-cut full beard. He smiled as he laid a menu in front of me. He had a towel thrown over one shoulder. "Whatcha drinking, buddy?"

I looked across the back of the bar, and it seemed they had every single brand of liquor I had ever heard of and some I hadn't. I rarely drank anymore. I guess I looked overwhelmed. He leaned over the edge of the bar and tapped the menu, I looked down and they had a separate drink menu from the food menu. Almost every single specialty drink had Bourbon in it. I looked up at him, "Bourbon, huh?"

"It's what we do best. We've got some special ones that are really hard to get."

Wasn't that just fitting? Abby wasn't here, but she was. I read over the drinks and ordered one and of course, it had bourbon in it. I decided there was nothing that I could do to get away from her. Might as well enjoy it. He moved down the bar to make my drink. I had just chosen one and hadn't looked at the full line-up. Almost to the bottom of the list was a drink called "Spirit Animal."

"You've got to be kidding me," I said to no one in particular. There were several televisions showing a baseball game, but the volume was down on all of them. My neighbor on the stool to my right was a gentleman who appeared to be in his late 50s. He wore a casual navy suit, but I could see the sparkle of a diamond cufflink poking out of his sleeve. He sipped yellowed liquor out of a brandy glass.

"They do have a lot of bourbons here," he spoke up. I guess he thought my outburst referred to the extensive list of bourbons on the back of the menu.

"That they do. I have a friend who would love this place. She loves bourbon," I said and turned to him. I offered him my hand, "I'm Tadeas."

He shook my hand. "I'm Milton. Folks call me Milt."

"Nice to meet you Milt. Is the food good here?" I asked.

"I hear it is. I rarely get past the drinks," he said lifting his glass to his lips. He had salt and pepper hair and dull blue eyes. He looked tired. The bartender returned with my drink. "Here you are, Sir. You eating with us, too? Would you like to start a tab?" he asked.

"No, tab, but I am hungry." He traded the drink menu for a food menu. It was only one-fold, and he still stood there. I ordered quickly.

"Just the tavern burger please with cheese, hold the mayo," I said handing the menu back to him.

"Sure thing. Won't take long," and he walked away to a nearby kiosk to place my order.

"First time in here, then?" Milt asked.

"Yeah, I work nearby, but I don't get out much. I just picked the first place that looked good and had a bar," I said carrying on the friendly conversation. "You come here a lot?"

"Yea, every Sunday to meet a lady friend," he said.

"Oh, very nice. She here?" I asked not seeing a woman seated by him or hovering nearby.

"No, she's not here yet. She'll be along shortly. I like to get a few drinks in me before she gets here," he downed the rest of the brown liquid. The bartender instinctively looked up and Milt tapped the edge of his glass. The bartender nodded, immediately pouring him another in a fresh glass.

"Is it *that* bad?" I asked chuckling.

"No. Not at all. I enjoy spending time with her. Just getting the night off to a fun start," he said. He looked at his watch. "Yep. She will be here soon." The bartender brought his new glass, removing the old one.

"What about you? Are you meeting someone? The lady you mentioned?" he asked.

"No. Not tonight. I just went out on a spur of the moment. Nothing to eat at home," I said lying. He raised his eyebrows at me and smiled.

"Oh, you are in the doghouse," he laughed.

I shook my head. I supposed in a way I was. I laughed. "I guess I am," I said.

"Then you should have one of these," he said nodding to his glass. He looked at the bartender who had moved to the end of the bar. He talked to some younger women there. He turned to look back down at his patrons and locked eye contact with Milt. Milt then tapped his glass and pointed at me.

"No, no Sir, that's not necessary. I'm driving. I really shouldn't have more than one," I said. The bartender walked up and handed me an identical glass.

Milt spoke up. "He won't be needing that other one. And I'll cover his bill."

"You've got it, Milt," the bartender responded.

"I can't let you do that, Sir. I am appreciative, but really you don't have to do that." I didn't know what to think about a guy randomly buying my drinks.

"Tadeas, you said, right?" I nodded. "Well, Mr. Tadeas, you are in the doghouse, and that's a rough spot to be in. I've been there a few times myself. And just before you go home, and say your apology, cause that's the only way you are getting out of this, you need a good drink and a solid meal. In a little while, you won't have time to drink, and you'll be eating shit before the night is over. Or perhaps if you are lucky, something more intimate." He laughed heartily.

I had to laugh, too. But there would be no luck for me. "I concede, but next time you must allow me."

"That's a deal. Next time bring the pretty lady with you. I don't mind looking at the pretty ones even if they aren't mine," he laughed again, and I joined him.

"I'll do that," I said as I took a sip of the liquor. It was very good. I could taste a hint of orange and honey, but it was strong and burning all the way down to my gut. I smiled. Abigail would love it. She'd probably had it before, but it seemed to match her.

"It's a 10-year Eagle Rare. They have a 17-year, but that's a bit extravagant for a pre-date drink, or in your case, a session in humility." He smiled again and looked at his watch. "Time to meet my girl. You have a nice night, Tadeas. And good luck with the lady. Next time the drinks are on you," he said as he got up to leave.

"Thanks, Milt," I said as he walked away.

"Anytime," he said over his shoulder. The bartender arrived with my burger, and it looked pretty good. I took another sip of the drink, looking out the front glass. He had his arms around a woman who looked much younger than him. She pulled back from the embrace and smiled. I blinked because I couldn't believe what I was seeing. The young woman hugging Milt was Samantha Taylor. I stared at them as they crossed the road, and he put her in a blue BMW.

"Everything good, Sir?" the bartender asked.

"Yes, yes, it looks great," I began to eat. The place was packed, and I was taking up a seat. I supposed Milt had paid for everything. The bartender was probably eager to fill the spot with another paying customer.

As I ate, I had a lot to think about including the little scene I just witnessed. Who Samantha saw on her own time was none of my business, but it was strange to see her with an older man like that. I had sincerely hoped she wasn't mixed up in an escort service or heaven forbid, a prostitution situation. A lot of the girls we got at the Agency had been in that environment, and unfortunately, they went back to it sometimes. I sincerely hoped that isn't why she tried to contact Abigail. Milt and Samantha. Meredith and Travis. Lianne. Gregory. I picked up the glass and swirled the liquid inside. I tossed the rest of it back. The bartender promptly arrived and asked if I wanted another. I explained to him that I wouldn't be drinking anymore and asked for a Coke to drink while finishing my meal. He brought it to me, and I asked him before he walked away about the liquor. "Hey man, is that Eagle 10-year hard to find?"

"Not really. The Liquor Mart down on 15th Street usually has it. It runs about $65 a bottle. It's good stuff."

"Yes, I like it. I have a friend that would like it too. How about Milt? Does he come in here often?"

"Yeah, old Milt is here every Sunday. He waits on his girl and always has two glasses, then meets her outside. She never comes in. To be honest, she doesn't look old enough to be in here, anyway."

"She did look young," I agreed. I knew all too well that Samantha was only 18.

"Rich guys have all the luck, no matter how old they are, don't they?" he laughed.

"Seems that way. Thanks for the service, man. I know he paid for it, but I appreciate the attention," I said. I pulled out my wallet and dropped a $20 on the bar for the Coke and the service. "Have a good one."

"Come back again, and bring a friend," he smiled.

"I plan on it," I said walking out the door into the cool night air. The mountains in the distance loomed darkly over the city. I hopped in the Mercedes and headed back to the compound. I rarely went out, but it had been nice. I needed to do it more often. Maybe the guys from the training center would like to visit the bar. Maybe Abby would come.

As I drove back, I started to feel tired. For a moment, I even crossed the centerline of the highway. Thankfully, no one approached in the opposite direction. I centered myself and focused on the road. Needed to stop letting my mind wander. I hadn't had much sleep, and it was catching up with me. But the need to sleep was persistent. Overly so. I became concerned and found a small road to pull off of the main highway. I put the car in park and rubbed my eyes. I felt unnatural as if someone drugged me. I leaned forward, putting my forehead on the steering wheel. I lost consciousness for a minute.

The Jaguar started to stir. Danger was nearby. I bolted back in the seat looking around frantically. I reached for the door handle, but before I could open the door, a muscular man in silhouette opened it for me. I couldn't see him. He looked to be nothing but a shadow. I tried to pull away, but I felt like I was bound. He was a wielder. I started to panic, but my body felt numb. I had no way to fight back and had no hope of anyone helping me.

He spoke in a deep tone. "Yes, you will be a fine addition to my collection."

"Get the fuck away from me," I managed to get out of my mouth as he reached for me. He grabbed me by the shirt, dragging me out of the car. I hit the dirt beside the car. Every time I tried to move or kick him away, it was futile. My limbs weren't responding.

"Take the car. Lose it. Make it disappear," he chuckled to someone standing nearby.

I twisted, putting my hand on my chest. I could feel my crucifix there. I could not speak. I hoped a silent prayer would work, but before I could even start the prayer, I heard a storm moving in from the west. The shadow man turned to look at it.

"We must go. Forget the car." He bent down and spoke in my ear. "Next time, Jaguar. I'll take you with me." The person with him, also in shadow, joined hands with him, and with a whoosh of wind, they were both gone. The thunder rolled closer. After he disappeared into the night, I regained motion in my legs, slowly. Dragging myself back to the car, I tried to pull myself up into it to no avail. I searched my pockets for my phone but couldn't find it. A car pulled up behind me. A man's voice called out to me.

"Hey, are you okay?"

I shook my head, and managed to choke out, "No, I'm not." My arms and legs started to respond to commands again, and I felt more alert. I tried to push myself up off the ground. I was covered in dirt, as the man approached me.

"Let me call you an ambulance. You look rough," he said. He was tall and muscular. He looked young but seemed older. I could see his blonde hair reflecting with the car lights.

"No, please don't do that. I'm feeling better now. Thank you." I steadied myself next to the car.

"There are bad things out in the night, Tadeas Duarte," he said. He had dropped the young surfer boy tone. "You should go home."

My heart rate picked up, and I touched the edge of the spirit world. I would shift if need be. I looked back toward the man and his car, but they had vanished. The storm rumbled in the distance. I inched my way back up to the seat of the car. I should have known that this day couldn't end normally. Looking at Abby's car, I knew it needed to be detailed after all the dust I was about to put in the leather seats, but I didn't take the time to dust off.

"Abby is going to kill me," I thought. I pulled the door shut and sped off as fast as I could. Once I reached the compound, I got to my room as quickly as possible. Without taking off my dusty clothes, I crashed into the bed, falling asleep immediately.

I AWOKE TO MY CELL PHONE RINGING. I BOBBLED IT ONTO THE floor. I fell off the bed trying to reach it. I clicked the button, "Hello."

"Where are you?"

"Hey Mere, what's up?"

"Tadeas, it is 9 a.m. and your class has been waiting for you for an hour. Please tell me you aren't with that whore."

"Meredith, please stop yelling," I mumbled. Why was she yelling?

"I'm not fucking yelling, YET!"

I jolted with her scream in my ear, and it all started to register.

"Holy crap. I'm on my way." I hung up the phone, rushing over to the dresser. There was no time to shower, but I changed out of the dusty clothes quickly. When I looked back at my phone, it hit me that I couldn't find it last night. Apparently, I was completely out of it. The whole thing felt like a hallucination.

RUSHING TO THE CLASSROOM, I PAUSED AT THE DOOR TO control my breathing. I pushed the door open and started barking orders for the opening of class. We always started with forms. I started calling positions but did not join them today as I normally would. When I looked around the class, I spotted Samantha in the back. She seemed fine despite my seeing her last night with Milt. I worked myself through the class in the same old fashion. However, I made none of the changes that I had discussed with Abigail.

Just before dismissing them, I spoke to all of them. "I apologize for my tardiness this morning. It is inexcusable. I hold all of you to a very high standard. I hold myself to the same. I failed in that today, and I will promise that it will never happen again. You are all free to go to lunch. Be back here at 2."

They all left the room except Samantha, and she stood at the door. "Miss Taylor, I'm sorry. I haven't spoken to Abigail. She stayed back at her home this weekend, and she has not returned my call."

"It's okay," she said. "I planned to tell you to forget about it, anyway."

"You sure?"

"Yes, Sir. Thank you for trying. Is she okay?"

"I believe so. I haven't spoken to her since before dawn Sunday morning," I replied, which sounded like I had spent the night with her. Idiot.

"Okay, cool. See you this afternoon," she smiled, then hurried out of the room.

I started walking for the exit myself when Meredith came in, and she put her hands on her hips. She was kind of cute when she was mad. "What the hell, Duarte?"

"I am sorry. Thank you for calling me. I had a very strange day yesterday, and I went into Boulder for dinner," she cut me off.

"Again! With her!"

"No, I haven't spoken to Abby since around midnight Sunday morning." I decided it was best to stick with Colorado time. "I had a drink and a meal at this nice tavern down there."

"You went drinking alone?" she asked. "You have lost your mind."

"What? Why?" I said.

She walked toward me looking very concerned. She put her hand on my forearm and squeezed. "The Tadeas I know doesn't go out to bars. He doesn't go following a fairy witch all over the place. He's steady. He's routine. I don't want to see something bad happen because she's come into your life and tried to wreck it."

"She didn't do that, Meredith."

"The way I see it, she did. She is. It's scary. Please don't let her ruin your life."

She was almost in tears. "Meredith, it's not like that. I think you've got a few questions to ask yourself, too, about the boy."

"Travis is something to have fun with, a toy. Did you turn us in? Did you tell *her* about it?"

"I have not spoken to her, Meredith. I haven't told anyone, actually."

"You didn't go upstairs yesterday and report me?" she asked.

"No. I didn't." I fully intended to, but after Lianne and Gregory, I honestly forgot about it. "But you need to be careful. Break it off. There are plenty of frivolous flings you could have without breaking the rules."

"I wouldn't have to if you would just..." she trailed off. "Oh, never mind." And with that, she stormed off.

My head pounded. I wandered back to my room to clean up the dusty clothes and change my sheets. I sat on the couch with headache meds and a coke. I called Blake, one of the other instructors.

"Hello?"

"Blake, hey man, it's Duarte."

"Hey, what's up?" he said.

"Can you take my afternoon class? I'm not feeling well. I'm going to get some sleep," I said.

"Get some sleep, huh?"

"Yeah," I muttered. I already knew where this was going.

"What's her name?" he asked.

"Her name is Karma, and she's a bitch," I said.

"Damn straight, she is. I'll cover the class. Get some rest, man," he laughed.

"I appreciate it."

"No problem," he said, then hung up. Much like last night, I stumbled into the bedroom and hit the bed. I was out in a matter of seconds.

I WOKE UP TO THE PHONE RINGING AGAIN.

"Ugh, who is it?" I growled.

"Master Duarte, it's George." I perked up at the sound of his proper British. It was 11 a.m. I'd been asleep since close to noon on Monday.

"Oh, hey George. Is everything okay?" I was happy to hear his voice

"Sir, she is awake, but she went for a walk. I think you might need to come here if you can get away," he said.

"What's wrong, George? Is she okay?" I was fully awake now. Something inside me clicked, and I felt like I needed to get to the island as soon as possible.

"It's hard to say, Sir, but if you would please," he continued.

"Yeah, sure. I'll be there soon. Bye, George," I said, hanging up the phone. Opening my closet door, I found that it was full of clothes like the ones at Casa del Sol. "Creepy as hell, Abby," I said, but I smiled. I decided on a pair of dark tan slacks and a navy button-up shirt.

Realizing I had neglected my personal hygiene, I jumped in the shower, shaved and combed my hair. I still needed a haircut. After dressing quickly, I took a quick look in the mirror. I seemed presentable enough. It hit me that I hadn't made a decision, but I was rushing off to see her anyway.

Forty-five minutes had passed since George called. He had sounded concerned, but not so much that I should have left immediately. I didn't have to worry about classes today. I could be back in 24 hours in time to teach on Wednesday. I entered her office without even checking and went straight for the closet. Without hesitation, I stepped through the portal to Casa del Sol.

CHAPTER 23

VANESSA

*M*wenye and I were having company over tonight. I tidied up a bit while Mwenye showered. Thinking about my childhood, I remembered my mother having company over quite often after my father left. Then, one day, the company turned out to be a necromancer. John took me from my mother when I was sixteen. He offered me the world, and I took the chance. I had no idea what I was getting myself into. It wasn't so bad to begin with because he taught me how to wield magic. I wasn't even sure how he found me, but he had. John didn't care for man's rules on things, and I wasn't in his care long before he took me to his bed. I enjoyed every minute of it. He hadn't forced me. I went willingly. Now, every time we were together, I had to force myself to enjoy it.

Ever since I got the info about Duarte, he had been rather tame. I suppose this whole endeavor weighed on him. He generally did not work well with other people. This was a definite step out of his comfort zone. I eased my anger toward him, and over the last 24 hours I tried to enjoy my time with him. Old Trujillo would be here in a few minutes, and I would have to endure his advances. But perhaps with Mwenye here, he would not be so bold.

I sat out candles and opened wine. I set a tray of crackers, cheese, and meats on the coffee table. I wore a simple black dress which was cut low in the front. The truth was, I didn't think I owned anything that didn't show cleavage. Even with my tee shirts I had cut the neck out until they hung just right. I used all the tools in my arsenal.

Mwenye entered the room wearing black slacks and a charcoal grey dress shirt. He looked wonderful. He even smiled.

"You should do that more often," I said testing the waters.

"Do what, my love?" he asked.

"Smile," I said looking up at him. He smiled more. It made me happy. Maybe we were through this rough patch. I wanted to adore him again as I once had, but something in my gut told me those days were over.

"Ah, well, anything you for you, my lovely," he said. The doorbell rang.

"Let me get that," I said passing him. I kissed him on the cheek as I passed.

I opened the door, and there stood old Milt. "Please, Mr. Trujillo. Come in. We welcome you to our home. There is food and refreshments this way." Mwenye instructed me that this would be an official hospitality-observed meeting. They both were formidable beings. Trujillo was a shifter. I'd never seen him shift, but I'd heard the stories.

"Why thank you, dear Miss Vanessa. You do look lovely tonight." He took my hand, kissing the back of it with a slight bow.

"My goodness, Milt, when did you become so debonair?" I teased.

"My picture is in the dictionary next to debonair, Miss

Vanessa," he laughed as he walked up to Mwenye. "John, very pleased to see you. Thank you for the invite and the hospitality."

"Please come in and sit," Mwenye motioned to the living area.

I grabbed two glasses and poured each a glass of Casa Del Sol Merlot. I gave one to each man, Mwenye first. Then backed away to the chair removed from the main sitting area. I started to sit when Milton protested.

"Now Miss Vanessa, please sit with us old men. Let us see your pretty face as we discuss business. If that is okay with you, John?" he asked his host.

"Why yes, of course," he nodded to me. I picked up another wine glass and poured myself a half glass and sat down on the couch at the opposite end from Milton. John sat in the leather stiff-backed chair on the end.

"How's Colorado?" John asked.

"Well, I found a pretty little piece of ass out there. She is young and beautiful. And useful," he said.

"I like useful women," Mwenye said, winking at me. I blushed out of habit. He certainly seemed to be in a good mood.

"Yes, I see," Milt responded. "She has confirmed the info you gave me regarding the jaguar shifter. It seems Miss Davenport is recruiting. Perhaps it's time we make a move on her."

John waved his hand in the air dismissing the thought, but he did it with such ease that it did not come off as a slight to Milton. "No, I want to keep her in play a little longer. She is predictable. She has a pattern. We don't need to concern ourselves with her until she starts *breaking* the pattern. When Lincoln died, we all rejoiced, especially you, old Eagle."

"Aye, I did. My old nemesis finally laid to rest. Although I admit, I do miss him a little. He was a formidable foe and honorable. You don't find many like that anymore," Milton said swirling the Merlot in his glass. "The girl said that Duarte and

Davenport have had a couple of meetings. She is not in a posi-tion to get a lot of information."

"What is her position just out of curiosity?" Mwenye asked.

"She's a canvas recruit that I met in Boulder," he said.

"A canvas recruit! She can't be more than 18, Milt! You dirty old man!" Mwenye teased.

"That I am, and I love every minute of it. So, she only hears what she hears. I don't want to push too much out of her right away. She is just turning tricks for money right now."

"Oh, you are paying her. That makes much more sense," Mwenye said.

"I admit my good looks had an expiration date that has long gone by, but my charm and pocketbooks are deep," Milton admitted. I giggled a little at this but tried to stay quiet. "I hear you giggling there, Miss Vanessa. If Mr. Mwenye gets tired of you, you just come to see Old Milt, and I'll take care of you."

I started to decline his offer when Mwenye spoke up. "I will never tire of her Milt. She is magnificent."

I blushed hard at this and turned my head away and spoke quietly. "Thank you, my love." I cut my eyes to Mwenye, and he smiled at me. He admired me like he did when I first met him. I was younger then and inexperienced. He adored me then. I missed that relationship. Things were much darker now, even though these smiles were here now, I knew the blacker parts of our relationship would return. Pushing away the hopes of my heart, I reminded myself that I had decided to leave him. I was here for information.

"Mr. Mwenye, what do you suggest is our next move?" Milt asked. Then there was a knock at the door, "Are we expecting anyone else?"

"No. Vanessa, if you would please get the door. Perhaps it is someone we can just send on their way." He looked at me, and I rose to check the door. I reached out with my magic and felt a cold dark presence there. It was a familiar one. I opened the door to find Nalusa Chito.

"Hello Mr. Chito, may I help you?" I asked. He started to speak, but then he looked over my shoulder and saw Milton there with Mwenye. "Oh, I do apologize. I did not realize you had company. I will return later."

"No, Chito, don't be daft, please come in," Mwenye called over my shoulder. Chito smiled at me, and as he passed me he squeezed my hand. I'm sure Mwenye noticed because when I turned around after shutting the door he glared at me. I shrugged. I was not sure why Chito felt the need to touch me, but hopefully, it wasn't enough to set Mwenye off. The night had been good so far. I didn't want an incident.

"Come here and sit down, Chito," Milton called. "Miss Vanessa, get this man a glass of wine." I looked over to Mwenye who nodded. Milton caught the exchange and shook his head.

I poured him a glass, giving it to him with a smile. I went back to the chair in the corner to let the men talk. I knew all the modern sensibilities about male chauvinists and the roaring feminism in this country, but I've found it's easier to make a fool of men if you just let them talk. So, that's what I did. I sat and listened to them talk about the shifter and Miss Davenport. I refilled their wine as needed as a good host would. Mwenye caressed my hand the last time I filled his glass. Maybe, just maybe, we were on a long good streak. The three men spent about an hour discussing their next moves. All the while I listened and took mental notes. Mwenye smiled at me several times, and I returned them.

"Well, Chito, the two of us old men should probably get out of here. Let these two have some alone time," he winked over to me. I just smiled back at him.

Chito laughed, "Milton Trujillo, you do realize there is more than sex to a relationship, right?"

"At my age Chito, sex is the only thing that matters."

"You are too old," Chito accused.

"The hell I am not. In fact, I need to get back to Boulder, there is a lovely young woman waiting for me there," he stood up, bowing to Mwenye and Chito. He blew me a kiss, and I just shook my head. "Miss Vanessa, if you get bored, you come on out to Boulder. I'll let you meet my new little friend."

"You are too kind Sir, but I am quite well here," I explained. What old Milt didn't know was that I sent Miss Samantha Taylor to him. I kept an eye on Miss Davenport as well as the old man. I smiled at my cleverness, not at his slick tongue.

Mwenye shook his hand before leaving. Chito also stood, and they exchanged a few words then both of them were gone. I gathered up the glasses and went to the kitchen. I rinsed them out and placed them in the dishwasher. Mwenye came up behind me and whispered in my ear. "I'm going out for a bit, my love."

"Oh, okay," I said shyly. I was not going to pry. I had no desire to provoke him.

"Get some rest. I won't be back for a little while," he explained, pressing against my back. He leaned to my ear again, kissed it, and then my neck. I moaned. I hoped he would not leave. But he backed away, picked up a suit coat from the closet and went out the front door. I sighed. I knew where he was going. Perhaps it was good he decided not to involve me in his darker activities. I walked down the hallway to the bedroom. I removed my dress and shoes. I slipped into the bed and waited silently for him to return. I hated to admit it, but I missed him.

My mind and desires were a blender. It was like I knew what I needed to do, but there were still desires of old habits. I needed a new habit. My mind drifted to the sweet face of Cassidy. I would love to make her my new habit.

CHAPTER 24

TADEAS

From my best guess, it was just before noon on the island. George waited for me as I entered the house. "Welcome, Master Duarte. Thank you for coming."

"Hey. Where is she?" Refusing to admit it outloud, I was eager to see her.

"She's still out walking," he said. "Please come with me."

In the distance, I could hear thunder. "Storm coming?" I asked.

"Yes, there is," he replied. He walked to the room across from the sitting room. There was a beautiful wooden bar there. The recliners looked extra comfortable. "Can I offer you a drink or a cigar?"

"A cigar? She has cigars?" I said in disbelief. He picked up a small humidor and held it up to me. He lifted the glass lid and the tobacco smell wafted up to my nose.

"I don't smoke, but that's impressive," I said.

"Please sit," he said, motioning to the recliners. I sat down. It was soft leather and worn perfectly. I enjoyed the comfort for a moment, then a large clap of thunder rumbled the house.

"Is she out there in this?" I asked, looking toward the double doors that led to the patio. Even though I knew that Abigail was perfectly capable of taking care of herself, I still worried about the storm. Her grandfather said she needed this place, and that she needed a partner to protect her. Protection was a basic instinct for me. I had always attributed it to my Guardian Jaguar nature.

"She is out on the property, but I believe the storm will pass around us. She is in no danger," he assured me.

"If you say so. Why did you need me here? What can I do for you, George?"

"You can stay out of Boulder, drinking in unfamiliar bars. Especially if you are going alone."

I sat stunned. "How do you know about that?"

"You prayed for help. Did you not?" he asked knowingly.

"I didn't, actually. I never got the words out before the shadow guy split."

"You were in grave danger. One of my former brethren interrupted a very unfortunate situation. You must take better care and pay more attention to your surroundings. I know that the two of you aren't on good terms but losing you even at this point would be devastating to her. I think it's best that you don't go back into Boulder alone. It might be best to avoid it altogether," he warned. I wondered if this fell into the non-interference category, but I was sure he would break all the rules for Abigail.

"I agree. I didn't think any of it out clearly. Sunday was a mess," I said.

"Want to talk about it?" he asked. He appeared very fatherly to me. He looked at me, not with disdain or disappointment. He genuinely seemed concerned about me.

"After leaving I was propositioned by a Fae goddess, threatened by a Greek Titan, drank from a glass that I didn't pay for, watched an extremely young woman get in an expensive car with a much older man, and had a shadow man try to kidnap me. I think that about covers it," I said.

He didn't seem surprised, but then he sat back in the chair. He seemed to relax for just a moment. "Theodoard threatened you?"

"Heh, yeah. I hate to admit it, but I almost wet my pants."

"He is formidable, especially when it comes to Abigail. But I can assure you, if he thought you were any danger to his grand-daughter, you would have never left that office alive," he said firmly.

"That doesn't make me feel any better, George."

"No, I suppose not, but it is a compliment in a way. He allowed you to return to her, and here you are," George said.

"George, I'm here because you gave me the impression something was wrong."

"Something is wrong."

"Well, what is it? Please stop toying with me," I pleaded.

"She wants to apologize. I'm just giving her the opportunity to do it. She's too stubborn to do it herself. I'm interfering," he admitted.

I couldn't help but laugh at him. "The non-interference thing is conditional?"

"If I chose it to be, I just have to be able to explain it. Officially, I brought you here to discuss the bill for having her car detailed. It is my understanding that you left it in quite the mess."

"George, you do beat all." He smiled. I got up and walked to the window. I could see the storm in the distance. We seemed to be just on the edge of it. "I'll admit it, George. I am eager to see her. I want to talk to her to clear the air between us. It has been a burden on me since I left. We left things very badly."

"We all say things we do not mean when we are frustrated and confused. Especially when we are afraid. She opened a whole new world to you. It happened rather quickly. I cannot say I approved of her method, but she knows that. She also has done you no wrong, Sir."

"No. She hasn't. Not really. For so long I've worked at the Agency. Living each day, each the same way. It was comfortable and easy. I liked it that way," I said.

"Humans are creatures of habit. I know you've heard that, but it is absolutely true. But the world is always changing and humans always adapt. It's the way they were made and created. Free thought, free will, adaptation and for the most part, a sense to strive to be better or better the world."

"Not everyone is that way, George," I said. His ideals sounded pretty lofty considering he once was an Angel of God. Perhaps he was blind to the darkness in all of us.

"No son, I am not blind to it."

"That's weird, George. You shouldn't do that in public," I teased him.

"No, Master Duarte, I won't. I do see the whole picture. I know that good is greater than evil, and hope is within every creature. Even the darkest hearts have hopes and dreams." I wasn't sure I agreed with him considering the evil that was in our world. Evils that most people did not know existed. The thunder got louder, and lightning flashed across the sky in ribbons of purple light. I had waited as long as I could. I wanted to talk to Abigail.

"Where is she, George?" I could tell he started to give me a vague answer, but then he shut his mouth. He seemed to zone out for a moment. I thought maybe he was having a stroke on me. It was like those commercials you hear on the radio. After a tense moment, his eyes focused back on me.

"She is in the chapel. But, Sir, I am concerned about her health. It was not simply a lure to get you here. She hasn't eaten since your last meal together. I believe she will make herself ill if you both do not reach an understanding one way or the other."

I smiled and put my hand on his shoulder, "Thanks. Don't

worry. I am here now." My instincts have always been to care for other beings, especially those as unique as Abigail Davenport.

I walked out the door swiftly. I didn't want to seem too overeager if she returned from her walk as I went out. I tried to seem casual and calm. It worried me too that she hadn't eaten. My refusal of her job offer had affected her far more than I expected it to. I knew in my heart that I should not have refused her.

As for her health, no matter what she was, her body was human and blood sugar can do bad things when you haven't eaten for some time. Add in the stress over the last few days and it would be a wonder that she was not comatose. I walked down the arched corridor, standing in awe of the storm. We were on the edge of it. Lightning flashed in the distance and the rumble of thunder followed after a moment or two. The clouds swirled dark and grey. I don't think I've ever seen anything more ominous.

As I looked down the hill to where the little chapel sat, a huge bolt of lightning struck the ground just outside the church. I threw my arms in front of my face, turning away in an utter survival reaction. I turned back to the church. Had she been outside the church? I could not tell from this distance.

"No." I took off running. The strike landed extremely close to the chapel. She could be inside hurt or worse if she had been standing outside of it. "*Madre de Dios*, no, please no," I pleaded as I ran and placed my hand on my crucifix. The chapel sat a good half mile away. I wasn't running fast enough.

Out of pure instinct, I focused on the jaguar inside of me. I gently pulled on the tether to the spirit world and quickly morphed into my beast. The shift was easier than I'd ever tried before, something about this place was unusual. Unlike most shifters, my shift was like ripping open a small piece of the spirit world, and I would switch my body with my spirit animal. No ripping off clothes and destroyed shoes. And thankfully no nakedness at the shift back.

I picked up speed on all fours. Digging my claws into the earth, I rounded the last row of vines to see her standing there outside the church staring at the storm. I dug deeper into the earth to slow my sprint to a walk. I stopped about 10 feet away from her. She hadn't turned to look at me. She still focused on the storm. The wind gently blew her hair around her face and her dress around her legs. Then I noticed it, her face glowed with strange iridescence. Like the powder girls put on their faces to go out to the clubs and bars, she practically glowed. I grew more concerned and stepped closer to her. I could smell honeysuckle and cinnamon. However, with my senses, I could tell her heartbeat was calm.

The most important thing I noticed standing here in my jaguar form was that I had no instinct or desire to harm her. No animal urge to rip her to shreds. I waited for her to respond to me. I was controlling the beast just as she said I could.

She started to turn toward me but stopped suddenly. She tilted her head sideways and said, "Tadeas, is that you?"

CHAPTER 25

ABIGAIL

*A*s the storm began to recede, I caught movement out of the corner of my eye. Slowly I turned to face a sleek black cat. His yellow eyes showed concern and patience. He had to be over 200 pounds standing about a foot and a half tall at the shoulder. His structure was lean and muscular. His spots, even though he was black, could still be seen lining his body from head to tail. He was magnificent. I was in awe of the utter strength and power. Had he wanted to strike; I am sure there would be nothing I could do to stop him. Instead, he waited for me to recognize him. "Tadeas, is that you?"

I felt a sharp tug on the surrounding environment. With a small exertion of magic, he morphed back into the handsome Hispanic man I knew. Why was he here? And why had he shifted? He shuffled his feet, refusing to look at me. This made me hurt on many levels. He didn't embrace that part of himself. Surely, he knew what a powerful gift he had.

"How many jaguar shifters do you know, Abby?" he asked quietly.

"Just you," I responded. He looked up to me. His human green eyes studied me. I suppose he was gauging when I'd start yelling at him again.

"I saw the lightning hit very close to the church. George said you were out here. I panicked and shifted to get here quicker. Seems pretty crazy, I guess," he shrugged.

Suppressing the urge to gush over his animal form, I held back knowing it made him uncomfortable. As I walked toward him, I swayed a bit. Putting my arms out to steady myself, I watched as he leaned forward on his toes ready to lunge if I fell. I looked up at him and shook my head. "No, I'm fine. It's not crazy. Thank you for your concern for my well-being."

"I don't think you are fine. Your face is covered with some kind of weird makeup. Plus, George said you have not eaten, and he told me you should before you got sick," he explained.

"I ate food yesterday when you were here," I said. He stepped closer still. His eyes filled with concern.

"I was here two days ago Abby. It's Tuesday just before noon."

"No. It's Monday," I argued but then thought about when he left. I must have slept completely through Monday. No wonder George made the statement about eating. He watched me put it all together. I looked up at him, "I guess I've lost time."

"Yeah. I think so. Let's get back to the house. Get you some food." He offered his hand to me, and I just stared at it. Tadaeas had come here for a reason but had shifted to his jaguar form even though he hated it so much. He did it all to help me. I needed to get over myself and accept whatever he was offering.

"I am so very sorry for the things I said to you," I said sincerely. I didn't want to add anything to it. It needed to be simple and clear. No lofty explanations. An absolute apology.

"I know. I am, as well." He returned it in the same manner.

"Now please, let's go back to the house. We have plenty of time to talk. You are worrying me. You look very unwell."

Looking back to the church, I remembered that Gabriel had just been here. Did he do something to my face? I turned back around to Tadeas. I turned too fast. I felt myself waiver with vertigo.

"Abby, dammit." I heard him say as everything went black.

I WOKE UP ON THE COUCH IN THE SITTING ROOM. MY HEAD WAS on a pillow. George hovered at the end of the couch. Tadeas sat on the couch next to me, studying my face. I looked back at George.

Tadeas was the first to speak. "Just stay there for a bit, okay? George has fruit here, and you are going to eat it."

"Yeah, yeah. I just didn't realize I slept through Monday or I would have eaten. Why are both of you looking at me like that?" They continued to stare.

"Abigail, you had a visitor," George stated, not asking. Tadeas looked back at him and then at me.

"Someone got on the island, but I thought—" he stopped.

"Yes," I said quietly. "Gabriel."

"Who is Gabriel? How did he get on the island? Are wards compromised?" Tadeus asked in quick succession. Something inside of me stirred as he inquired about those things. As if he had come to realize how important the island was to me. I wondered what had happened since Sunday that changed him so much. I tried to raise up. He gently pushed me back down and shook his head.

"I'm fine," I protested

"And I don't care. Lay down until you eat something," he said forcefully.

"Then give me something to eat." He shoved the bowl of

fruit at me and glared. "Bite me," I added out of simple childish pleasure. I'm not sure where he got the impression he could order me around, but I didn't have the energy to fight him on it.

"Mature. Very nice," he scolded. I ate the fruit and handed him the bowl. He handed it to George. "More please, George."

"No, I want real food," I said. "May I please have permission to sit up now, Mr. Duarte?" I poked my lip out at him. Finally, the serious stare broke, and he smiled. When he started to get up, I put my hand on his leg and shook my head no. The truth was I still felt pretty groggy. I didn't want him to move in case I got woozy again. I make stupid jokes when I'm out of sorts. I pushed myself up to a seated position with my legs still laying on the couch.

"Gabriel?" he prompted.

"Gabriel, as in The Gabriel," I explained.

George came back in the room and this time he had a platter of meats, cheese, crackers, and fruit. "Did he touch you, Abby?" George asked.

"Yes," I said and pointed to the crackers and cheese. Tadeas handed me some of it. "He put his hand on my chin." I lifted my head and showed them my chin.

Tadeas leaning closer to look at it, tilting his head sideways. As he raised his hand up to touch me, my eyes widened in antici-pation. The pad of his thumb brushed the bottom of my chin sending a shiver down my spine. He looked down at his finger, then up at me.

"Tadeas, what is it?" I asked.

"You have a strange mark there. Like you were burned, and it left a scar." He looked back at George, and George nodded. Tadeas turned back to me. "What did he say?"

"I looked in his eyes, and—" I paused to finish chewing the crackers and cheese. They watched me closely. I didn't want to repeat what I saw. The terrible, heartbreaking and extremely tragic vision flooded my mind again. I felt Tadeas take my hand.

"And what?" he asked as if he knew I'd seen something terrible.

"A vision of the future," George said.

I winced. No, it would not be the future if I had anything to do with it. I closed my eyes and spoke. "I saw the world in chaos. The continents were broken off at the edges, and whole cities fell into the oceans. People died by the millions. I could hear them screaming and crying for help as they sank into the dark depths of the sea."

"*Madre de Dios*," Tadeas said and crossed himself. He turned back to George. "Is it for real? Can we stop it?"

"We?" I asked. He ignored me.

"He would not have shown her if he didn't think she could prevent it," George stated flatly. He sat down in the chair facing the couch, and his eyes went out of focus. I never understood what he was doing, but I always left him alone when it happened.

Tadeas looked at me. "We will stop it, right?"

I repeated, "We?"

He looked serious, but squeezed my hand. "Yes, we."

I squeezed back. A rush of relief flowed over me. Finally, I could get back to business. I sighed.

"But I've got the feeling I'm going to lose my entrails in the process," he smiled weakly.

"What?"

"Gregory."

I burst into laughter. "He threatened you?" I continued to laugh because it sounded like the kind of threat my grandfather would lay down. In fact, I was pretty sure he threatened Lincoln often.

"I find it disturbing that my entrails coming out of my nostrils is a comedic topic to you, Abby." He wasn't mad.

"He scared the shit out of you, didn't he?"

"Almost, literally." I died laughing again. My side started to hurt.

"Did he make you sit in the chair?" I asked because I knew my grandfather's tactics. They were tried and true.

"Fucking chair." This time I lost it for a good minute, and he just shook his head at me.

"You survived it. Well done," I managed to say between giggles. I put my hand up for a hive five. He half-heartedly obliged.

"Thanks, I think. Sunday probably ranks as one of the craziest, weirdest, scariest days of my entire life," he said.

"Welcome to my life. I definitely want to hear all about it. But I need to get up, go take a shower and eat real food," I said.

"George has spaghetti. The carbs will be good for you." He stood to help me up. He guarded me all the way to my room.

"I'm fine now. I promise," I said. "I really didn't realize I slept all day. I'm not the kind of person to do harm to myself over such things. I might smash a mug or two, but nothing really harmful."

"You smashed the mug."

"Yeah."

"Good. I hated it." I started giggling again.

"I blame George. He brought it to me. He knew you were still here." I pointed back down to the sitting room where we left him. He laughed too. "I won't be but just a few minutes."

"Abby, please leave the door open or the wards down. Just in case."

I nodded. Even though he joined my laughter, I could tell the prophecy affected him, and he was still concerned for my well-being. I hoped he didn't make a spur-of-the-moment decision, but he did look confident for a change. If I had known all it would take was to threaten to rip his insides out, I would have sent him to Grandfather before I did anything else. One of Grandfather's brilliant ideas for recruiting Tadeas included him forcing him to work with me or face death. He could go a tad bit overboard from time to time. I left the door open even though I knew my wards wouldn't stop him if he really wanted in this room. I watched as he walked back down to his room.

When I went into the closet, I realized that I was covered in dirt. However, my hair wasn't dirty. Tadeas must have caught me before my head hit the ground. He was fast. I'd fought with him, so I knew how deadly he could be. Stepping into the shower, I stood under the warm spray. It felt good to wash off the storm. It washed my giggles away, too. I suppose the last few days had taken a higher toll on me than I thought. I needed to regain the fortitude I once had. I wasn't sure how much time we had to counteract this problem. I didn't exactly know what the problem was outside of global disaster and chaos. I would assemble the team. We needed to start yesterday, tracking everything down that we could.

Washing off faster than I would have wanted, I finished so that I didn't faint in the shower. The last thing I needed was Tadeas rushing in here to fish me naked out of my own bathroom. Ducking into my closet, I could feel his presence leaning against the wall outside my door.

"You can come in the room, Tadeas. Stop hovering. Just don't come back here." He didn't answer me, but I felt him move into the room, then sit down in the chair opposite the end of my bed.

Jeans, t-shirt, hair back and slip-on shoes. I looked at myself in the mirror. I finally saw why they were staring at me. My face glowed with a strange iridescence. I moved my face back and forth and watched the spectrum of colors as they shifted back and forth.

"Um, how long has my face looked like this?" I asked as I stepped into the bedroom. He looked over at me from the chair.

"Since the church," he answered.

"No wonder you both were staring at me. It's weird."

"It's faded since I first saw you."

"I guess you get a face full of glitter if you lock eyes with an angel. You thinking about the prophecy?" I asked, knowing that he still was.

"Yes. I guess you could say I'm disturbed. I just know we have to stop it. I hope you have a plan," he said. Now it was time to be me.

"I do have a plan. It's not a complete one, but I know where to start," I replied. He smiled a little. He would have a role in it, too. I looked forward to saving those that we could together. Sometimes these things didn't turn out the way I expected or hoped, but Lincoln and I always did our best. We had lost good people along the way. I lost Lincoln. Then I lost myself. Part of the plan included doing just that, finding myself and my place again in this rapidly changing and dangerous world.

"Does it start with spaghetti?" he asked.

"It can. It's a flexible plan," I joked.

"Good. I'm starving."

"You seem to always be starving," I observed.

"Well, I burned a lot of energy shifting," he admitted.

"I'd like to know more about how you do it. Maybe watch you do it in the magical spectrum. It would be something new for me to learn. I didn't know shifters could change and not rip their clothing to shreds."

I saw a glint of deviousness in his eyes, then he said, "You were disappointed then. It's okay. It's not every day that you get to see a body like this." He put up his right arm and flexed. Honestly, it looked pretty deadly to me. Tadeas wasn't a hulking brute, but I knew that tight and fit was a brutal combination.

"Don't hurt yourself," I smirked.

"Your loss. Let's go eat, and I'll try to explain what it feels like. What I do when I make it happen," he explained as I followed him down toward the kitchen. These moments were exactly what I was hoping for in our partnership. A little give and take. We would find our way now. I was sure of it.

WE DECIDED TO EAT INSIDE THE KITCHEN AT THE SMALL TABLE there. No need for formality now. It was like having an old friend over to get caught up on stories. We talked all through dinner, and it was nice to be able to have a conversation with him now that we'd removed the tension between us. He told me about how he shifts. The way he does it is quite remarkable.

"It's like I can concentrate, and I can feel the edge of the spirit world near me. I can pull my jaguar form into this world to replace my human form. I can cross over and change as well. I could take you with me if needed," he explained.

"What happens to your human body when you shift? Can you feel it?" I was enthralled with the magic discussion.

"Honestly, I'm not sure. It's like it's there on the edge of my fingertips or claws, and I just pull it back if I want to shift back."

"Remarkable. Do you mind me watching you do it? Through the spectrum, I mean," I prodded. I hoped not too much.

"If you would like, sure. I'm sure it's not impressive," he dismissed it.

"Tadeas, I live and breathe magic. Something I don't know about is fascinating to me, and I want to learn as much as I can," I explained.

"It's not magic like you do," he said.

"Well, of course not, otherwise I wouldn't want to see you do it," I smirked.

He looked at me, then looked at my plate. I'd barely touched the food. I took the hint and began to eat again. "I need to tell you about your car," he said just as I put a large bite in my mouth. I'm pretty sure he did it on purpose just so I couldn't respond. My eyes widened, and I began to chew faster. "I'll have it detailed. It's just a little dirty on the inside."

I put my hand in front of my still half full mouth and mumbled, "What did you do to my car?"

"I went out to eat last night. Wait. Was that last night? No, it was Sunday night. The last couple of days have been a blur. It isn't like my life could get any more complicated or strange."

I had finished my bite and swirled pasta around my fork for another, "Sorry."

"I don't blame you. Well, maybe a little," he grinned. "But with the things going on here, Meredith and Travis, your Aunt Lianne, Gregory and other things, I decided to go grab a drink. By the end of the night, I was half-conscious on the side of the road with a shadow man trying to take me. I think an angel intervened, but I got your car a little dirty on the inside. I'll pay to have it cleaned up."

I dropped my fork. "You didn't tell me your life was in danger," I said.

"Well, I was concerned about you and the archangel's message. It had slipped my mind," he confessed.

"It's going to be a long night. I want to know everything that happened. It might be important to our job. You never know what kind of spies the enemy has within the network. It's happened before. We are too big for our own good sometimes," I said.

"Yeah."

"A shadow man?" I focused on the part that concerned me the most.

"You look worried. Don't worry. I'm fine. It was stupid of me to go out, and just assume everything was safe. As I was driving, a wave of exhaustion hit me. I felt bound up when he showed up to take me."

I felt sick at my stomach. "Sounds like a lethargy spell. People connected to me get hurt. It's why I don't have many friends. To think that just after a couple of days of contact, they already know about you and me. It makes me sick to think of it. Shadow magic is always dark. I can do it myself, but I don't. The elements and life forces you draw on for shadow magic can corrupt the wielder. It rips your whole being apart until you are nothing but a shadow. What happened? Tell me everything, please."

"I will, but you chose me, remember? I have to think that part of that is because you know I can take these kinds of things. I'm not helpless. I did lose focus, but no more," he assured me. I did choose him because I was sure he could handle himself in any situation. He told me the whole story from the Bourbon tavern, an old guy named Milt, Samantha which threw me for a loop, and finally the car ride home. I listened and watched him tell it. He grimaced in frustration with himself for not being more careful. When he finished, he looked at me, waiting for me to process it all.

"I think you promised to take me on a date," I half-heartedly smiled at him. This business rarely warranted smiles. I endeavored to get them where I could.

He half-smiled back, "I suppose so."

"But I want to go on a day that isn't Sunday. I want to see who else goes in and out of there. Perhaps a hub for nefarious creatures, and so close to home base. With Milt distracting you, there very well could have been a witch or other wielder there. A shadow man could have even just stood next to you and blended in. Milt, of course, is the obvious choice. I've found it's rarely the obvious, and almost never simple. It's too close to the compound not to investigate. We would be crippled in the United States if the compound was compromised." I drifted off into dark thoughts. Perhaps I'm making my moves too late. If they already had a solid hold on Boulder, it was too close to HQ for comfort. Whatever they were trying to do that would cause the continents to break apart, they would have to take us out. I needed to make some phone calls. Gabriel had warned me. Surely, I had time. What if I didn't? While spending my solitude working on things that didn't really matter, the darkness was winning.

"Hey, come back," Tadeas said. He leaned back in the chair, patting his belly. "You were off in some dark place."

"I drifted in thought. Sorry. You full?" I asked. "You look it."

"You saying I'm fat?"

"I didn't say it, you did," I laughed. Gathering the dishes, I went to start filling the sink with water. He pulled open a drawer like he lived here and pulled out a towel. I started washing, and he dried. I heard George pass by the door several times. "What do you want, old man?"

"I was just making sure the two of you weren't making a mess in my kitchen," he said from out of sight.

"Your kitchen!" I feigned anger.

"Yes, ma'am," he replied flatly.

"Well, your kitchen is in good hands," I replied smiling at Tadeas. I gave him credit. He paid attention the last time we washed the dishes. He knew where each item belonged. I wondered if he didn't have an eidetic memory. It isn't abnormal for a shifter to possess some form of higher brain function.

Over the years I've seen all sorts of rare talents pass through the Agency. In my team, I have a man who has always been labeled autistic, but he has the uncanny ability to tell if someone is lying or not. He's a human lie detector. The first time I met him, I was sure there was a type of magic involved, but looking through the spectrum there was nothing abnormal other than his shift abilities. He does not shift, but the ability is there. He's a giant golden eagle. Lincoln and his people hold the golden eagle in high regard. Lincoln could always see his animal when I could not. He taught me the skill over the years. Most shifters never know their abilities, which is probably a good thing. If they actually shift for the first time, a traumatic event usually triggers it. Otherwise, it just lies within them as a dormant ability. There is just no way to control or anticipate such a thing.

I thought of Tadeas and how his shift created a tragedy that would haunt him for the rest of his life. He let me ponder, but he did not speak. He watched me closely which also made me wonder if he could read my thoughts or at the very least empathic abilities, too. Animals know when someone is afraid, bad or good.

My mind twisted in ten different directions, offering no solutions. No answers. I sighed because I felt the darkness creeping into me. Part of fighting it is knowing it's there and refusing to give in to it. Darkness is a place without hope, and I felt myself losing hope.

"That's enough. Come back," he said softly nudging me on the side with his elbow.

"There's just too much to consider. I've got to get organized, or I am going to go crazy," I said.

"You already are crazy," he said, then quickly added, "but you can't wallow in doubt. I see it in your face." He leaned with his back against the counter drying off his hands, then offering me the towel. I faced the small window above the sink looking out into the vineyard. It was late afternoon, and all was still. Part of me wanted to crawl up into one of the big recliners with a drink. No time for that anymore. Well, maybe later on this evening.

"Right." I tossed the towel across the sink and headed to the downstairs office, lab, exercise room, and vault. I'd show him, then give him full access.

CHAPTER 26

TADEAS

ollowing her to the door to the basement office, I wondered if part of my role here would be just to keep her grounded. She no doubt had a brilliant mind, but sometimes it seemed the longer her thoughts were left uninterrupted, the darker she got. The brilliance in her eyes weakened. Her confidence seemed to decay. My words pushed her into mission mode. She took my hand and pressed it against the wall where the door should be. Disguised by magic, it looked like an ordinary wall.

"*Clavem*," she muttered. Having felt her power in the corridor, it was easier for me to recognize it again. Each wielder I've ever met had a signature much like their individual smells. Her power was warm like the sun shining down on a cool spring day. Darker wielders are cold. Hers had a steady strength to it.

"At this rate, Abby, I'll have access to all your hidden rooms."

"Honey, you are pretty, but not that pretty," she said with a touch of the devil in her eyes. Sharp tongue indeed.

"I knew that one would haunt me," I laughed.

"Come on, no counter retort? You've got to work on your banter," she said, allowing me to open the door. She followed me down the steps, and the whole place lit up the moment her foot touched the base of the steps. Monitors and computers came to life. "Ready to work?"

I nodded. She walked up to the screens, then her lithe fingers touched a few things on the main keyboard. The entire panel of televisions went black. She walked over to the corner, pushed up a comfortable chair, and plopped down in it.

Looking down at her, I asked. "Where's mine?"

She nodded back to the corner where she got hers.

"Shoddy hospitality in this place," I muttered.

"Welcome home," she said. Home. I stopped in my tracks. Was this home? I've washed the dishes. I've got access to every room in the house except her room, and I had been in there. We ate in the kitchen instead of the dining room. Maybe it was home. It felt good. I pushed up a chair next to her, watching her grin as I sat down.

"Did you bring popcorn?" I asked.

"No. Did you?"

"No."

"Bummer." She pointed a remote at the wall of screens and the individual images formed one big one. "Time for a crash course. Hold on."

"To you?" She turned her head, glaring at me. "Okay, okay I'm done, but you did say more banter." At that, she huffed, knowing I was right. She flicked to a series of slides that completely defined the Agency and all the different departments. The whole operation consumed every aspect related to power in the world: money, politics, weaponry, research, and people. She emphasized the people. All the other things were merely the tools we used to get things done.

After the history lesson ended, she flipped through slides of contacts for the various purposes within the Agency. She told me where to find all of this later on. When I entered my employment at the Agency, we went through a cursory orientation. The information Abby gave me was far more in depth. Apparently, none of her computers here at the house had passwords, and she welcomed me to use them anytime.

After we finished going through the slides, she motioned me to her office chair at the table. I sat down, and she clicked through files showing me, where they all were, and the things that I should look at when I had time. She let me look for a minute while she looked over her emails.

"Aunt Lianne emailed me again about that paperwork," she said

"Yes, please tell her I told you about it, therefore I have fulfilled my end of the bargain," I pleaded.

"Don't worry. I wouldn't have you under her thumb. Or under her anything for that matter," she said lifting her eyebrows.

"Yes, I would like to avoid further entanglements with her," I agreed.

"We will do some magic exercises tomorrow. Teach you a few useful things." This information shocked me.

"Abby, I'm not a wielder."

"Shifting is its own kind of magic. You have it in you, and if you will let me, I'll show you how."

"What's next?"

"Come on, I'll show you the rest of the basement."

"So, we are superheroes with a secret underground lair? It's not very original," I pointed out.

"At least it's not in the Arctic," she replied. We walked to a set of double doors that was to the left of the computer displays. She opened the door and held it for me. I walked through and she switched on the lights. We were standing in a huge multi-use practice room. The soft mats covered most of the floor, but the far-right side of the room was covered in hardwood flooring. A floor to ceiling mirror covered the entire wall. Speakers hung on the wall in the corners of the room. There were various punching bags and striking dummies. The left wall was lined with practice weapons in sets of twos. If she knew how to use all of them, she was far more impressive than I realized.

"We need to practice more together. Learn each other's movements and attacks. If you learn to beat me, or I learn to beat you, it's an area of improvement for both of us. In the process, we will fight better together. Sometimes it's not all magic, in fact, I'd settle for a good fistfight over flinging spells any time."

"Impressive room," I simply said.

Across from the first set of double doors was a second set. We walked through those into a long hallway. She pointed down to the right side. "There is a small kitchen down there, and a decent-sized bathroom with a walk-in shower identical to the one in your room. We will go through here." She pushed open another set of doors into a cage-lined room full of every hand-gun, rifle, and shotgun I've ever seen. The bottoms of the cages held boxes of ammunition. I turned to my left, and there was a shooting range with two stalls.

"Looks like you have one of everything," I commented.

"Not yet, but I'm working on it. Feel free to use any of them at any time. Use the range as much as you like. There is plenty of ammo. George keeps everything stocked up. He cleans all the weapons too. These are all practice pieces. We will probably never use them in the field. If you see something that is lacking, please let me know, and I'll get it. You may know of newer tech than I do."

We went back through the door into the hallway, and she started walking toward the area where she mentioned the kitchen and bathroom were. We passed another door. I stopped at it, and she turned and looked at me.

"What's in this one?"

"It's a bedroom."

"Oh, okay."

"It's down here because there were times I just didn't feel like going back upstairs. I admit that the last 25 years have been pretty dark for me. I do not use it now and haven't used it in a couple years. But if you are ever down here, and just want to crash, feel free," she said. "George takes care of everything, as you have probably noticed."

I nodded my head, and she turned a corner into a dead end. "Hidden door?"

"No. There is no door. Give me a moment I have to alter the wards so they don't fry you to a crispy kitty. Be right back," she said, then faded out of view. That was different. I could still smell her. It was like she was there, but not. I felt a weird nausea from the portal, and she faded back into view.

"Well, this is my vault. No one enters, but me. Consider everything in the vault to be deadly. It's not just where I keep weapons and such, but also ancient tomes, grimoires, artifacts, imbued objects and the like. I set the wards to recognize you so, no deep-fried jaguar tonight. It's going to be harder to teach you how to get into it if you need to, but eventually, I'll figure out a way to do it. Once I learn how you shift, perhaps I can alter the entrance to fit your magic more than mine. Also, I should warn you that you were about to break like seven of the TCAs magic rules."

"They are all pricks anyway," I said. She liked that answer and smiled.

"I'm about to invade your personal space," she warned.

"Well, okay, thanks for the warning."

"The entrance is a time shift of 2 seconds in the past. The room behind the wall is in real time with us, so it's just the doorway that is a time shift. So, we have to time travel to enter. I admit it's been a very long time since I've taken anyone inside with me. I built the thing, and besides Lincoln, George is the only one that has ever been in it. George doesn't need to use the entrance. He can go where he pleases on this island or in time for that matter. Don't let him fool you next time as if he couldn't find me himself."

"If the room isn't in a time warp, can't just anyone walk through the wall? I can walk through walls in the spirit world."

"They could but for two things, the vault is tied to this plane, which if you haven't noticed is a little different from Colorado. It cannot be reached through any other plane. Secondly, if you go in there, the wards will instantly kill you. I do not take chances with the items that are in this room. I have collected things over the years. Some are very evil. Most evil books and objects that I've acquired, I had to destroy. However, if the book contained knowledge that might help me fight someone with those particular talents, I kept it here. It cannot be breached. I'm going to need to have skin to skin contact with you. Your arms are fine, but roll up your sleeves, if you don't mind."

"I don't mind," I said.

"Put your hands on my elbows, and I'll put my hands on the top of your arms creating a bond between us. Our own little circle in a way. The other is, I trained the wards inside the room to a bit of your DNA. I got a stray hair from you as you sat at the desk. Eventually, I will be able to put a spell on you. If any part of your DNA separates from your body for more than 5 seconds, then it will burn to ash. That way we can keep all the witches from trying to grab some for a curse or spell. It sucks if you need a blood test because the blood will burn once outside your body. You got any medical tests coming up?"

"None that I know of. Is this going to hurt?"

"No, you big baby."

"Well, how was I supposed to know? I've never time-traveled before."

"Yes, you have, through the portal to the island, but as far as anyone outside of those on this island, you never have or will," she said, implying that no one else needed to know the true nature of her safe haven. I wouldn't dare jeopardize that for her.

"Loud and clear."

She took a deep breath, closing her eyes. I felt the power building around us. When she opened her eyes, the sparkling gold edges appeared like I had seen before in the corridor. She spoke in a clear voice, *"Tempus est via ad iter mihi placent: Aperi ianuam, cum ire ad otium."*

I felt a small tremor, and the world smeared like an already wet painting splashed with more water. Colors and light shifted. Shadows moved. When the blur cleared, we stood in a room that was only 20 feet by 20 feet. I started to move, but I felt her hands clamp down on my arms. "Wait for it." And the walls ignited in runes and glyphs of all different languages and cultures. I recognized several from my own country that were Mayan symbols. I watched as they slowly faded out, and she released the grip on my arms. "You can look around now," she said as shook her arms a little because I was still holding onto her elbows.

"Oh, sorry. This place is amazing!" The floor was marble, but it had a compass rose laid into it with different colors of marble and lined with gold. The ceiling high above was dark blue, and along the full expanse of the room was an accurate depiction of the night sky with little illuminated stars forming constellations. I wasn't sure how she got all the little orbs to float, but the effect was impressive. The East and West walls were lined with rich cherry wood shelves. There were various artifacts and books. The bottom of the bookshelves contained small glass cases like the ones in jewelry stores. Inside I saw guns, knives, crystals, wooden sticks like wands and jewelry. The collection impressed me. It would impress anyone. Against the back wall, four female human forms stood. Each one draped in a different outfit. One had a long green flowing dress with a gold vine-like piece of jewelry that started like a choker and wrapped down around the arm, then down one side of the dress, and then around the waist and fell down like two ends of a belt. As I got closer to it, it seemed as if the vine was alive. Living gold.

The second mannequin wore jeans, a rather plain t-shirt, sneakers and a ball cap. The third mannequin wore sleek black fatigue pants that were tight around the legs and tapered to the ankles. A pair of $300 boots, ahem. A black combat-grade moisture wicking shirt. A black leather jacket that reached down to the mid-thigh and a sparse black utility belt. The last mannequin wore a sheer white gown with a wide brown leather belt. A sturdy leather loop held a long slightly curved scabbard encrusted with red jewels. It looked angelic with embossing on the belt and scabbard with religious symbols like the cross but with runes I'd never seen before. Abby stood behind me and watched me walk around the room, never talking about the items. She just let me take it all in.

I walked along the cases and saw a set of pistols owned by Wild Bill Hickok, a katana owned by Mochizuki Chiyome, a quill pen that once belonged to Sir Walter Scott, a compass owned by Hernando de Soto, a pocket watch owned by Winston Churchill, and a crucifix owned by Mother Theresa.

"This place is a museum," I muttered.

"Every object in this room has magical properties. Partially because they were dear objects to those who owned them, but also may have had a casting done on them for various reasons very much like your crucifix."

I reached up and touched my cross beneath my shirt. "My necklace is magic?"

"It has a magical casting on it. I would have to take a closer look sometime, but the impression I get from it is that it is a protection spell of sorts," she explained. Father Sergio had given me the cross. After the exorcism attempt, I laid in the bed for several days waiting for the right moment to leave. Father Sergio had said the necklace was for protection. At some point, they forgot to watch me, or someone made a mistake in changing the guard shifts. I didn't think I was a prisoner, but there is no way I intended to let them do that to me again. When the opportunity presented itself, I left the church hoping to find a new life to start over.

That's when I met Isabel. I ran into Father Sergio after I had proposed to Isabel. The church had moved to the city I was in with her, and Father Sergio was there setting things up before the other priests arrived. I introduced Isabel to him. He said the necklace would protect both of us. I wore it all the time, except that night. I had worn it into the market. An old drunk grabbed it trying to steal it but broke the chain in the process. I wondered if Father Sergio knew exactly what I was and gave me this to keep me from becoming the jaguar. I would never be able to ask him those things because I was told that he died of Yellow Fever in 1929 while visiting Venezuela. Perhaps Abigail could tell me if it had held me back all those years.

Abby waited for me to stop my introspection before she continued to tell me about the items in the room. She watched me with kind and concerned eyes but held back from asking any questions. This was just another of the things I liked about her. She didn't pry into my head demanding to know what I was thinking. I hung my head because I was just the opposite. I wanted to know what was going on in her head to the point that I might demand it if curious enough. I supposed we both would get used to each other's quirks and idiosyncrasies. It would take time. We just needed to make sure we didn't get frustrated with each other before we got it figured out. Somewhere in the chaos of the last couple of days, I had just accepted that we would be working together on this. I wondered how it would affect my teaching. Something told me that my teaching days were over.

There were many questions, but I couldn't learn it all in one day. I had to accept, too, that she didn't seem to be purposefully hiding anything from me. There were definite things I didn't know about her but wanted to know. I just had to remember that she had already opened herself up more to me than she probably has to anyone in a very long time. The same went for me too. I still had skeptical moments. From time to time I thought that she could have found someone better than me to do this, but I was in now. No turning back. "I'm sorry. Got lost in thought."

"It's quite alright. I do it all the time," she smiled. She was right. Several times tonight I watched her attention drift off. "All the items and tools that are here can be used for different purposes. I can call anything in this room to me as needed, from anywhere in the world. There is a magical tether from me to it. I open the entrance. Call the object to my hand, and in the blink of an eye, it's here. It's not really practical for impromptu battles, but good for well-planned assaults, I can use the room or the objects to house anything that we might need. The spell itself requires that I memorize this entire room, top to bottom. I took the time to know how long the cases and bookshelves are and the dimensions on each object as well as its weight. It took a long time for me to get it all memorized, but it works. There is an empty case there on the end. It's for anything you would like to put in that you think we might need in a fight. It is getting harder and harder to sneak into places with weapons because security is extremely tight these days, therefore, I store them here and call them to me as I need them."

The battle potential of this room gave us a huge advantage. I approached the north end which clearly contained the most prized possessions. On each end of the open display, an extensive collection of knives, swords, handguns and other weapons lined the walls. On the far right in a featured display, a native American bow, quiver, and tomahawk. Clearly, these had belonged to Lincoln. The quiver was empty, but all the other objects looked pristine. I knew that the weapons had to be exceptionally old if Lincoln was the famed Navajo Monster Hunter.

On the left, multiple handguns including a hand-engraved set of Desert Eagle 1911 pistols, 2 Sig Sauer P226 Legion 9mm semi-automatic pistols and a mean-looking .357 Mag Revolver the size of a small cannon hung on a vertical display with a bottom shelf full of loaded magazines for each semi-automatic. These must be her guns. I'd never gone to the range when my class was shooting, but I had to assume she was a good shot. The Desert Eagles were particularly amazing. Each one was engraved with angel wings and a cross in front of a sun.

In the center, an ornate stand holding a small shield about 48 inches in diameter engraved with angel's wings stood on a silver surface with white accents. Along with the shield, lay a slender gently curving sword. Blue sparkling stone was embedded in the hilt, and the blade itself shimmered with an engraving of a cross and a scale. I felt the power resonating off the blade. I kept my distance. It was almost as if this too, lived and breathed. Danger and power were held in one small blade. It favored a mameluke, the ceremonial swords carried by United States Marines, but was definitely older than that particular design.

Abigail walked up beside me to tell me about the sword. "It is called Vindicta, the sword of Vengeance. It was given to me by Gabriel. It belonged to an angel. It was broken when he gave it to me. I had to re-forge it. I rarely use it. Only when told to do so by Gabriel or one of the Archangels. It is the Vengeance of God."

"Vengeance is mine, I will repay," I quoted from the Bible.

"Yes, well, from time to time, I am tasked to complete that Vengeance," she said sadly.

"Why you?"

"There is a price to pay for every deal. When I died, Odin, and the Valkyries had to have permission to resurrect me. The permission came with a cost that once I was well again, I would take the sword, and use it as commanded. Once I remove the sword from its sheath, my free will is gone, and I am driven by the command of the archangel. I must admit that the command has always been a righteous one. Thankfully, I have only had to complete the task twice since it was given to me. Not having a choice is the worst burden to bear. I have to trust that Gabriel and his brothers send me at the behest of the Almighty." I saw her shiver a bit. It was not cold in the room but talking about the sword and losing her freewill weighed heavy on her.

"If you refuse to use the sword," I started to ask.

"It's a command. It flips a switch inside me, and I cannot stop it."

"Who did it belong to?"

"Raguel. The Angel of Justice. He was murdered by a fallen angel around the time of the crusades. I do not know the whole story, but I know the sword is the most powerful weapon I've ever seen on this planet. A sword forged by archangels and endowed by God to exact vengeance on those who are the most grievous of offenders that were supernaturally inclined. Never a human target." With that she stepped away from me, turning her back on the sword.

I truly did not know what to say. I turned to her and grabbed her elbows and said, "I've seen enough, let's go." Her hands shook as she grabbed my elbows to complete our circle. With a quick chant of the previous incantation with just a slight variance, the world around us blurred again, and we stood in the long, dead-end hallway. She looked at me and waited for me to speak. She started to look tired again. I pushed a stray hair behind her ear.

"You need rest. The day may soon come when we cannot rest. Take the time you can now. As for the vault, thank you for showing it to me. The sword is a pretty heavy responsibility, yeah?"

"It is," she looked down.

"Abby, thank you for trusting me with all of this. It helps confirm my decision. I've got a purpose here. I'm willing to learn whatever you want to teach me, and maybe along the way I've got a few things you can learn from me. It's all pretty overwhelming though. I admit it." There was so much more to her than I originally thought. I should have known that a being that lived as long as she had, wasn't simply a spoiled rich girl. I had equated her to her relatives like Lianne.

"It overwhelms me, too."

"I'm sure. But now I'm here, and we can talk about all of it together. We can start making moves to stop this disaster. It will be our purpose until the world no longer needs us to do it," I said feeling a little more confident. She still looked down. "Tell me what you are thinking about?"

"I am afraid we are too late," she admitted.

"No. Gabriel just warned you. He's trying to point us in the right direction. You will figure it out. It's who you are."

She looked confused. "I'm glad you know who I am because there are days that I don't know who I am."

"My partner, who is going fight with me to save the world." Cheesy but true.

She quirked a smile to the side. "Damn straight we are," she said. "So, what you are saying is you are my new BFF?"

I threw my head back and laughed. "Yeah, I guess so." She used humor to cover her lack of confidence. It would take time, but I would help her find her strength again. The world depended on it. The sword cemented that thought in my head. The Angels of Heaven entrusted *that* weapon into the hands of this human woman, at least semi-human, and somewhere along the way she chose me. She had given me confidence in myself, my shifting ability, and my purpose in the world. The least I could do was return the favor.

CHAPTER 27

ABIGAIL

*W*hen we returned upstairs, twilight had consumed the island. My phone rang. It was Ashley, my assistant. She gave me a bit of information as we walked down the hallway.

After I hung up with her, he asked, "Everything okay?" Tadeas, I had noticed, was curious by nature. I had the feeling that I wouldn't be able to keep anything to myself anymore. Mainly because I didn't want to lie to him. Not ever again.

"Yes, that was Ashley Montgomery, my assistant. She told me that my team has already dug up some information." George had opened the double doors around the sitting room and my bourbon room. Showing Tadeas the basement vault had taken a huge weight off my shoulders. I still had plenty of secrets to keep, but if the sword did not scare him away, nothing would. "Let's grab food, and then I'll tell you everything." He nodded, and we turned our attention to George.

George smiled at both of us. "I laid sandwiches out in the bourbon room. I've opened a bottle of wine, as well."

"George, I love you. Thanks," I said as I kissed him on the cheek. He blushed. When I looked back at Tadeas, he grinned as he took it all in.

"You are most welcome, child," George said. I nodded toward the room, and Tadeas followed me in. On the small bar was a platter with enough sandwiches to feed an army.

"I hope you are hungry," I said.

"He overdid it a bit." He walked behind the bar and poured the wine into glasses. "Who drinks wine with sandwiches?"

"We do." I held up my glass, and Tadeas touched his to mine. We both took sips. A bright pinot grigio.

"It is good," he admitted.

"The people here take great pride in a hard day's work, and a job well done," I explained. I grabbed a plate that George had placed out and put two half sandwiches on it. One looked like ham and cheese, and the other was bacon and tomato. I sat down in one of the recliners with my wine glass and plate. I leaned it back. I pulled my legs up into the chair and began to eat. He sat down in the other chair and shook his head. "What?"

"Why sit in a recliner with the footrest up, but your feet in the chair?"

"Bugger off," I exclaimed. He laughed, and we ate. We talked more about his crazy day. I did warn him that Lianne could not be trusted. None of the board of directors who entailed some of the oldest living offspring of Hyperion's children could. "I need to throw a welcoming party if you are truly taking up the job."

"Why do you not believe me? You already showed me everything downstairs."

"I don't know. I lost hope. It's hard to find it again once it's gone," I said. "I want to introduce you to my team. The people I trust most outside of George and my grandfather. I have my own little network. They need to know they are working for you as well, now."

"Working for me?" he asked with a mouthful of sandwich.

"Yes, eventually you will get the hang of what we are doing, and you will become comfortable having them work for you. They all have special talents and are extremely good at their jobs. There are also moves I've been making with a few accounts that are owned by the Agency and I personally manage. I'd like to tell you why I'm doing these things, and hopefully, it will give you some insight on future events," I explained, and he turned and gave me his full focus after draining the wine glass.

"I saw the monitors when I was here on Sunday. You manage the savings accounts," he said.

"Yes, I do," I replied.

"I was wrong," he said.

I didn't want him dwelling on the past. "You were right about everything else though," I said.

"No, I wasn't. You aren't a spoiled, rich granddaughter of a Titan," he said.

"I am a rich granddaughter of a Titan," I said smiling. "Two out of three isn't bad. I promise from now on that I will tell you everything I can about our operation."

"Any insight is appreciated. I would hope that you'd tell me as much as you can. I know that you can't possibly tell me everything I need to know in a single night, or for that matter, it may take months. I am a quick learner. I can keep up," he said.

Part of the reason I picked Tadeas was that I knew he could keep up. That wasn't completely accurate either, because I didn't pick him out for me. Someone else did.

Starting with the offshore accounts, I told him about the money I had moved around in addition to all the aliases I used to move it. If we needed access to cash in a hurry, the accounts would provide us with what we needed in an emergency. As for all the aliases, they were all documented valid identifications, but all owned by me.

"The team has found interesting moves in the geo sector. Mostly mining, fracking, and refining industries. There has been a spike in demand for an element known as Osmium and the metals that are mixed with it. Osmium is the densest element on earth. Iridium and Platinum are second and third. Osmium is volatile when at room temperature and when it's exposed to oxygen. The team has followed these leads to the items it would take to transport and protect such an element. We are also investigating the uses. I instructed them to focus on the geo-business sector. It would be the perfect front for a group of individuals who might want to chop off edges of the continents and cause chaos."

"Have they found anything specific?" he asked.

"Yes, but not much. A newly created company was registered as a non-profit organization that fit these certain criteria. It's called Geo-Enhancement Alliance. They have a simple website that states their mission is to facilitate geo-sector businesses with relations to the public and sponsor fundraising to prevent disasters or aid when geological disasters take place. Our IT expert is digging into the registry of the website and company to see what he can find. I should have some information about that soon."

"Do you think you've found it already? This quickly?" he asked.

"Perhaps, but I imagine that if there were a large conspiracy honed to destroy so much life, that they wouldn't be extremely blatant. Then again, if you didn't know what to look for, I doubt a non-profit geological society would be your first guess. Perhaps we just got lucky," I admitted.

"So, what's the plan for tomorrow?" he asked.

"I'll show you a few basic magic techniques and see if you can pick them up. At the same time, I'd like to see you shift. Perhaps we can do that, then head back to Boulder around noon tomorrow. When we get back, it will still be early, and we will have some extra time in the day. If I'm going to be spending more time in Boulder, I'm going to have to find somewhere to stay."

"You don't mean outside the compound," he stated. Not asking.

"Not necessarily. I'll speak to grandfather and see if he has anything pre-warded nearby if not, I'll find a place in the compound even if I have to put a bed in my office."

"After my trip into Boulder, I don't think it is safe to stay outside the compound. You are welcome to stay in my apartment until you find something. My couch is comfortable. I can sleep there," he offered.

"Tadeas, I would no more invade your private space than poke my own eyes out," I said firmly.

"Why? Am I not invading your space? Yet, you said I should consider it mine as well. I know my apartment isn't this place, but it's still mine to share if I want," he said sincerely.

"There is a difference between your apartment and an estate with ten bedrooms. We will see. Perhaps there is something I can find quickly. I know you need your own space. This is all very new, and I really do appreciate your kindness. I don't want to intrude. I still feel the need to be delicate with this whole situation. We both have very strong personalities and each have a stubborn streak," I explained.

"Not pressing your luck, eh?" he asked.

"Something like that. How about this, if we go back and that first day there I can't find anything, I will gladly sleep on your couch. But no more than that, okay? One-time deal and only if necessary. Plus, you have a friend that I truly do not want to upset any more than I already have," I said alluding to Meredith.

"It's a deal and don't worry about Mere. I can handle her." He got up and stepped out onto the patio. I followed him. It was cooler after the storm had blown through. A light breeze still blew. "Will you go with me to class tomorrow?"

I could see this was a sticking point for him. Perhaps if I did return, it would validate him to them. Show that he could pick out someone who did not belong and build his reputation. I'm sure he didn't see it that way, but I could look at it that way. I'd do it for him. "Yes, I will."

He turned to me beaming. "Really? You will?"

"Yeah," I said.

"Awesome. You can help me explain the new stuff to them. Help me show them. I mean, if you don't have a lot of other stuff to do," he added.

"Tadeas, we are partners. The stuff I have to do involves you. Where you go, I go," I said genuinely.

"Thank you so much, Abby." We stood listening to the sounds of the night. My mind raced through all the scenarios I could think of involving the geological alliance. I thought of things to have the team look for tomorrow. I made mental notes of them all. I took Gabriel's warning to be a metaphor, but perhaps this one time it was quite literal. A very scary thought that somehow humans could cause the continents to fall into the oceans. I thought about the warnings over the years about the San Andreas Fault. The scientists believed it was only a matter of time and the "Big One," as they called it, would strike the coastline. Maybe these people were looking for the same sort of thing. A man-made earthquake. I held my breath for a moment and noticed him watching me.

"What are you doing when you do that?" he asked.

"What does it seem like I'm doing?"

"Looks like you are lost."

"My brain works in overdrive. I thought about earthquakes, and if it was possible for someone to cause a man-made quake big enough to cause the kind of disaster that Gabriel showed me."

"I don't even know how you got to that line of thought, but I suppose it is a valid question. But you do you think Gabriel's vision was literal and not a metaphor for something?" he asked.

"Funny you should ask that because so far I have operated under the impression that it was a metaphor. But what if it *is* literal? What could cause continents to break up?"

"Those are scary thoughts," he stepped closer to me. "Doesn't your brain ever rest? I see you zone out a lot. Especially today."

"Frankly, no it doesn't."

"How do you sleep?"

"I had to practice techniques to calm my mind."

"Is that what you were doing the night I watched you do forms in the dark? When Meredith told me about your magic being bound?"

"Yes, I did it every night before bed. I did not realize the isolation in the training areas would be so hard on me. I kept trying to plan every move, and think ahead like I always do, but it didn't work well. Plus, I had no access to the magic. It is a part of me as much as your arms or legs are to you. I was well on my way to becoming downright non-functional," I admitted.

"After I confronted you in the hallway, you went there?" he asked.

"Yes, I tried to think of all the things you must have thought of me at the time. None of them were good. I tried to think of ways to make it better. I gave up. I knew it was over. I just hoped it wouldn't be too devastating," I explained. "I started planning. After everyone left for class, I wrote the notes for you. I placed the note in your room, and the two for your suit in the elevator, sending the elevator to the fourth floor. That's where my assistant Ashley picked it up and got your suit. She put the notes on the suit and after our fight, it waited on the elevator for when I got in. I went up one floor and slipped it into your closet. And just so you know, it's not normal for me to intrude into people's personal apartments, but I was desperate. And I certainly wasn't thinking clearly after the fight."

"Which you let me win," he interrupted.

"I did. I had to. I couldn't put you down in front of all of them. I had already undermined your authority enough," I said.

He looked down at his hands. "You let me hit you. I tried to pull the punch, but you were extremely good at avoiding my other strikes. I had gotten into a rhythm." He put his open hand up to my jaw, lightly touching the place where he had hit me. Heat rushed into my face. I forgot what I was saying for a moment.

"It healed the moment my grandfather removed the binding. Seriously, it was no big deal. I calculated the punches and tried to pick the one least likely to hurt. Unfortunately, I had a prior smack to the jaw the day before, also my own fault. I do not hold any of that against you, Tadeas." He still looked pained. I pressed my hand on top of his. "I promise. I deserved it."

"No," he said quietly. "I was angry and provoked you on purpose. You responded to me."

I looked at him in the eyes. "We can continue to hash this out or we can just let it go. I learned something about myself through all of it. I learned wonderful things about you. And thankfully we both aren't poised to kill each other. At least not at this moment."

He smiled a little still holding my face. "Not at this moment." He blinked and seemed to shake off whatever it was, then backed away from me.

"As I was saying, after the fight, I got in the elevator and the suit was already hanging there. I went into your apartment leaving it for you. I felt intrusive. I'm sorry. I just didn't have time to plan it all out. But I knew I'd owe you an explanation."

"You are right."

"Of course, I am, but about what specifically?" I teased.

He chuckled, finally getting my humor. "We can't keep saying we are sorry. I'm not sorry you came to my apartment by the way. Dinner was great that night. Tension and awkwardness. Fabulous food. It was awesome," he teased back. "I don't know about you, but I'm ready to sleep. What about you? Ready to shut down the brain?"

"Yes, I am." I really was, but I had little hope of calming my brain tonight. I headed into the house. We had made it to the hallway, and I said, "Watch this." I paused and said, "*Ostia!*" All the front double doors eased to a close in unison. I winked at him.

"I hope you can do more than close doors," he teased again.

"I can open them, too," I said.

"Fantastic. I can't wait to be fighting a two-headed dragon, and you can close the doors for us," he laughed at his own little joke.

"Silly boy, there are no two-headed dragons." I paused again, "Everyone knows it's only one head or four."

"Four!" he exclaimed.

"I'm joking, just one head, generally," I pondered. I did not need to start thinking about dragons. It had been a very long time since I saw one. Let's hope we didn't see any for a very, very long time. I had heard recent rumors of a dragon or dragons in St. Louis but had concluded that would be an unlikely place for a horde of dragons. We reached his door.

"There she goes," he smirked.

"What? Oh, heh, brain in overdrive," I said.

"Dragons?" he asked.

"Dragons," I replied.

He touched my face again. "Get some sleep." He leaned down and kissed me on the forehead.

"Goodnight, Abby." I felt a twinge of something that I hadn't felt in a long time. The warmth of knowing someone had my back again. Someone I could count on.

"Goodnight, Tadeas," I watched him go in the room and shut the door. Then he opened it again to my surprise.

"Leave your door open. I won't sit by if you have that nightmare again."

I blanched white. "Oh, you heard that."

"Yeah, I did. The animal in me wanted to rip the door off the hinges and get in there. I thought someone was hurting you, but George stopped me."

I sighed. "Tadeas, the first day you stepped into my house, I removed the wards that would keep you out of my room."

He shook his head. "What? You are a crazy woman."

I nodded in affirmation. Over the years, I had approached things differently than most people did. There were times when I thought that made me special, but other times it just made me crazy. I had told him the truth. Once he stepped foot in my home, I trusted him completely. I knew he would never harm me. Even through the arguments and disagreements, I still trusted him to always do the right thing. At that moment, he had access to everything. I wasn't holding back. Never again.

It took a while to calm my mind, but I drifted off to sleep. The nightmare didn't return.

CHAPTER 28

VANESSA

*M*wenye did not return that night. I got up and made coffee. I sat on the couch watching the clouds rolling by wishing I had something better to do when there was a knock at the door. I approached it and stopped to see if I could sense what was on the other side. A human male stood on the other side, but near him, I felt a magical element. I loosened the belt on my robe allowing the curves of my breast and the full length of my legs to show through the robe's opening. I had nothing else on. It would not be hard to distract the man if I needed to do so. Perhaps I could use him for a release.

I slowly opened the door to a nervous delivery man. He wore those awful brown shorts that looked like chopped-off dress pants, a button-up shirt with a company logo and a nervous, but handsome smile.

"Well, hello handsome," I smiled at him.

His eyes bulged out of his head. I imagined it wasn't the only thing bulging. "Um, hello ma'am, I have an envelope here for you. I need you to sign, please," he said as he offered me a clipboard to sign. Clearly, the magic I felt was in the envelope.

"Sure, no problem." I reached for the clipboard and my robe fell off my left shoulder exposing my naked left side to him. "Oops," I said sliding it back up onto my shoulder. I signed the clipboard, then handed it back to him.

"Have a good day, ma'am," he said nervously as he reached for the clipboard. I didn't let go of it.

"Isn't about time you had a break?" I asked him.

"Um, s-s-s-sorry, no. I can't take a break right now. My truck is downstairs, double-parked, and they don't like me to leave it very long," he started to walk away. I walked toward him and backed him into the wall on the other side of the hallway. I could satisfy the urge I had, erase his memory, and send him on his way.

"Please, won't you come in for a drink? Just a glass of water perhaps," I begged.

"I really shouldn't," he said.

Very nice we've moved from can't to shouldn't. I pressed harder against him and jerked the clipboard out from between us. I leaned into his mouth and locked him into a deep kiss. He moaned. Ah, yes. I felt the bulge in his shorts. Men were so easy.

"Let him go, Vanessa," Mwenye said stepping out of the elevator. The guy looked shocked and grabbed the clipboard. He ran so fast he made it to the elevator door before it closed behind Mwenye.

"I was just having some fun," I smiled at him.

"I saw that. What do you have there?" he asked as he walked toward me. He looked refreshed and happy. His eyes sparkled with life. His smile seemed genuine. Good thing he wasn't the jealous type, but I was. There was only one thing that could make him glow like that.

"Mr. Delivery Man brought us an envelope. I had hoped he

had a bigger package though," I grinned, walking back into the condo.

"How crass, my dear. You don't need a bigger package, anyway. You have me," he said.

I poked my lip out, and pouted. "Yes, but I got lonely without you last night."

His eyes glittered again. "I'm sure I can remedy your loneliness."

I sauntered up to him, dropping the robe as he started to open the envelope. His eyes admired me as I approached him. He looked down at the letter in the envelope. As his smile faded, I stopped my seduction. The last thing I wanted to do was set him off.

"What is it, my love?" I asked.

"An invitation. To an auction in Paris on Monday evening," he explained.

"What sort of auction?"

"These things are never specific. I will have to make some calls to see what is up for sale. I may have to send you in my place. I have meetings with investors every day over the next week. The Director would not approve of a detour to Paris," he explained.

"Can I take a guest?"

"Yes, the invite is for two people. Would you like to go? There would be a room full of like-minded individuals. I think you would enjoy yourself meeting some of the people in this world that are more powerful than you. Perhaps it'll make you give up these petty intrigues you have seducing delivery men and such. Your talents are wasted on such things," he scolded.

"I'd like to waste my talent on you right now," I purred into his ear.

"Are you going to Paris or not? I must respond immediately." He turned, pulling me to him.

"Why, yes. I'd love to go to Paris. It will be a nice little vacation. I will miss you though," I added that bit at the end just to make him smile.

Seducing him, I was well aware that he had been with someone else last night. I also knew that I had to keep up appearances. I would fuck him as many times as needed until I could get to the point to free myself from his hold. Then I could seduce any delivery man I wanted. Or sweet little redhead.

"No worries my dear, we know how to make up for lost time," he said before kissing me hard. As he hoisted me up, I wrapped my legs around him. He continued the violent kisses all the way to the bedroom where I played the good, little slut responding to his every command.

As we laid in the bed exhausted from our romp, I noted that he still had an abundance of energy. I could barely keep up with him. He decided to make a few calls and inquire about the auction and what exactly was for sale. As he made the calls, I snuggled next to him. It felt like the days before our relationship got very dark. The darkness didn't bother me. I would miss this. Sort of.

He talked to a female on the line. "Ah yes, I am aware of the item," he explained. I listened to her talk but didn't use magic to overhear. It would make him angry. "Thank you very much for the information. Please call me anytime if there is anything I can do for you. Goodbye."

I looked at him waiting to see if he would tell me what he had found out. He looked at me, caressing my face after our rough scene. "Did you find something out, my dear?"

"Yes, I did. And you will go to Paris and buy the item for me," he said.

I raised up in the bed and sat there looking at him curious

about what the item was that had intrigued him so much. "What is the item, may I ask?"

"It's a book. A magical tome. The blackest of magic. It contains spells and rituals that can destroy the earth," he said smiling. "My favorite kind of book."

"How interesting that such a book has become available considering our activities," I remarked.

"It is no coincidence, I assure you. Whoever owns the book either wants to lure us out with its sale or wants to maximize profit on the book when it would be in high demand. There will be plenty of abominable creatures there. You must stay safe while there. You must come home with the book. Is that clear?" he demanded.

"Of course, my love," I said. He got out of the bed and headed for the bathroom. I heard the water start running in the shower. I'd have to make a few calls myself. I would need a dress, shoes and a date. I was thrilled he was going to let me go out and do this on my own. I heard him humming in the shower. He must have had a wonderful evening. That made me a little sad, but I suppose if he was eating souls I didn't want to be involved. Either way, this was my chance. If I could obtain the book for him, then perhaps I would just keep it myself.

I got out of the bed and went into the other bedroom where I kept all my clothing and belongings. I jumped in the shower. When I got out, he was already gone. He had left a note on the counter saying he'd gone to speak with the Director about the auction and not to expect him home tonight.

That's okay. I had plenty to do myself. Time to make plans to free myself from John Mwenye's hold.

CHAPTER 29

TADEAS

When I awoke in the warm bed, I smelled bacon cooking. I loved Casa del Sol if for the bacon supply alone. I jumped in the shower. Afterward, I threw on black utility pants and an army green t-shirt. I made up the bed. I did not want George cleaning up after me all the time. I put my boots and socks on the chair next to the bed and padded down to the kitchen in my bare feet. The cool tile floor felt good against my feet. My nose led me to the kitchen.

Abby stood there over the stove using a fork to turn bacon in a frying pan. She wore khaki utility pants, but they were shorter than mine. They cut off at her calves. She wore an off-white t-shirt, and her hair was up in a ponytail. She was barefoot, too. I smiled at the coincidence.

"Good morning, handsome," she said. I blushed but recovered quickly.

"Good morning, bacon maiden," I said. She threw her head back and laughed.

"There is some on the table already with eggs and coffee." She pointed to the table with her fork, and I went over and sat down.

"You sleep okay?" I asked.

"Yes, better than I thought I would," she said, scooping the last of the bacon up and laying it out on a plate. "Go ahead and eat. You don't have to wait on me."

"No, that's rude. I can wait," I said as she washed her hands off and sat the second plate of bacon down.

"George, it's ready if you want some," she called out to the house. I did not see George on my way to the kitchen which was unusual. He was always cleaning.

"Go ahead and eat. I'll eat later," he called back from the direction of the sitting room. She sat down and put several strips of bacon on her plate.

"Oh, I forgot my tea," she got up, picking up a plain white mug from the kitchen counter before sitting back down to eat. "Now eat!"

"Are you going to cuss at me for eating your bacon?" I poked fun at her.

"For your information, Tadeas Duarte, I made that bacon that day, but once it was done, I didn't have the appetite to eat it. But right now, I'm going to eat your share for you if you don't hurry up," she poked back.

"Thank you for breakfast, Abby. You will have to let me cook for you sometime," I said as I shoved a whole piece in my mouth. She shook her head laughing at me. We chatted about the class later on today which would actually be early in the morning in Boulder. This time zone change stuff could be complicated. I was excited that she planned to come to class with me.

"Perhaps we can have a real match now," I said.

"You wouldn't want that," she said as her green eyes smiled over the mug.

"Oh please, I went easy on you," I smirked.

"I know. Good thing, too. I'd hate to have to hurt that pretty face," she said putting the last bite of bacon in her mouth.

"I accept your challenge," I said.

"Oh good, come on let's go fight," she said, putting her napkin down. She headed toward the door.

"Wait, what about the dishes?" I asked.

"Don't make excuses Duarte, just because you are scared to be beaten by a girl," she said as she rounded the corner out of sight.

George appeared in the small doorway to the back of the house on the other side of the kitchen, "Go. I'll clean up." He grinned at me.

"Thanks, George," I said as I sprinted after her.

BY THE TIME I CAUGHT UP WITH HER, SHE WAS ALREADY AT THE end of the hallway.

"George said he would get the dishes," I explained.

"I know. You have no excuses now," she teased.

"I suppose I don't."

We descended into the basement. I supposed I didn't need my shoes if we were going to spar. We walked into the large training room, and the lights automatically turned on with the motion in the room.

"Well, how do you want to get started?" she asked. "Kata, Wushu Taolu?"

As I stretched, I said, "No, I want to fight."

"Okay. Whatever you want," she shrugged.

"Unless you *need* to warm up," I added.

"No, I don't *need* to warm up, Tadeas," she said.

We faced each other on the mat and bowed. We began to spar. Neither of us giving up much room to the other. She was extremely skilled. We didn't talk; however, I enjoyed myself. I rarely had the chance to go against someone who had as much or more training than myself. I took a lot of my time off from the Agency to travel to new teachers and new disciplines. She obviously had traveled around a great deal herself. She presented forms of Karate, Ju-Jitsu, Tae Kwon Do, Judo, Aikido and many others. Throughout the entire workout, her heartbeat remained steady. Strong. She was a wonder. She remained very calm in a fight. I got tired rather quickly. "Where in the world did you learn all of this?" I asked between heavy breaths. I had the feeling that our skills were evenly matched, but she might have more stamina than I. Perhaps it was something magical that kept her going.

She stopped and bowed to me. I returned the bow.

"When Samara taught me magic, we traveled all over Asia. Every town we went to, he made me learn whatever flavor was most revered in the town," I said. "You would have thought it would have taught me a little more discipline, but it was hard for me to connect the real-world obstacles to the training. In hand to hand fights, yes, but when magic got involved, I didn't understand it until much later on."

"You are very good," I said.

"You are the best I've ever sparred with since Lincoln. The animal instincts help, yeah?" She walked to the back of the room where there was a small counter. She threw me a towel from it and opened the cabinet underneath to reveal a mini-fridge. She got two bottles of water. She gave me one and sat down on the mat.

"They do. It's how I initially saw you holding back."

"The whole reading the muscle thing. Honestly, that's amazing to me," she said admiring my talent.

"I'm not sure it's all that great," I said as sat down across from her.

"It is. I see it. One day you will too," she said confidently. "I would like to see you shift. I figured here was as good as any. It's

286

quiet, and I can concentrate on how the environment changes to determine exactly what variety of magic is going on there. It will help us in the future if I know more about your gifts."

"I wouldn't call them gifts," I muttered. She continued to praise this side of me that I kept hidden. That I kept restrained. In this small space, I was nervous to shift. What if I turned on her? She wouldn't be able to escape.

She continued to gush about my ability. "I would. It's magnificent. Shifters are all very special. You are one of a kind, Tadeas. I looked it up in the Agency records. There are no other black jaguar shifters in the world. There are very few leopards and jaguar shifters at all, but no documented cases of a black jaguar."

"I don't think my coloring makes me special," I said as I stood up. I couldn't look into her eyes, so I studied my feet.

"What's wrong with your feet?" she asked leaning over to look at them.

"Nothing. Why?"

"You keep looking at them," she said trying to get me to smile. "Tadeas, if you don't want to do this, I'm fine with that too. If you aren't comfortable with it, I don't want to upset you at all. Honest. I won't be angry if you say no."

"I'll do it. It's just that I've always considered shifting a bad thing. And you came along and to hear you praise it like you do, it's just different," I admitted.

She stood up and put her hand on my shoulder. "It is a good thing. It is not a curse. And the only way you can ever learn to control it completely isn't really magic at all. It's learning to accept it for what it is. I just propped it all up but put it in perspective what you do is no different from my magic. It's a very unique talent. You can use it for good or bad, but you can't really use it at all until you accept it and try. You know your Bible, right? The parable of the talents?"

"Yeah, I've heard that one. Two servants took their talents

and multiplied them. One man put his talent in a hole, and the master took it away from him."

"That's actually the best-condensed version of a parable that I've ever heard," she laughed. "No one is going to take your talent away, but it could take you away to a very dark place if you don't control it. You've kept yourself in an isolated place and on a routine. And the last few days all of that has been ripped from you, thanks to me," she paused, acknowledging the fact that she had interrupted my life. I knew I would never be the same no matter how all of this panned out. "But now you have the opportunity to make this wonderful talent into something you can use for good. I already know how capable you are without even seeing it in action."

I heard what she said. And parts of me knew it to be true, but there was that nagging voice in the back of my head that kept saying I was a murderer. If I ever did anything to hurt her or Meredith or even one of the students, it would destroy me. Finally, I gathered myself up enough to speak.

"I want to try, but I still can't see it that way, Abigail," I admitted. It felt nice to be truthful with her. She didn't flinch or back down.

"Then we will try. And eventually, you will see what I see. Now, are you shifting for me or no?" She winked at me.

I nodded. Reaching out to feel the coolness of the spirit world, I pulled on that edge and my jaguar body morphed into place. She circled me, studying my body. I stood there twitching my tail as she shifted her sight between the magic spectrum and reality. The golden edges to her eyes glowed. I noticed like before when I shifted, I had no urge or desire to harm her. It was a relief because I was growing fonder of her every day. I wouldn't allow myself to carry on if I hurt her.

She bent down in front of me, looking into my eyes. Then, I heard her voice muffled in my head, and jumped backward several feet, startled. I turned my head sideways to indicate,

"*What the hell?*" She laughed at me as she sat back down on the floor and crossed her legs. She was not afraid of me at all. Such confidence in me caused me to rethink everything I had ever thought about my animal form.

"*Can you hear me better now?*" It was like her voice filled my entire head. I twisted side to side and shook my head. "*Oh, it's too loud,*" she said in almost a whisper. I sat down where I was looking at her from the distance.

"*What the fuck?*" I thought very clearly. She rolled back on her back laughing. "*Seriously, you can talk in my head. Fan-freaking-tastic!*" She laughed some more.

"*Yes, I can, but I can do this while you are human, too. However, I couldn't do it if you weren't willing.*"

"*How can I be willing if I don't know you are going to do it? Don't go poking around in my brain,*" I let out an audible whine.

"*If you were afraid of me or hated me, I wouldn't have been able to make the first contact. I imagine it came through kind of muffled. But once you concentrated on it, it was like giving me permission to communicate with you in this way. And I promise I would never poke around in your brain. I can't do anything other than what you let me do. If you want me to stop talking to you this way, just say so.*"

"*You promise you aren't in my brain?*" I asked her, baring my fangs. She grinned, still not afraid.

"*Easy kitty. I promise. I swear it on my power.*" I felt a rush of the oath swirl around her and bind it to me. In my form as the jaguar, I could physically see the swirl of glittering gold power wrapping around her, then forming to a little glowing ball flying into me. A power oath meant that she just gave me a small bit of her power. It's basically like I can hold it over her head and destroy it if she breaks her promise.

I thought back to the orientation when I joined the Agency. We had to sign a non-disclosure agreement, but there was a binding oath there too. It said if the Agency had any questions about a major crime or questionable activities that one of their wielders would have the power to enter my mind. They could retrieve any information they wanted to. It made me uneasy, but everyone that entered the Agency signed the paperwork. I figured I'd be training students for the rest of my life and signed it. I realized that Abigail was probably one of the people that could enter a mind and take what she wanted. However, in just the few days I've known her, I know she would never do that without permission. Her oath to me was strong. I could feel its warmth in my chest.

"*Wow, but that wasn't necessary,*" I said.

"*Sure, it was. I wanted you to know I was serious. Meddling in people's minds is a big no-no. And while I generally ignore a lot of what the TCA has to say, they are absolutely correct on that one.*" She looked like it pained her to admit it.

"*If I'm ever like this you can always communicate with me by just thinking the words?*" I asked.

"*It's a little more than that, but I have to focus on you and your aura, and there is a small communication spell involved. Like I said, I can do this while you are human. It's helpful in many situations, but of course, you have to allow me to do it.*"

I prowled over taking a seat across from her. "*Do you want me to switch back?*"

"Yes, please," she spoke out loud.

I pulled on that unnamed place where my human body waited and switched bodies. I had watched myself do it in the mirror before to see what it looked like. It was a shimmer, a bit of a blur, and the bodies just switched. I sat across from her in my human body and mimicked the crossed legs. "Do the head thing with me like this," I said.

"*Communico,*" she said in Latin. Then her voice lightly brushed around in my head like a breeze, "*Hear me?*"

"Yes," I spoke.

She held her finger in front of her mouth like she shushed a child. "*No like this,*" she spoke again in my head.

I concentrated on her, *"Better?"*

She smiled, *"Much. It will get easier. It's harder as a human. Humans are far less trusting than animals. Your spirit form, which is what it is, by the way, trusts me more than you do."*

"Spirit form," I said out loud again, "Damn it. I'm sorry."

She laughed and spoke out loud, "No, it takes time. We have time to practice it. I'm going to break the bond of the spell. That way, I'm not sitting here holding a spell in place for no reason. *Adimo.*"

"You will have to teach me these Latin words so I will know what you are doing. Sorry, Latin isn't one of my known languages," I said.

"Sure. *Adimo* is to take away, or withdraw, to steal. I withdrew the earlier spell which was *Communico.* It is not simply communicating, but it's actually more like sharing because we both have to be willing to share our minds for it to work."

I nodded. "The other day you said *Quies* in the corridor." I hesitated to bring up the memory, but the word stuck in my head. Much like the one the dark figure at my exorcism used. I would never forget it. I tried lookingup that word once, but I was never able to determine how to spell it or its origin.

"*Quies* is peace. And yes, that will stick with you," she explained. "It was not a request like the communication spell. It was a demand."

"There was a word, a spell someone used on me many years ago, and I wonder if you might know what it meant," I decided to ask. She knew a lot about magic maybe she knew.

"Sure, what was it?" she asked willing to help.

"I might not say it right, but I've heard it twice before. *Hodéezyéél.*"

You would have thought I told her something horrible. Her face went pale, and she scrambled to her feet. She covered her face with her hands, turning away from me. Her body started to shake. I stood up, stepping toward her.

"No, don't. Wait," she choked out. She lowered one arm to her stomach and held it like she might be sick. The other she still held in front of her mouth.

"Abby," I said quietly. I wanted to apologize, but I had no idea she would react that way.

"No, it's okay. Just give me a second," she said quietly. Tears streamed down her face. "Where did you hear that word?"

"Twice in my life, a dark figure approached me in the spirit realm. Father Sergio tried to tell me it was a demon. Once was during an exorcism. The other when I killed..." my voice trailed off.

She winced. She took the back of her hand, wiping the tears. She drew several deep breaths, steadying herself. I resisted the urge to wrap her up and hug her. Whatever I had said was extremely painful to her.

She looked up at me with those green eyes sparkling with tears. "That was no demon."

CHAPTER 30

ABIGAIL

*A*fter he spoke the word, it took me a while to gather my senses.

Grief was a sneaky bastard. If you ever had a great loss in your life, you learned to cope with it, and over time the pain would ease. However, occasionally a smell, a song, a memory, or a word could trigger that long hidden grief. The pain of it would rush back on you, stabbing you in the heart all over again.

I tried wiping the tears away, because of the pained look on his face. He hadn't meant to hurt me. He honestly didn't know. I needed to get myself together to explain it to him.

"That was no demon," I managed to say. I felt a little light-headed. I sat back down on the mat, and he sat across from me again. His kind heart showed all over his face. He was going to beat himself up if I didn't start talking.

"Just tell me when you are ready," he said not pushing.

I tried to smile at him, but I'm pretty sure it came out as a wince. "The word is Navajo. There is a reason the United States used Navajo for code talkers in World War II. They continued to use the language through the Korean War for code. It's barely understood by any non-Navajo people." I had to stop for a minute and gather myself again. He moved closer to me on the mat, putting his hand on my knee. It reminded me when I awoke from passing out after the storm. He held my hand then. It was oddly reminiscent of having a loyal pet that instinctively comforted you when you were in pain. Perhaps it would seem weird or kooky to anyone else, but for me, his instincts to comfort me in a non-obtrusive way was amazing. I would have to pay more attention and see what other animal instincts besides purely fighting he exhibited as a human.

"You drifted off again," he said patiently.

I tried the smile again, but it still wasn't much of one. "Yeah, sorry. It wasn't a demon. The word is identical to my *Quies* spell. It means peace. I didn't realize he was at your exorcism," I choked up again.

He squeezed my knee. "I see now."

I gritted my teeth. I would get through this without being a basket case. "It was Lincoln's spell." There I said his name. The weight lifted a bit, but I could feel that gaping hole in my heart.

"So, he stopped me from shifting at the exorcism," he half-stated and half-asked.

"It seems that he did. He had not told me that about you." I thought back about all of our conversations involving Tadeas and his gifts. Lincoln had interacted with him several times. I knew he was the one that arrived to pull Tadeas out of the room where Isabel died. I wanted to avoid that subject with him because Lincoln told me that I was to find Tadeas if something ever happened to him.

"What I saw while sitting in that chair when they branded me looked evil," he said not understanding.

"You saw him in the spirit world. He probably walked into the room that way to avoid confrontation with the priests. He had the ability to travel through multiple planes. Back then he was assigned to seeking out and collecting shifters. The Agency endeavored to save as many as possible. But at times there were too many to save. Lincoln was one of the few operatives that had a gift for seeing a shifter. That ability he taught to me. I don't understand why he didn't take you from them then." I bowed my head, trying to understand. If Lincoln was there, he was there to remove Tadeas before he shifted. Why didn't he do it? "If it isn't too painful, can you tell me as much about the exorcism as you can? But if you don't want to that's fine."

"No, it's okay." He proceeded to tell me about it. It was eerily similar to mine. They even called him an abomination. He knew now that the first shift tried to happen right there in the exorcism chair, and I knew that if he saw Lincoln in the spirit world and he used that word, then he did not shift. I listened to the story.

"It sounds a lot like mine. Very much like mine. Despite their lofty beliefs, neither of us is an abomination." I looked up to his eyes to make sure he was okay. He had moved his hand from my knee while he told the story. That whole thing where he couldn't tell a story without using his hands. The thought made me smile.

"Why are you grinning now?" he asked confused.

"I just thought about how I used to watch you in class talk with your hands, and how you always tried not to." I grinned, even more, admitting to it.

"Aw, come on, I've worked on that. Why you gotta bring it up?" he teased, easing the tension in the room.

"Sorry, it just occurred to me."

"Crazy, wandering mind," he said as his smile faded. It was a temporary respite from our intense conversation. "Do you do that on purpose?"

"Do what?"

"Deflect when something gets serious or uncomfortable."

"I suppose it's human instinct to avoid uncomfortable topics.

Right? But this time I honestly just let my mind wander a bit. My face just gave me away that time."

"Hmph," he grunted.

"You don't do it though. Let your mind wander. That I've noticed. You generally seem to want to confront things head on. You could teach me how to do that or at the very least point it out to me when I start to deflect."

"He looked like a skeleton in the spirit world," he started back into the conversation. A subtle way of pointing out that I had tried to move the conversation away from Lincoln.

I smiled because I did ask for him to point it out. "Yes, Lincoln was the legendary Navajo Monster Slayer. Ever heard those stories?"

"No, I don't think I have," he said.

"Lincoln and his brother Thomas, which were the names they adopted in more modern times, were twin brothers. Lincoln was the Monster Slayer, and his brother was known as Born for Water. He hunted and killed monsters for his people, then later on for all of us. He and his brother could be described as brutal. I admit the first time I saw him in the spirit realm, it scared the crap out of me. He and his brother were extremely formidable. They were war gods."

"Wait, your ex-partner was a god?! That's quite the standard to live up to," he said playfully, but it felt like it did bother him.

"I guess, but he really was no different than you and me. The Mayans considered a Jaguar Guardian to be an angelic-like creature, and part of southern Mexico in the Olmec traditions worshiped the were-jaguar as a rain deity."

"I am not a god," he said.

"Lincoln said the same thing. He would say that just because someone did not understand your true nature and worshiped you for your talents did not make you a real god. But we both know that belief has a lot of power. As the years went by and the Navajo nation dwindled, Lincoln too, had less power. By that time his experience and talents carried him. He also said that Grandfather's faith in him, and mine to an extent after I learned to tolerate him, gave him power as well. His enemy's fear of him also made him powerful. He had plenty of enemies. Think about it like your students. Every time you take an extra moment with them or encourage them through a difficult sparring match, you are placing faith in them. The belief that they can do better. Your faith in them gives them power. It gives them confidence." I watched him take it all in.

"You had to learn to tolerate him?" Out of that whole diatribe that's the one thing that he latched onto and asked to know more about.

"Well, more like he had to learn to tolerate me, and I had to change. After training with Samara, I felt invincible. I was a royal pain in the ass. And he got saddled with me. He felt like he was babysitting. Technically, I was an adult, but he had lived on this earth much longer than any of us. After getting smacked down a couple of times, I realized I was a little fish in a big sea. Samara taught me spells and power. Lincoln taught me control and constraint. Grandfather put me with Lincoln because he knew that I would fail over and over, and I would need someone to bail me out. He always saved me. He and I..." I had to pause as the memories flooded over me. I missed him very much. I pulled my knees up and buried my face in them. I couldn't hold the onslaught back anymore.

Tadeas moved next to me, wrapping his arms around me. "Don't talk about it anymore. It can wait," he whispered.

I had restrained myself around Tadeas, but now I leaned into him. He just held on and didn't move away. All the tension and unresolved issues between us just melted away. I tried to gather my emotions. I raised my head, and I guess I didn't realize how close he was to me. He wiped my tears. My emotions raged back and forth. I didn't want him to see me as weak. I wanted to move away from him, but I was transfixed looking at him. I was not used to anyone being that close. It had been so long since I allowed anyone to be that close to me. And although part of me fought against it, the other part wanted to just accept the comfort for what it was.

"Abby, I know you are tough and powerful, but you are human. You hurt just like the rest of us."

"Do you read minds?" I blurted.

"What? No, why?"

"There are times it seems like you do," I muttered.

"No," he pushed himself up off the floor, offering his hands to pull me up. I put mine in his. He pulled me to my feet. "But I will tell you this. After talking to your Grandfather, I have a better perspective of my purpose here."

"I should have just let him threaten you in the beginning."

"It might have worked."

"My way was much more fun, though right?"

"No, it wasn't." I had to look up at him, then realized he was joking again. Maybe because the loss of Lincoln was fresh in my mind at the moment, I didn't catch on to the humor immediately. "We've got to be getting back. The magic lesson will have to wait."

"Yep," I agreed. "Let me grab a few things including shoes, and we can go through the portal. We will have a few hours on the other side. But I want to get back and see if I can find out if any of the upstairs apartments are vacant." I started to walk away but realized he still held my hands.

"Abby, anytime you want to talk about all of that stuff, I'll listen," he offered.

"I'm not the only one with pain. The road goes both ways," I said squeezing his hands, and he let go. "But thank you. Guess I didn't realize I needed to let some of it out. You too, right?"

"Yes, sometime soon. I will," he said. We headed back upstairs, and George stood there with my black duffle bag, my boots, and Tadeas' boots.

"I took the liberty of packing the things you wanted," he explained.

I looked over to Tadeas and whispered, "Ever seen an Angel blush?" I turned back to him, "George, I told you to stay out of my lacy underwear drawer."

"They are just so pretty," he replied.

I stood in shock, and Tadeas almost hit the floor rolling in laughter.

"You dirty old man," I walked up and hugged him.

"You will be back soon," he said. It wasn't a question.

"Hopefully, but I have no definite plans. You need anything from here, Tadeas?" He was putting on his shoes. I picked mine up and just carried them with me.

"No, ma'am," he replied.

"Take care, George," I said as I hugged him again. I opened the closet door to the portal and stepped through.

CHAPTER 31

TADEAS

I watched her step through the portal with confidence despite the breakdown she had had. George offered to shake my hand. I met his grip.

"She is important to me, Master Tadeas. Please take care of her. Thank you for what you did down there. She's needed someone besides me for a very long time. I had my doubts about you, but you are proving yourself to me daily. We are watching, Son."

"I understand, George. I think she's taking care of me more than me taking care of her though," I replied to him. I genuinely liked him. I didn't know any angels. I didn't know what to expect, but he was like a wise, understanding father who loved his daughter.

"It's a partnership," he said.

I smiled and patted him on the shoulder, then went through the portal. Abby waited there for me. Unfortunately, she wasn't alone. Meredith sat in the one office chair.

"Hey, Mere, what's up?" I said nonchalantly even though her presence there set off every alarm in my body.

"Just needed to talk to you about your class, and I decided to wait for you to return," she said.

"Do you lock your door?" I asked Abigail who sat behind the desk tapping on the keyboard. She shook her head no at me and grimaced. I suddenly saw the benefit of the communication spell.

"I'm right here. Did you have to ask that in front of me?" Meredith practically yelled at me.

"Tadaes, I have a few things I need to do here. You can go with her and discuss the class, and I'll be down in a bit. I'll come by your apartment. If that's okay with you?" She frowned at me. I could tell she didn't want me to go.

"Okay, I'll see you in a bit," I said, motioning Meredith to the door. I turned with my back to Meredith and mouthed, "I don't want to go." I hoped she could read lips.

She smiled at me and held up 3 fingers and then made a zero indicating she'd give me 30 minutes.

I mouthed back, "Fifteen."

"Are you coming?" Meredith insisted from the hallway. I shut the door, but I heard her laugh just a little inside the office.

"Meredith, it is 4 a.m. in the morning. What is your problem?"

"Not here," she shot back at me.

We got to the stairwell, and she was not the least bit quiet going down the steps.

"Meredith, people are sleeping. Could you please stop stomping?"

"I'll stop stomping when I get to stop babysitting your people every time you run off with that tramp."

"We cannot have a conversation if you continue to call her names. I'm sorry, Mere. I would never let anyone talk about you that way. I can't let you do it to her either," I said.

"Fine," she said walking a bit more quietly. We exited the

stairs, and she walked to my apartment door. She wasn't asking to come inside. She practically demanded it by standing there waiting for me.

Avoiding the fight, I opened the door and let her enter. The moment the door shut she went off like a bomb.

"I am sick and tired of covering for you. Yes, I know we didn't have traditional classes, but there's all kinds of crap going on with your class. You let that little whore upstairs ruin a completely good class of recruits. Samantha has been in tears all day. A man she met in Boulder dumped her. I went to check on her since no one could find you. On my way there, I ran into Travis and another girl from another class fucking in a closet. He actually asked me to join them. I got Samantha calmed down finally, and I went to the cafeteria to get a drink. When I came back by, Samantha was in the closet with Travis and the girl. These people have lost their damned minds and you are off in a fancy portal with little Miss Witch."

"You done?" I asked.

"No, I'm not even close to being done. Do you realize who she is? Yes, she's *his* granddaughter, but there have always been rumors about who she is and what she is. Her father is a wizard, big whoop. But her mommy? Who is her mommy? Rumors say her mother is Fae. That makes her a Halfling. She is a Fae witch whore."

"You can leave now," I said firmly.

"I am not done!" she yelled.

"Yes, you are. Get out!" I felt my anger rising. I suppressed the animal.

"See. That's the other part of Tadeas Duarte. In the nice little confines of this building, you are a great instructor and a good friend. But the moment you leave this place, you are a freak. Everyone that looks at you will see that you are an animal on the inside. What happens when you can't control it? What happens when you kill her like you did Isabel?"

I clutched my hands into a fist, thinking about Abby in the corridor on the island. About her power and how it calmed me. Focusing on the moments where I didn't attack Abby at the chapel and in the training room. I knew I could control the animal, but my body shook as I tried to prevent myself from losing my temper with Meredith. Abby said I had to believe in myself. I had to accept what I was, but Meredith was right. I was a murderer.

"He told you to leave," I heard her steady voice behind me. I felt the calm wash over me.

Meredith threw her hands in the air. "We will finish this when you come to your senses, but until then stay the hell away from me." She stomped out the same way she stomped in.

"She is insane. What in the world?" I muttered.

Abby walked around to face me. "That's putting it lightly. What she said…"

I waved her off. "No, I know. She tried to provoke me. I don't get it. She knows me too well to be doing that stuff to me."

"Why would she do it on purpose?"

"I'm not sure." I plopped down on the couch, and Abby sat down next to me.

"Nice TV. We should watch it," she said.

"Deflecting," I said.

"I can deflect about you. I just am not allowed to deflect about me," she stated.

"We probably should discuss the rules of this game before-hand," I smirked. She had made me smile. In fact, overall, I was much calmer. Her belief in me made me stronger. I saw exactly what she meant when she talked about faith.

"Nah, I'm making them up as we go along." I turned the tv to late-night reruns of Night Court. I don't think either of us watched it. I took my phone out and set an alarm for class tomorrow. I felt myself getting sleepy. The timezone change affected me. It was time for a siesta on the island.

"You find anything in your emails?" I asked.

"I didn't have time to read them. I felt the hatred coming off her, and I followed down pretty closely. I'm getting weird vibes from her. I can't pin it down," she said.

"You look at her in the spectrum?" I asked. I just assumed she was always looking.

"In general, I don't, but when someone is that angry it helps to look. The colors of an aura can sometimes define the source of any emotion. And yes, I looked."

"See anything?"

"Her aura is black right now, which means she knew I would look, but blocked it somehow. I'm aware of her magical talents. She probably just didn't want me snooping. I can understand that completely," she said dismissing it.

"Every once in a while, she gets wound up. She will calm down and apologize for it all soon," I assured her. Meredith was mostly harmless.

She moved across the couch to sit next to me with her legs pulled up under her like in the recliner at the island. "You sure you are okay? Big tough man doesn't want to talk about it," she mocked, and I saw her shiver a little.

I got up, went to the closet, and brought back a blanket. It did get cold down in this underground bunker. I handed it to her. "Thank you," she said, curling underneath it.

I sat back down, propping my feet up on the coffee table. "No, it's okay. I know what she said isn't true, but there are things that I will eventually have to come to terms with. I'll discuss it with you. Just not right now." I felt guilty. She had made herself vulnerable with me earlier, and I wasn't giving her an inch. She moved back to the other end of the couch, positioning a pillow on the back of her head.

"I'm will always be here for you," she said quietly.

"I know," I said as I reached up and turned off the lamp beside the couch. The TV was the only light in the room. As it flickered, I drifted off to sleep watching Abby at the other end of the couch. I think she was asleep the moment the last word came out of her mouth.

THE ALARM ON MY PHONE WENT OFF, AND I GROWLED AT IT. I looked down at Abby. She pulled the blanket over her head. "Turn the damn thing off," I heard her muffled voice.

"I think we should have breakfast again before class," I said.

She pulled the blanket down and said, "I'm not hungry. Plus, I'm not sure me showing up in the cafeteria with you is such a good idea."

"I'll go grab something and bring it back. You want anything?" I asked.

"No. I think I'm fine."

"Ok, well help yourself to anything in the fridge. The bathroom is in there. You can even go lay down on my bed if you would, rather."

"I'm fine," she repeated.

I hurried down to the cafeteria, grabbing my second breakfast for the day. I felt like a hobbit. Maybe they were time portal travelers, and that's how they had so many meals. I got her a cup of tea, too. By the time I got back, she had commandeered the couch and slept again. I sat the cup of hot tea down on the coffee table. As I plopped down at the small kitchen table to enjoy my bacon, egg and cheese biscuit, I watched her sleep. She was peaceful there. No signs of dreams or nightmares. She had no fear of sleeping in this room with me despite what I could do to her. I couldn't comprehend the faith that she had in me.

I had eagerly wanted her to come to class, but apprehension started to rise up in me. The students developing their skills meant a lot to me. They had plenty of distractions thus far. Hopefully, this would be a good move. I heard her moving around behind me. She sat up and said, "Ooo! Tea!" She scooped it up quickly taking a sip. "Cold tea."

"I'm sorry. I didn't know you'd go back to sleep," I said, laughing at the things she took as simple pleasures.

"It's ok. I know how to use a microwave," she explained. She put the cup in the microwave which was on the end of the counter next to where I sat at the table. Then, she stared at the keypad. I reached over and hit a couple buttons to start up. "Perhaps I overestimated my microwave skills."

"I see," I smirked at her.

"You mind if I use your computer?" she asked.

"No, go ahead. I'm gonna get a quick shower and get ready for class. How do you want to do this class thing?"

"I was thinking about that. I considered a grand entrance with an invisibility spell, but I think just let me be in there when they come in. I'll even take my old spot in the lineup if they leave it open for me."

"You aren't my student anymore, not that you ever were," I said.

"But I am. And I promise to be a better one now. I have a lot to learn from you," she said trying to encourage me.

"I don't know what you could learn from me," I said finding somewhere to wallow again.

She sat down at the computer and logged in to the Agency network using her credentials. I imagined she had a lot more access than I did. She opened her email. The screen filled with unopened ones, "Ugh. I'll just hit the highlights. Mind if I use the shower too when you are done?"

"Yeah sure." I walked over to her. "What exactly are you gonna learn from me, Miss Deflection? Or should I say Miss Change the Subject?"

"Compassion. I think you have a lot more heart than I do. I can be extremely calculating. Sometimes I can't predict the human response much like my entering your class. I didn't see the problem until it was too late. To be honest, Meredith is a ticking time bomb, and I don't handle that kind of thing very well. She deliberately tried to force you to shift to prove a point. You, however, because of your friendship with her, are willing to endure a lot to save the friendship. I'm not sure I'd have that much compassion. I know that I wouldn't. I have walked the edge of evil too many times," she admitted.

"Abby, there is nothing evil about you," I said.

She hung her head, not watching the screen now. "Yes, there is. I fight it back daily. I keep it confined. I keep it suppressed."

I realized now how much she actually identified with me, then I asked a very dangerous question. "Have you killed? Like me?"

She swallowed and took a deep breath. She let it out slowly and quietly said, "Yes. I have."

I just stared at her. I didn't know what to say. I saw her bite her lip because she did not want to talk about it. I put my hand on her shoulder, and she put hers on mine. I felt it shake a little, and it was cool to the touch. I knew there were no words. I squeezed her shoulder before heading off to the shower. I knew we had many days ahead to discuss it further. Now wasn't the time, for either of us.

When I got out of the shower, she waited patiently on the couch. She sipped tea while staring at the television. It was off.

"I'm done, if you want to use it," I said.

"Thanks," she said as she walked past me into the bathroom, shutting the door.

The shower must have made her feel better. She smiled when she came out of the bathroom. Of course, she didn't have any clothes here that I knew of, so she wore the ones that she had on at the island. While she was in the shower, I picked through my full closet of clothes courtesy of Abigail. I hadn't figured out how she managed to do all of that. I had gotten over the creep factor of it. I supposed it was par for the course when your partner was a crazy wizard. Partner. Yep, I was all in now.

I thought back to Meredith's rant about Abby's lineage. If she was part Fae, it wouldn't surprise me. She was related to Theodoard down the line. There had to be something supernatural there. But she had told me her Aunt Lianne was extremely dangerous because she was Fae. Abby, I suppose, was dangerous too. I knew I hadn't seen her really throw down with magic, but I wasn't afraid of her. Once again proving her point that sometimes a little faith was all you needed. She was earning my faith daily.

"You good?" I asked.

"Yep," she said.

"You are going to be late for class if you don't hurry up," I teased.

"Can't have that, my teacher is a real prick."

"Hey! That's not nice. You need to learn to respect authority," I teased.

"Yes, I do. Please teach me, O Great Master," she said with a bow.

"Oh enough, let's go." I think she could banter with me all day if I kept coming back. I would run out of witty retorts, eventually. I wasn't sure that smart mouth of hers would.

THANKFULLY, WHEN WE ENTERED THE ROOM, NO ONE HAD arrived yet. We also avoided seeing anyone else in the hallways. Sometimes I wondered if she didn't arrange everything. Samantha was the first through the door, followed by Travis. She squealed and ran to Abby. Abby stood in her normal spot on the mat. Samantha hugged her.

"Miss Taylor, please take your spot," I spoke firmly. Abby grinned at me. The other students walked in. Travis walked past Abby and said something quietly. She blushed, then fist bumped him. There was something strange about the exchange that unsettled me. I already had a bad opinion of Travis with all his extracurricular activities.

"Mr. Reed," I said.

"Yes, Sir," he said as he jumped in place. I bowed to them, and they all bowed to me.

"Naranhi Sogi." They all popped into a ready stance. We used a lot of basic stances from Tae Kwon Do. Over the year's we've found that if any had any martial arts at all that they were exposed to some form of Karate or Tae Kwon Do. I chose to use mostly Tae Kwon Do stances for teaching. "As you all see, Miss Davenport has joined our class today. I thought it would be beneficial for you all to know why she was here in the first place. A lot of the reason she came to our class was for each of you. Over the last few days, I've been privileged to see her vision for the canvas crews going forward and honored that she wanted my opinions and ideas. Over the years our teaching methods have changed, but never before has the world changed as rapidly as it does these days. With the booming technology and the immediacy of the world, our methods need a complete overhaul. Miss Davenport, would you please join me?" She walked up and stood next to me. She bowed to all of them, and they to her. "Please tell them why you are making changes and what classes will look like from now on." We had talked about what she wanted to present to the class. I wanted to hand it over to her. I hadn't seen her in this kind of setting. I stepped to the side to watch my new partner work her magic.

"Good morning, everyone. Thank you, Mr. Duarte, for allowing me to return to your class." She looked over at me. "He is right. I came into the class as a mundane for two very specific purposes. The first was Mr. Duarte, himself. Most of you know, and if you don't you should, that you are fortunate to be under the teaching of the best instructor that the Agency has ever had. I disguised myself as a student to learn more about him and his methods. Most of you know or have heard that I am a wielder. This is true. However, for the purposes of this experiment, I allowed my grandfather to bind my magic. While in this setting, I could not access it even if I wanted to. I wanted to be on the same playing field as the rest of you. Because of the skill of your instructor, it wasn't very long before he knew something was off about me. His instincts are beyond any of us in this room, including me. All in all, he handled the situation in an extremely professional manner," she said.

I looked down. We did not discuss her bragging on me to them. I felt embarrassed. I cut my eyes up at her, and finally, she caught me looking. I slightly shook my head, so she changed course. No one had ever praised my methods so openly. I didn't know if she was genuine or if she was stroking my ego. Perhaps both.

"I have asked Mr. Duarte to become my new partner on a much greater scale. My team and I have for many years worked directly with proxies and regents to fight the bad things that would rise up in the night. The very things that each of you will find when you enter the streets. He and I will be making changes to the way you train, as well as establishing new proxies and new policies on the streets. The whole system needs a revamp starting right here at the core with all of you." As she spoke to them, she moved across the mat gracefully. They all watched her every move, locking into everything that she said.

"I mentioned my team. Mr. Duarte, by way of object lesson, I have invited a few guests. If you would please, get the door." She had gone off-script, and I gave her a half-hearted evil eye. I heard her in my head very quietly, *"Trust me."*

I focus on her, *"I do."* She smiled.

"And you better get used to me complimenting your skills," she said.

"*Abby,*" I groaned, but she continued to smile at me. I let it go.

We had started the communication spell just prior to class just in case. I opened the door, and seven very diverse people walked into the back of the class. She motioned them to the front of the class.

"Ladies and gentlemen, this is my team. Along with our newest member, Mr. Duarte, I'd like to introduce them to you. These two hulking brutes are simply known as Tony and Tommy. They are my Polynesian hit squad. They cover all security and related measures while in the field. This tall drink of water is none of other than the formerly famous race car driver, Jeremy Stafford. When you drive the circuits as a non-aging being, people start to notice that undying youthful glow while everyone else grows old. Mr. Stafford retired from driving in circles and now handles all vehicles and driving duties including planes and helicopters. He's expanded his repertoire while with our team." Stafford leered at her. I gritted my teeth. She looked back at me like she could hear me grinding. I motioned for her to continue.

"Vincent Volkov, the mad Russian, and Aiden Haider, the Arabic alchemist are my geek squad. They cover all sorts of - ologies. If it's science related, these guys know about it and are on the forefront of research that even the American government doesn't know about. Dr. Ichiro Maki is the doc. He patches us all up and keeps us from getting hurt in the first place. Miss Ashley Montgomery is my personal assistant, but I fondly call her the 'party planner.' We move across the world as needed, and that takes a lot of contacts and savvy skills. Miss Montgomery makes sure we all have what we need when we need it, whether it's a designer suit for an unexpected dinner or a whole closet full of clothes for a longer stay somewhere. She makes the impossible and improbable happen." She turned and grinned at me, knowing the examples she used applied to me even though the class had no idea. She walked up to the last guy in the line. He was a jittery waif of a man.

"And finally, this Mr. Matthew Oliver." She put her arm around his shoulders and whispered something in his ear. He calmed his jitters. "Matt is autistic. He is extremely special. His skill has saved my life, and the lives of everyone on this team multiple times. He is a human lie detector. Hey Matt," she said looking at him.

"Yes ma'am," he answered clearly.

"Mr. Duarte is wearing white shoes," she said. I dumbly looked down at my shoes. Matt became agitated.

"No, Miss Abby, his shoes are black, you shouldn't lie," he said.

"You are very right. Let's try one more, okay?"

"Okay, sure, that one was easy," he said.

"You are right, however, this one is a little tougher. This morning I had eggs and bacon for breakfast with Mr. Duarte in his apartment." If they weren't tuned in, they were now. She had them all wrapped up.

"No, ma'am. You had breakfast somewhere, but not here. But the part about bacon and eggs is true, and Mr. Duarte was with you," he said with an awkward smile. The class was astonished.

"You are absolutely correct. Thank you, Matt. You are very good." He smiled with her compliment. Ashley then took him by the hand, and one by one they filed out. Stafford stopped and whispered something to her. She frowned.

When the last one left, she continued. "That's my team. We work as a machine. Thankfully, Mr. Duarte has agreed to join us. All of this made me think about all of you going out into the field. If I won't go into the field without a team, what kind of person am I to send each of you out into this world alone?" She paused and let it sink in. She had me wrapped up at this point, too. She mastered the room. I should have known she would school me on presentation. There were no wild hand motions or awkward sentences. It was as if she had practiced this speech one hundred times.

"Not anymore. In fact, I will tell each one of you right now, you will pass this level of training. No one will wash out." Their faces brightened, and they all looked at each other. "But it's time to learn something new, and your very survival will depend on it. Time for another object lesson. Travis, please join me." Travis blanched but followed her instruction. She pointed to her right. He stood next to her.

"Penelope, please join us." Penny, as we fondly called her, was tiny, but she would knock your teeth out. She was all quickness and finesse when fighting.

"Now, Travis here is all brute force. He can knock you out with one punch," she said, knowing very well he had knocked her out. The image of that moment flooded through my mind. I had watched her take that hit. I watched her let it happen. I *let* it happen after yelling at her. She said we needed to let those things go, but I was angry that I hadn't trusted my instincts sooner. More than one of the students chuckled, and I cleared my throat.

"*Tadeas, stop,*" she said in my head.

"*I know,*" I replied. She knew exactly what I was thinking. It must have been written on my face.

"Can anyone tell me Penny's strengths? Samantha?" she continued with the class.

"Yes, ma'am. Penny is fast and deceiving."

"Correct. Now if I were taking bets, I'd put all my money on Penny kicking Travis's ass."

"Hey!" Travis interrupted. She turned to him quickly, and he stood back to attention.

"If you are going to participate, Mr. Reed, I suggest you learn to keep your mouth shut and not say everything that comes into your head." Whatever he said to her before class, she just got him back for it.

"Yes ma'am," he gulped.

"You both can return to your spots. Each of us has strengths and weaknesses, but when we work together, we are all strong.

From now on you will never fight alone. That goes for here as well as on the streets. When you get your assignments, you will at the very least be paired up with one of your fellow students. As you train over the coming weeks, one day someone will be your enemy, and the next they will be your friend. You will learn to adapt your attacks and reactions based on the skill set of your team. Once you get into the field, you will know the value of life. Not just yours, but whomever else is out there with you. You will be the ambassadors of this new philosophy and carry it out to the crews. I expect a lot of all of you. As does Mr. Duarte. We both agree that each of you are up to the task. Mr. Duarte." She handed the class back to me.

"Alright, let's test this out. The first fight will be split down the middle of the room. Each section has 6 people. Pick a partner. You will face off against two people from the other side of the room. You have 30 seconds to pick a partner."

That started it all. They engaged in the teaching and the philosophy of working together immediately. I was proud of them. Abby was pleased, too. She stepped in to show techniques. She would have made a great trainer. We mixed them up again after several rounds. They were adapting and putting forth a good effort. There were a couple of mishaps. I think Travis was a bit off his game. He doesn't play well with others unless it's in a closet, apparently. He tried though. I'll give him that. I dismissed them from class. When the last one left, I looked at her.

"Well?" she asked. I walked up to her and hugged her, and she laughed. "I guess that means you are pleased."

"Yes, it was awesome." I spun away from her, pumping my fists. We had made a huge difference in their lives in just a couple of hours. She had trusted me to do it.

"Well, I'm excited they all responded to it," she said.

"And good grief, you know how to hold a room. They were all tuned in. Nice to meet the team by the way," I said.

"There will be a formal meeting tomorrow evening," she said.

"Oh yeah?"

"I'm throwing you a welcoming party. Of course, Grandfather has taken it over, but it will still be a party, just a huge one. If that's okay with you though, I don't want to put you in a strange situation," she said.

"Why stop now?"

"Touché."

"What did Travis say to you?"

"Ugh. He's a pig. By the way, both he and Samantha are marked, which means someone upstairs is watching them both." Marked meant they were picked as favorites by someone in the Agency, and that person would ultimately decide where they were assigned.

"What did he say?"

"I guess he thought since I stood with students that he could talk to me like that, but I'll adjust his attitude as needed. Or rather you will. Unless you want me to come back," she said.

"Of course, I want you to be here as much as possible. This is your idea as much as mine. No need to hide behind the glass. Now, stop with the diversion tactic, and tell me what he said," I pushed.

"I don't even want to repeat it. Basically, suggested I should join his closet activities, and that he was sorry for punching me out. I fist bumped the pig just for show," she said.

"Why on earth would he say that in my class?"

"I don't know. But I think we might need to revisit the whole 'live and let live' of fucking all over this damn training center," she said. "That could get out of hand very quickly."

"I agree with that," I said. I never understood it either. Get a room on the weekends. I thought this whole place should be about training. Let them do that on their own time. "What about Stafford?"

"Mr. Stafford said my car was brought back this afternoon from being detailed after someone got dirt all in the inside of that beautiful machine." She lifted her eyebrow at me.

"Who would do such a thing?"

"A moron that decided to go out and drink alone."

"Guilty," I said. "I'm glad it's cleaned up. I told George to send me the bill."

"Oh, all George did was call Ashley. She really does arrange everything."

"Like my whole new closet of clothes?" I asked.

She nodded. "Just like that. You look good in green."

I wanted to say that she looked good in everything. It was the truth, and I had more than noticed. I kept my cheesy comment to myself. "So, what's the plan for the afternoon?"

"I've got to get up to my office and get some work done. You have class this afternoon?"

"No, they are in computer training this afternoon," I said.

"Great, you are welcome to hang out with me. I've got to get the emails taken care of and see what my guys found overnight about the GEA. And I'm hungry. A good time to get that delivery number," she said.

"Sounds like a plan. How will I be of any help?"

"Well if I order food, you can help me eat it."

"I suppose that's something," I admitted.

"No, you can go through the emails with me. I want you to see it all. Let's end this communication spell too, *Adimo*."

"Okay," I said. Having the spell was extremely helpful. I could see where in a tense situation or fight having it would make a huge difference.

We went to her office and spent the rest of the afternoon and evening working on information that the team sent us. We focused on the GEA and the man-made earthquake theory. We did our own research on the net trying to find as much info as we could on all of it. She ordered pizza which didn't require the number, but she gave me the number anyway. I went upstairs to get the food while she closed everything down in the office. We had decided to go check out the apartment that Ashley fixed up for her in the Agency.

I stepped out of the elevator on the surface in the abandoned airfield office, and immediately my hairs stood on end. Reaching down to my boot, I pulled out the knife I kept hidden there. It was only a 3.5-inch blade, but it was better than nothing. I could do damage with it, if needed. A car idled just outside the gutted building, but no one was in it. I slowly walked into the open. I never saw him coming, but I felt him. A large figure hit me on my left side sending us both flying into a stack of old desks. I kicked the invisible thing off me. It grunted like a man. Taking several blind swings into the air, I hit nothing. If I shifted into the spirit world, I knew could see him. I pulled on the edge of the plane and pulled my body into it. Before me stood a tanned Native American man with long black hair, he grinned at me with bright white teeth.

"Come on buddy, play fair," I said, ready for anything he could throw at me.

"You are a predictable boy. You are mine. She can't save you here," he laughed, and I felt shadows pour out of the floor and up around me. I could not move. I had played right into his hand. He was right, too. Abby couldn't shift to the spirit world without me. I couldn't even pull her through, because I was slowly being bound by the shadows. She didn't even know I needed help. I focused on her hoping the connection we had earlier would still work. We had spoken to each other in the class-room. Maybe that spell had a lingering effect. My life depended on it working now.

"Abby! Help me!"

CHAPTER 32

ABIGAIL

"*Abby,*

I know you are extremely busy with that sexy new partner. At the very least, I hope you are enjoying his company. Don't hold back my dear. You are in a long line of immortals that get what they want. Just take him. I seriously doubt he would protest. And if you don't want him, I do. I need you to sign these papers before your grandfather roasts me. I'll catch you tomorrow at the compound. - Aunt Li"

I WAS SURE THAT ALL MY AUNT EVER TRULY THOUGHT ABOUT WAS sex. It didn't matter how much I tried to explain to her why I was not sleeping with him. She just couldn't understand. Grandfather said the whole world had gone Fae. I laughed, but he was right. Everybody was having sex with everybody. I'll make a point to see Lianne tomorrow and see what papers she needed me to sign.

I let myself entertain for a moment a relationship with Tadeas. For that moment, I came up with fifty excuses why it should not happen. Top on the list was his relationship with Meredith. I had the feeling that once things settled down, and he admitted to himself he wasn't going to hurt her that there would be real feelings there. Clearly, there were on her side, but he held back. The more he accepted his role as a guardian, he would see that a relationship would only enhance that role. You become a better protector when you have more to protect.

What was taking so long? I stood up in my chair, and I felt a wave of fear rush over me.

"Abby! Help me!"

His voice sounded like a choking panic. My adrenaline kicked in, and I sprinted out of my office. I hit the button for the elevator. This was one of those moments when being in an underground bunker didn't help. I started focusing on my magic, as I drew power from the surrounding earth. I couldn't use any sort of earth magic inside the facility, but I knew Tadeas was on the surface. I would not want to shake the whole facility down.

It was safer if I pulled within myself. I knew there was power there, despite knowing it would exhaust me. I called the four orbs to my hand, and they appeared. Cold iron, hollow steel, quartz crystal and molten sun, all elements I could control easily. I could mold, morph, conduct and flame anything with them. No matter what I faced. I had an answer right in my hand.

By the time I reached the top, the power inside of me thumped. I stepped out of the elevator but saw nothing. I could feel him though. His aura was fading quickly. I switched to the magical spectrum, and I saw the man. Nalusa Chito, a Choctaw soul eater, stood laughing at a figure that only barely pulsed with a dying light. He could not see me. The darkest parts of his form leaked over into this plane. A seething black smoke, a shadow man. I knew who had tried to take Tadeas on his way home from Boulder.

Suddenly, I sensed a second presence nearby. There were two of them the night they tried to take Tadeas. I centered my focus on the crystal orb. *"RESONO,"* I shouted. The power in my voice amplified and resonated through the derelict building. The rafters shook as a wave of visible sound reverberated through the building.

"I have you now," I said, moving toward the hidden figure in the back corner of the room. I pulled the steel ball to my left hand and closed my hand around it. I formed my hand into a gun like kids do when playing cops and robbers. I pulled the fake trigger, and said, *"Ecfundo."* The steel orb shot out of my hand like a bullet from a gun. At the last moment, the figure threw up a shield, and the orb ricocheted off into the darkness. I could feel it as I had all three of the physical items marked, but I let them think I ran out of ammo.

The echoing crystal continued to pound the sound of my voice, echoing over and over the Latin command. Tadeas' aura continued to fade, but I could feel him fighting the darkness that surrounded him. I reached deep for the edge of the spirit world like I had felt Tadeas do when he shifted. I could feel it on the edge of my hand. I concentrated on touching it. It kept slipping out of my hand. I shouted his name in my head, *"Tadeas!"* I felt the fringe as if somehow, he pushed it to me and grasped it with my left hand and yanked it across me like a cool, dark blanket. I wasn't sure he had pulled me in or if I managed it myself.

I tried to pull the sun orb to me, but it winked out. It didn't work in this realm. I only had the hollow steel left, and I wasn't sure it would do any good for me here. I closed my right hand, and it too disappeared.

A black tornado of smoke swirled around Tadeas. I tried to call his name, but the smoke started filling the room. I took a deep breath just before it consumed me. Everything was cold here. I tried to come up with a translation of my magic here. I did not want to pull the sword, but I would not let him take

Tadeas. I made my way to him in the chaos. I could hear Chito laughing. He believed he had won.

"Oh, dear Abigail. If only my friend Lincoln could see how weak you've become, how desperately you fight for this one who is nowhere near his equal. I miss him. He always was a good fighter. This is almost too easy," he taunted.

I spun around to where I heard his voice. Silently, I prayed. Please don't let me hurt Tadeas. I put my hands out wide and spread my fingers, and called the sword, "*Vengence mea, et ego retribuam!*"

A purple flash of light strobed through the shadows. The hilt hit my hand. The white dress from the vault encircled me and a loud report of thunder echoed through the spirit world. I waited for the angel to take over my body, but nothing happened. I stood with the sword to a middle fighting stance. It sang in my hands.

"*Et erit lux,*" I called. The purple glow stretched out beyond me, and as it pulsed outward, it consumed the darkness. The light spell was not one that I had learned how to do. It was as if the sword taught me to use it. Once the light reached the edges of the building, I could see Chito clearly. He looked human. No more shadow. No more darkness. I lowered my eyes to him. "You have one warning. Drop your spells and walk away. If you do not, I will destroy you here and now."

"Where did you get that sword?" he growled.

"It was given to me. It is far more powerful than I," I said as I took a step toward him. I could hear Tadeas moving behind me, then he shifted. The light had broken his bonds. He walked up next to me, crouched, and growled a low continuous rumble. The figure, clearly a woman, darted out the back door. "Go, I've got this," I said, and he sprinted off after her.

"*Who is she?*"

"*Couldn't see her well. Don't know. Be cautious. Don't chase her too far,*" I warned.

"*No scent. She's gone. Abby, is that the sword?*"

"No time. Circle around behind him."

Nalusa thought for a moment, and it occurred to him that in a second that this sword could strike him down. I saw it register in his face. I had an implement that could erase him. His many years would be laid to waste at my feet. He pulled power and a ball of shadow hurled toward me. I did not move. It hit the sword and dissipated.

"It seems you've won this day, my fair angel," he bowed to me, winking out in shadow. I felt the pull of our reality surge over me. Tadeas shifted us back. He walked toward me in human form and stopped several feet from me. I slid the sword into the sheath attached to the leather belt.

I hadn't noticed the storm had arrived other than the clap of thunder. It was violent and loud.

"Did Gabriel or one of the other angels come?" he asked.

"No, why? Are you okay?" He was bruised. He must have struggled so hard against the bonds that he hurt himself. I walked over to him, and finally used the earth power that I pulled in, *"Consano."* I waved my hand over his arms, chest, and legs.

"Stop. I'm fine. Look at me," he said. He reached up, touching my face.

"What is it?" Then I remembered the island when Gabriel had come, my face glowed with a luminescence that none of us could explain. I looked away because before it was extremely strange. I had only seen it after it started to fade. "He wasn't here," I whispered.

"It wasn't him. It's you," he said.

"I don't understand," I said. "When the sword hit my hand, the angel didn't take over like before when I used it."

"Before you were commanded to use it. This time you chose to use it. Right?"

"Yes."

"I can only tell you what I saw," he said.

"What did you see?" I asked.

323

"You looked like an angel to me," he said.

I shook my head. "No that isn't possible. I'm human. Well, I mean wielder, yes. Maybe partly Fae, but not celestial in any way, shape, or form. I can't be an angel. What just happened?" I started to feel overwhelmed. The thoughts in my head raced. What was I? Why would my grandfather lie to me about my parents? It couldn't be. I physically shook. The thoughts swirled through me like Chito's shadows. I felt like I was being crushed from the inside out. They were that close to the compound. They were waiting on him as if they knew he would come to the surface. Why would Chito take his soul? Where did Chito fit into all of this? Who was the woman?

"Come back," he said gently. "Abby, you gotta come back to me." His voice was as fearful as I felt. I could barely hear him from the depths of the thoughts that overwhelmed me.

"Can you send the sword back to the vault, Abby?" He grabbed my chin firmly, trying to force me to focus on his eyes. "Look at me, come back. You've gone too far. Please."

"*Fit iustitia*," I muttered. The sword and dress winked out. I stood there as I did before in my utility pants and shirt. The storm ceased around us and only the calm pattering of rain echoed on the roof. I leaned into him and put my forehead on his shoulder. "What am I?"

"I don't have the answer to that, but to me, you were my guardian. You came for me when I called," he said. "Come on, we should go back inside." He gently guided me toward the elevator. I stepped in and leaned against the back wall.

"Is my face really glowing again?" I asked, dumbfounded.

He didn't answer.

I STOOD IN FRONT OF THE MIRROR IN THE NEW APARTMENT I HAD acquired within the compound. Apparently, it was the only vacant one in the whole building. I was on the third floor. Ashley had the whole thing furnished for me. I asked her to make it comfortable, not fancy. It had two bedrooms, that way if Tadeas ever needed to stay, he could.

I didn't even know what to say about the iridescent look of my face. I would have to call George and get answers. While I inspected my face, Tadeas stood behind me watching me. He leaned against the wall. He grimaced, looking down at his feet like he did when he was unsure of himself.

I spun around and looked at him. "No, don't you dare do that right now."

"Do what?" he muttered.

"You feel like you did no good in that situation." I knew exactly what he was thinking.

"Abby, I was out the door for all of 60 seconds, and he had me bound," he protested.

"No, please don't do this right now," I walked over to him.

"You can question yourself, but I can't, is that it?" he said frustrated, but not angry.

"You are right. Are we both having a pity party, or are we both getting over it?" I asked.

"Ugh," he said in frustrated man language. "You make me want to scream sometimes." We were both searching ourselves for answers.

"We will figure it out. It takes time. It's never easy," I said.

"What? Easy to learn to trust you? I trust you completely, Abby. You saved my ass up there," he pointed out.

"No. It takes time to learn to trust your own abilities. Chito knows you haven't done a lot of fieldwork. He used your lack of knowledge against you. I just had no idea they would be so bold to take you on our doorstep," I said.

"How am I supposed to learn everything? I was just trying to get pizza, dammit."

I reached into the dark part of my soul that I know existed, and I pulled the shadows around him just like Chito had.

"What are you doing? Abby, stop. Please stop," he begged.

"No. Get out of it," I said firmly.

"I don't know how," he panicked.

"Yes, you do." Holding the dark spell that long pulled on my heart, and it started to ache. It pained me to do it. I felt the anger rising up in him, and the cold blanket ripped over us again. He shifted to his jaguar form. The shadows around him dissipated. I went to my knees before him. "You are more powerful than you know. I will spend every moment teaching you what I can. I have failed you to this point. I am so sorry."

I slumped from the darkness of the spell. I had pulled the power from myself to create the shadows, and I was already spent from the fight above the surface. He pulled us back into our home plane, and he sat on the bathroom floor with me. I stumbled trying to get up, but he continued to sit there staring. I needed to get to the bed. The spells had taken more out of me than I had realized. I didn't switch on the light. My weakness pulled me to my knees just before I got to the bed. I grabbed the blanket, trying to pull myself closer to the bed.

Suddenly, his arms linked under mine, and he gently lifted me up. He helped me have a slow descent into the bed. My head hit the pillow. He pulled my boots off. Then he arranged the covers so I could slide my legs under them. He leaned over me with a sadness in his eyes that I wanted to make go away. I just didn't have the energy to do it at the moment.

"I don't blame you. I blame myself for hiding away in a basement for so many years," he said. I didn't know what else to say to him. He hurt. I hurt. We were one big ball of hurt. I slowly faded into blackness.

As I woke up, I became immediately aware of someone in the bed with me. I let out a bit of a gasp when my eyes opened. "Oh!"

Tadeas laid on the other side of the bed on his side facing me. His eyes were closed. He was laying on the edge of the bed as far away from me as possible. He slowly opened his eyes. "The glow has faded," he said. He didn't move.

I closed my eyes tight and tried to recall the last bit of last night. He had made sure that I got to the bed, and to my surprise, he didn't leave me alone. However, I remembered the sad statement he made before I drifted off to sleep. I didn't want him to blame himself.

He eased up and turned his back to me sitting on the bed. "I did not want to leave you since you saved me last night. Felt like I should at least make sure you were okay after the sword and shadows."

"Thank you," I said quietly. He worked his way to a speech to say something I knew would not like.

"I need some space today, Abby. Please see if you can call off this party thing for tonight. I just can't do it today," he said.

"What about class today?" I asked.

"It's only a half day. They have final weapons training today. I'll cover it if you don't mind. Then I just need a little space, because I don't know what I'm doing here. You pulled a stunt last night to save me, which you would not have had to do if I weren't completely incompetent. Fighting and instructing these kids is nothing like what's out there. Right now, I don't think I'm ready for it. I'm not backing out on you. I just need to think."

I was crushed. I had a feeling our differences were completely resolved, but we needed more time with each other. I needed to teach him. That way he would know what was out there. Not less time. He still sat facing the wall with his back to me. I got up and moved toward the door.

"If you are going to work with me Tadeas, there will be days that I pull power to save you. Then there will be days when you keep me focused, shift, and save me. And on-the-job training is brutal but extremely effective. We need more time together, not less if we are going to do this." I turned back to look at him. His back was straight as a board. The tension in his shoulders was evident.

"It won't be today," he said, walking toward the bedroom door with me. I honestly was not trying to block his way at least not consciously. I moved a little aside so he could go through. He stopped right in front of me. He leaned over and kissed my forehead and went out of the apartment.

"Bloody hell," I cursed the empty room.

I stood there for a minute not knowing what to do. I knew I'd have to make a visit to my grandfather that I didn't want to make. I'm sure he would have all sorts of awful things to say. I was also sure he would not cancel the party tonight. He loved to throw a good party. After taking a shower, I put on a white A-line midi dress with a touch of black lace on the bottom hem. I added matching black pumps and pulled my hair back out of my face. Grandfather would not want me showing up in a t-shirt and cargo pants. I looked at myself in the mirror. The strange iridescent was almost gone. I tried my best not to think about Tadeas, but I did. I just did not know what to do anymore. I took a deep breath and went to visit a Titan.

As I entered the office, grandfather stood up from his desk and hugged me as he had in recent days. He stopped in his tracks. "What the hell is on your face?"

"A piece of heaven," I said. Sounded good against his swear.

He walked up and touched it. "It's not makeup."

"No, it isn't. Something happened last night," I said.

"Sit down and tell me about it," he said.

"I'm not sitting in that chair," I said. He chuckled.

"You, my dear, are immune to the chair."

"Sort of," I agreed, but I sat down anyway.

"Tell me what happened? And where is your new partner? The party tonight is going to be grand!" he exclaimed. He was excited. It had been some time since we had a real party around here.

I proceeded to tell him about Gabriel's visit to the island. Then I told him everything about last night and everything about this morning. His excitement turned to displeasure.

"I am not canceling the party," he proclaimed as if that were the most important thing in all that I had told him. Of course, knowing him, he probably knew most of it anyway.

"I don't care about the party," I exclaimed. "I called an angelic sword to my hand, and instead of it controlling me, I controlled it. Only an angel could have done such a thing. I think you have some explaining to do."

"You are not an angel, my dear." He looked pained for a moment. I had sat in the chair willingly which meant I had him. If I sat in the chair knowing its purpose, he had to be truthful with me. He grimaced with the realization. I narrowed my eyes at him.

"Yes, you have me," he admitted. He wasn't dumb or oblivious. And honestly, I didn't think I could pull it off. It was time to find out some of the things I wanted to know. However, I knew if he was bound by oath, it didn't matter what questions I asked, there were some that even the chair could not force out of him.

"What am I?"

"You are many things, Abby. You are an extremely powerful wielder. You are the daughter of a powerful wielder. Your mother's secret I am bound by oath not to speak, but I think you know that she is a powerful Faerie. In your heart, you know. There were deals we had to make to ensure that you were returned to us after your death. I do not know the angels' purposes in giving you the sword, but they did give it to you, Abby. They trusted you with it. I would think that included using it as you saw fit as long as you used it for a righteous reason. I cannot think of anything more righteous than saving the life of another. You will have to talk to George to get the answers you seek," he suggested.

"George isn't going to tell me anything," I spouted in frustration.

"As for canceling the party, I'm sorry, but there are too many invites that have gone out. We have guests here from all over the world, and I will not be an inhospitable host. I will talk to Duarte. Let me handle it."

"Please don't make things worse between us," I begged.

"I'll try not to. You will just have to trust me."

"Could you not threaten him, please?" I pleaded. "I know you did before which was inappropriate."

"I will make no promises, Abby. Now go see your Aunt and sign the paperwork that she has, okay?" He was a Titan. He was used to getting his way. There was nothing more I could have gotten out of him. I failed in mission number one today.

As I got up to leave, he said before I opened the door, "I love you with all my heart, Abby. I am deeply proud of you. Please do not let this darken your spirit. It's been extremely nice having you here. I don't want to lose you again."

"I love you, too," I said, then I slipped out the door. His speeches to me were becoming more and more kind. It felt like he was trying to make up for lost time. I went to the elevator and pressed the button for the floor with Aunt Lianne's office.

When I reached the door, I found a hand-written note for me.

"A, went for lunch with a handsome man, be back soon, L."

Mission number two. Failed.

I got back in the elevator and went down to my office. When I opened the door, a man sat in the chair opposite my desk. My heart jumped for a moment because I thought it was Tadeas. It wasn't. It was Jeremy Stafford.

"Hey Jay, what's up?" I tried to sound cheerful.

"Hello, beautiful. Wow! You look great in that dress. I thought I'd drop by and see if you wanted to go grab lunch with me?" He flashed me a toothy smile. He had a Fae mother, too which made him a Halfling. He stood about 6 feet tall. He had a strong jaw and deep-set dark blue eyes. They had a bit of an almond shape to them as if he had just a twinge of Asian in him.

"I'm not feeling up to it today. I've got things to get done before this evening. You are coming, right?" I asked as I sat down at the desk.

"Absolutely. It's been too long since I've been to a good party. I'm hoping I can find a partner for the evening, and perhaps the after party," he grinned at me slyly. He was good-looking. Jay and I had a long relationship. We might have even tried to go out a couple of times, but he always wanted more than just dinner.

"I'm sure there will be many willing and beautiful women there tonight. You have a knack for finding the available women," I laughed. Jeremy could be described as a playboy. Handsome, rich, smart, witty and from what I heard very good in bed. He was also my driver. He had gotten all of us out of extra-ordinarily dangerous spots. I always knew he had my back even if it was just to catch the view.

"Actually, I had hoped it would be you," he said.

"Oh no, don't you start that suave game with me, Jay," I warned him.

"Honest. It's not a game. I really would like a chance, Abby. I know that when we've gone out before I pushed for things I shouldn't have. I'm getting old even though I don't look it. Sleeping with all the different girls all the time, while fun, does nothing for me the next day. You are amazing and have always been amazing to me. You've been isolated from us for too long. Seeing you yesterday in the class, owning that whole room, it reminded me of how attracted to you I am even after all this time." He sounded sincere.

I shook my head. I didn't believe him. He just thought if he pulled at my female sensibilities I'd give into him. "Jay, I've known you for too long. It's not going to work."

"I know that's what you think, and I will prove it to you if I have to. Will you at least dance with me just once tonight? I know you've got your new partner. Maybe you are with him already. I don't care. I'll wait for you, Abby," he said.

"I'm not with him," I said admitting it to him. I could have strung it along. I had warned Tadeas yesterday that everyone we come across will think we are together. Just something we would have to deal with along the way.

"So, you aren't going to the party with him tonight? You don't have a date?"

"I don't need a date, Jay. I don't want one."

"One dance, please."

"Okay," I gave in. "Just one, and during it, you keep your hands where they should be."

He let out a whoop and jumped up. "Just remember where I think my hands should be and where you think they should be are probably two different things!"

"Dammit Jay. You almost had me believing you wanted to change," I said shaking my head at him.

He walked around to the back of my chair and hung his arms around me being careful not to touch anything he shouldn't. I flinched a little with the touch. "I don't *want* to change, Abby. I *have* changed." He kissed me on the cheek. I looked up at him trying to determine if he was just playing around again. He wasn't. He was serious. I stood up in front of him, and he didn't budge.

"I see," I said.

"Do you see? Doesn't matter if you do or not, I will show you," he said as he stepped closer. I couldn't move backward because my chair was behind me. He slid his right hand around my waist and pulled me closer to him. My heartbeat raced. My emotions were all over the place. If he was being this forward, then he had not changed. 'He's just playing the game a different way', I told myself. He leaned over until our noses almost touched. I could feel his breath on my cheek. Then I felt it. Someone was coming down the hallway. I knew exactly who it was and I didn't want him to find me this way. Jay didn't let go. I locked eyes with him. He watched me panic. A smile spread across his handsome face. "I'll see you tonight, beautiful."

Jay stepped back as the door swung open, and Tadeas came in without knocking. His eyes were wide, but he seemed surprised as if he expected to find something other than Jay and I talking. I didn't know how he knew something was going on, but he did. Another animal instinct.

As Jay walked out, he patted Tadeas on the shoulder and said, "See you tonight, big guy."

Tadeas didn't respond to him and didn't take his eyes off of me. I was completely out of sorts.

"What are you doing here?" I said. It sounded angry. I was a bit upset with him, but it came out all wrong because I was rattled by Jay's overt behavior. It had never really bothered me before, but this time seemed different.

"Did I interrupt something? If I did, I can come back later," he said. He sounded hurt.

"No, Jay is just being the Half-Fae bad boy that he knows how to be. That's all," I tried to brush it off.

"He's trying to be a bad boy with you?" he asked.

"Yeah, he's always trying to." I didn't want to come out like I was bragging. Jay was just being Jay though. It didn't mean anything.

"Trying to what, Abby?"

"You know," I said and waved my hand around trying to dismiss it. I was even more uncomfortable now. I was definitely not to the comfort point where I could talk about sex with Tadeas. Not even close.

"He's trying to sleep with you," he blurted.

"I guess. I dunno," I still tried to dismiss it. I wasn't sure why that mattered to Tadeas either. He was the one that wanted some space.

"Has he before now?"

"Has he tried before?" I asked. This was going to hell in a handbasket very quickly.

"No, have you slept with him?" he growled at me.

"I'm pretty sure that's not any of your damned business," I said.

"Oh, how many others on your team have you been with?" he said, assuming I had slept with Jay.

"Why does it matter to you, Tadeas? You are the one that wanted some space this morning. Yet, here you are in my office. This is not the space I thought you wanted." I stood up, clicking off my computer. I marched around the desk and got in his face. If he wanted to fight, I was more than willing. "It isn't your business, but because I care about you, you should know that I've never slept with him nor any other person on my team. I'm not even sure you deserve that little tidbit of information, but there it is. Unless you have some other business beside who I am not fucking, I'm gonna go back to my apartment, because my grandfather is not going to cancel this damn party and even if you don't show up, I have to go. I have no choice." I gritted my teeth. He just looked at me dismayed. I marched out the door to the stairwell. When I got halfway he followed me into the stairs. I stopped and looked at him waiting for him to say something.

"I left my boots in your apartment, and the door was locked. I wanted to get them back," he said simply.

I marched back up the half flight to him. "No, you don't get to throw this back on me like you were doing something innocent. You came into that office knowing someone was in there with me. You knew a man was in there. I could feel you in the hallway the moment you stepped out of the stairwell. Don't play games with me, Tadeas. I'm *done* with the games. Jay was in there practically throwing himself at me like he *always* does, and I *always* tell him no. You have no right to ask who I am with, who I have been with, or to assume who I will ever be with." I turned back around and went back down to the 3rd-floor doorway and stopped. "Come get your damn boots."

He followed at a distance. When we entered the apartment, I went and poured a glass of Buffalo Trace. He went back into the bedroom and picked up the boots. When he headed to the door, I decided I wasn't done with him yet. "Tadeas?"

He stopped in his tracks. "Hm?" He didn't look at me.

"How many pairs of those boots do you own right now? How many are in this building?" I pried, knowing the boots were an excuse.

"I got over myself and wanted to talk to you."

He stabbed me in the heart. I oozed hurt, anger, and frustration. "Talk about what?"

"Never mind," he said, walking out the door.

I had already broken enough drinking vessels, but I sure wanted to throw this one.

CHAPTER 33

ABIGAIL

By the time Ashley arrived to check on me before the party, I had finished off about half of the bottle of bourbon. Somehow, I managed to get dressed and fix my hair. I opened the door when she knocked.

"Hey Ash," I said. She rolled her eyes at me, walked in, and pulled my glass away from me at the same time. Technically, I was not drunk. It took a lot for me to be drunk, but pair the half bottle with an empty stomach, and. I was well on my way to happy town.

"You've got to be kidding me!" she exclaimed. I shut the door behind her, rolling my eyes.

"I'm not drunk," I said fairly convincingly.

"Oh really? Just tipsy then?" I laughed at her.

"Tipsy is a funny word," I laughed at myself.

"You aren't funny. What happened?" she said. She had known me for years, and really was the only woman I got along with for any extended period. I walked over to the soft leather couch that she picked out for my apartment and plopped down.

"We had an argument. By the way, this couch, yeah, it's great."

She shook her head at me and sat down on the side chair. She wore a lovely dusty rose tea length dress with a spring floral motif wrapping around her waist and up over her right shoulder. She had on pearls. Her deep auburn hair was curled, falling down around her face. She was gorgeous. "Is he coming tonight?" She sounded concerned.

"I don't know. Probably not. You look lovely," I said to her. "You don't usually wear pink." I had always told her she would look good in a rose color, but she was afraid it would clash with her red hair.

She looked nervous all of a sudden. "Oh, yeah I see you. Spill it!"

She smiled, quirking her lips to the side. "I've been seeing someone."

I moved to the edge of the couch. It had been a while since she dated anyone, and I didn't know anyone that could convince her to wear pink. "And this someone is?"

"Ichiro."

"You are dating the doc! It's about damn time!" I squealed, moving down to the end of the couch. There were times I could be an all-out girl. "He's adorable. When did this start? And why didn't you tell me?"

"It happened while you were downstairs. He offered to take me for a drink since my best friend decided to chase a cat." I laughed at that one.

"You liked the idea," I accused. "In fact, I think you were the only one who did. You were wrong by the way. It was a bad idea." I pretended to blame her.

"Doesn't matter, he's hot," she said.

"Yeah, well, he's hot and angry at me. Truthfully, I'm not

really happy with him at the moment. He can just go be hot somewhere else," I said. Women can talk about hot guys, and the other woman realizes you have no intention of sleeping with him.

"Did you sleep with him?" Okay, maybe not.

"Bite your tongue," I said. "No, I didn't. In fact, the fight started over him asking me if I slept with Jay."

"Oh, he didn't like that you had," she said.

"What! Ash, you know I have never slept with Jay Stafford," I shot back at her. "But I didn't tell him that to start with. I pretty much let him think what he wanted. I was pissed he even asked."

"What made him ask?"

"He walked in on Jay in my office with me being Jay," I said.

"No wonder Abby! Were you making out or something?" she asked.

"Hell no! But Jay is acting weird. He said he's changed, and he wanted us to make a real go at it," her eyes got wide. "What do you know about that?"

"He asked me if I thought you would. He said he's tired of a different woman all the time. He said you are the only one he had ever considered for something long term. He seemed genuine," she explained.

"Oh please. He has never done anything except try to get in my pants, or up my skirt or whatever," I said.

"Are you wearing that?" she said changing the subject.

"What's wrong with this?" I said. The dress was a high-low dress. It was a royal blue and hung to my knees in the front and to my calves in the back. I had on black high heel sandals.

"Well, at least your hair looks good. I'll go pick out a different dress," she said going into my room. I got up, following her. She knew more about fashion than I did, and what I know I learned from her. There was no use in arguing with her. She was going to dress me whether I liked it or not. At the moment, I really didn't care what I wore to the party. The guest of honor wouldn't even be there.

"Back to Tadeas, do you like him? Like that, I mean," she asked.

"No. I haven't had time to think of him like that," I lied.

"Really? Your brain can think about 10 different things at once. A dozen if you try hard," she said.

"He's amazing, but we are never on the same page. It's only been a few days, but I've wanted to throat punch him at least twice. I've lost my temper twice. I should have never tried to find a new partner," I groaned.

"So, the answer is yes. Gotcha," she said.

"Ash, please don't." I suddenly felt really sad, watching her go through my closet and looking back to the shoe rack to match up an outfit.

She stopped for a moment and looked at me. "I had hoped that you would find someone you trusted again. That maybe in the future you could fall in love. Abby, it's been long enough. Don't hide your heart away forever. To be honest, you work better when you have someone with you."

"It's not that I don't trust him. We are just like oil and water."

"This one!" She pulled out a sleeveless nude dress with a slate blue chiffon overlay. Slate blue sequins and embroidery shaped like vines accented the dress from the neckline and dwindled to the bottom of the full-length dress. She added a strappy pair of slate blue pumps.

"Where did that come from?" I asked. "That is not one of my dresses."

"Sure, it is. I bought it for you," she admitted.

"When?"

She smiled devilishly. "This morning."

I just shook my head as I started taking the navy one off. I really didn't care. It was a pretty dress. A new dress to wear might make me feel better.

I looked at myself in the mirror in the bedroom. "You did well."

"Of course, I did," she replied, "now let me do something with your hair."

"You said nothing was wrong with my hair," I exclaimed. She produced a glittering comb in a matching blue that was shaped almost identically to the vines on the dress. No sense in stopping her now. I sat down in a chair at the dining room table, and she sat down a glass of ice water and a peanut butter sandwich.

"Eat," she said. I ate as my surrogate sister fixed my hair for the party.

The alcohol started wearing off, and I was just sad. "I'm going to move to Jakarta or Edinburgh."

"Stop being a drama queen," she said finishing up. "You guys will work it out. I've got to get going. Ichiro will be waiting on me."

Looking at myself in the bathroom mirror, I was impressed with the choices. It looked very nice. My golden locks were swept up around my head and braided in spots. The comb aligned perfectly with one of the braids. Little loose strands fell around my head. "It looks great, Ash. I'm incredibly happy for you, too."

She hugged me from behind. "I love ya, Abby. Hang in there." I walked her to the door.

"Thanks again, Ash. Not for the dress and hair, but for just being here," I said.

"Anytime," she said. "Besides you know what the two of you need to do?"

"What?" I laughed at her playful tone.

She reached for the doorknob and said as she opened the door, "You two just need to kiss and makeup."

I started to laugh until I saw him standing at the door just about to knock. He wore a black suit and a slate blue tie which was the exact color of my dress hung untied around his neck.

"Damn Ash," I said wincing. I knew then she had set me up.

"Oh, hello, Mr. Duarte," she said inviting him in with a hand wave.

"You can call me Tadeas," he said to her, but he didn't take his eyes off me.

"I'm Ashley or Ash. What about Tay?"

He looked at her with a "you've got to be kidding me look."

"Um, what about Deas?" she suggested.

"No, Ashley. I like just Tadeas," he laughed at her.

"Jag," I said.

Ashley cooed. "Oh, I love it! Yes, you look like a Jag."

"No," he said shaking his head at both of us. I saw the glint in his eye though. He liked it.

"Too late. Jag it is," Ashley said as she walked out the door. "See you two in a bit."

"Seriously?" he said to me. I just shrugged.

"I didn't think she would take it and run with it," I said. "You are going?"

"I will if you know someone who can tie this damn thing for me," he said pointing at the tie.

"Come here, I'll do it," I offered. He walked up to me, and I tied the tie as I had many times before he came along. Lincoln hated ties, and I always had to tie them for him. Tadeas' cologne floated around me. He smelled wonderful, and his hair looked great, too. When I finished, I pushed down his lapel and straightened the slate blue handkerchief in his pocket. He looked unbelievably handsome. I gritted my teeth. This was ridiculous. Ashley was ten times worse than me about sneaking around and doing stuff. Of course, that's what I paid her to do.

"You look gorgeous, Abby," he said kindly. I still felt the tension between us.

"You look very nice, too," I returned the compliment. He left the 5 o'clock shadow, and it gave him a rugged look. His hair hung just a bit on the left side of his forehead. I reminded myself he said he wanted a haircut, but I loved it like that. I did not know what else to say.

"Have you eaten?" he asked.

"Huh? Yeah, Ashley made me eat a sandwich," I said. "Why would you ask that?" I tried to tone down the edge in my voice, but it was still there.

"She said you've had a few drinks. I didn't mean anything by it," he said backing away from me.

"Yeah, well, unfortunately, the alcohol has worn off," I said.

"Maybe we can agree to get through tonight without ripping each other's heads off," he suggested.

I closed my eyes and winced. "Yeah, maybe we can."

"Alright." He held his hand out to me. "Let's go."

I took it, and we went out the door cursing my best friend for setting me up.

CHAPTER 34

TADEAS

When she took my hand, hers felt like ice. Ashley told me when she brought the tie by that she spied on her earlier, and that she had made her way through half a bottle of bourbon. I'm pretty sure I could have put down a whole bottle. She seemed fine now though. The most unusual thing at the moment was her heart rate. Her normal steady rhythm had disappeared. Instead, it pulsed quickly. She was genuinely nervous.

As we rode the elevator, I tucked her hand into the crook of my arm. She smelled like honeysuckle to me. "You cold?" I asked.

"No just nervous," she admitted.

"Why? Something you want to give me a heads up on?" I asked.

"This is grandfather's party. I don't know what he has in store, but I promise that I'll help you through it if he pulls anything. Do you dance at all?" she asked.

"Not really," I said. "I can sway to a beat."

"Okay, that will do," she said. She looked up at me. "Did he threaten you?"

"No." Surprising her, I reached over and hit the emergency stop on the elevator. It jolted to a stop.

A voice came over the speaker. "What's the emergency?"

"Barry, this is Abigail Davenport. I just needed a moment to talk to my friend. Please don't restart the elevator," she said quickly. She picked up on things easily.

"Yes, ma'am," he said, then I heard the speaker click off.

"He called me up there this afternoon and said that he appreciated me giving it a good try. He offered me a job to be the new director of training and canvas crews for the Agency. He said it was a position he made up just for me since things didn't work out between us."

"Oh," she said quietly.

"My thing is, where did he get the impression that we weren't going to resolve our issues and move forward?" I looked at her for a reaction. Shock rolled over her face.

"I haven't spoken to him this afternoon. I did this morning before we argued, but not since then," she said. "But he has a way of knowing things. Perhaps he just assumed."

"I told him I didn't want the job. I *told* him that we are partners and that we may fight, but we would figure it out." As she backed away from me, I couldn't believe it, but I heard it. Her heart skipped a beat. Occasionally, they do. The songs and poems aren't wrong. Sometimes they skip. I moved toward her. Her lip quivered.

"Don't cry. Please don't. You look too lovely to go into this with red eyes," I said, hoping to keep her from shedding a tear. I should have come to her earlier, but I let myself stew after the argument. I knew when I walked out her door with my stupid boots that I would come back to her.

She took deep breaths and fought back tears. "We are going to figure it out?" she asked.

"Of course, we are," I said. I spent the entire morning dying to get out of class to go talk to her. We had spent too much time, including the time she masqueraded in my class, that should have been used to get me caught up on the big picture of things. But being away from her, I knew one thing for sure. We had a bond. The bond between a jaguar and his wielder even though at times she was more like a *bruja*. I was ready to get to work, but I couldn't do it without her. "Give me a quick rundown of what we are facing here."

She took a deep breath, switching into business mode. Her heart rate steadied as she spoke, "I'm not sure of the exact details, but don't be surprised to see a hundred people or more there. They will be from all sorts of affiliations and supernatural communities. I'm sure the Six will be there. They are the representative offspring of Hyperion's children. At some point, formally in front of everyone, I will have to introduce you to all of them. Your response should be a bow to each person. They will return the bow. Everyone in that room, for the most part, will assume that we are together. Like together, together." She paused a moment to let it sink in. I nodded at her, and she continued. "These people are all various parts of the Agency. When we go out into the world, we are kind of the face of the Agency to the proxies and regents. Do not trust anyone in that room. Besides me, and you know you can trust me, right?"

"Of course," I said without hesitation. "Let them think whatever they want about us. I don't want either of us to have to get into an awkward conversation. If we can avoid it, fine. If not just roll with it."

"You want me to pretend we are together?" she said.

"Yes. In fact, Ashley suggested it, and it makes sense. It will keep any propositions from Fae or whoever else is in there at bay. She said if they think that I'm yours they won't even try because they would be afraid of you. Except for Lianne. She said Lianne can't help herself," I said.

"I'm going to kill Ashley," she said.

"No, you aren't. You admit it makes sense?"

"Yes. It does, but most of them in that room will know we are not really together. It doesn't matter what we say or how we act," she said. "Especially any Fae, they go by scent. Like if you are with someone that person leaves a mark on you."

"That I understand, too. Ashley said the same thing," I moved toward her quickly that way she wouldn't fight it. I wrapped my arms around her, pulling her to me. The heart skipped again. I was sure of it this time. She trembled for a moment, then looked away.

"That's what she meant," she said. She didn't pull away from me, but she tensed up.

"Yes. Just for tonight, you are mine," I said, and she turned to look up at me. I couldn't tell if it was fear or anxiety. She continued to tremble, but she looked me in the eye. Ashley was insistent that this be done. I hated that we had fought and hated that it bothered me so much with that man making moves on her. She was not mine. I had listened as Ashley explained it all to me. About how the women and even some of the men here would see me as fresh meat, but to avoid any distractions, I just could claim to be with Abby. However, she insisted that we make it in the form of a Fae deal. She assured me Abby would agree to it. She also said it had to be more than just the two of us parading around this party. And now I was at the moment when I needed to do this with her, and I wasn't sure I could do it. Then I felt her cool hand on my cheek, and I focused on her. She understood.

"It's okay," she muttered.

She had agreed. It was all I needed to solidify my resolve. The animal inside me stirred. I pushed it back. I leaned into her lovely face, and my lips met hers. The kiss lasted longer than I expected it to. Her heart stopped beating, and when I pulled away, she let out the smallest of sighs. I didn't realize I had her pressed against the wall of the elevator. There was no heavy breathing or surges of heat. Just a very good kiss. I stayed close to her. "We good?" I asked.

"More than," she replied. I backed away to hit the emergency release button, and the elevator started to move.

"Ashley tried to explain this Fae deal stuff to me, but perhaps you could clarify it," I asked as I looked at her. She still stood there against the wall with her fingertips on her lips.

"You just made a deal with a Half-Fae and sealed it with a kiss," she said. "You suggested the deal. I agreed, and we sealed it."

"What exactly is the deal?"

"For tonight, you own me. I am marked just like Samantha and Travis, basically. You give me an order, and I have to do it," she rolled her eyes.

"Huh, interesting," I said. She glared at me daring me to do it. "Okay, I'll refrain from ordering you around, but please scratch your nose."

Immediately, her hand went up and scratched her nose. She growled at me, then punched me in the arm.

"Ow," I said, rubbing my arm. Finally, she cracked a smile. A big, lovely smile.

"Baby," she teased. I knew then that we would be okay.

"Who is here that we need protection from?" I asked as the elevator doors opened, and she took her position to my right with her hand on my arm. We walked out into a large ballroom on the tenth floor. It was the top level closest to the surface. A mini-orchestra played and beautiful people swirled around the dance floor. I felt her hesitate.

"Cast the communication spell," I said.

Without hesitation, she said, "*Communico*. And Jag you have got be careful with your phrasing."

Shit. I hadn't realized that was a command, but it was. I

would have to think before I spoke, "Are you really going to call me Jag?"

"Yep," she said.

"*Why the hesitation when we came in the room?*," I said in her head. The connection was easy. No focusing on her or major concentration involved. I assume that was the deal.

"*The blonde-haired man over at the bar with the ladies. That's Lukas Castille. My ex-fiancé.*" she said.

"*The incubus?*"

"Yes," she said out loud. Ashley and Ichiro came up to us. Ashley hugged her, said something in her ear and she blushed.

"Thank you for your help this evening, Ashley," I said.

"I see you got everything squared away," she said.

"Yes, we did." She was quite pleased with herself. I guess she assumed there was more involved than the deal, but I knew there wasn't. However, it would keep the wolves away. Ashley's endeavors to fix her friend up was endearing in a way. She tried her best to make Abby happy again. I can't say how misguided she was, but the gesture indicated a sweetness in her for her friend. Ashley had even suggested that Abigail's biggest problem was that she needed to get laid. I didn't dare bring that up to Abigail. Ashley was very forward, which was something I would have to get used to.

"Everyone else is over here at a table. Come join us," she said.

"We should go say hello to Gregory," Abby said.

"Okay. Come over once you've done that," Ashley said. Ichiro didn't speak the whole time. He just watched Ashley talk. He had it bad. I couldn't blame him. I didn't know what Ashley's lineage was exactly, but she was extremely pretty.

I looked over at Abby and tried to find the right words to say. I started to say "Let's go," but that could lead to a lot of places. I didn't know what to say.

"Oh, just say something, I'm not going to be mad," she said.

"We should go see your Grandfather, now," I said. She smiled, locking arms with me again. We went to find the Titan who blew a small welcoming party into a huge celebration. We passed through lots of people. As we walked through, I listened to the conversations with my enhanced hearing. Many people spoke to Abigail. She would politely and briefly introduce me, then we would try to keep moving.

I could see the crowd watching us as we made our way through. It made me uneasy. I could hear whispers. Bits and pieces of conversations of what a wonderful-looking couple we made and of how much of a whore Abigail was which pissed me off. The truth was I didn't know if it was true or not. I hoped it wasn't. She didn't seem like that type of woman. One older woman, in particular, talked about how she wished I wasn't marked, because she'd like to do things to me. We had to stop for the caterers moving across our path.

"You have to tune it out. I hear them. Just remember they can't touch us tonight. It really was a good idea. I had no idea so many would be here," she whispered in my head. I didn't respond because the path reopened, and we were approaching Gregory. He dressed as dapper as an older man could. Black tuxedo, crisp white shirt, black bow tie and a huge smile on his face as he talked to those standing around him. His presence was intense. As we approached, he waved us closer.

"Please excuse us, ladies and gentlemen, I need to speak to my granddaughter and her partner. Tadeas and Abby, it is good to see you both. You look wonderful tonight. Please follow me for a moment," he walked through a double set of doors and into a side room which was empty.

"He's pissed. Just hang in there on this one," she said.

"About what?"

"The deal," she said. Suddenly a wave of force slammed me against the wall, and I felt my air being choked off. He didn't move. No words were spoken. No hand motions.

351

"Stop now!" Abby shouted. I felt dizzy and clawed at my neck. "Gregory Theodoard, Hyperion, master of the watch and rising of the sun, I said stop!"

He turned to her and snarled. "What have you done?"

"It was a precaution," she stammered. "Please let him go. He's not done anything wrong. I swear it."

When he released the power holding me, I slid down the wall gasping. She hurried over to me and started to fuss over me. I brushed her away a little and rasped, "I'm fine. No big deal." I stood up, and she helped me. She rounded on him. I was happy to see that ire going in a direction other than toward me.

"How dare you?" she said. "Do you have no faith in me at all?"

"The mark on you is forced," he said.

"No, it's not forced. It just was a last-minute decision," she explained.

"I would never do that, Sir," I said still trying to catch my breath.

He pointed his finger at me and said, "You shut up."

I held my hands up in surrender. *We are going back out to my friends. I'm not playing his game anymore.* She spun to walk out the door, and I grabbed her arm gently. There was nothing I could say that wouldn't be a command.

"Hey, I'm fine. It's okay," I said. I wanted her to talk to him. To avoid confrontation later. I had the feeling it was going to be a long night.

"It's not fine," she spouted. She grabbed my hand to lead me out of the room.

"Abby, stop. Come back here this instant," he demanded.

"Tonight, I'm his and you can't command me to do anything," she glared at him, and we went back into the party. She composed herself before we started meeting the crowds and took her place on my arm.

"He has you marked?"

"Yes, but the bond between us tonight is stronger. A deal for a specific amount of time. I'll pay for it I'm sure in the future, but it can't be helped."

"He can order you around?"

"Yes, but generally he doesn't. It's from a long time ago when I was a little less agreeable. He's just mad. He thinks you...."

"*I know what he thinks. I would never, Abby,*" I tried to explain.

"*I know that and he should too,*" she said. I could see Ashley, Ichiro and the others sitting around a large booth table. They slid around, letting us sit on the end. There was barely room, and Abby practically sat in my lap. No complaints.

We all sat and chatted about the party and the food. I got the distinct impression that you didn't talk about work at these kinds of functions. Ichiro asked Ashley to dance, and we moved out of the booth so they could get out.

"Where's Jay?" I asked, and Abby elbowed me in the ribs. "I was just asking."

Vincent spoke up. "He told me he would be a little late. You can call me Vince by the way." He reached across the table to shake my hand.

"We call Vince the mad Russian because he's crazy as hell," Abby said grinning at him.

"Mad scientist," he added.

"Yeah, you got a monster in your basement?" I asked.

He lifted his eyebrows and tried to look sinister, "Maybe I do."

I laughed. He had a good sense of humor. Tony and Tommy, the brute twins, sat and drank their beers. I believed they were of Polynesian descent. They had little to say, but Tony joined the conversation occasionally. I assumed this sort of event would not be good for Matthew, and I did not see him anywhere. Aiden, the Arabic Alchemist as Abby called him, was a wielder and a chemist. He sat next to a very lovely Nubian beauty. Her dark skin glistened in the dim lights. It was smooth and radiant. Aiden introduced her as Fayola, his wife.

353

"She's an honorary member of the team," Abby smiled at her.

"I am only considered as such because Aiden cannot function unless I tell him what to do," she said with a grin.

"Oh, you have a deal," I said.

Abby smirked at me, "Yea, it's called marriage, doofus."

"Oh," I said, and they all laughed. I laughed too. *I'll get you back for calling me doofus.*

"*I look forward to your efforts,*" she replied.

Ashley and Ichiro returned. Tony and Tommy excused themselves, and I saw them approach a couple of women on the other side of the dance floor. I liked all of them. Well, that was until Jeremy Stafford showed up. He lumbered up to all of us with his arm around a woman wearing a completely see-through dress and no underwear. I turned my head away even though there were plenty of scantily clad women at the party, none of them were as close as this one.

"*Dear God, he's drunk.*"

I looked up at her. "Would you like to go with me to get a drink?" She smiled because I found a way to phrase it.

But before we could slip away, Mr. Drunk Swagger spoke up. "Well, looky here. Damn Tadeas. This afternoon she wasn't marked and now she is. Good for you ol' chap. Fuck her good for me."

I started across to him. He put his hands up, and Abby got in between us. "*No. He's doing it on purpose. Let him talk. We can go. Please let's just go.*" I looked at her. I could see the pleading in her eyes.

"I didn't know cats marked their territory. I thought that only dogs did that," he laughed at himself. No one else did.

Then she turned on him. "Jeremy Stafford, so this is you changed? What a liar. To think I almost believed you. You need to shut the fuck up before I…" People were turning to see the commotion.

"Come away," I whispered. I felt a chill run up her arm. I

had given a command. Crap. She complied, and we walked over to the bar closest to us. The bartender poured us two glasses of champagne. "I'm sorry."

"No, you were right to pull me away from him. He and I have a long history. Don't apologize for speaking as we normally do or if it's something that needs to be said. It's hard to understand the bond. I'm seriously not going to hold anything against you," she said as she took a sip. I saw her eyes moving across the crowd. She froze. I followed her gaze to a woman dressed in a long purple gown. She wrapped herself on the arm of an older man who looked as well-dressed as Theodoard. It was Meredith. They stood with several other people and talked. One of them was Lianne.

"What in the hell?"

"Did you know she would be here?" she asked.

"No."

"She's with Cyrus MacCormack. He's Lianne's brother. He's one of the Six," she explained.

She meant the six board members of Kenward, Blake, and Shanahan. Each one was a direct descendant of one of Hyperion's children. "I didn't even know she knew any of the board members."

"This whole night is going to be a disaster," she muttered, finishing off the glass of champagne. Then she picked up another. I knew commanding her to stop drinking would get me in a deeper hole, so I just stared at her. "Last one, I promise."

"*It's not going to be a disaster. It's going to be fine,*" I assured her, even though I didn't believe it myself.

"*Good try, Jag,*" she said with a smile.

I finished off my glass but declined another. The music came to an end. The dancers and the crowd clapped, as a spotlight turned on toward the front of the room. Out of the floor rose a stage with seven chairs. Once the stage reached full height, seven people positioned themselves, one in front of each chair then sat down in unison.

"Showtime," Abby said, slamming down the last of the champagne. She turned to me to check my suit and her dress. She smoothed her hands over it nervously. "I look okay?"

I touched her face, as her anxiety grew. Her heartbeat raced again. I felt every single pounding beat of it. "I told you, you look beautiful. You always look beautiful." She was mine tonight. I could say it if I wanted to. Then I heard it again. Skip.

Gregory began to speak. "Ladies and Gentlemen, honored guests, I hope each one of you will take full advantage of our hospitality tonight in celebrating this great occasion. For many, many years Kenward, Blake, and Shanahan has directed the movements of the world. In recent years, we took a step back and re-evaluated our interests in the world and the goals we set forth for ourselves. Life is our greatest treasure. All life. Whether Celestial, Permutation, Fae, or Human, we value them all. Our goals have always been to preserve it and this world to which all planes are tethered.

"Many years ago, my granddaughter, Miss Abigail Davenport crossed this globe with her partner. She controlled the face of our esteemed agency. She was the force that moved us into the current era. Times are changing as they often do, and the world's perceptions are changing. Technology has advanced far more and far faster than we have adapted. I am pleased to announce that Miss Davenport will once again become the face of our agency in the field with her new partner. Ladies and gentlemen, please welcome my granddaughter, Miss Abigail Sophia Davenport, and her new partner, Mr. Tadeas Nahuel Duarte."

The room erupted in applause.

"*Escort me to the center of the room right in front of the stage,*" she instructed.

"*You are more nervous than I am.*"

"*I never know what he is going to do. Hopefully, he plays nice.*"

Already arm in arm, we walked toward the stage as the crowd parted for us as we approached the seven sets of watchful eyes on the stage. When we got there, she made a long deep curtsy, and I bowed. The crowd's applause faded out.

"I would like to welcome you, Mr. Duarte to the inner circle of our agency. Miss Davenport will now introduce you formally to the six board members."

"Bow to each one as I introduce them," she looked up to her grandfather on the stage. I watched her steel herself. "Thank you, Grandfather, for your kind words." She took my hand, leading me down to the end where her Aunt Lianne sat in the first chair.

"Lianne Theodoard, descendent of Helios, son of Hyperion, I would like to introduce to you and present for the inner circle, my chosen partner, Tadeas Nahuel Duarte." We both bowed. Lianne nodded her head and winked at me. Crazy Fae woman.

"Cyrus MacCormack, descendant of Helios, son of Hyperion, I would like to introduce to you and present for the inner circle, my chosen partner, Tadeas Nahuel Duarte." We repeated the bows. This went on for each of the board members. Joyceline Shinar and Muraco Philyra, descendants of Selene, and Zoran Maruti and Li-Mei Xing, descendants of Eos, all nodded at our bows and smiled. I then led us both back to the center, and we stood once again before the whole group.

Gregory spoke again. "Thank you for your formal presentation. I would like to welcome you Mr. Duarte and give you a fair warning. Miss Davenport is the light of my life, tread lightly, Son." I nodded and bowed again. Abby squeezed my hand.

"Before you are allowed into the inner circle, you must complete a rite of passage."

I gulped, but Abby smiled. *"Unless he changes something, it's not a big deal."*

"You must prove yourself a worthy partner not only for my granddaughter but for the Agency itself. Are you up to the task?"

I spoke as clearly and as strongly as I could. "I am up to the task, Sir." My mind raced at the possibilities of having to prove my worth to this room of people. Perhaps a fighting demonstration or a weapons test. Abby's anxiety stilled. She once again proved that she had faith in my abilities. No matter what test they threw at me, I knew that she knew, I could handle it.

"Very well. Please clear the floor." The dance floor opened up behind us as people moved to the edges of the room. "If you can fight, you can dance. If you can dance, then you are worthy. Please show us your worth."

Dancing. I took a deep breath and tried to remember the lessons that I had taken forty years ago. One of my martial arts instructors said learning to dance would help my finesse and grace in my movements. That class was the extent of my dancing knowledge. I stepped slightly away from Abby and put my hand up. She took it, then we walked to the middle of the floor.

"*I can use a spell if you want, but you must decide now.*"

"*You have a dance spell?*"

"*I have a spell for everything.*"

I laughed out loud. I'm sure I looked crazy, but she giggled, too.

"No, I've got this." I stepped away from her again, bowing formally to her. She curtsied to me and held it. I put my left arm behind my back, walking toward her. I offered her my right hand, and as she took it, the orchestra started. She raised to her feet, and I placed her right hand on my forearm and wrapped my right hand around her waist. She grinned at me. I thought she was enjoying it too much. She said that it was show time. I decided to make a show. We joined left hands, and I pressed my right hand into her back, gently forcing her body to mine. She lifted her eyebrows questioning my sudden confidence. Yes, I remembered how to do this. I lead a simple waltz. As we started to circle the room, there was a little applause in approval of our start.

"*You do know how to dance.*"

I leaned close to her ear, "Yes, I do." She laughed as we turned around the floor. I didn't even think about the steps. I had spent six months in that dance class for this moment. As if no one else was in the room, I focused on her. I could physically feel the bond between us. My mind drifted over the last few days. I remembered the moment she walked into my class. I remembered struggling with how to confront her. The thought of her helpless on the streets plagued me. Coming to know that she was a formidable wielder, turned out to be a relief more than anything.

"*Hey where you at?*"

"*I'm dancing with the most beautiful woman in the room.*"

"*Since when do you become such a flirt?*"

"*Since you kissed me,*" I said.

She laughed. "*That's not how I remember it.*"

I pulled her close and said, "I could remind you." Her eyes widened with surprise at my answer. The heart skipped again. With that, I planted a foot and spun her away from and back to me. Then continued the normal steps to the waltz. The crowd clapped.

"You have got to be kidding me," she said.

"Nope," and I planted and spun her again. I was having a blast.

"Ok enough, Mr. Astaire, I had two glasses of champagne before this rite of passage," she scolded.

"No, I've got to make a good show of it." I turned her around, and we took several steps in an open position. She just shook her head. "*Now just shut up and finish this.*" I felt the tingle run down her arm. I took my eyes off her. I had commanded her, and my steps wavered with the command. She took the hand on my shoulder and moved my face until I met her eyes again.

"*As you wish,*" she complied. We continued to dance until the music ended. We stood there locked together, face to face, and the crowd roared. "*Well done, but don't get used to this,*" she said.

"You know how to ruin a moment." We bowed again to each other and turned to bow to the stage. All seven were standing and clapping. I could hear Ashley and the team back there whooping and whistling. Once the crowd ceased, Gregory spoke again.

"Well done, Mr. Duarte. You have passed and are welcomed into the inner circle."

I placed my right hand on my heart and bowed to him in thanks. He could have tortured me, but he did not. I have to assume that he didn't because he would not torture Abigail.

The music started again, and the crowd filled the dance floor. We moved back to the table with the team. Ashley squealed and hugged Abby. "Oh my god, I had no idea he knew how to waltz. That was fantastic, Tadeas."

"Thanks," I said.

"He surprises me every day," Abby said. That statement meant more to me than she realized. I hoped to continue to surprise her. Even though she was technically mine for the night, I wanted to be worthy of that. Worthy to be her partner, which meant all the craziness had to fade away. We had to roll with the punches because I was sure it wasn't over yet.

We sat and talked with the rest of the team. It was great getting to know all of them. As the night went on the music became more and more modern. I enjoyed every moment with her. After a couple of hours, I got up, and she looked at me. I offered her my hand, and she took it. I pulled her away to a quieter corner.

"How long does the deal last?"

"Until dawn, when the night ends. If you want me to wash your clothes or clean your apartment, now's the time to get that order in before it becomes daylight," she said.

"No, don't be silly. I just didn't know. We've had a good night, and I didn't know if the deal pushes all the other stuff out of the way or if, I don't know how to explain it."

"You want to know if I'm still going to be mad at you in the morning?" she asked.

"Yes."

"No. I won't be. I'm not mad at you now, and it has nothing to do with the deal. I'm very thankful you are here tonight, even if grandfather threatened you."

"He didn't. Ashley convinced me to come." She looked over to Ashley all snuggled up next to Ichiro. I had the feeling all of them were about done with the party. Jeremy had long gone off with a pretty redhead.

"She's a good friend," she said.

About that time, the man she pointed out as Lukas Castille approached us. I had watched him on and off during the night. This was the first moment I saw him without a woman hanging on his arm.

"Good evening," he greeted us both, then looked at Abby.

"Tadeas Duarte, this is Lukas Castille, regent of the United States West Coast and Pacific Islands," she said in monotone.

"Nice to meet you, Duarte. I've heard a lot of great things about you. It's about time Abby got back to work," he said in a jovial manner. He seemed pleasant enough. I felt Abby wrap her arm into mine.

"Nice to meet you as well. Hopefully, we are making moves to make the crews and the whole agency more modern and effective," I responded.

"Very nice dance earlier, too," he said.

"I had a beautiful partner," I said, looking at her.

"You did, indeed. I wondered if I might have a word with her in private. If you don't mind, I am well aware of your mark on her. I promise that I will not compromise that bond in any way, on my honor." Again, I looked back to her for some sort of guidance. She seemed lost with him standing before us.

"It's up to her, Mr. Castille."

He looked at her and pleaded. "Abby, please give me a moment. That's all I ask."

"Excuse me for just a moment, Tadeas," she said. She looked pained. I watched her walk to the other side of the room with him. I kept my eyes on them both. I didn't know if it was the bond or just my instincts. I did not want her anywhere near Lukas Castille.

CHAPTER 35

ABIGAIL

"*One word and I'm there,*" Tadeas said in my head. I could tell he didn't like me walking off with Lukas. I didn't want to talk to him either, but I felt obligated. My history with Lukas was long and sordid. We had ended badly.

"*Alright. It's fine, though. He's got to get his annual word in edgewise,*" I assured him. I looked back across the room, and he never took his eyes off us. I suppose the deal had a lot to do with his behavior tonight. It was fun. I was afraid it would all end by dawn though. That's how these things work. The bond was supernatural. It's magical, and when you participated in one like this, it could cause you to act differently. I had enjoyed his attention, even the bit of possessiveness he displayed. It had been a very long time since someone had been that connected to me. I reminded myself that it was the bond, and it would soon go away. I just hoped we didn't fight anymore. The fighting was taking the life out of me.

"When you are done speaking to him across the room let me

know," Lukas said flatly. Lukas and I had once shared a bond close enough for us to communicate that way even though he was human at the time. He knew exactly what I was doing when my gaze faded over to Tadeas.

"What do you want, Lukas?"

"Forgive me if I am concerned with this new partner. I've never seen you marked other than Theodoard's claim on you. Lincoln never marked you, neither did I. I never thought you would ever allow yourself to be in such a deal, therefore I have to assume that he forced you into it. I want you to stay in sight until dawn, and then I'll get you out of here," Lukas, the white knight said.

"You have lost your mind, Lukas Castille," I said. "I went into this willingly. He and I are not together."

"You could have fooled me. You are all over him," he said. His words stung. They hurt me deeply because he knew exactly what I had been through. He knew things about me that even Tadeas didn't know yet.

"I am not! How can you see anything with five different women hanging on you?"

"Abby, you know all of that is a show. Just like your little dance with him. It was a show. The crowd clapped and hooray, Abby is back to save us all," he said bitterly. I unleashed my hand and struck him across the cheek.

"Get away from me," I said through gritted teeth. In an instant, Tadeas pulled me away from him. I struggled against his grip. I wasn't finished talking to Lukas. I knew Tadeas didn't want to order me in front of Lukas.

"Hey, Duarte," Lukas called after us. "You take care of her, or you will hear from me."

"Get in line," Tadeas said. I choked back a laugh. He continued to lead me out the doors into the hallway.

"He's an ass," I said.

"You still love him?" Tadeas asked.

"No. I don't. It was a long time ago. I mean, I believe that if you truly love someone that no matter how life goes and if you split up, a piece of that love always stays with you. Love means giving a piece of yourself to someone else. There was a time when he held a piece of me. However, that thing in there is an incubus, not *my* Lukas Castille. It's complicated. There is love there. *Was* love there, but not for *that*," I said pointing my finger back in the room. Word vomit. I had just word vomited.

"Will you tell me the story sometime?" he asked in a steady tone unfazed by my spew.

"It's not a good story," I said.

He brushed a piece of hair out of my face. "I want to hear all your stories. Good and bad."

"I'm tired. I'm going to break the communication spell. I think we are out of danger. *Adimo*." I had changed the subject again, but he allowed me to do it.

Ashley and Ichiro came through the doors.

"I think we are both done for the evening. It was an enlightening party," Ichiro said. Ashley looked exhausted.

"You take care of her Ichiro," I said to him.

"I will. I promise," he said, letting her lean on him as they went to the elevator.

"You ready to go?" Tadeas asked me.

"Yes, but I need to say goodnight to grandfather. Did you want to speak to Meredith?" I asked.

"Absolutely not," he said. That answer pleased me greatly. More and more I felt like she was not who she claimed to be. She had been in the Agency for years, but something seemed very off with Miss Meredith Spence. Seeing her here tonight on the arm of one of the Six confirmed it in my mind.

We walked back into the ballroom, and the crowd had dwindled down to a few dozen partiers. We walked up to grandfather. He turned to us with a smile on his face.

"Impressive dancing, Mr. Duarte."

"Thank you, Sir. I believe we are going to be retiring for the evening. Thank you very much for the party, and your acceptance of me."

"You are welcome, Son. I apologize for earlier tonight. I completely overreacted," Gregory said.

"That's putting it lightly," I said. Tadeas squeezed my hand, and I shut up.

"Goodnight, Sir."

"Goodnight."

As we turned to walk out of the ballroom, a slow ballad started playing. The orchestra had turned music duties over to a DJ earlier in the evening.

"One last dance?" Tadeas asked.

"Sure, why not?" I obliged because for tonight I belonged to him. It had been a very long time since I was deeply connected to someone. It felt good, and I knew dawn loomed just around the corner. No waltzing stances or formal steps. He just pulled me close to him, and I relaxed, laying my head on his shoulder. We swayed to the slow song. I looked around the room to see the remaining guests. Some danced. Most were at tables laughing and drunk. One thing for sure was grandfather knew how to throw a party.

Lukas stood in a corner watching us intently. I missed the man he used to be. He was the only reason I survived after Lincoln died. He wore his hair as he always did, sandy brown locks long enough to cover his face and his stunning blue eyes. I had placed him in Los Angeles as a proxy because of his looks. He fit in with that crowd, but when he was human, he had a heart. That fact alone made him stand out among the glittering celebrities of that town. Los Angeles was always hard to place a proxy and get good results. Lukas turned out to be the best proxy we ever had that was why he had been moved up to regent even though they turned him into a beast.

We have never been able to track down who turned him. We

did not think it was possible, but someone did it. I knew they had done it because of me. Because I loved him. It tore us apart. As I leaned on Tadeas, Lukas' dark stare was a stark reminder of why I could never fall in love again.

"*What are you thinking about?*" he asked, even though I had ended the communication spell.

"*How are you doing that?*" I asked.

"I dunno," he replied. "Are you okay?"

"Yeah, just thinking too much about the past," I replied.

The song ended, and Lukas made eye contact with me once for just a moment. He claimed many times before that his change in desires never changed the love he had for me, but I could not tolerate his extracurricular activities which were essential to his life now. I split with him for our own good. He had to survive.

"*Thank you, for tonight,*" Tadeas' voice in my head brought me back.

"Perhaps it's the bond," I said looking up at him. I couldn't figure out how he was still able to talk in my head.

"You heard me the night the shadow man was here, too."

"Of course, in the mad rush of things, I had forgotten that. I'm tired," I said, as he led me out of the room to the elevators.

The doors opened, and to my relief, no one was there. I let them close, then I leaned over putting my head on his chest. He rested his hand in my hair, holding me against him. His heartbeat was steady inside his chest.

Once we reached the floor with my apartment, the doors opened again. I held his hand, and I went to my door. He stopped as I went in. I pulled him inside with me. "*Bulla,*" I said putting a privacy bubble around us.

"What's wrong?" he asked. His instincts were on point.

"I had to shut everything out for a bit. It's been a whirlwind of a couple of days." He reached up and started pulling off the tie. He took off his jacket, then laid them on the arm of the chair. He took a seat on the couch.

"What are you thinking about now? In general, I don't need to know all the dirty thoughts you were having about Castille," he winked at me.

"No dirty thoughts about Lukas. I promise. I've just been devising a plan to lure these earthquake makers out into the open. I'm going to need your help though, and I need to know that we are okay. It will be officially dawn in a few hours, and until then we are still connected. I'm not going to be mad at you, but there are things we need to be clear about," I explained.

"Then come over here and sit with me, and we can reach clarity together," he said.

"Damn," I said as my body forcefully moved me over to the couch and I sat down.

"Oh crap, Abby I'm sorry."

"It's okay. It will be over soon. It's not like you asked me to perform a lewd act."

"If I told you to do something like that, you would have to do it right?" I narrowed my eyes at him. "Hypothetically, of course."

"No comment," I replied. He got a good laugh out of that one. "May I have permission to go take these shoes off and this dress?" He had ordered me to sit. I couldn't move until he allowed it.

"Yes, of course, this bond thing really is stupid," he said.

"Oh please, you love it," I said as I headed to the bedroom. When I shut the bedroom door, he tried to get in the last word.

"Just let me know if you need any help to get out of that dress," he teased.

"You are pushing your luck, Jag," I replied. Removing the shoes was easy. However, I almost didn't get the dress unzipped. Ashley had helped me put it on. I didn't realize how awkward the zipper was until I tried to take it off. Thankfully, I didn't have to ask for help. I slipped on a pair of yoga pants and a tank top. I grabbed a throw blanket from the top of the closet, rejoining him on the couch.

"Are you really going to call me that?" he asked as if I hadn't been gone from the room for ten minutes.

"Would you like a bottle of water?" I said ignoring him.

"Yes, please," he said.

Grabbing a couple of out of the fridge, I walked back toward him. "If you don't want me to, you have your chance to order me not to do it." He just sat there grinning at me. "That's what I thought, you like it," I said.

"I do not, but I'm not going to order you to do anything on purpose. Are you going to tell me your plan?" he asked. I sat down on the couch with the blanket.

"You know that room is the extra room, and it's full of your stuff," I said.

"Not my stuff, just stuff you got for me," he said. "And no, I didn't know that."

"What would I do with a bunch of boy stuff? Technically, Ashley does the legwork on all of it. It is all yours, Tadeas," I said. "There are clothes if you want to get out of that suit." He did not hesitate. He jumped up and started unbuttoning his shirt before he even got to the door. "Let me know if you need help getting out of it."

"By the way, it's man stuff. Just so we are clear," he said, then shut the door. I laughed at him.

It only took him a couple of minutes to change. I was always jealous of men. They could change clothes in just a couple of minutes. As women, it takes much longer. He walked in and clicked off the lights.

"What are you doing?"

"Light some candles, please," he said.

"*Ignacio*," I said without thinking. Fucking bond. "This must be what it's like to sit in that stupid chair."

"Thank you, and yes, it is a stupid chair," he said.

"Why the candles?" I asked.

"Because we've been in a dark room all night and being in here with all these lights bothers my eyes. You have to remember that my eyes aren't just human eyes. I have a lot of abilities to see in many ways. Adjusting from the darkness to the light can be taxing. There really isn't any reason to have all the lights on," he explained.

"I'm sorry. You are right. I've never thought of it that way." I thought about his abilities and how I still didn't fully understand what he was capable of doing.

"Sorry to disappoint you. I didn't intend on seducing you tonight," he teased.

"Okay, that's one of the things we have to talk about," I said as he sat down on the couch with me.

"Abby, I was just teasing."

"I know you were, but to be honest, I do care about you very much. The bond between us, even after the deal evaporates, is still pretty strong. I believe that is because of what we are, wielder and shifter. We just have to make sure we don't mistake that bond for something it isn't. I don't know how to explain it without being harsh. I, we, can't have a relationship like that."

"I get that. You have said that, and even though I have no intentions for that, explain to me why it is that we can't?" he asked

I paused. Everything that I thought of to say sounded self-deprecating or like a lie to me. I did not know how to explain it to him. Hell, I wasn't even sure I wanted to admit the reasons why he and I couldn't have a relationship, even though I knew exactly what they were.

He looked me in the eye. "Don't hate me," he said.

"Hate you for what?"

"Tell me why, Abby. Tell me the truth." His words rippled over my skin like stepping out into a blizzard. I felt anger well up inside me. "No, you have a terrible tendency not to fully explain yourself. And for once, for this once, I want you to be truthful to me."

I tried holding my anger back. I fought the words as they tried to explode out of me. I got up from the couch thinking that if I could make it to the circle in the floor of my room, maybe I could cut myself off from the influence of the bond. I made it to the door of my bedroom but sunk to my knees. My body demanded that I answer him. "Damn you, Duarte," I said through gritted teeth.

He got up, lifted me off the floor, and carried me back to the couch. My body was repulsed by him. He sat down close to me, wrapping his arms around me. I wanted to shove him off, but he was warm. It felt good. What a mix of emotions, I thought to myself.

"Abby, I know why, but you need to say it out loud," he explained in a soft, apologetic tone. "You are more stubborn than any woman I have ever known. You hide things from me because you think you are helping me or protecting yourself. If we are truly going to be partners, you've got to stop holding back."

At this point, my body shook as I fought the command. "Because every person I care about gets hurt or dies."

The command released, and I was back in control. I tried to shove away from him, but he didn't let go. He was right. I knew that he was right. If we were going to be partners, I needed to learn that I could tell him anything. Up until now, I was always afraid he would leave if I really spoke my mind. And he might still, but I couldn't try to protect either of us anymore.

"You aren't going to hit me?" he asked.

"No, but I want to," I said.

"I was willing to take the risk to get you to let go," he said.

"I had no choice."

"I know. Perhaps it wasn't the wisest time to push you on it."

"You think?" I said quickly. "Tadeas, please, I don't want to fight you anymore."

"Then don't. I have a few more hours of you being mine. I'm going to enjoy it."

I turned and looked at him. "What?"

Releasing his hold on me, he put his feet up on the couch and almost pushed me off. He put his hands behind his head with a grin. Then he said, "My dear, if you would please, get me another water. It seems I've finished this one."

I rolled my eyes and went to the kitchen. I brought him back the water. When I handed it to him, he grabbed my wrist, pulling me down to the couch with him. It was awkward, to say the least. "What are you doing?"

"Now lay here with me and tell me your plan," he smiled.

I shook my head, but my body obeyed. This bond thing was a terrible idea, and I planned to berate Ashley the first chance I got. I curled up next to him, resting my head on his chest. I refused to admit that I liked it. Besides, he didn't even drink the damn water. It was only a ploy to get me into a position so he could pull me down to the couch. Clever devil.

I started to tell him about my plan. We discussed options and how to handle the trap. He liked it and agreed it was a good plan. It felt good sharing it with him.

"I guess we are going to Paris," I said.

"Seems so," he replied with a yawn.

"Do you have class in a few hours?" I asked.

"No, your grandfather called downstairs and canceled all classes for tomorrow. I thought we might go visit the tavern I told you about," he suggested.

"Sounds good," I replied, as his yawn made me yawn. We were quiet for a long time. I started drifting off to sleep. I could tell he was, too. I didn't get up. I didn't want to leave his side.

After a long silence, he said, "It was a good kiss though."

I sighed. "Yes, it was," I admitted just before we both fell asleep on the couch.

CHAPTER 36

VANESSA

"He marked her!" I shouted excitedly into the phone.

"Yes, I don't know if she let him do it, or if he's more devious than I expected," she said.

"Oh, my dear, that's wonderful news. I know the mark won't last past dawn, but that means she trusts him. Now if someone in Boulder, like one of our operatives, could convince him to do it again, perhaps for her own benefit, we could take them both. She would be under his control and not free to act. Depending, of course, on how strong the bond is between them. So many possibilities." I was giddy with the prospect of ruining that little bitch. She had been in this world for far too long. It was time to put her down. Just knowing she was weak enough to allow it to happen, even if it was a willing act, it meant that even though Abigail Davenport was back in the game, she needed a man to protect her.

"Perhaps you can get in good with him, use your womanly wiles," I suggested to her.

"I am pretty sure that isn't going to work," she said.

"Why? You are gorgeous and smart, my dear! Do it. I'll let you practice on me," I suggested.

"You do not count, V. You would fuck anything," she accused.

"I would not! Well, maybe I would," I said. "Well, let me go. Keep me informed and get your fine ass back to Philly as soon as possible. I do miss you," I said. I really did miss her. One of the few women in this world I truly got along with, but partially because I wanted to make her mine, too. "I'm off to Paris on Saturday. Got business there. Bye, sexy."

"Bye, V."

Abigail was really slipping. There was no way in hell she would have ever let anyone including Lincoln put a bond oath on her. This jaguar must have quite a bit of power over her. Or it was as I suspected and she wasn't nearly as powerful as we were lead to believe.

I walked around the condo naked, packing for Paris. Sweet Miss Cassidy would be here soon. She had agreed to be my assistant for the trip. I was so excited. Mwenye has spent very little time in the condo over the last few days. Good riddance.

I got the impression he'd found a new toy. Last night before he left he got pretty rough with me. I love rough sex, but this was different. I did not enjoy it at all. Once I started consuming souls, I wouldn't need him anymore. The ultimate would be to consume him. Oh, the power, that would be. I'm not naïve enough to think I could defeat him, but it was a wonderful daydream.

Progress continued at the office on the earthquake project. They were selecting sites and acquiring the materials and personnel needed to set each of the sites up. I was also working on a side project. I hoped to acquire some of the materials for myself. I just hadn't had a chance to do it. My friend in Boulder would help me. I wanted to make a statement. One the rest of these weasels are too afraid to make. Oh, yes, they talked big about dropping the coastline into the sea, but they won't do the dirty work. That's why I was here.

What would the Agency do if the entire Boulder facility went poof?

The doorbell rang. Hurrying to the door in my excitement, I had forgotten that I was naked when I opened the door. Edgar Donovan stood there with Cassidy. "Oh hell," I said. "I wasn't expecting you, Mr. Donovan. I just got out of the shower. I thought it was just Cass. You both come in and I'll grab some clothes."

I really hated that man. I would be glad to take Cassidy away from his domineering presence. I hoped to have her before she went back west to spend time with her mother. I had no idea who her mother was, but it didn't matter. If she was the kind of woman that Donovan would fuck, then she must be a bitch or Fae. I threw on a light dress and I heard them talking softly.

"Dad, I'm not a child. I want to go to Paris. I've never been. Please, daddy," she purred. That's my girl, wrap him up.

"Child, this woman is dangerous," he said, as I walked into the room.

"Pish, posh, Edgar Donovan, I would not hurt a hair on her head," I said.

"I am not concerned about you hurting her, Vanessa. I don't want you seducing my daughter," he said frankly. I liked a direct man. I found it to be extremely sexy.

"Eddie, please, I would never. She is your child. And I know what you would do to me if I did anything inappropriate to her," I lied. He couldn't touch me. Mwenye would fry him alive.

"Do not call me that," he said forcefully. There was a little magic behind it, and it made me sway in place.

"Now, now, Donovan, no need for that," I smiled, then winked at him. The angrier he got, the more turned on I became. I knew how to get under a man's skin. Despite hating him, some part of me wanted to feel his power, and I didn't mean in a magical sense.

"Swear that you will return her to me as she is right this moment," he demanded.

That put a damper on things. It might push my timeline back a bit, but I did want her to go with me. I'd just have to swear it and get in her good graces. That way, she would willingly do the things I wanted her to do. "I swear on my power that I will return her to you as she is right this moment," I said, as I winked at her.

"See Daddy, she swore. I told you she would," she said.

He growled. "Alright."

She jumped up and kissed him on the cheek. "I'm going downstairs to get my bags. I'll be right back."

"Cass, sweetie, the doorman will help you get them. His name is Dixon. Tell him I will pay him for his services later," I instructed her.

"Okay, thanks, Vanessa," she giggled in glee and went out the door.

I sauntered over to Donovan and got in his face. "You make me so hot when you get angry."

He grabbed me by the neck and held me against the wall. "Shut your whore mouth. You may have sworn, but I assure you, I will cut out your pretty tongue if you harm her."

I wrapped my leg around his and moaned. "Oh yes, choke me, Eddie. I do have a pretty tongue, let me show you." I ran my hand up his leg to the bulge in his pants. He bucked forward with the touch. Ah, yes, a man couldn't resist a bold woman who wanted to feel him up.

He clamped harder getting in my face, "Don't call me Eddie."

He was close enough. I latched onto his lips with mine, and he squeezed harder. I rolled my hips against him and he responded. My eyes flashed open to his, and I saw hunger there.

Oh yes, Edgar Donovan would know my power, too. He pressed his whole body against me, returning the kiss. It was lustful and hot. He pulled away, released my neck, and slapped me across the face so extremely hard that I hit the floor.

He stood over me and said, "You are nothing more than a filthy whore. That's all you will ever get from me. Good try, sweetheart, but I've been in this game far longer than you. I could break you with a single breath. You remember that as my daughter travels with you. She's an adult woman, and capable of making her own choices. I will not hinder her, but I swear to you that there is nothing Mwenye could do to stop me if I chose to put you down like the bitch you are."

He turned his back to me and headed to the door.

"Oh, baby, talk dirty to me," I laughed as I laid on the floor. The hit hurt. He put something besides just his hand behind it. He had never frightened me before, but I could see the darkness welling up inside him as he talked about his daughter. Perhaps I should rethink my plans for sweet little Cassidy.

I got up and cleaned my face before Cassidy got back. We piled into the car later on and went shopping for our girl trip to Paris. Maybe just for a few days, I could tone it down a bit. Be the person I once was. The good person. I laughed out loud at the thought.

"What are you laughing at?" Cassidy asked.

"Oh, me, lying to myself." I left it at that and gave her no further explanation. It was a lie. I was never good. Every girl with a sexual deviation like mine has a sob story about their daddy, or perhaps a boyfriend, beating them or raping them. Not me, I just liked to fuck. I wanted it all the time from whoever would give it to me. I liked it rough. None of that sensual stuff for me. Mwenye said that once I started consuming souls this "broken" part of me would settle. The souls would calm the desire in me and feed it from within. It would make me more in control and more dangerous. I'm not sure I wanted to be in control. And I was sure that I was pretty dangerous already. I smiled at the thought.

"You are still smiling," Cassidy noticed.

"I'm just very happy that you are going with me to Paris," I said to her and added as any silly girlfriend would, "I'm extremely excited."

CHAPTER 37

TADEAS

I probably shouldn't have thought it, but I did. I woke up on the couch with Abby curled up next to me sleeping quietly. The mark was definitely gone, but it didn't cool my desire completely. I just had better judgment, now. With the bond, I could barely hold back my desire for her. And I thought to myself how nice it would have been to make love to her.

I shouldn't have thought it because the wonderful thought was shattered by her opening her mouth to breathe. Morning breath was one of the world's most karmic devices. Every time you find a girl and sleep with her, it was inevitable that one of you would wake up with stinky breath. Just a fact of life. I turned my head away from her, trying not to laugh at my nonsense. I couldn't help it. She stirred. I slipped out from under her, then rearrange the blanket over her. I went into my bedroom and shut the door. It seemed I was collecting bedrooms and closets full of clothes. I'd get a shower and hopefully just relax today before we did some recon in Boulder at the tavern.

I thought about all the things I wanted her to teach me on the magical side of things. Maybe finally we could do some of that today. I looked at my phone when I went into the bathroom. It was just before noon. I had 3 messages. They were all from Meredith. She wanted to talk, but I did not want to talk to her. Abigail was right. If she was there with MacCormack last night, then she had been in contact with him for a long time. The Six couldn't be trusted. Ignoring her messages, I threw the phone on the bed and jumped in the shower.

When I got out and got dressed, I went into the kitchen and there was a pot of coffee. Abby was in the shower. I could hear the water running. There was a knock at the door. I opened it up, inviting Ashley to come in.

"Morning, Jag," she said with a grin.

"Morning Ashley, or afternoon rather," I said.

"I know. I slept late, too. But the party was good. Is she in the shower? You did great. I doubted that she would actually let you do it. I'd give anything to have been a fly on the wall in that elevator," she rambled on. "Was it good? The kiss? She did not seem to mind being under your power at all!"

"Slow down and take a breath, Ashley. What do you mean you doubted she would do it? You told me last night that you were sure she would agree!" I said.

She lowered her voice to a whisper because the water stopped running in the bathroom, "Well, I may or may not have pushed your buttons a little. But it worked out great! Right? So, what happened when you got back here?"

"That is none of your business. If she wants to tell that's fine. But guys aren't allowed to talk about that kind of thing," I said leaving her hanging. She deserved it after toying with us.

"You have got to be kidding me. You are a tease, Tadeas Duarte," she accused. "Good thing though she did let you do it. I talked to Tommy and Tony and they got several conversations on their reviews of the security tapes this morning. There was more than one person there who had designs to seduce you. The people we work with sometimes are just as dangerous as our enemies."

"You mean besides Lianne?" I asked.

"Fae are very sexual beings. They rarely pay attention to common decency when it comes to getting what they want. You may be up for some of that, but you don't seem the type. Neither of you needed that kind of attention last night. After all, it was only a few hours before that you were at each other's throats. Last night it seemed as though both of you finally reached an understanding. And on that note, I'll say, and I know it's probably a touchy subject, but Lukas means well. He still loves her. She left him, and he's never gotten over it," she continued.

"I wish he hadn't been there. It bothered her," I mumbled.

"Morning, you two. You conspiring against me again, Ash?" Abby accused as she entered the room.

"You have to admit it was a good idea," Ashley defended herself.

"Perhaps, but I hope we don't have to revisit that any time soon," Abby said.

"Was it really that bad?" I asked.

She smiled at me and said, "It was awful. Anything new this morning, Ash?"

"Um, well," Ashley hesitated.

"Anything you want to say, you can say in front of Tadeas," she said as she sat down on the couch and put her feet on the coffee table. She had on a tank top and shorts. It reminded me of her in the robe in the basement of Casa del Sol.

"It's not that, I'd rather tell him than you," Ashley said.

"Oh, good grief, just say it," Abby said pressing her, but not harshly or in anger. I walked over, sat down on the chair, and sipped my coffee. The both of them did enough talking that I could just sit back and listen.

"Castille brought a serum that Jacqueline Vargas has been

working on for him. She wants Ichiro to test it on the incubus and succubus we have here or back in Europe. See if it works," Ashley explained.

Abby leaned forward, and she paused before she spoke. "What is the serum supposed to do?"

"He's had her working on it for years. Testing his blood before feeding, after feeding, after fasting, to come up with a serum to suppress the urge to feed. It would be like an insulin shot for a diabetic. It would fill in the gaps and he would no longer need to feed on humans," she explained.

"I'm not up on my incubus facts," I interjected. I could see Abby trying to process it. I thought I'd give her a second. "What is he actually feeding on?"

"He feeds on life force. He literally sucks the life out of people, and the best way to do it is during sexual intercourse. But Dr. Vargas and Ichiro seem to think there is a very specific formula of hormones and pheromones, a certain chemical compound that is the actual food. And if they can replicate it, then they would not have to feed on humans," Ashley explained.

"Intercourse is the only way to do it and survive. Just casual contact isn't filling enough, but if the serum works, then he could live a normal life," Abby said.

"What happens to the person he feeds on? Does he kill people?" I asked starting to get angry. Why in the world would the Agency let the West Coast regent kill people?

"Lukas does not kill people. He has always restrained himself from going that far, but that means he has to feed regularly. It's because he was once human. All the others of his species are born that way. He's gone long amounts of time without feeding, but it's always harder on the person he first feeds on after the fast. He keeps a strict regimen. That way no one gets too deeply hurt," Abby explained.

"What happens to them?" I asked again.

"They usually pass out. They quickly recover. It's like getting the 24-hour flu, and it goes away after a couple of days," Ashley said.

I looked at Abby. "Go ahead and ask," she said.

"Did he feed on you?" I asked.

"Damn, you are bold," Ashley muttered.

"No. I'm immune to him," she said, hanging her head. Everything made more sense now. I understood why she hadn't tried to stay with him. He needed to feed, but couldn't feed on her.

"How are you immune?" I asked.

"Ichiro did some tests, but he never could figure out why Lukas never had any effect on me. We speculated it must be a magical element. A protection ward on me, or something in my blood. It's not like I know exactly who my parents are therefore it could be hereditary. We just don't really know," she explained.

"What's the plans for this evening?" Ashley said to change the subject. I was thankful she did. Abby looked pale.

"Did you get the ball rolling on my little project?" Abby asked.

"Yes, everything is taken care of. I called George and gave him all the info for the hotel in Paris, and you both are set up to attend the auction," Ashley said.

This was all part of the plan she had to lure out whoever worked on the earthquake disaster. She had told me the full plan last night. I believed it to be a good plan. I was glad to have a role in all of this. We would get to Paris Sunday, and the auction would be on Monday night.

"Are you going to the tavern tonight?" Ashley asked.

"I think we are," I said looking at Abby. She nodded that we were. She still thought about Lukas and the serum. I suppose it would open a door up for the both of them to resolve their issues and pick up where they left off. A part of me wanted that for her very much. I wasn't sure of the timing, but from what I could gather within about a four-year span of time she had lost both

Lincoln and Castille. It's what forced her into seclusion and working in the background for too long. The Agency had suffered for it. But the other part of me didn't want her anywhere near him. I've never known any diabetic that followed their regimen completely. I imagine it would be the same for someone with the evil of an incubus inside them. It seemed like a disaster waiting to happen.

After a minute she finally spoke again. "We should rest up for the trip to Paris. I've got the feeling we won't get any rest there."

"Ain't no rest for the wicked," Ashley said.

"Good song," I replied.

"Yes, it is," Ashley smiled.

"What song?" Abby said.

"Buy her an iPod please, Ashley."

"I tried. She won't listen to it," Ashley claimed.

"I'm not going to be able to stand the both of you hounding me about things. You need to decide who's going to do what," Abby playfully said.

"Me," Ashley and I both said at the same time and laughed at each other. Abby rolled her eyes. I was beginning to see that was a signature move for her. That and she bites her lip if she's nervous. I'm pretty sure I could beat her at poker.

"*You ever play strip poker?*" I asked.

"WHAT?!" she yelled out loud. Ashley looked surprised. "Oh, this moron is talking in my head."

"Ah, commune spell, yeah that's cool. You leave it running all night, Abby?" she asked.

"No, it doesn't go away. He can do it whenever he wants. It just happens," Abby said. I laughed. She eye-rolled again.

"You are bonded then," Ashley said.

"Not sure," Abby said.

"Bonded?" I asked.

"And that's my cue to go. See you both later," Ashley said and headed out the door.

Abby bit her bottom lip. "I don't know if it's a bond or not. I'll have to let grandfather look at us in the spectrum and see. I personally can't tell."

"What does it mean?" I asked.

"A soul bond is a connection between two people or a person and an animal. I imagine if there is one between us it is because of your shifting ability and the inherent connection to the wielder for your specific species. It does not generally happen unless the two people agree to it usually with intimacy involved or they have a genetic bond," she said.

"If you turn out to be my sister, I'm going be sick," I said.

"I sincerely doubt that, but if it concerns you, Ichiro has the DNA record from my blood. He can check your DNA against it."

"Otherwise we'd have that whole Luke and Leia thing going on last night," I said.

"Who?" she asked.

"Ok, you are getting a TV and an iPod for Christmas, Princess."

"But it's more likely attached to your spirit animal and me as a wielder," she continued ignoring me.

"Say for instance, when I was in the shower, I could tell when you got up and started coffee?"

"Can you do that?" she asked.

"Yes, I knew when you got up. I knew you started coffee for me, then went to get in the shower," I explained.

"That could be just animal instincts."

"No, it wasn't like that before," I said.

"When did it start?"

"When I shifted for you on the island, or maybe it was the fight with the shadow guy. I'm not sure exactly," I replied, honestly not knowing how to pinpoint when it started. I could almost trace it back to the moment I decided to be her partner which meant that it probably did have something to do with the wielder/shifter connection.

"And you just now decided to tell me, that you can feel me walking around," she said.

"Well, you would have to feel it too for it to be a soul bond, right?"

"I already feel it. I could feel it before just from my magic," she admitted.

"Oh, you just now decided to tell me, that you can feel me walking around," I shot back. I was just joking.

"I can't admit to all my abilities. A girl has to have some secrets," she stated.

"I see. How do we know?" I asked.

"Let's go do the blood test. It won't take a minute, then we will go see Gregory. You can sit in his chair again." I had made his blood inaccessible, but the Doc had ways around it to do blood tests when necessary. I had to trust my own people.

"No thanks. Abby, does it matter if we are related? It's not like we are together or going to be."

She was so insistent on that point last night. I thought if I pressed the issue she might want to talk about it more. Maybe it was all remnants of the mark, but I did not want to shut that door.

"It matters if I have family that I didn't know about before now."

Perspective. I worried about kissing my sister, and she longed to have a real family.

CHAPTER 38

ABIGAIL

"I've got to change before we go up to see grandfather," I said. "He doesn't go for casual. You probably should, too. We can go do the blood test, go see him and head out to the tavern."

"What about the magic?" he said.

"Right, the soul bond, if it is one will help this out a lot," I told him. "You should be able to feel what I'm doing when I cast spells. The biggest thing you need to learn is to put up a protective circle. Are you familiar with them?"

"Yes, but I'm not sure how you set it up."

"It's the simplest thing. Most mundane humans could do it. It's simply a circle made by writing, pouring a powder—which can get moved easily—or using a premade circle. There is one in my bedroom." I walked into the bedroom and moved the rug at the end of my bed. "Step inside."

In the floor, there was a silver circle embedded in the concrete. He stepped inside it. "You are going to need blood;

387

therefore, you will have to cut yourself or something else to get it. I have this small knife we can use." I handed it to him and he pricked his finger. "Now focus on the world around you. Focus on keeping yourself safe and keeping everything else out. Then touch the circle with your blood."

He closed his eyes, bent down, and touched the silver circle. I felt a small swirl of wind as it went up. "How do I know it's in place?"

I picked up my hairbrush on the side table by my bed and threw it at him. He ducked, but the brush rebounded off the barrier around him.

"It's there. Easy peasy," I said. "Now you can only break it from the inside. Or if you trap something in it, only you can break it on the outside. However, if you run across an extremely powerful being, it can be broken, and there isn't much you can do about it then. It's hard to know how powerful that being is until you really get out there and see what's there."

"What else?" he asked eager to learn something new.

"The communication spell, it seems, we won't have to worry about because of the soul bond," I said.

"You seem pretty confident now that there is, in fact, a soul bond," he said.

"Yes, it explains so much," I said. The soul bond, if there, was a complication I hadn't anticipated. It made me nervous. A soul bond could either make us a force to be reckoned with or it could tear us apart at the seams. One thing I knew for sure was that I needed to protect him as much as possible. We couldn't have another incident like the one with Chito. "I would like to place a personal protection on you by my own hand. Your crucifix has some protective qualities. I made you something before we ever met in hopes that I could give it to you one day."

"Okay. What is it?" he asked.

I held my hand up, palm up, and said, "*Armilla.*" I pulled a leather woven bracelet from my vault on the island. It had a cylindrical silver adornment on it. Carved into the silver was the Celtic shield knot for protection and wrapping around it a blazing sun motif. I made it myself. "Would you wear it? I know it's a bracelet. I tried to make it look masculine."

"Yes, of course, put it on," he said and offered his right wrist.

"No, the left. The left is your weak hand. I will put the protection on your weakest side. It's mostly symbolic. The Celtic knotwork is a shield knot for protection. The sun is a symbol of my branch of the family. I fall under Helios' line. If for some reason the soul bond isn't working or if you are incapacitated, I should know immediately. Because I crafted it and put the spells on it, I will know if you are in trouble. I should have given it to you before the other night."

"Do I need to do anything with it?"

"Just don't take it off," I said. "Now get out so I can change."

"Thank you, Abby," he said looking at it intently. He kept studying it as he walked out of the room. I saw him go in his room and pick up his phone off the bed to make a call. I put on a cute sleeveless turquoise-colored maxi dress with a long necklace plus my sun pendant necklace and some gladiator sandals. I grabbed a cropped jean jacket and put it over it. I pulled my hair half back and clipped it up. It would work for a faux date, plus it was dressy enough not to set my grandfather in a tizzy because I had dared approach the Titan in casual dress. He was a stickler about some things.

WHEN I RETURNED TO THE LIVING ROOM, I FOUND A BOX ON THE kitchen counter. He sat on the couch grinning at me. He wore a pair of dark blue jeans and a grey tee and a black leather jacket. "What are you grinning about?"

"I got you something. The box came today. Ashley just brought it in," he said. He got up and walked over to the box and waited for me to join him. I opened the shipping box and found a black cube-shaped box with a white ribbon tied around it.

"Tadeas, you shouldn't be buying me anything."

"Oh please. Just open it."

I took off the ribbon and there was a glossy black coffee mug in it. I pulled it out, and it had matte black jaguar spots on it. There in white vinyl script letters, it said, "I love Jaguars." I started laughing so uncontrollably that I almost dropped the mug. He had a huge, adorable smile on his face. I hugged his neck. "I love it," I said continuing to laugh.

"I saw it online and thought you needed one to replace the other one. Happy house, um, apartment warming gift. But you gotta promise not to smash this one," he smiled as we still stood arm in arm. I hugged him again.

"It's my new favorite mug. No smashing. I swear," I said.

"You ready to go?" he asked.

"Yes, let's go," I said setting the mug down on the counter. It was really great. For the first time in a very long time, I felt genuinely happy. It felt good. We rode the elevator to the sixth floor which was basically research and development. We went into the lab where Dr. Maki worked on experiments, and Ashley sat at a desk typing on a laptop.

She looked up to us and said, "Did you give it to her?"

"Yes," he said smiling.

She looked at me waiting for my response. "It's great. I love it."

"It was such a cute idea. I say you keep him, Abby," she suggested.

"He's useful for now," I shrugged off.

Ichiro decided to speak up. "We are just chopped meat, man."

"I see," said Tadeas.

"Abby, what can I do for you?" Ichiro asked.

"Please do a DNA test on Tadeas, and cross check it with my DNA. See if we have any common ancestors please," I asked.

He looked shocked and looked over at Ashley. "Why do you need to do that?" Ashley said.

"A common form of soul bond that is a natural connection is between close relatives," I said.

"Gag, and you kissed him," she said.

I laughed. "Actually he kissed me and you made him do it. I doubt any connection considering our racial differences, but you never know. You saw the racial diversity of the Six. Just want to rule it out."

"Yuck, yuck, yuck. You kissed her," she said emphasizing it to him.

"Oh, Ashley, we aren't related," he said.

"You hope you aren't! I've already picked out names for your children," she said continuing to tease him. A dark thought washed over me. Ashley knew I couldn't have children. She was just teasing him, but it was a painful point for me that I didn't talk about to anyone but her. She saw the look in my eyes, and I could tell she regretted saying it. I couldn't be mad at her. I made a waving motion at her as to push it away. I didn't want her to be upset over a slip of the tongue. She was just having a good time torturing Tadeas. I loved seeing the friendship between all of them bloom and grow. We all needed friends in this business. I had forgotten that while isolating myself from everyone. I loved my team. I had missed my friends.

Ichiro walked up with a small needle and drew a small amount of blood out of his arm. I put my hand on the bleeding spot and said, "*Consano*" and the small spot healed.

"Thanks," he said.

"No problem."

"It will only take a few minutes, Abby," Ichiro said.

"Okay, we will wait," I told him. We sat down on the small couch near the desk where Ashley was and she started going over some of the info she had gotten about those who were inquiring about the auction in Paris.

Ichiro walked up with a serious look on his face. I stood up. "What's wrong?"

He said, "I can't believe it, but he *is* your brother."

Tadeas jumped up and shouted, "*What?*"

I felt light-headed. "No, it can't be." Then I looked over to Ashley. She tried to stifle a laugh. I turned around on Ichiro. "Ichiro Maki, I am going to kick your ass. That is not funny!"

He died laughing, and Ashley couldn't hold it a back anymore. I walked up and jerked the results paper away from him. No common ancestry at all. I wadded it up, then threw it at him. He batted it away, as they kept laughing. It wouldn't have been bad to have a brother. But I did not want to be related to Tadeas in any way, shape or form. Partially because when he kissed me, I liked it, and my name wasn't Lannister. I may not watch TV, but I do read books. I looked at Tadeas, and he smiled at their fun.

"*You okay?*" he asked.

"*Yes, relieved actually.*"

"*Me, too.*"

"Okay, you two. Before I strangle you both, thank you, Ichiro."

"I'm sorry, Abby, I had to do it. The looks on both of your faces was priceless."

"I videoed it with my phone," Ashley said.

"You what!" I exclaimed. We both walked around to the desk and she replayed it.

"Good grief. Do not put that on the internet," I said.

"Oh, I won't," she said. "But I did send it to Aiden, Tommy and Tony."

"Dammit, Ash!"

"Tadeas, save me before she kills me," Ashley played, using his body as a shield.

"We should go," he said laughing at her.

"I will get you for this," I said.

"Oh, I'll count on it," she said. Tadeas grabbed my hand, and we went out to the elevator to visit Gregory.

GREGORY GREETED US, COMPLIMENTING US AGAIN ON A FINE PARTY and dance the night before, "Except for you slapping the west coast regent, I'd say it was a good night overall."

"Sorry," I mumbled.

"One day you will stop being hard on him. You don't love him anymore. Fine, stop torturing him. Find a way to be friends."

"Yes, Sir," I complied. I didn't want to be friends with him. It was much easier pretending that I hated him.

"Tadeas, have a seat."

I looked at him as he turned white as a ghost. Grandfather really scared the crap out of him with that chair. Gregory slapped him on the shoulder and laughed.

"I'd rather not sit, Sir."

"You got something to hide?" Gregory asked. Tadeas fell for it, plopping down without a second thought.

"You dummy," I said. He scowled at me.

"What brings you two by here today?"

"Soul bond," Tadeas blurted out, and I giggled. "Shut it."

"Yes, what about it?" Gregory asked.

"We would like to see if you could tell if we had one," Tadeas said.

"Yes, you do," Gregory said.

"Wait, don't you have to look or something?" I said.

"I did look. Last night while you were dancing. It is a very strong bond. It's why I calmed my anger against both of you. I hadn't realized your relationship had progressed to such a physical level."

"No!" we both said.

"Grandfather, we haven't, you know, done that," I said. Talking about sex with your grandfather was the most epic form of uncomfortable. I remembered when he realized that Lincoln and I had been together. Awkward. I thought Lincoln was going to crawl under a rock which was saying a lot considering he was one of the most powerful beings on the planet.

"That's interesting. It seems very much like a sexual/physical bond. Let me look again." He put his hands flat on the table, and his eyes turned completely white. "It's there. It's very strong. Son, have you done something to her while she slept? Did you drug her?"

"What! No! I would never, Sir," Tadeas exclaimed. "Tell him, Abby!"

I bit my lip, ignoring Tadeas' chair induced panic. It didn't make sense. "Is it possible for you to show me what you are seeing?" I asked him.

"We can try. I'm not sure you can see it the same way as I do, but you should be able to see something. Come over here and hold my hand." When I held his hand, I felt him pull power. It was subtle and clean. Effortless. When I looked I could see red and purple strands of light swirling back and forth between Tadeas and me. It was mesmerizing. I shook my head as I let go of Gregory's hand.

"What is it?" Tadeas asked.

"It's like glowing red and purple ropes tying us together. They were moving and twisting around each other," I tried to explain.

"Kinky," he said. "I hate this damn chair."

Gregory roared. "You can get up, Son. The colors are significant. The red generally indicates unconditional love, Agape. I've never seen purple. I'm not sure what that is."

Tadeas jumped up. He clearly had reached his maximum level of uncomfortable, and said, "Well, we can talk about it more on the way to the tavern. I want to make sure we get a good seat before it gets too busy."

"Kinky, huh?"

He shrugged. "What? I'm a guy."

I rolled my eyes and hugged my grandfather.

"You two be careful out there," he said. "Abby, did you sign that paperwork?"

"Ugh. No, I forgot. We will go down there and see if I can find her."

TADEAS AND I WENT DOWN TO THE OFFICES, AND AUNT LIANNE was nowhere to be found. I knew she didn't live in the compound, so the paperwork would have to wait. We were waiting on the elevator when Meredith stepped out of the stairwell.

"Hello, Tadeas," she said to him. She didn't speak to me. I just ignored her.

"Hey Mere, did you have a good time last night?" I believe he asked genuinely. He hadn't figured it out yet that she would never be a true friend to him again.

"As a matter of fact, I did. Mr. MacCormack is a very interesting and delightful man. I'm supposed to meet him tonight. Where are you two heading?"

"We are going out to grab some food in Boulder," he said.

"Well, you two kids have fun," she smirked. I figured my best option was to keep my mouth shut. The elevator door opened, and I stepped in. I put my hand up and held the door open for Tadeas.

"*One minute,*" he said.

"*Okay,*" I said and put my finger on the open-door button.

After a minute he came back, "Did you listen to that?"

"No, I didn't want to intrude."

"I'm just worried about her hanging out with him," he said.

"You should be worried. I would worry if you took up with Aunt Lianne. Same danger, different person," I said. His concern for her was legit. The Fae, especially these particular ones, should not be taken lightly.

"Did she listen to you?" I asked knowing that she probably hadn't.

"No, of course not, she just said some rude things about us and stomped off."

"I'm sorry."

"No, it's okay. I've kept her at arm's length for too long. I thought maybe there was something there between us, and I was just afraid. But I know now that I just kept her around because she did like me. Maybe it was an ego thing. I'm ashamed of that," he admitted. I wondered if it was more that he liked her attention and wondered if he would ever get to the point where he trusted himself with her. It didn't matter either way. Since she was tied up with one of the Six, she was dangerous.

"No need to be, Tadeas. We all make bad calls on relationships whether it's just friendships or more. It's part of living life. I've made quite a few bad choices in my life," I admitted.

"I'd like to hear about that," he said.

"You want to know about my bad relationships?" I asked.

"If you made a mistake and did something wrong, yes, I do," he grinned.

"I should smack you," I said.

"See, I knew you wanted to kiss me again," he said.

"Keep thinking that Romeo," I returned.

"Sin from thy lips? O trespass sweetly urged! Give me my sin again," he laughed quoting Shakespeare.

"Thus, with a kiss I die," I returned and made a gagging motion.

"That's not the next line!" he protested.

"I wasn't going to compliment you. Your ego is already larger than life," I said knowing full well the next line was "You kiss by the book." I'd already said too often that it was a good kiss. We needed to move on. The banter was fun, but underneath it all there was a red strand of soul bond between us, and that could be very troublesome.

"You know how to cut me, Abby," he sounded hurt, but his eyes laughed.

The elevator doors opened, and we walked off to the right side of the building where the parking garage was located. As we approached where the Mercedes usually sat, he stopped in his tracks.

"You have got to be kidding me?" he exclaimed as he looked at the car sitting in the parking spot. He turned and looked at me with a huge grin. I held up the keys to my fully-restored Mustang. He grabbed them and kissed me on the cheek and took off running to it. He stopped at the passenger door, "Come on let's go."

"Slow down. Do not wreck my car," I warned.

He helped me in, then jumped in the driver's seat. "Oh hell, yes! Let's see what this baby can do."

I groaned. He drove it wide open on the road from the compound to the outskirts of Boulder. He smiled, enjoying himself completely. I loved watching him. I thought about the bond between us. Obviously, I was overlooking something within myself when it came to him. I probably built the bond myself or partially just by following him closely for the past two years. I put all of my hopes for the future in him, in us, and because of it, we were intimately connected.

CHAPTER 39

VANESSA

"Yes, I understand," I said over the phone to Mwenye. "I will make the call immediately. This is a perfect opportunity. Goodbye, love."

Somehow, he had gotten information that Tadeas Duarte and Abigail Davenport had left the compound together and were heading into Boulder for the evening. I supposed he had contacts on the inside as well. I would call my contacts and set up an interruption to their plans. I dialed another number. A man answered the phone.

"Hello, sexy!"

"I'll be damned if it isn't the black mistress herself. How are you Vanessa?" he said.

"I'd be better if you were in my bed," I retorted building his ego.

"There is only so much of me to go around," he said.

"And you do get around," I returned.

"What can I say? When it's good, it's good. What can I do for you Vanessa?" he asked.

"Travis, grab that little girlfriend of yours and the two of you get to Boulder. I have information that Duarte and Davenport have gone out that way for the evening. Locate them. Interrupt their little date or whatever it is. Get as much info as possible and keep tabs on them until I can get people into a position to take them out," I explained.

"Is that all?" he said. "Because things are getting out of hand here, we can't just keep parading around here. We are drawing too much attention."

"What are you parading around? Your dick? I told all of you that this was my plan. Putting you there, getting you inside. Do not fuck this up! I will have you, Travis Reed. Quit fucking around and get the job done!" I yelled through the phone.

"Oh, Vanessa, you are so amusing. Get over yourself. It's handled," he said.

"I'm going to handle you. Get to Boulder! Now!" I said, hanging up the phone. Travis exemplified the ultimate robust man. He had it where it counted in all the right places. I never saw a woman that could turn him down. Not all of it was natural though. He was one of the sons of Asmodeus. Over the years the bloodline had thinned out, but those men in this world with perfect eyes, abs, and dicks, were generally sons of Asmodeus.

The demon Asmodeus walked the earth as the most sexualized beast known to man. He had a thing for Sarah, the Angel of Vengeance, Raguel's daughter. She would not have him. He managed to kill off seven of her husbands before she could bed them. The story was that she ended up killing herself. But over the years he had many offspring and in modern days, the sons were the captains of the football team and porn stars and men that reeked of masculinity. Travis was a specimen. I'd had him myself a few times, but I generally had whatever man I wanted.

I picked up the phone to make another call. I needed to get

the players in place to take out Abigail and her pet once and for all.

I finished that call when Mwenye came in. "Did you arrange it?"

"Yes, my love, tonight she dies," I assured him.

"Perhaps you should have gone yourself," he suggested.

"Oh, I can't my love. I'm off to Paris tomorrow, and I needed you one last time before I go," I built his ego.

"I'll see you when you get back. I have things to do tonight. If this plan fails Vanessa, I'm holding you responsible. I've given you far too many chances. This is it. You better hope it works. I can find someone else to go to Paris for me," he turned to me with his black eyes. Evil rolled off of him and choked me. "Do you understand, my love?"

"Yes, of course," I softly replied. Maybe I *should* have gone myself.

He walked over to me, touching my face. For a moment, I thought he was going to be rough with me, but instead, he stroked my cheek. "Vanessa, I have taught you much about magic and wielding it. Yet, you sit back and let these incompetent fools do your bidding. Sometimes you have to do things yourself. Get your hands dirty. You have yet to eat a soul because of a strange infatuation with that woman. I admit she is exquisite, but you were born for a much darker cause, and I will teach you no more until you start becoming who you were meant to be. If you can't move forward, then our time together has come to an end."

I thought of sweet Cassidy sleeping in the other room. Perhaps Mwenye was right. I needed to move forward in my development, and while Cassidy was an ideal, killing her would most certainly be the death of me by Donovan's hand.

"You are right, my love," I said. He kissed me on the cheek, then walked to the door to whoever it was that now held his affections.

"Don't come back if this fails," he said, as the door closed.

"See you soon," I replied. I sat down on the couch, staring out into the night. It was time to act, or I would lose him forever. Maybe that is exactly what I needed to do. Either way, he was right. This was something I needed to do myself. I needed to prove to all of them that my black heart went beyond the bedroom.

I went back to my room to put on dark clothing. I grabbed a few items including a gun from my dresser in the room where Cassidy was sleeping. She stirred a little with the noise I made in the room. I slipped out the bedroom door, then loaded the gun with enchanted bullets I had acquired at an underground shop in Cleveland. I pulled out a dark obsidian crystal, spoke a few words, and a black smoke surrounded me. When it cleared, I stood in the dark night. The Rocky Mountains loomed over me to the west. In the distance, I saw the flickering lights of Boulder, Colorado. I waited on the call. Then, by my own hand, Abigail Davenport would die.

CHAPTER 40

TADEAS

*D*riving that car was a dream come true. It handled like a boss. I looked good driving it, too. Abby just smiled at me while I took it all in. I needed to forget about what Meredith had said to me. I told Abby that she had said things about her, but she said them about me as well. She called me weak. She called me a toy soldier. I was glad things were settled with Abby and me. It was time to move on and be a better self.

I slowed down as we got into Boulder. I didn't want to get a ticket in her car. Abby looked more simply dressed compared to last night. I preferred her like this. Simple and beautiful. Parts of me wished our relationship could be more. I would be happy with whatever we had. The soul bond red strands were probably because somewhere inside me I wanted it to be more. I just didn't realize how strongly I wanted it. The kiss was amazing. Perhaps I was building it up too much because I knew it wouldn't happen again. I had too many thoughts about doing it again. Maybe one day she would get to the point where she could conceive of us having a relationship, but until then I'd be whatever she needed me to be. It would probably never work out, anyway. We seemed to constantly be at each other's throats. However, I consigned that to sexual tension as well. One day. Maybe.

I found a spot for the car about a block from the tavern. I walked around the car as she got out. "I was going to get the door for you," I said.

"It's okay. I am not helpless," she said.

"Of course, I know that, but this is supposed to look like a date, correct?"

"You are right. Shall we, Mr. Duarte?" she grinned.

I took her hand and we pretended to be in love.

When we walked into the tavern, the same burly red-headed chap was behind the bar. He noticed me and nodded to a booth near the back. He gave me a thumbs-up and pointed at Abby. I gave him the confident look guys give each other when they appreciate the other's woman.

"I had a booth saved for us," I explained and we walked to the back. She started to sit opposite of me. "You aren't going to be able to see the room over there."

"I thought it was best I feel the room, and you watch it," she said.

"If you say so," I said as I sat down with full view of the door.

The bartender walked over with the menus. I noticed this time his name was Finn. "Good to see you again, Finn. This is Abby."

"Hello, Finn. It is nice to meet you," Abby said.

"Good to meet you too, ma'am. Thanks for letting him out of the doghouse. Now, what can I get for you two?" Finn asked.

Abby looked at me and laughed. "Doghouse, huh?"

I shrugged. "Give us two glasses of the Eagle Rare, and we will decide on food in a bit." I handed him five one-hundred-dollar bills. Abby's eyebrows shot up. "Finn, we might be here a while tonight. This is to cover the loss of you turning tables."

"Thanks, Tadeas. Whatever you need, just let me know," Finn said as he tucked the bills into his pocket and hurried away to get our drinks.

"That was awfully generous. But good thinking, if we are here a while I would hate to see him not get compensated," she said.

"I learned that from you from our first date," I said.

"I see. And how many dates have we been on by your count, Tadeas?" she said having fun with it.

"The horseback riding date. The visiting the old church date. We've had several dates where we had meals together, doughnuts, lunch, lamb, and spaghetti. Too bad we didn't get that pizza date in."

She laughed. "That one was a disaster."

"It happens. We made it through it," I said.

Finn showed back up with the drinks. We both ordered barbeque sandwiches and fries. Finn hurried off to put in our orders.

"*He's a shifter. Wolf, I think,*" Abby said in my head.

"*Is he dangerous?*"

"*Not sure. He seems to be working and living a life, but he could be just the lookout for a boss. An informant. Just keep an eye on him.*"

"I enjoyed the dancing date," she said with a smile.

"Meh. I'm a terrible dancer," I said.

"Actually, I thought you were an excellent dance partner. I can't wait to do it again. Maybe there will be dancing on our trip this weekend," she said. I got the feeling at this point she spoke sincerely.

"Maybe so," I said taking a sip of my drink. I watched her close her eyes. I could just barely feel her power stirring in the room. "*Anything else?*"

"*Not in the building, but something is approaching. Something close,*" she said.

I heard a squeal from the door, and I tensed up reaching for the knife in my boot by instinct. I saw the source of the shriek and sank down in the seat.

"Samantha and Travis," I said to her.

Her eyes grew wide, and she sat utterly still. It was too late. Samantha saw us and dragged Travis back to where we sat.

"I knew it. I knew it. You two are dating, aren't you?" She beamed at both of us.

"Um, no. Well, we are just having a drink and talking," I stammered. "*What the fuck do we do?*"

"*Play the game, Jag,*" she said. "Sam, it's good to see you. Hello, Travis."

"Hello, Miss Davenport," he mumbled.

Finn showed up with our sandwiches.

"Just a drink, this is a date," Sam said. "Can we sit with you? They have no tables available."

"No," I said.

"Sure," Abby said, and I gave her a dirty look. "Tadeas, it's not like it's our first date. I'll sit with you." She got up and moved to join me on the bench. My anxiety skyrocketed.

"*What are you doing? We are supposed to be working. They are a distraction.*"

"*They are the work. They are the ones I felt coming.*" She looked me in the eye, and I saw pain. I realized that somehow these two were tied up in whatever mess was going on with the shadow man, perhaps even with the GEA.

Samantha jumped into the seat on the other side of the table, and Travis sat down beside her. She went off with a barrage of questions. "I knew you were going to start dating. You look totally good together. How long have you really been going out? Were you together when you were in the class, Abby? Oh, my! This is exciting."

I cringed and wanted to crawl in a hole. Abby took my hand, then squeezed it. I guess she did it to ease my apprehension, but it didn't. I liked touching her entirely too much.

"Samantha, slow down. No, this is very new for both of us," she said. Samantha started to continue on, but Finn brought them menus.

"I'm going to have to see some I.D. from the both of you," he said.

They each produced I.D.s to show him. He looked at them closely. Then he looked at me, recognizing the girl as Milt's hot, young friend. I just shrugged, again. I was tongue-tied at the moment. He handed back the I.D.s.

"Ok, what can I get for you?"

"I just want a coke," Travis said.

"I'd like what they are having," Samantha said. Finn returned to the bar to place their orders. "Please don't say anything. Sometimes we just need to get out of the compound."

"We can discuss it later," Abby said. "Sam, tell me how things are going for you."

"Oh, I'm fine. I love the new training. I hope you guys put me with Travis. I love him. I'd hate to be separated from him," she said.

Travis turned red and tried to look like he watched the baseball game on the television hanging over the bar. Occasionally he would look down at his phone. Looked like he played a game or something. He showed no interest in Sam's excitement or any of the conversation at the table.

"You know we don't have any control over that," Abby said. I was glad she continued to talk. It gave me time to calm down.

"You should. Perhaps that's something you could change," Sam suggested.

"Perhaps so. Maybe I can look into it," Abby offered. "Now let's not talk about the compound. Tell me what you guys do for fun here in Boulder."

Samantha went on a rant about the lack of good clubs in Boulder, and how they go down to Denver a lot, hence the need for fake identification.

"*Get yourself together,*" she said, but she looked at me with a teasing smile.

"*I was not expecting company,*" I said.

"*The whole point was to draw attention. We succeeded. Just be ready for anything, okay?*"

"*What are they?*"

"*Human, I think. It's hard to tell sometimes. There are just too many possibilities out there, but they are bonded.*"

"*Like us?*"

"*Yes and no. They are bonded to each other, but each has tethers to something else. I just learned to see this with grandfather. I'm not sure exactly what I am looking at. Our bonds look red and purple to me. Theirs are green and black.*" She moved closer to me in the booth seat, and I put my arm around her shoulders. "*There you go, play the part.*"

I was not playing. I wish she had sat on the inside next to the wall. If something came after us, it would get to her first. I should have thought of that. I knew she could take care of herself. I guessed I was just a chauvinist. It used to be called chivalry. Times changed, and no one liked a knight in shining armor anymore. I looked up, and Samantha beamed at me.

"Sam, what kind of clubs do you like? Any certain kind of music?" I could do this. Just keep them talking and see what happened.

Samantha started talking about clubs and music, and Abby and I just kept the conversation going. Occasionally Travis would speak up. We all ate food, but Abby and I both switched to water after the first bourbon. I knew I was uneasy, but I could tell she was too. The tension in her body radiated off of her as she sat next to me. I could feel the subtle power she pulled in and held it ready to unleash at any moment. I occasionally reached out to feel the spirit world to make sure I could pull us through if I had to. I tried to keep a part of me in contact with her at all times just in case if we had to, we could shift through quickly.

After an agonizing hour, Samantha said, "We should get back before curfew."

"Good idea," I said giving them both my instructor tone. "You ready to go, Abby?"

"Yes," she looked at them. "We will cover the bill. It was nice talking to both of you outside the compound."

We all piled out of the booth. I stepped away to the bar but kept them all in my sight. Finn gave me the bill. I gave him double what was on the receipt, "I'm covering theirs, too. Thanks, Finn. You ever need anything let me know," and I scribbled my phone number onto the back of the receipt.

He picked it up, then looked at it. "Thanks, Tadeas. You never know."

Abby came up behind me, putting her arms around me. Damn. I wasn't sure if I hated or loved this game. I turned around to face her, finding a huge smile on her face. Samantha and Travis had made it to the front door, but she looked back at us. I leaned down and kissed Abby on the forehead.

"*Boring!*" she said.

"Come on, let's keep an eye on them for a minute," I said.

"Good idea," she said, then nodded at Finn who watched us. We walked out the front of the building, and I held her hand. We looked both ways, but they were gone.

"Well, that can't be good," I said.

"Nope, let's get to the car," she said, pulling me that way.

"Why did you give the wolf your number?"

"Abby, I know what it's like to be alone and a shifter in this world," I said.

"What if he isn't alone?" she said.

"Instinct. Please trust me," I said.

"I do. I just try to be cautious with everyone," she said.

"We are supposed to be helping people, Abby. You can't help anyone if you are suspicious of everyone."

"Okay, we'll make a deal. You be the open one, and I'll be

skeptical. That way we have both bases covered," she said. She was serious. We made it to the car, and I started to open the car door when I smelled something off. It smelled like a dead body. I tensed and moved closer to Abby. "Hold on a minute," I said to her.

"What is it?" she said. I could feel her pulling more power.

"I smell death. Putrid rot." I looked both ways up and down the street. It was darker now, and there were a few groups of people walking up and down the sidewalks. I looked through feline eyes to each of them. They all looked normal. I looked down at her, and she clutched my jacket. She closed her eyes as she felt around for any sort of magic around us. I put my hand over hers. "What do we want to do?"

"I feel something, but it's not good. We might be better running in this situation," she said. I could feel her tremble a little. Despite her power, I knew she hadn't been in the field for a long time. My urge to protect her jumped into high gear.

"Get in." I opened the door of the car and practically shoved her in. I ran to the driver's side, getting the car started as fast as I could. She directed me through side roads and before we knew it we were on the long road to the compound on the outskirts of town. The foothills of the Rockies rose along our right side. She sat with her eyes closed.

"Faster," she said, and I slammed on the gas. The car lurched forward. I looked over to her again, as her eyes shot open. "Tadeas, look out!"

I looked back forward, and there was a black shimmer. The next few things happened very quickly. I heard the bending and crunching of metal as the car started to flip. I reached over to her. I just needed to touch a part of her. As I felt her cool skin, I could tell that she had thrown a golden shield around us like a bubble. When I touched her, I ripped the cord between the planes, shifting us to the spirit world. We both tumbled separately from the car which was still on the other side. I tried to wrap her up as much as I could with the momentum. If we survived this, we would both be bruised up pretty badly. She landed on top and quickly shuffled off of me, standing up ready to fight. I stood up to look around. I could see the smoldering carcass of the car about 10 feet away.

"Damn, she's going to kill me," I thought.

"You hurt?" she asked.

"Not too bad, you?"

"No, but whatever it was isn't on this side. I can't feel it anymore. The moment there is danger we have to go back to our world."

"No, we are safer here."

"No, we aren't. I don't know how to use my magic here. And I don't want to use the sword unless I absolutely have to," she said.

"Ok, but we are still a good 15 miles from the compound," I said. Then I caught a flash out of the corner of my eye. I dove to protect her. The report of the gun cut through the eerie silence of the spirit world. When I hit her body, I shifted us back, and she put the shield back up around us. Several more shots rang out, and I could feel their impacts on the shield. Then it was quiet. I put my hands on her face. She had gone pale. "Abby, talk to me."

She moved her mouth, but I couldn't hear her. I looked down, and her chest was covered in blood. She was panicking. I heard her heart racing. She put her hand up to my chest, pulling it back red. I looked down at myself. It was my blood. It was all my blood. She pushed me off of her with effort and started ripping my shirt off. I could feel her pulling in power.

"It's not bad," I said. I felt no pain. There was a hole in my chest, and I just didn't feel it at all.

"*Don't you dare fucking die on me,*" she cried in my head.

"*It will be fine. It's not bad.*"

She stripped out of her jacket, then ripped the bottom of her

411

dress. In any other situation that might have been extremely hot. She shoved the cloth down on my chest. She chanted in Latin. I could not make out the words. But as she chanted out loud, I could hear her calling my name in my head. I couldn't speak, as I realized that I couldn't breathe either.

"*Tadeas, please stay with me. I can fix this. Just hang on. Tadeas. Please. Tadeas.*" The sound of her voice faded. The light faded. The last thing I saw was her panicked face chanting and a swirl of golden light around her eyes.

CHAPTER 41

TADEAS

*T*he bright light blinded me like an oncoming train, but when I looked closer, I saw a beautiful angel with white glowing wings. The angel had piercing green eyes and golden hair. On her side, she wore a long sword. I knew it was a dream. Or maybe I died. I was just glad that whichever one it was; she was here too.

"How do you feel?" she asked.

"I'm not sure," I said. "Are you okay?"

"That shouldn't be your concern, you have to get well. She needs you."

"You are her, aren't you?"

"Not exactly, but you need to go back now. Thank you, Tadeas, for saving her life." The light around her spread, and I winced at its brightness. Once it faded, I could tell that I laid on a bed in a hospital room. Several monitors beeped around me. The uncomfortable poke in my arm indicated that I had an IV attached. Sitting in a chair next to the bed with her head down and asleep was my partner, Abby. I picked up my hand to touch her hair. She was real. I was awake now. She stirred, looking up at me.

"Maki, he's awake," she called back to the doc. "Lay still. You lost a lot of blood." She looked tired, and her eyes were red. Behind her, Ichiro approached wearing a doctor's coat and a stethoscope. Ashley and Jay stood further back, looking concerned. Abby stood up, moving away to let him look at me. I didn't want her to move. Even though Maki started talking to me, I kept my eyes on her.

"Hey man, you scared the crap out of us," Maki said checking all the monitors and looking in my eyes with his light.

"I'm fine. Abby, are you alright?" she nodded at me, but didn't say anything.

"He looks fine, Abby. Whenever he's ready to leave, you can take him," Maki said. He lightly pulled the IV out of my arm. I didn't even feel it.

"What about the gunshot wound?" I asked and put my hand on my chest. I raised up to look. I was astonished. There wasn't anything there. I looked up to Abby. She put her hand in mine, and I felt something metal. I turned my hand over. I looked at the copper-jacketed hollow point bullet charred around its edges. It bloomed out like it had hit a steel wall.

"I am glad you were unconscious when I pulled it out, or you might not be happy to see me right now," she said quietly. I realized that everyone else had left the room. "You threw yourself in front of it. I didn't get the reinforced shield up fast enough to stop the first one. It cut right through the shield I already had up, but on the other side I haven't figured out the best way to pull energy. Once you moved us back, I could do more. I'm sorry I failed you. I almost lost you, but you saved me. She was aiming for me." She hung her head down like she had done something wrong.

I raised up to sit in the bed, and she sat down on it facing me. "Seems to me that while I bled out because of a gunshot wound, you pulled the bullet out of me, and somehow saved my life."

"Once I pulled the bullet out of you, I could tell it had an enchantment on it. I started working a counterspell and healing the wound up the best I could. You still had your cell phone in your pocket, and I called Jay to come get us. We collected the bullets that hit the shield. Aidan is analyzing them. They were all enchanted. We went asking for trouble and got it." She was blaming herself for this one all the way. I couldn't let her do that. It was our life now.

"Seems like that's what we would be doing in Paris, too," I said.

"Yes," she admitted. "Part of the reason I'm afraid. You can back out if you want to."

"What! No, I can't believe you would even suggest it. We have work to do." I climbed out of the bed and had the awful realization that I was completely naked. I jerked the sheet off the bed almost causing her to fall to the floor. I struggled to wrap it around me. She started giggling, but she turned her back to me.

"There are clothes for you on the table. Ashley brought them for you," I could hear her smiling in her voice.

"You could have told me before I got up," I said embarrassed.

"Honey, you haven't got anything I've never seen before," she bragged.

"You haven't seen me," I said.

"Seen one, seen them all."

"Completely not true," I said pulling the jeans up and buttoning them. She bantered with me to help me relax.

"Prove it," she said.

I spun around as I put my shirt on. She still had her back to me. "Dammit, woman!"

She laughed, and said more seriously, "Meredith came by

here a bit ago checking on you. She really did not want to talk to me and left pretty quickly. I did not want a confrontation. I let her just go."

"Guess I should go check on her," I said.

"Probably a good idea," she said. Which I was surprised she would say because she clearly did not like Meredith. She deferred to my feelings though. Even though I had told her my feelings for Meredith were nothing more than friendship, she still thought I cared for her. But I felt ashamed for leading her on even if I didn't realize that as it was happening. I'd go talk to her and clear everything up.

"Are we going through the portal? What day is it?"

"It's early Saturday morning. The auction in Paris is Monday night. We can head to the island and rest up today. We will leave for Paris tomorrow," she explained.

"Sounds good. I'm going downstairs. I'll meet back up in your room right after I talk to her," I said. I walked around the bed and hugged her tightly. She returned the embrace. She had been very scared. I just wasn't sure if she was scared to lose me, or that someone came after her. "I'm sorry about the car," I said to take off the pressure.

"I'll just take it out of your paycheck," she said. I pulled back to look at her. "I'd rather have you than the car, anyway."

"Thank you," I said, putting my hand on her cheek.

"We save each other. I could not let you get one up on me," she quipped.

"I'm not joking, Abby."

"I know. I thought I lost you there for a minute. It was awful."

"It will take more than a bullet to stop both of us," I said fully confident in her abilities and for once in mine. Had that first bullet hit her, I couldn't have pulled it out of her and healed her. I was glad it hit me. "See you in a little while. Okay?"

She nodded but didn't speak. She was afraid of what she

would say. As I left the room, Ashley went in. "Don't screw this up, Duarte," she said.

"I'm trying not to," I said. She smiled and went into the lab.

CHAPTER 42

VANESSA

"Hello?" I answered the buzzing cell phone in my pocket.

"Hey, we just left the bar. They are leaving too," Travis said.

"Leave the rest to me, dear boy," I said.

"When do I get my payment for this?" he added suggestively.

"I'm taking you on a trip to Paris with me. I'll call you in a bit," I said, then hung up the phone. Travis' usefulness had worn out. I was ready to terminate his employment.

I moved out to the edge of the highway and waited. He had texted me earlier and said they had arrived in a restored silver Mustang. An engine like that wouldn't be hard to mistake. I would be ready for them when they passed this way. I cast a shadow spell on myself and lurked by a large spruce tree.

The shadow allowed me to blend in with any shadows or actually become the shadow of an object. It was a great way to hide in plain sight. Nalusa had taught me the trick. Mwenye did not approve of me learning from other masters, and I paid for it with a beating. Nalusa refused to teach me anything else after that happened. He had a few honorable bones in his body and didn't want to see me beaten. Nalusa's shadow magic came naturally to me and wasn't as distasteful to me as Mwenye's necromancy.

As I sat in the darkness, I thought about my relationship with Mwenye. I didn't realize it until this moment, but it came to me that I did not need him anymore. I knew he was almost done with me anyway. He clearly had moved on considering he never spent nights at home anymore. Whether he consumed souls or fucked his next whore, he no longer needed me. Killing Abigail Davenport and taking the book from all of them in Paris would put me on the map. I would no longer be the necromancer's apprentice. The darker circles of the world would chatter the name of Vanessa Vaughn.

I heard the low rumble of a V8 engine. Pulling power from the surrounding darkness and from the black crystal in my pocket that held the souls of long dead men, I stretched my arms out before me. I uttered the word, *"Murus!"* A shimmering almost transparent wall stretched from my hands across the entire road. It blended with the darkness. I cast a spell on it to make it look transparent, like tinted glass, *"Sepculo."*

I heard the brakes engage on the car as it sped forward, but it was too late to stop. The car hit the wall and crumpled. I dropped the wall, and the momentum of the vehicle caused it to surge forward and roll. I pulled the .40 caliber pistol out of the holder on my back, aiming toward the car. I approached it slowly as it steamed and leaked fluid on the grass along the side of the road. The car was empty. I turned, reaching for my senses. They must have shifted planes. "Fine. You want to jump around, I can play too," I said to the darkness.

I reached for the edge of the spirit world and tugged. I

pushed my arm through the rift, and I could see them standing back to back. The wreck had barely scraped them. This was the first time I saw Tadeas Duarte. He was magnificent. The picture on Cassidy's computer did not do him justice. His handsome features and green expressive eyes were godlike. His lean muscular form tensed, and he stood alert protecting her as much as he could.

Suddenly, I wanted him alive and underneath me. It was a shame he would have to die. I raised the gun and dropped my shadow spell. As I pulled the trigger, his eyes flicked to a golden yellow, and he lunged for her. I had decided to take her out first. She posed more of a threat to me than he did. The moment he touched her, they shifted back to the real world, and I followed. I fired multiple rounds, but they bounced off the glowing golden shield she cast around them. Before I got close to them, I heard her gasp. I saw the large red spot expanding on his back. The poor girl cried as she tried to save him.

I cast the shadow spell quickly and watched, waiting for another chance to move on them. She rolled him over on his back and tried to cover the wound on the front of his chest. I could feel her power as she pulled it in. She would do all she could to save him, but you can't come back from that kind of bullet. The bullets were enchanted bullets. They housed the basic 4 elements. These particular ones contained fire. Once inside a body, it would start to burn them from the inside out. I had stolen the gun from Mwenye's room before I left.

It was a shame to watch the jaguar die there on the dirt. He should have been loved and protected. Not assigned to the one woman in the world that was sure to get him killed. I laughed inside as she dug into his chest trying to dislodge the bullet. The large red spot of blood grew on the ground. No amount of pressure on his chest would stop the bleeding from his back. His beautiful green eyes rolled back in his head.

"Such a waste," I said to myself. Killing him would kill her. I saw the way she desperately fought to save him. Another partner down the drain. It would be entertaining to watch her suffer more. She was on the phone calling for backup. I wouldn't be able to finish her now with all the power she pulled in to help him, but one thing was for certain, he would die. She would either go back into seclusion or kill herself. Either way, I was happy and had completed my task at the moment.

ONCE I GOT SEVERAL MILES AWAY FROM THEM, I DROPPED THE shadow spell and hitched a ride into Boulder. I found a cheap hotel out of the main part of the city and called Travis.

"Hey babe, I just got a room at the Foothills Motel out on Highway 119. Why don't you come join me? Bring your little girly with you if you would like."

"Sam is off with the old guy. But I'm on my way. I'm not going back to the compound. I'm done with that bullshit," he said.

"Aw, too bad. Well, you come along, honey. I believe I owe you payment for services rendered," I said to him. I didn't have to lure him. He'd come for sex no matter what I said to him. I needed a good roll. It would be nice to get it without Mwenye being involved too.

"On my way," he said, and I hung up the phone. I laid back on the shitty bed in this shitty hotel and daydreamed about a redhead who was going to Paris with me.

I DOZED OFF WAITING ON TRAVIS. ABOUT 45 MINUTES LATER HE knocked on the door. I barely had the door open before he was all over me. "Slow down there, tiger."

"No way! I've been waiting on this for a long time," he said ripping my clothes off. It was nice to have someone want me like that. We had only gotten started when my phone rang. It was Meredith. I rolled over to answer it, and Travis groaned. I swatted him away.

"Hey honey," I said to her.

"You shot him!" she screamed. "You fucking shot him!"

I played dumb. "Meredith, what on earth are you talking about?"

"No. You can't lie to me, Vanessa. I know you are in town. You were supposed to kill her!" she screamed.

"It is not my fault he took a bullet for her. Honey, there was no way you were ever going to get him. Why don't you come out here to the hotel and have some fun with me and Travis?" This unhealthy infatuation with Duarte was always her hang up. But after seeing him I understood why she had it bad for him. He was sex in a big cat package.

"He's not dead. If he were dead, I would hunt you down and kill you with my bare hands," she said.

This shocked me. I pushed Travis off me completely. "What do you mean he's not dead?"

"She saved him. I hate her guts, but she saved him. You stay the fuck out of this, Vanessa. I've got this handled. Go back to your necromancer and your masochistic games," she spouted.

"What are you going to do? You have no real power, Meredith. Chito carries you. Get yourself down here with me. I'm done with Mwenye. It's just us girls now." Travis grunted. "And Travis," I added.

"Fuck Travis," she said.

"I was trying to until you called. Look Mere, you know I adore you. This is our chance. Come with me to Paris," I begged her. I really did care about her.

"No, my plan no longer involves you. You know when he

catches up to you he's going to kill you, right?" she said almost like she cared.

"No, he won't. He's got a new whore. It was time to move on," Travis took that as an indication to start back up on me. I let him. He was useful at the moment.

"Goodbye Nessa, stay away from me," she said quietly, then hung up the phone. I tossed the cell phone over to the nightstand and turned my attention to the son of Asmodeus in my bed.

I would have to come up with a new plan for Abigail Davenport and her jaguar. Maybe this time I could get her and then have him. That would show Meredith. She would come to me if I had him. I don't know what Meredith's plan was but once it failed, she would be calling me back. However, with her ties to Chito and the GEA, it was probably best we cut off our friendship.

TRUE TO FORM, IT WAS ONLY A COUPLE OF HOURS AND THE PHONE rang again. "I need help," Meredith said.

"Sure, Love. Come join us," I said.

"No please send Travis back. I need help. I need it now," she said.

"Unless you are putting a knife in his heart, I don't think you need any help," I said.

"No, he's not the one I want dead. I want her dead," she protested.

Travis untangled himself from me and rolled out of the bed.

"Where are you going?" I said.

"I'm going to help her," Travis replied putting on his pants.

"No, you aren't. You are staying with me." I said.

"It won't take long. I'll be back, and I'll pick up Sam on the way," he said.

I did need the girl for part of the plan in Paris. "Alright fine, but you promise to come back, right?" I pouted.

"Yes, Vanessa, you know I will come back, I can't resist you," he said with a smile.

I kissed him one more time to ensure that he returned to me when he had finished with Meredith. It almost felt genuine for a few seconds. Travis was a means to an end. Samantha was a means to an end. They were all my means.

CHAPTER 43

ABIGAIL

Sitting on the couch in the dark, I waited for Tadeas to return. It had been 2 hours since he went downstairs to find Meredith. More than anything I wanted to get out of the compound and back home. This was the longest I'd been away from the island in a very long time. I needed my peaceful place to focus on the task in Paris. It made me calm and helped me think more clearly. Everything here seemed a tumult all the time. I felt like a boat tossed about in a storm. I got up, fixing a small drink. I thought back to the car, and the black figure that shot at us. It was not Nalusa Chito this time. The figure looked clearly female. It looked like maybe the woman we had seen before with him. A knock at the door shattered my concentration on replaying everything that happened in my mind.

"Come in. It's unlocked," I called. It wasn't Tadeas. It was Jay.

"Oh hey, I wish I could have caught you earlier. Thank you for coming for us," I said.

"Kind of dark in here, you okay?" he asked.

"Yeah, just trying to figure out who shot at us. What can I do for you, Jay?" I had to be nice to him. I called him even though I wish I could have thought of another way out of the situation. He showed up. He helped me get Tadeas in the big Tahoe, then together we collected the bullets that we could find. He drove us back to the compound quickly as I tried to stabilize Tadeas. I knew I could rely on him, despite whatever was going on between us. He had been with me since even before I met Lincoln. He was there the night I died.

"I wanted to talk with you," he paused for a moment. "Mind if I fix a drink?"

"Of course, I'm sorry. I should have offered."

"No, it's okay. I know how your mind is. You are going over everything over and over," he said.

He was right. He did know me. He poured himself a drink then sat next to me on the couch. He didn't even take a sip of it.

"What do you want to talk about?" I asked. I knew he wanted to talk about us.

"Your car. I have a friend in Boulder. He's going to take a look at it and see if he can salvage it. He can work wonders on vehicles. He might be a wielder," he joked.

"Auto mechanic, an interesting profession for a wielder," I said. "Thank you for doing that."

"I know you love that car," he said.

"In the grand scheme, the car doesn't matter."

"You are right. You could have died out there if Duarte hadn't taken that bullet for you. I'm glad he was there," he said.

"Me, too. But I hated that he got hurt."

"Abby, all of us know this job. We know that something could happen to any of us at any point. I myself have my fair share of scars." He continued to speak the truth. We all had been in quite a few fights together. "He knows that too. You can't assume he doesn't get it now."

"I know that he does," I said.

"You still seem upset. What can I do?" he asked.

"Nothing. You've already done a lot. Thank you, Jay, really for coming after us."

"I'm here for you. Whatever you need," he said and stood up. "I'll leave you alone. I just wanted to check on you and tell you about the car. Please be careful in Paris. You just came back to us. I know whoever that was out there was trying to kill you."

"Thanks for seeing to my car. I'm aware of the dangers just like the rest of you," I said.

"Did you consider what we talked about in your office?" he asked.

"Well, after the party and your comments there, I decided you were just being the same old you," I replied. I didn't mean to be hard on him, but he was obnoxious at the party.

"I apologize for the things I said at the party. When I saw he had marked you, I got pissed," he said, hanging his head. "Ashley explained things to me. I knew why you guys did it, but I still hated the idea of it. Never in all the time we've spent together would you have allowed anyone to do that to you. I've known you longer than any of them. I worry that you are following a path that will just get you hurt again. I've seen you hurt too much."

I got a large lump in my throat. I didn't know what to say. He has known me longer than anyone else. He had seen me through each pain and hurt over the years. "I'm on the right path, Jay. I'm sure of it. I would like your support."

"You know that I always have your back." It seemed like he wanted to say more, but he didn't. He just silently left.

I was tired of waiting. I dialed Tadeas' number. It rang several times, and I got his voicemail. I did not want to bother him, so I didn't even try to contact him through the bond. Maybe Meredith and he were resolving their issues. I just hoped resolving them didn't involve them getting together. I could not think like that though. If he was happy, then I would be happy for him.

"I can lie to myself like the best of them," I said to no one. I curled up on the bed and went to sleep.

About two hours later, I woke up. I looked at my phone. No messages from him. I could not feel him either. That meant he wasn't nearby. I got worried. I put my shoes on and headed downstairs. I got to the door of his apartment, but I could only barely feel him inside. Perhaps Maki underestimated his healing abilities, and he needed help. I started to knock on the door when Samantha came around the corner.

"Don't," she said.

"Why? Something is wrong. I need to check on him."

"Abby don't. She's with him," she said.

"What do you mean with him? How do you know that?" I asked.

"I came up here earlier to try to talk to him about last night. I felt like we intruded on your date. I wanted to apologize. When I knocked on the door, she answered. She wasn't wearing clothes. She said they were busy. I apologized and went back downstairs, but I came back up because I didn't want you to find them. I'm sorry, Abby. I know you both looked completely happy last night together. I never thought that he would cheat on you."

"He's not cheating, Sam," I said. My heart exploded in pain, but I couldn't explain it. "We were pretending. We were practicing for fieldwork. We never thought we would run into anyone from here. I'll leave them alone. Thanks for the warning. That would have been awkward." I turned as fast as I could, heading straight to my office. Back to the portal. I needed to go home right now.

I opened the door to my office. A note hung on the door from Aunt Lianne about the paperwork. "I'm so sick of the damn paperwork," I shouted.

"Yeah, I never liked paperwork either," Jay said.

"Bloody hell, what are you doing here?"

"Leaving you the number for the shop where your car is at. I thought you were already gone. What's wrong? You look terrible. I mean, I can tell something is wrong," he stood in front of me to keep me from going to the portal. "I thought you were going to Paris with Duarte."

"I am. He's a little busy right now, and I've got to get back home to get things ready to go."

"He's with her," Jay said. There were days I really like his frankness on things, but right now I just wanted to go.

"Yes, but it doesn't matter. He will be along in a bit, and we will get to work."

"It does matter. I can tell that it matters," he said still preventing me from getting to the portal.

"Move Jay. I'm not talking about this right now," I yelled at him.

He put his hands up in surrender and moved out of my way. I reached for the door and stopped. "I'm sorry. I'm not angry at you. I just can't talk about it right now."

"When you are ready, I'm here," he said. Taking Jay to Paris never crossed my mind. I needed Tadeas, and he would be along when he finished what he was doing which was none of my business. I had gotten mad at him for the very same thing. I needed to forget about it.

I pulled the door open, stepping through the portal. George waited on me as if he knew something happened.

"What's wrong?" he asked.

"Nothing. I'm going to get some stuff ready downstairs," I said. I had to find something to keep my mind busy until Tadeas showed up. If Tadeas showed up.

CHAPTER 44

TADEAS

I woke up in my own bed. I was groggy and felt dazed. I reached for my phone. I picked it up, and the screen was smashed. "Crap." I didn't remember breaking it or laying down in my bed. I rolled out of the bed, and I heard her.

"Tadeas, come back to bed," Meredith said.

"What?" Standing over her laying in my bed, I struggled to remember the night before. "What's going on?"

"Stay with me a little longer. We don't have class today," she said.

I closed my eyes, trying to remember. I remembered coming to my room. I remembered her being here waiting. She wanted to talk. She had made coffee. We talked about the gunshot and the job with Abigail. She apologized for being stupid. Then that's it.

"Why are you in my bed?"

"Stop playing games, silly," she said with a giggle.

"I'm not," I started to walk across the room and everything started to spin.

"You should really lay back down," she purred.

I leaned on the door to the bathroom. "I don't remember."

"I can't believe you are doing this to me, Tadeas. We finally get together, and you are claiming you don't remember being with me," she pouted.

"What did you do to me?" I looked back at her. Her face was not sad or upset. She smiled.

"I told you that woman would be the end of you, and I will do whatever it takes to get you away from her," she said.

"Get out! Leave," I shouted. But every time I spoke my head pounded. I looked at the clock on the wall. It was 6 p.m. I just hoped it was 6 p.m. on Saturday. I had to get to Abby. Why hadn't she come looking for me by now? Maybe she did, and I didn't remember.

"One day, you will thank me for this, Tadeas," she said as she got up and put her clothes on.

"I never want to see you again. You will be fired," I said.

"I don't care. I quit. It was worth it to see your face," she said, walking out the door.

I put on jeans and a shirt as fast as I could. Splashing water on my face didn't help. I looked at myself in the mirror. The car accident left me bruised all over. My eyes were bloodshot. Maybe I shouldn't go. I sat down on the bathroom floor. It felt cool and good. I leaned my head back against the wall. If I didn't go, I'd let her down. I'd already let her down by not going back to her last night.

What happened to me? My mind raced and traced my steps. Gaps filled my memory. I got up and went into the living room, then the kitchen. The coffee cups were washed. Maybe Ichiro could find something in my blood. With my head still spinning, I ran as fast as I could to the elevator. There was no way I was making it up the stairs to his office. I leaned my head against the doors until they opened. I stumbled in and hit the button for the floor of Ichiro's lab.

The elevator doors opened, and I stumbled all the way into the lab. Ichiro and Ashley were mid-makeout session. I started to turn back out.

"Tadeas, what's wrong? Aren't you supposed to be with Abby?" Ashley said.

Turning back to them, I teetered. "He's sick," Ichiro said.

They both rushed over to me, and Ashley guided me to the couch.

"Something happened. My phone is broke. I need to call her," I said.

Ashley produced her phone and dialed. She handed me the phone. It just kept ringing. I looked down and hit the button for it to redial. Ichiro looked into my eyes. "Did you take some kind of drug?" he asked.

"No, but I think someone drugged me," I said. Ashley gasped and covered her mouth like she knew who had done it. "I need help. I need Abby."

Ashley said. "We will figure it out."

The phone kept ringing. I looked at Ashley, shaking my head. Ichiro drew blood and hurried away to his equipment. "This might take a little while. Ashley, get him to the portal. I'll call when I have the results."

I kept dialing. "Abby, please answer."

"You can dial and walk," Ashley said, guiding me toward the door.

We stepped into the hallway, and the elevator doors opened. Jay came out and his jovial face turned to pure hatred. He swung at me before I could react. His fist hit the side of my face, and I went to my knees. Ashley's phone slid across the tile floor. Blood poured out of my nose. Every nerve in my face screamed in agony. My dizziness returned with vigor.

"You, sorry son of a bitch. How could you do this to her?"

Ashley jumped between us. "Jay, have you lost your mind? Stop it right now."

He kept yelling. The room kept spinning. Ichiro came out of the doors, and got in front of Jay, "Help him." Ashley turned from Jay and helped me stand up.

"You didn't tell them, did you? You didn't tell them what you did! Tell them, Duarte. Tell them what you did to her? I should kill you!" Jay kept yelling.

Big Tony stepped out of the lab. "Shut up now!" His big voice boomed in the room, and I covered my ears. It worked. Jay stopped shouting. Everyone was quiet.

"He's right," I mumbled. "It's my fault."

Ashley turned to me. "What is he talking about?"

"I woke up a little while ago, and Meredith was in my bed with me."

Ashley had been steadying me, but she stepped away from me like I had the plague. Tony cracked his knuckles. Ichiro barely restrained Jay. The doc saved me at that moment. "He has been drugged. His pupils are dilated. If she drugged you, we need to get her out of the compound or into containment."

"Tommy and I will find her," Tony said, going back into the lab to find his brother.

"You cool, Jay?" Ichiro said, not really asking.

"Not even close, but I will back off for now. For her sake, not yours, you rotten bastard." He stormed off into the lab.

"Get him to the portal now," Ichiro told Ashley.

I stumbled into the elevator, and Ashley followed. I leaned against the wall and let her push the buttons. My hands were covered in blood. She would not look at me. "I swear to you, Ashley. I did not sleep with her. I couldn't have. I don't remember anything. Abby is never going to forgive me for this. What am I going to do?" I slid down the side of the elevator wall and sat down. My head pounded.

"You are going to suck it up and do your job. If you think this

436

is the first time a partner has let her down, then you are wrong. Lincoln had his faults. She's faced all kinds of things. She will forgive you eventually. My advice is to not lie to her."

"How did Jay know?" I asked.

"I don't know, but I'll find out. Let us handle this end. Take my phone. I'll call you from Ichiro's," she said.

"Thank you, Ashley," I said. The doors opened, and I went straight to her door. I still felt dizzy, but the haze started to clear. Blood from my nose dotted my shirt. We went into her office. I hesitated before opening the closet door. I looked back at Ashley.

"Tadeas, I know you mean well, but this will crush her if you don't figure this out. If you hurt her again, you won't have to worry about these guys doing something to you. I have yet to show you my true nature. Now suck it up, big boy. You can do it, just go. She will forgive you because that is who she is. You owe it to her to go. You have to at least try," she said.

Her threat scared me more than Hyperion's, but I hoped that she was right. I opened the closet door and stepped through the portal. I came out the other side as a wave of nausea hit me. I tried holding it back, but the intensity of the attack forced me to my knees. I barely choked out her name, "Abby!"

I heard running footsteps from the front room. I looked up and saw her barreling toward me. In that moment, her only concern was getting to help me. If she were mad, I couldn't tell, because she was all over me in an instant. My feelings rushed to the surface, and I almost made a blubbering fool of myself. However, in true Abigail fashion, she cut me off before I could speak.

"Good God, you are bleeding," she said as she hit the floor next to me. George handed her a handkerchief. She held it to my nose and squeezed.

"I'm going to puke," I said. She and George hoisted me up, dragging me to the bathroom in my room. As soon as we got to the toilet, I could not hold it any longer. I hugged it and heaved into the bowl. I sat back on the floor. She had a cold washcloth wiping my forehead and face. No matter what, she was caring for me. I held on to hope.

"You finished?" she asked. I looked into her eyes. They were cold and distant. She already knew about Meredith. I didn't know how, but she knew. My heart sank.

I just nodded. Because I didn't trust my voice. She pulled me up off the floor, then guided me to the bed. I laid down on my back. The room did not spin in here like it had back in the compound. She walked back into the bathroom, then returned with another cloth.

"Here, this is for the blood on your face," she said dryly. "I'll be down in the bourbon room when you get cleaned up." She walked out. The tone of her voice cut through me like a million knives. George stood there just inside the door. I looked at him, and he shook his head.

"I'll be down in a minute," I muttered. George left. I sat up on the bed. My blood covered my shirt. I had no choice but to tell her everything. She was extremely upset. I could feel her pain as if it were my own pain. I had to convince her that I did not do this on purpose. Returning to the bathroom, I brushed my teeth and gargled mouthwash to get the acid taste out of my mouth. I went into the closet and got out a pair of shorts and a t-shirt. I didn't put on shoes because the tile floor felt good on my feet. I looked at myself in the mirror. I had a huge bruise forming on the side of my face where Jay had hit me.

I walked slowly down to where I knew I'd find her. George hovered out in the hallway. He handed me an ice pack as I walked by. "Give me some space, George, please." He nodded and headed off toward the kitchen. She stood in the doorway looking out onto the tiled patio. She had a glass of dark liquid in her hand. She stood tall and straight, like a statue of a goddess in blue jeans. Her heartbeat seemed distant. Steady, but weak. She had been preparing herself for this conversation.

"Abby, something happened. I'm waiting on a call from Ashley, but I need to tell you what happened. What I can remember of it anyway," I said as plainly as possible. I tried to leave my emotions out of it.

"You don't have to explain anything to me, Duarte. What you do on your own time is your own business," she said coldly. She used my last name. It stung. I swallowed and armored myself for I knew this would be painful for us both.

Abigail Davenport was meant to be in my life. She was stubborn and headstrong, and I was probably the worst match considering it. However, I needed her, and I knew she needed me. Swallowing my pride, I decided that I would go to whatever lengths necessary to get her to listen to me. If it was a fight, then so be it.

I walked up next to her, but I didn't dare touch her even though I wanted to feel her skin. "Please listen. I know you are hurt. I know you are upset with me. I can feel it coming off of you waves, Abby, but I *need* you to listen to me."

"Doesn't matter. We have work to do," she said. "Unless you are bailing out on me which is fine. I knew that might happen anyway."

"No, I'm not, but I *need* to talk about this. I *need* you to listen, even if you don't want to," I said firmly. The phone in my pocket started ringing. I pulled it out. The caller info said Ichiro. "Hey doc, what did you find out?"

"Tadeas, it's Ashley. Give her the phone please," she insisted.

"But…"

"You aren't getting out of this without my help," she said. "Give her the phone."

"It's Ashley. She wants to talk to you," I handed Abby the phone. She took it and walked out into the twilight.

"Hello," she said. She walked in circles as she listened to Ashley talking. I stood back hoping that Ashley could help, then maybe I would have a chance to work this out. She mumbled words that I couldn't make out back to Ashley several times, and she went over to one of the benches to sit down. She looked up to me. Her eyes were still cold. Whatever Ashley said wasn't working. I walked over and sat down near her. She handed me the phone.

"Hello," I said.

"I did what I could. You have Ketamine in your blood. She definitely drugged you. Tony and Tommy have her locked up for you guys to deal with after the trip to Paris. Be honest. Tell her everything. Do you hear me? Make her understand," Ashley urged. Tall order.

"Yes," I mumbled.

"We have the security tapes from your room. You probably didn't know we record everything down there, but I would not let the guys watch it unless you gave us permission. You are one of us now. I won't break that trust," she said.

"Thanks, Ashley. Please look at the tapes. Let me know what you find," I said. They knew everything anyway. Might as well know the truth. I shut off the phone, laying it on the ground. I put my head in my hands. I should have known with the way Meredith talked that she had done something to me. I growled in frustration, stood up, and paced around the patio. The fountain splashed a quiet rhythm. I tried to focus on it. Tried to calm my mind. I finally got the courage to look at her. Her eyes were distant and removed. I didn't even know where to start.

"When I got to my room, right after I left you, Meredith was already in the room. She had made coffee and wanted to talk. She apologized for being angry at me and for all the things she said about you. She said she was happy for me and the new job with you. The drugs must have been in the coffee. I don't remember anything else until I woke up. And when I woke up, she was…" my voice trailed off.

"She was in your bed," she said. "I told you before, Duarte. You can fuck whoever you want to. It's none of my business."

None of it swayed her. Not even that Meredith drugged me. I was the victim, but Abigail had thrown a wall up to protect herself. To protect her own emotions from teetering off into an oblivion. Somehow, I knew that she wasn't doing this to hurt me —by instinct she was protecting herself—but right now, I needed to her to engage. I needed her help. I needed my partner.

I gritted my teeth and tried to remind myself that she was in pain. Some of which I had caused, but there were other pains in her life. A few of those pains I knew, but I imagined there was much more beneath the surface. In the days that I had known her, I'd seen supernatural strength in her character and endurance, but even so, she'd been through a lot of fucked up stuff. Also, I knew that she had a sharp tongue. If we fought now, our partnership could be over before it really got started.

"There is no way in this world I slept with her. If I was drugged, which Ashley said I had Ketamine in my system, then there is no way anything was going to happen. Things don't function down there when you pass out like that. I hope," I added.

"It doesn't matter," she insisted.

"Abby, look at me. Please. It matters to me. *That* woman drugged me. The woman I've considered my closest friend for many years put enough Ketamine in my system to knock me out. She said she did it to break us apart. Please don't let her do that to us." My words were impassioned now. Desperation slithered and settled in every single word that came out of my mouth.

"You knew she drugged you before you went to Ichiro and Ashley?"

"No, but when I got out of the bed, I was dizzy and my memory was foggy. It still is, but she was happy I kicked her out. She told me she would do it all over again if it meant getting me away from you." I stopped and took a breath. The dizziness returned with my adamancy, and I sat down on the edge of the fountain. "I admit that I went down there to try to talk to her one last time. I did not go down there to be with her. I've never wanted her like that, ever. I don't know how you even knew, but it's obvious you already knew before I ever got here. How? How did you know?" If I sat here in desperation, she would have to explain herself as well.

"Because when I came looking for you, Samantha stopped me at your door, and said she came up to talk to you. When she knocked, Meredith answered the door naked. She said you were busy. Meredith implied very clearly to her what the two of you were doing. Samantha waited to tell me in case I came looking for you. She thought we were dating because of our charade in Boulder. She is the one that told me. I never even knocked on the door. I just went to my office and through the portal."

"Jay knew too. He hit me." I rubbed the edge of my chin where the bruise was forming. Finally, she looked up at me with a twinge of sympathy.

"He sat in my office when I got there. I was upset. He was dropping off the number to the shop where they took my car. He asked where you were because they all knew we were going to Paris. I told him you were busy with a friend. He guessed where you were, because of the way I acted. I didn't talk to him any longer than I had to. I just went through the portal. It's my fault he hit you. I'm sorry," she said, giving me the tiniest bit of sympathy.

"I probably deserved it," I said, putting my head in my hands. "Wait, you said 'were' going to Paris. Are we not going?"

"You've been drugged and beaten up. Considering those things and the car accident, I think I should just call Paris off and think of something else," she said.

"No. I want to go. It's a good plan, Abby, please," I pleaded with her. I got up and went back to the bench. She didn't turn to look at me. She just sipped her drink.

"I'll sleep on it and decide tomorrow." She got up, leaving me on the bench.

"Where are you going?"

"Somewhere you aren't!" she exclaimed. She needed to get angry and let it all out. I could not believe I was about to do this.

"Fine then. Just run. Leave me here when I've been drugged. I've done *nothing* wrong. Who knows what she did to me! From the moment, I woke up all I thought about was *you* and getting back here. I need my partner, but you are bailing on me when I need you the most," I said.

She paused but didn't speak. Then she walked into the room and put her glass on the bar. Her wall stood firm, so I had to push more. I needed one of the trumpets that the Israelites used to bring down the walls of Jericho because my only hope was an act of God.

"Wow! You know, Abby, you have wanted me to trust you. I came here because I trusted you with everything just now. Your friends jumped to my aid. Ashley immediately believed me. Ichiro took my blood. They even got between us when Jay tried to beat my face in. I never took a swing at him because I knew you wouldn't want me to. I just sat on the floor like a weakling and bled. Maybe what Meredith said about you was true. You have turned me into a toy soldier to line up and do with as you wish!" That did it.

She spun around. Her eyes lit up like green flames and she stomped toward me. "How dare you! I have endured your whining ass for a week now. Finding every excuse *not* to be my partner. Do you want to leave? You think that's what I think of you? Then fucking leave, Duarte. Maybe then I won't have to worry about you anymore. I won't have to care. You can train canvas crews in the basement for the rest of your life. I will not bother you ever again. I will never speak to you ever again. Is that what you want?"

"You know it isn't," I said.

"You could've fooled me. You should have never gone back down there with her. She is messed up in the head. For the life of me, I can't understand why you couldn't see that. She's acted like an irate idiot ever since I became a part of your life. She wanted you, and she got exactly what she wanted. You can go right back to her."

"No, Tony and Tommy have her locked up for drugging me," I said.

"Oh, even better, you can go back to your life and not have to worry about any crazy women anymore." It was a thought, but I knew entertaining it wouldn't do me any good. Neither would a smart remark.

"The only one I worry about is you, Abby."

"Oh. please, you don't care at all. I don't care what Ashley says. You have sabotaged this over and over, and you are just waiting for the next chance to do it. Just pack your shit and go. Or better yet, just go. I'll have it sent to you," she raged. I continued on because I knew that she was doing it to protect herself from losing another partner. She had been through too much, but we had to get through this together. An angel had warned us. We had bigger things to worry about than this, but for us to work together, we had to get it all out. All of it.

"I'm not leaving Abby, and you don't want me to leave."

"You think if you make me mad, and make me shout, that I would get it all out of my system and everything would be square? You are wrong." Her voice wavered at that time. She was too smart. She knew I had provoked her on purpose. I had counted on it because she needed to see what lengths I would go to in desperation to mend things between us.

"That's exactly what I did. You needed to get it out, and I needed to hear it."

"Fuck you, Tadeas." My first name. The wall started to crumble. I needed that trumpet.

I walked toward her, and she put her hands up to stop me. "Abby, let's fix this now. Don't push me away. You've spent too many years alone. This world needs you."

"You are right. It does need me, but it doesn't need *you*," she said quietly. She didn't mean it, but when she got like this, there was no stopping that vitriol.

"No, *you* need me," I said.

"You are full of yourself. No, I don't," she said, still holding her hands up between us.

"What do you want to do? We could go downstairs, and you could kick my ass if it would help."

"Nothing is going to help."

"Why? If you don't care who I sleep with, why does it matter?"

"You are right it doesn't matter. Excuse me," she said, then left the room. She didn't cry until she got into the hallway. I looked up at George standing in the sitting room.

"Don't give up, Son," he said, pointing toward her.

Damn it. Apparently, I hadn't abused myself enough. "Abby, wait!" I ran after her. She got to the top of the steps at her bedroom door before I caught up to her. I turned her around to look at me.

Putting my hands on her tear-stained cheeks, I dared to speak into her head. *"You should know that I would never do anything to hurt you on purpose. After the party, with the bond, everything we've been through, you should know,"* I said. I wanted to remind her that no matter what happened. We were still bonded.

"Don't do that," she said.

"Why? It's part of us."

"There is no *us*," she said. The tears had already dried on her face, and she barely held more of them back. There were times when I knew she just wanted to let it all go. She fought it so much. The problem with that was that she had let it build up inside her, and it came out harsh and angry. I had known her long enough now to know that she wasn't really that person.

"Yes, there is. In just a week's time, the world has tried to break us apart or kill us no less than three times. Four, if you count this. They are scared of us. There is an us."

"Stop talking in my head," she said, backing away from me. "Please, Tadeas."

"Tell me what to do. I want to fix it, Abby."

"I don't think it can be fixed. Not this time."

"You don't trust me?"

"No, I don't."

"Why? I went straight to our people for help. *Our* people. I came straight to you even though I could hardly stand up. I hit the portal, and the jump made me sick I almost puked all over George's carpet. I didn't care. I had to get to *you*. I needed *you* to help me. I need *you* to trust me. I can't get through this without *you*."

"Tadeas, I just don't know that I can help."

I could feel her anger easing. I am the one that provoked it, and her words stung. If I ever had any doubts at all about her intentions toward me, I now knew she valued me more than just filling a job position. She cared about me even if she wasn't up for admitting it at the moment. She had shed tears over me. Her heart ached because of me. No matter what happened to us in the future, I knew right now beyond the anger and sharp words that our friendship, our bond, meant something to her. It had been a very long time since someone cared that much about me, and I knew I felt the same way in return. I desperately wanted and needed her friendship right now. I needed her strength. The whole situation came to full realization to me right then and there. I looked at her, and even through her stoic gaze, I felt hope. It had been a very long time since I had a real source of hope. I would do anything to get through this. I made the choice. I offered her everything. No holding back.

"Look in my memories."

"What? No, I can't do it."

"You can do it, can't you? We sign the papers when we join the Agency. It can be done. If that is what it takes, then look. Maybe you can see things that I don't remember. Maybe there is a way to see past the drugs. To see what happened to me. I want to know, and you are the only one I trust to do it. Please don't turn away from me now. Please help me," I pleaded.

She shook her head.

"I am willing to let you look at anything you want in there. You can dig around all of it. I have nothing to hide. Please, Abby. I need you to trust me."

"My child," George said from the bottom of the steps. I didn't know if he directed it to me or her, but his eyes were fixed on her. His face looked grave and solemn.

"Don't interfere, George," she said.

"You know it doesn't work like that child. Look and see. Your heart will never be settled until you know the truth," he said. There was my heavenly trumpet. George had blown it loud and clear.

"Please, Abby," I pleaded.

She turned without a word and walked down the stairs to the basement door under the steps. George motioned for me to follow her. I walked by him and he muttered, "I did what I could. The rest is up to you."

"Thank you, George. Dios mio, thank you."

I followed her downstairs into the sparing room. She sat down on the floor with her legs crossed. I sat down facing her and crossed my legs.

"There is no good way to do this," she said.

"What do you mean?"

"I have to touch you. I have to get close. Just give me a minute to calm my mind," she said.

I sat quiet and still, trying to settle my mind, too. I did not know what she would find there. If I had really been with Meredith or not. I couldn't remember. How could it be in my memories? But maybe at the very least, she will see that I truly didn't remember. We sat quietly for about five minutes, maybe longer I wasn't sure.

"Are you ready?" she asked.

I nodded at her. "What do I need to do?"

"Just sit still, I've got to move closer," she unfolded her legs and took her hands and moved my legs to make me unfold them. She moved between them on her knees and placed her hands on my temples. "It won't hurt, and it will only take a minute. If you want to back out, now is the time."

"I'm not backing out if you aren't," I said.

She took a deep breath, closing her eyes. "Tadeas Nahuel Duarte, do you give me permission to look at your memories? I swear on my power not to do you any harm."

"I give you permission," I said as her oath swirled around me. It felt warm and comforting.

"*Memento.*"

I felt wind stir around us, and her hands turned to ice. She sat on her knees deathly still. Her heart beat a steady rhythm. Her eyes were closed, and I prayed. *Dios, let this work.*

CHAPTER 45

ABIGAIL

I focused on the last time I saw him in Ichiro's lab. I could connect my last memory to his as a starting point and go from there. Everything inside of me said I should not do this. I was angry and hurt. This was not going to help anything. I did not want to see him with her.

I whispered the word, "*Memento*." I focused on my memory. I saw him standing there after he put his clothes on in the lab.

"It will take more than a bullet to stop us. See you in a little while," he said, turning away from me. I latched onto the memory in his head and felt myself follow him out like a ghost stalking its prey.

"Don't mess this up, Duarte," Ashley said to him. God bless her. I wouldn't even be doing this if she hadn't insisted on the phone that I give him a chance. That he truly had been drugged, and that he was scared and desperate when he showed up in the lab.

"I'm trying not to," he responded and got in the elevator. I did not want to enter his head. I did not want to know his full thoughts and emotions. Even though he told me I could see whatever I wanted, there are things that are sacred. I would not go there. He got to his floor and stepped out of the elevator. The door to his apartment was cracked open. He approached it cautiously. He slowly opened the door to find Meredith sitting on the couch smiling widely at him.

"Come sit down," she said, patting the cushion next to her.

"How did you get in here, Meredith?" he asked, suspicious of her from the moment he saw her in his room. I hadn't wanted to connect to his emotions, but they came through loud and clear. I suppose it is because he trusted me with them. Or perhaps it was the bond which I knew was still there. As he pleaded with me on the steps, I looked at us the way my grandfather had shown me. The ribbons of red and purple still pulsed around us.

"The door was unlocked. I thought you were home. I know about the accident. You look terrible, and your handsome face is covered in bruises," she said.

"Yeah, I was with Abby out working, and wrecked her car," he said.

"Are you okay? Is she okay?"

"Like you care about her," he said sharply to her.

"Actually, that's why I am here. I do care. Besides getting into car accidents and neglecting your class, I think this job offer has been a good thing for you. You seem excited about it, and I wanted you to know that I'm sorry I've been such a pain. Perhaps I misjudged her, but this job will be extremely dangerous. I'd never want anything to happen to you."

He moved over to the couch and sat down. He tried to keep his distance from her. He did not believe what she said to him and that at any moment she would unleash her fury on him again.

"I made some coffee. Be right back."

He watched her go in the kitchen. He looked back at the

door of his apartment. The impression I got was that he was suspicious mainly because he knew he had locked the door when he left. She came back with a steaming mug, handing it to him. She did not have one. "Thanks," he said as he lifted it to his nose and took a long whiff.

"After visiting you upstairs, I felt like I needed to talk to you. They were all very upset about your condition and taking good care of you. I wanted to talk to you because I realized that they were becoming new friends to you. That you haven't made friends in a very long time. I came here, and I decided to wait. You said she's okay?"

He set the mug down without drinking. She winced. He noticed it. "Yes, she's fine. I got shot. It's all healed now."

"What!" she exclaimed and moved next to him on the couch. He moved away from her a bit. "Where did you get shot?"

He pointed at his chest. She tried to lift up his shirt.

"Meredith, stop, it's fine. She healed it." He pushed the shirt back down and didn't let her look. She didn't move away from him. He wanted to get up and move away from her. She ran her hand down his left arm, resting it over the bracelet that I gave him. I knew why she had done that; she was undoing my spells to protect him.

She looked down and pouted. "I hate you getting hurt like that. You aren't used to being in the field. You've got to take better care of yourself if you are going to do this. What would I do without someone to yell at for no reason?" she said playfully. He did not laugh or even smile at her.

He picked the mug back up. "I'm fine. We are going to do a lot of good. I would really like you to support it. You have been my friend for a long time. It would mean a lot to me." He blew on the coffee.

"Cyrus called down to me and told me you were in the accident. He told me to check on you in Maki's lab. I'm sorry if I intruded, but I needed to know you were okay."

"Meredith, why are you *really* here?" He still didn't drink the coffee. She was confusing him. She talked in circles, stalling the conversation.

"Because I wanted to know if you would lie to me about being out with her. She looked pretty upset that you were harmed," she whimpered.

He set the coffee back down. "I have never lied to you, Meredith."

"Really? Because you know I'm in love with you, but you just keep me around just in case you get bored or until something better comes along. You have to know by now that you aren't going to shift and hurt me," she said.

"Meredith, you may be right about leading you on. But honestly, I didn't do it on purpose. I've only ever seen you as a friend. Nothing more," he picked up the coffee cup and took a sip. He looked down at it and back up at her. He took his coffee black, and he knew immediately something was wrong. I could feel the alarm going off through his whole body. "What's in this coffee?" he demanded.

"We are having a serious conversation, and you are talking about your coffee! You are breaking my heart, and you are worried about your coffee! Well, you *should* be worried about it." His eyesight started to blur. As he tried to set down the cup, it missed the coffee table, spilling on to the floor. He tried to get up. I felt the wave of fear and desperation roll over him. He looked over at her and tried to speak. He fell over on to the floor, and she stood over him. She shook my bracelet in his face and waved goodbye. *Heartless bitch.* He groaned and tried to fight the drugs. His body would not respond to his commands. It made me ache inside. I felt him think about me. He tried to reach my mind as we had been doing over the last couple of days since the bond really took hold of us. But his mind clouded and he couldn't concentrate. He tried to call my name, but his mouth wouldn't move. His memory blurred at that point. It was not completely black though. I could hear voices. I definitely heard another man. I could feel his body being moved, dragged across the floor. The man grunted. Tadeas mumbled something. Tadeas' face jerked to the right, and his cheek started stinging. Someone slapped him. And the memory went dark.

I could feel my anger welling up inside me. Anger at myself for distrusting him and immediately thinking the worst of him. Anger at her for everything she was doing to him, a man she claimed to love. Anger at him for being too kind and giving her the opening. Pure utter rage ripped through me. I reminded myself that I couldn't be mad at him for being kind to her. It was part of him. One of the things I most liked about him. There are too few kind-hearted people in the world, but this was a stark reminder of what happens to the kind-hearted in this world. In the midst of all of it, he had thought about me. He had tried his best to reach out to me, but the drugs worked too quickly.

When he opened his eyes again, I saw him grab his phone in a panic. It was broken. I heard her mutter something. He turned to see her in the bed, and he jumped out and away from her. He yelled at her. I had seen enough, but I heard the last thing she said to him, "I told you that woman would be the end of you, and I'll do whatever it takes to get you away from her."

I pushed myself out of his memory, sitting still for a moment with my hands on the side of his head. He did not move. It was almost like he wasn't breathing. I tried to calm myself. I had to decide what to do. If he had slept with her, he didn't remember it. She clearly intended to rape him, at the very least she violated his trust and his body. Most guys would never admit to that. Just the fact that he sat here with me indicated he was willing to do whatever it took to get the truth and prove it to me. I had not treated him any better than she had. He came to me, and I gave him hell.

I dropped my hands to his shoulders and opened my eyes. He waited for me to say something. I wrapped my arms around his neck, holding on tight. He put his arms around my waist and pulled me to him. Neither of us said anything. She did this to him on purpose to hurt me more than him. I vowed to kill her if it was the last thing I did.

"*Talk to me*," he said in the quietest whisper, using the bond between us.

"*I am going to kill her,*" I said back.

"*No, you aren't.*" Ever too kind.

"*I want to,*" I assured him quietly.

"*What did you see?*" I let myself finally hear the fear in his voice. The desperation. I let his emotions that I had blocked roll over me. I deserved to feel all of it at once after ignoring him for my own pain. I had been a complete asshole.

"*I could not see any more than what you told me. You told me everything you knew, except for one thing, there was someone else there.*"

"What?" he pulled back from me.

"It was a man," I said. I told him what I had found out beyond his memory which wasn't much. I told him that I knew he had tried to reach out to me. He sat there on the mat. I could tell that it relieved him that I had come to my senses. My anger turned to self-hate. I had given him hell upstairs, and he continued to push me. It hadn't taken him long to figure me out. I needed to become a better person for him.

"Upstairs, I failed miserably as your partner and friend. From the moment I met you, I've pushed for you to trust me. When you finally did and needed me the most, I let you down. You would think that someone my age would have just a tad bit of perspective and maturity, but as you can see, I still have many lessons to learn. Thank you for coming to me. Thank you for going to Ashley and Ichiro for help. I promise in the future I will learn to get over myself," I said, swallowing that bitter pill.

"Let's not talk about age, because I'm pretty sure that the last time I checked we are the same age. I knew you would come around. It's why I pushed. I believe in this now. I'm not letting it go," he said. We reached the point where the apology was not needed. He leaned in and put his head on my shoulder. My brain kicked into overdrive as I sat there, holding him. Mindlessly, I brushed my fingers through his lengthening hair.

Meredith had a man there. It would either have to be Cyrus MacCormack or Travis Reed. Those were the only two suspects. It also occurred to me that Samantha Taylor was outside that door for the sole purpose of upsetting me and sending me on my way. I heard a cell phone ringing. George came into the room and nodded at me. I reached out for the phone and clicked it on. Tadeas did not move. I could feel how exhausted he was.

"Hello," I said.

"Hey, I am sorry to bother you, but I sent the security videos to your email. You need to see them. We have a bigger problem," Ashley said.

"I know. We need to get Travis Reed and Samantha Taylor out of the training center and in lock-up along with Meredith," I said.

"How did you know? Never mind. Tony and Tommy already went down there after them. They are gone. Meredith is gone, too."

"What? How? She was in the warded room, correct?" I asked. Tadeas leaned back and looked concerned.

"Yes, she was, but when Tommy and Tony went downstairs, we left her alone. Surveillance showed a shadowed figure surrounding her, and she disappeared," Ashley said.

"Meredith is working with Nalusa Chito," I said out loud for Tadeas' benefit. He cringed.

"It would seem so," Ashley said.

"Does Gregory know?"

"Yes, Ichiro went up to tell him a little while ago."

"Ash, we need to start the first stage of Code: Decedo," I said.

"What! No, it's not that bad, is it?" she asked in astonishment.

"Yes, it's that bad."

"How is he?" she wanted to know about Tadeas.

"I've got him. It's going to be alright. I hope," I said, looking him in the eyes. He nodded that it would.

"Abby, thank you for hearing him out. I know it was hard for you, but we need you both right now. This is serious," she said, sounding afraid.

"Don't I know? Decedo. Do it now. Wait for further instructions," I said.

"Talk to you soon," she hung up.

"What is Decedo?" Tadeas asked.

"It's a pre-evacuation protocol. All non-essential personnel have to be moved out of the compound, and all data transferred to an alternate location. It's precautionary. We had not one, but three traitors in our midst. The compound by my standards is compromised. Perhaps beyond salvaging. My team will start a quiet and discrete pre-evacuation," I explained.

"This is far more serious than we thought. I mean continents falling off in the ocean is serious, but this really hits home," he said.

"She said the security videos are in my email. That we should watch them."

He groaned.

"Hey, look at me. We will do whatever you want to do. I'm with you now, no matter what," I said to assure him.

"It needs to be done. I want to know. You will stay with me?" he said. I touched his cheek and nodded. I couldn't abandon him now. I could tell he was extremely tired. I whispered my healing spell and touched his bruises, and they each faded away. The one on his face was especially bad. Jay had hit him extremely hard. "Thank you."

I stood up, helping him stand with me, but he teetered a bit. Clearly whatever she had given him was strong. "We'll watch the tapes, then we will get you in bed. I feel how exhausted you are. The emotional rollercoaster can take a lot out of you." He nodded. He walked with me back to the office with all the moni-tors. I accessed the smallest one closest to the desk. I motioned for him to sit in my chair. He sat down, and I leaned over him and started up the surveillance footage. The first clips showed her sneaking into his room and starting a pot of coffee. She took something from her pocket and poured it into the coffee pot. I stepped away from him, sitting on the desk not looking at the screen. I did not need to see. No matter what was on that tape, I was here for him. It took too long for me to realize that, and I'd do whatever I could to make it up to him.

His eyes were glued to the monitor as I reached down taking his hand from the mouse. I held it to reassure him that I was here. I closed my eyes and concentrated on his emotions. I could feel the jaguar in him now. It was restless. It occurred to me then that the jaguar did not fight out against her. He had controlled it. He probably didn't even realize it. I felt him flinch, and I looked down at him. He shook his head. He leaned over on the desk and put his other hand up through his hair. He rested his head on his palm. I watched his eyes as the screen flickered reflections through them. The video ended, and he said there for a moment. I would sit there with him as long as he needed me too.

"She tried," he choked out. "But nothing happened. She called someone on the phone and was angry. She cleaned up the coffee that spilled, and the cups, then just laid in the bed waiting for me to wake up." He looked relieved. I could see it in his eyes and feel it in his touch. "Travis and Sam both were in the room once I passed out. They helped her undress me and put me in the bed."

"I should have known they were involved. The tavern experi-ence should have been a loud and clear warning. I've got to get my instincts back for these kinds of things," I said. "What can I do for you now?"

"I need to sleep for a little while, then we can plan our next moves. Maybe a shower to wash all of this off of me," he said as if a shower could clean off the hurt, pain, and confusion. Showers were good, but I didn't think they were that good. He stood up and looked at me with kind, but painful eyes. "I still need you to help me with all of this."

"Good thing I'm not going anywhere," I said.

"Good thing," he murmured. I wanted more than anything to see him smile. Now was not the time, but soon I wanted to see his face light up. I jumped off the desk and took his hand. I led him upstairs to his room. He let go of my hand without looking at me and went into the shower. I walked over to the door that went to his private balcony patio, opening it up to let the breeze in. George came in with clean linens. Together, he and I put fresh ones on his bed while the shower ran in the bathroom. George touched my face, kissed me on the forehead, and disappeared into the house somewhere. He never said a word. He didn't have to say anything.

Tadeas came out in jogging pants, no shirt and a wet mop of hair. He rubbed it with a towel.

"Was the shower helpful?" I asked.

"Yes. Made me feel a little better." He looked over to the bed where George and I had it turned down waiting for him.

"I can shut this door if you would like, but I thought the breeze felt nice." He didn't respond, so I left it open. I went over to the main light switch, flicking it off. I watched him lay down on the bed and curl up like a child. I walked over, then pulled the covers over him.

"Will you stay with me?" he asked.

"Of course," I shut the hallway door, walking over to the chair next to the bed to sit down. He reached over, grabbed my hand, and tugged. To be honest, I didn't think having a woman in his bed is what he needed. But then it occurred to me, he needed a friend as close as possible. Someone he trusted. Someone that cared for him. For him to think that of me after everything I had said to him tonight nearly broke me. I fought back a sob, and I climbed in the bed next to him as he rolled back over, curling up in a ball. I pulled the covers back over us both, listening to him fall asleep. My mind did not slow. The ball was rolling now. The question was who all were the players, what was the game, and did we have time to stop it? The Paris auction now meant everything.

CHAPTER 46

VANESSA

Sitting in the dark waiting for Travis to return, I decided to alter my plan a bit. Since the Jaguar and his bitch seemed to survive my first attempt, I hoped Meredith would come to her senses and just kill the cat instead of trying to fuck him. Even I know when to fuck them or when to leave them. I needed to get back to Cassidy. I left her asleep in Mwenye's condo. I pulled in power, and with a whirl of black smoke, I stood at the end of the bed. She was still asleep like a little goddess of beauty. I sat on the edge of the bed. She opened her eyes and looked at me.

"Hey where have you been?" she asked.

"I had to take care of some things before we left for Paris. I need you to do something for me, okay?"

"Sure," she said sweetly.

"Go ahead and get dressed. Get the luggage together. Here's my credit card. Call a cab and go to the airport. Take the earliest flight you can to Paris, and I'll meet you there."

"I don't want to fly alone," she said.

"I know, sweetie, but I've got a friend joining us. I've got to go pick the friend up, and I'll meet you in Paris," I said. I got up and wrote down the address to the hotel in Paris. "This is where we are staying. They will be expecting you. I'm sorry, sweetie. I hate that it's happened this way. But we are going to have a great time in Paris. I want you to see it all."

"I'll do it," she said smiling.

I kissed her on the cheek, and she blushed. "I'll see you soon, beautiful goddess." I stepped back and the black smoke engulfed me again.

When I arrived back in the hotel room, Travis and Samantha were there. It surprised me that they weren't having sex. "Something wrong with the both of you?" I asked.

"No, we were just waiting on you," Travis said.

"Well, lover boy, we are going to have to postpone any further nocturnal activities. We have to get to Paris. There is an auction there with an item that I desperately want, and I want to kill the person that is selling it."

"Kill?" Samantha said.

"Yes, my dear, there is a very evil woman out there who likes to manipulate people. She plays games and hurts people. She's killed people. I've decided that I will be the one to put her down," I proclaimed.

"Who is it?" Samantha said.

I sauntered over to her and bent down to her ear. I whispered, "Abigail Davenport."

"No, she didn't do anything to you," Samantha protested.

"Oh, but my dear, she used you. She pretended to be your friend. She let you think you could help her with her failing efforts in the canvas trials. She manipulated Tadeas Duarte. She has her claws in him now, and it will just be a matter of time before he is dead. Just think of what that will do to poor Meredith," I explained and watched the wheels turning in her head.

"She made a fool of me in front of the whole class. Made me look like a woman beater, then humiliated me when she stopped pretending," Travis added.

Samantha shot him an evil look. "You are a sex-crazed idiot, Travis. You are just mad she didn't want to jump in your bed." I laughed because I knew Travis wasn't used to being turned down. Apparently, Miss Davenport had the ability to see through his nonsense.

"Maybe so. But I wouldn't mind if she were dead," he responded.

"Well, I'm not going to participate," she got up to head toward the door.

"Where are you going?" I said to her.

"I'm going back to Milt. He's the best thing that ever happened to me," she said.

"Oh please, you are his paid whore. He's your sugar daddy," I threw at her.

"He's never paid me. I love him."

I did not know what to say. It was just too gross to even imagine. He had told us in Boston that he was paying her.

"Gag," Travis said.

"Shut up, Travis. You will never know what love is," she spouted at him.

"I sure as hell know it's not fucking some shriveled dick," he said.

I died laughing. He was right. She opened the door and stormed out into the night. I looked at Travis.

"Are we going to fuck or what?" he asked.

Leave it to a son of Asmodeus to get to the point. Perhaps we had time for one last roll in the bed. I just quirked a smile at him, and he was on me in a second. I would miss his vigor and thirst for sex.

I LOOKED BACK INTO THE ROOM AS I WENT OUT INTO THE NIGHT. His muscular form laid across the bed naked. His eyes were devoid of color. He had ceased to breathe, but I could feel his soul stirring inside me. I had finally done it. Sucking his soul into my body was a rush of power far beyond any I had ever felt. It boiled inside of me. I could use his strength as mine. I finally understood what Mwenye felt, and he had been collecting souls for ages. I wanted to find another one as soon as possible and start my collection. I walked out to the road. Perhaps a hitchhiker or a lost young woman would happen my way. My eyes settled on her as she walked toward me. I could see the tears running down her cheeks.

"My dear Samantha, what is wrong?"

"Milt said he had to go to Paris. He left me behind. I have nowhere to go," she cried.

I put my arms around her and hugged her. "Oh, sweetheart, you come with me to Paris. We will find him, and you can show him what he missed out on. These men don't care about us, my dear. We have to make our own way in this world."

She looked up at me and nodded. I pulled on the darkness, and we arrived in an instant under a bridge just outside Paris. She fluttered her eyes after experiencing the journey through the spirit world. We could see the city bright against the horizon.

"Oh wow, how did you do that?" she asked.

"Just a little magic my dear," I replied. "And the soul of a strapping young man," I added to myself.

"Where's Travis?" she asked on cue.

"Oh, he decided that Paris was a girl thing, and he didn't want to come," I explained.

"He's a man whore, anyway," she said.

"He can't help it, dear. It is who he is. He's rather good at it though," I said regretfully.

"Yes, he is," she turned and smiled at me with a glint in her eye.

"Well, let's go to the city. I have a friend I want you to meet."

I called a cab to pick us up on the outskirts of town. We would make it to the hotel before Cassidy arrived. I could not wait to take my girls on the town. This worked out splendidly. Samantha's soul would substitute for Cassidy's, and I could keep the red-headed goddess around a little longer.

ONCE CASSIDY ARRIVED THE TWO OF THEM MADE FAST FRIENDS. I loved watching them laugh and giggle. I missed innocence. Mine had been ripped from me by a man that I did not realize was utterly dangerous. I could live vicariously through them for the day. We loaded up, went shopping, saw the tower, ate French pastry, and generally lived the life of a common tourist. I felt antsy. It had almost been twenty-four hours since I consumed Travis. I hungered for my next soul. I know Samantha caught me staring at her many times throughout the day. She would just blush and smile.

'Oh, dear heart, if you only knew what I am going to do to you,' I told myself.

I would smile back and join their cheerful conversation. I would show John Mwenye that this world needed a new legendary necromancer. I would have to thank him for every-thing he had shown me to make it possible, but then I thought to myself, "I've already fucked him far more than he deserved."

I was a new woman. My life had just now begun.

CHAPTER 47

TADEAS

*W*hen I woke up, I laid very still. Abby slept next to me. Her heart pumped steadily. Her face was calm and serene. My dreams were awful. A mix of exorcism, death, and Meredith laughing hysterically at me, but even in the dream, I felt a hope that kept me steady. That hope was Abby.

She had been so difficult to deal with last night. She was unreasonable, but in the end, she came through, and she stayed here even though I knew she didn't want to lay in the bed with me. I did not want to be alone. My deepest desire was that she and I had finally reached a place of complete trust. I thought we were already there, but feelings make you irrational. Between our pasts and our present, we had plenty of pent up emotions. I knew how much time, effort, and soul that she had wrapped up in our partnership. Even if the feelings weren't romantic, her entire plan for the future rested on me. Meredith's game had cost us time and a step back in the trust we had built. I hurt like hell knowing what Meredith did and what she had tried to do. Every single bit of trust and respect I had for her evaporated. A twenty-year friendship ruined and for what? What was her ultimate goal? She should have known I would never be with her after she drugged me. Was the whole purpose to destroy my relationship with Abigail? If she worked with the shadow man, then she had tried to kill me already. And who shot at us on the road back from Boulder? I had to question her dealings with MacCormack too.

"No wonder Abby's brain never stops," I thought to myself.

I watched her sleep. Never in my life have I been completely confused about a woman. I supposed that's because outside of Isabel and Meredith, I'd not had any other close relationships. I went on a few dates here and there but nothing serious. I've never been comfortable with anyone. Perhaps because I grew up around a bunch of priests and monks.

At first, I didn't want to be connected to Abigail at all, but now I couldn't imagine my life without her even with how infuriating she could be. The bond may have tied us together, but even without it, I knew that we were fated to be here at this time and place for this purpose. We would see through together.

She stirred a little and turned on her side facing opposite to me. Her golden hair slid down revealing the cross brand on her shoulder. I thought about the night she pulled the sword on Chito. She illuminated the entire room holding that thing. I fully expected a pair of wings to sprout out of her back. There were no wings. No halo. She was just divinely impressive. Then, at times—like at the party—I knew she was completely nervous and out of sorts. The times when we were in danger she was confident and in control. When we were supposed to be relaxed, she seemed uncertain of herself. She was the epitome of juxta-position.

I considered our partnership and my role in it. Thus far, it seemed keeping her focused and on track defined the bulk of my responsibilities. Along with taking a bullet for her. I would take a hundred bullets for her, and I cannot give an absolute reason other than this world needs her. An archangel visited her and gave her a vision. Our survival depended upon her which meant my task was to make sure she survived. The jaguar inside of me seemed to concur with this conclusion.

I would protect her no matter what came our way. She was completely formidable on her own, but add me to the mix, and I knew I could keep her safe. I felt her breathing change. She started to wake up. We would head to Paris soon to a den of wolves, vampires, dark wielders, and God only knew what else. I was in it for the long haul now. I had no time to pity myself over Meredith's actions. One thing I knew for sure that Abby was wrong about was when she said the world didn't need me. I knew the world would need us both. No more time for parties, horseback rides, fancy dinners, or fake dates. We needed to get work. I had Meredith to thank for waking me up fully. Even my closest friends could be my enemy. I needed to move on, and I wanted to go forward with Abigail in whatever capacity that was.

"What are you thinking about?" she asked, shattering the silence.

I smiled. I had a million answers that would get her riled up, but instead, I just said, "Thinking about getting my hair cut."

"George!" she screamed, and he barreled in the door as if he stood just outside waiting for her to call out. "Please cut this man's hair so I don't have to hear him whine anymore." It startled me because that wasn't supposed to get her riled up.

"Of course, Miss Abby, I can do that," he muttered at her just as shocked as I was at her outburst.

I slid over in the bed, wrapped her up in the covers, and got close to her ear and said, "Abigail Davenport you are the craziest woman on the face of this earth." I kissed her on the cheek and rolled out of the bed, waiting on instructions from George the newly-appointed barber.

She raised up in the bed and said, "And don't you forget it!"

"You won't let me. George, let's buzz it all off," I said keeping my eyes on her.

"Oh, please don't," she said as she got out of the bed and pouted. "Just trim it a little."

"Nope. George, we are cutting it all off."

"As you wish, Master Duarte," he said, walking out the door. I followed him and looked back at her. She pouted, poking her lip out as far as she could, and I laughed at the nonsense, but it was the light in her eyes that made me happy.

I SAT IN A CHAIR IN THE KITCHEN AS GEORGE DRAPED A SHEET around me. I could feel her hovering in the doorway when George pulled out the buzz clippers. "I can't watch," she whined, skulking off to another room.

"Just trim it, George," I whispered.

"I had no intention of doing anything else. We both have to live with her," he said plainly.

"That we do," I agreed, and George trimmed my hair.

AFTER MY TRIM, I FOUND HER IN THE BOURBON ROOM LEANING on the bar talking on the phone and looking at pictures on a tablet. When she saw me, she smiled knowing very well I'd give into her. I winked at her and plopped down in one of the recliners.

"Ashley, please call Zuhair's people and beg them to deliver the dress to the hotel," she said and paused. I could hear Ashley talking but not exactly what she said back to Abby. "Fine, then I will wear the red Ralph & Russo." She continued to pause after each statement allowing Ashley to talk. "Yes, I know the split goes to the crotch."

I turned around looking at her wide-eyed because that statement got my full attention.

"Tadeas approves," she said.

"Leave me out if this. Whatever this is," I said leaning back down in the chair.

She talked over Ashley and said, "I'm picking out a dress for the auction. She sent me pictures on the tablet." She walked over and sat down on the arm of the chair. She handed me the tablet to see the pictures of dresses. I grimaced. Dress choices were not part of the job interview. There wasn't much dress to look at, and yes, the split on it went way up. At least the top was mostly covered. I shook my head no.

"Why not?" she said as Ashley kept talking.

"Because it is hardly a dress, Abby," I said. She looked at the phone scrolling through pictures while Ashley talked. She showed me another, and it was completely sheer like the ones I saw at the party in the compound.

"No, absolutely not!" I said.

I heard Ashley clearly say, "What's his problem?"

"Nothing. Tadeas is a prude," she laughed. I heard Ashley laughing too.

"Women," I muttered, and she lightly punched me in the arm.

"Just pick one Ash, just as long as I can get to a knife strapped to my leg, I'm fine with whatever you decide," she conceded to Ashley.

"Now, that's hot," I replied to the knife comment. She punched me again, harder this time.

"No, I have not shown him. I will. I'll do it right now. Not on the phone with you. Bye, Ash," she said and hung up.

"Show me what?" I asked.

"This," she said, and I turned to look into the violet eyes of a dark chestnut brown-haired beauty. It looked like Abby, but not.

"What the hell?" I said, jumping out of the chair to get a

better look. I touched her hair to see if it was real. It felt the same as when it was blonde.

"It's a glamour," she said.

"I know that, but why?"

"Did you think I would walk into that auction as Abigail Davenport?"

"It didn't occur to me," I said trying to see past the glamour. Most of the time my animal sight would let me. But not this one. It was too sophisticated. "Who are you, and why don't we take this to my room before my crazy partner gets back? She gets jealous."

"Cute," she said. "I go by Annalise Madden at these kinds of events."

"Do I get one too?" I asked.

"If you want," she offered.

"No thanks. I'll just be me," I said.

"You still need an alias. You can either pick or I can pick for you," she said.

"Just do something simple like Carlos."

"Carlos is boring," she said getting up and gathering her various electronic devices. "How about Alejandro or Sebastian?"

"Ew, no, Carlos is fine. Or Juan."

"We can decide once we get there. I've got to grab some stuff downstairs in the lab," she said.

"Lab? I didn't see a lab down there," I said.

"It's a small closet off to the side of the office," she said walking that way, and I followed her.

Beside the office there stood a door that I'd never noticed before, and the room was the size of the walk-in closets upstairs. It held various containers, rocks, crystals, jars, and books. On the concrete table, there was a small inlaid silver circle. She picked up a couple of blue colored crystals and handed them to me. "Those are teleport crystals. It's how we get back home. I'll show you how to use them. We'll have two just in case. If something happens to one of us, the other has a crystal."

"I'm not leaving without you," I said immediately. She stopped and looked at me stunned.

"Silly, no, I mean like if you have a fainting spell, I can drag you with me and use my crystal. Or if I like do this amazing feat of magic, and become too weak to come home, you can use yours," she joked.

"I mean it," I said. "I'm not leaving without you." She did not know what to say. I was not going to beat around the bush with her anymore about these kinds of things. If we went in together, we came out together.

I could tell she understood. She walked up to me and kissed my cheek. "I'm going to change clothes. I laid some out for you. Okay?"

"Okay. Then we go?"

"Then we go," she said.

I got to my room, and the clothes weren't anything special. A nice pair of black dress pants with a matching sports coat. There was a deep blue button-up shirt with black dress shoes. I figured everything else we would need would already be there. I learned that she planned ahead for everything. I walked out of the room buttoning up the shirt, and she stood there in her glamour with what had to be the sexiest black dress I'd ever seen. My jaw dropped, and I stood in amazement as my hormones went wild.

I closed my eyes and swore. "Damn it."

"Thank you," she said. When she started walking to the base-ment door, there was very little on the back side of the dress except what covered her butt. I gritted my teeth and forced back the raging hormones. I caught up with her that way I didn't have to stare at the rear view.

George waited downstairs and had pulled the main rug back in the room. It sat rolled up in the corner. A large silver circle was embedded in the floor. She picked up a small purse from the desk and pulled out the blue crystals. She walked over to George, hugging him. He shook his head at the dress, but she just smiled. I looked at him and gave him a pleading look.

He walked over and shook my hand, "Good luck."

"For what?" I asked.

"For that," he said pointing at her.

"Thanks, I'll need it. Say a prayer for me," I said.

"Already done," he said.

"You two done now?" she asked.

"If I wasn't, would it matter?" I asked back.

"No."

"That's what I thought," I said as I joined her in the circle. She pulled out a small knife from the purse and cut her finger. She put her finger on the silver circle. A cyclone of wind swirled up around us which was very dangerous in that dress.

"Both of these crystals are tuned to this circle. They can be used from any circle anywhere. See how they glow while we are here in it?" I nodded, and she continued. "You take one, and I'll keep the other." She handed it to me, then stuck hers in her bra. I gulped because it surprised me she even wore a bra. So little fabric to cover so much.

"Aw, damn Abby, seriously?" Maybe she was right, I was a prude. Not completely, because even though I wasn't trying to take a peek, I got one anyway. I looked up at George, and he shook his head. Perhaps the angel knew the meaning of blissful torment.

She grinned at me. She was doing all of this on purpose. "This crystal," she said as she pulled out a green one, "is tuned to a circle in a safe house in Paris. KBS has an operative there that has empowered the circle for us. Since I've been there, I'm going to use this one, but we need to be in physical contact."

Two could play this game. I walked up to her and put my

right arm on her bare back, pulling her to me. She didn't flinch at all. Damn, she was good.

"All you have to do is concentrate on the place you want to go. If you end up having to use your crystal, focus on this room and the island. Once you've focused on it, say the magic word."

"What's the magic word?" I asked.

"*Transilio*," she said, and the wind whirled inside the circle. It blew around enough that I squinted my eyes. When I opened them, we were in a small apartment with sparse furnishings. The circle in the floor glowed. Outside the circle, two rolling suitcases sat along with a hanging garment bag.

"That's really awesome," I said standing there in awe of jumping to an entirely different place through a circle.

"Here's the tricky thing though, jumping back to the island is different. The only way to get on the island is through the portal. Basically, we just jumped through the portal, and then here with no stops in between. As long as the portal is intact, the magic works. If not, then you can't jump to the island," she explained. "And you can let go of me now."

"No, not until you quit playing games," I said.

"I'm not playing games," she protested.

"Yes, you are. I know you are beautiful. You know that I think you are beautiful. You don't have to parade around for me. This is serious now. You need to concentrate on our task here and stop trying to throw me off," I said.

She looked hurt, but she said, "I understand." I let go of her, and she walked up to the edge of the circle. She told me that circles could only be broken by the person that put them up, or someone more powerful than the circle itself.

"*Rumpo*," she said as she touched the invisible barrier. A small gust of wind blew around the room and the protection of the circle dispersed. She went to grab the luggage, but I hurried over and got it before she did. We exited the room and went down several flights of stairs. I assumed the place did not have an elevator. When we got to the bottom, we stepped out on the street and a cab waited on us. I loaded in the luggage, opening the door for her. She got in and slid over in the seat, and I followed her into the cab.

"19 Rue de Caumartin," she told the driver. He said something in French, then pulled out into the thick Paris traffic. I'd never been to Paris before. I watched as the city passed us by.

Traffic was congested, and the ride from the safe house to the hotel took about 45 minutes. Abby pulled out a wallet from her purse, counting out Euros to pay the cabbie. When we got to the destination, she paid him and thanked him in French. "*Merci pour le tour rapide.*" He spoke to her again, and I watched him watch her get out of the cab. I couldn't blame the guy. I watched her walk down the hall earlier and then scolded her for it.

The hotel did not look like much from the outside. It actually appeared to be an apartment building. We entered the hotel, and while it had been a little while since we had done it, I heard her voice softly speak in my head. "*You take over. You are in charge. I'll follow you.*"

"*I don't speak French,*" I informed her.

"*The guy at the desk speaks English,*" she said.

We approached the check-in desk. "Good afternoon sir, how may I help you?" the clerk said in English.

"Afternoon to you as well. We have a reservation under the name Madden," I said remembering her alias at the last minute.

"Why yes, here it is right here. You will be in room 20. It is on the top floor. Here is your key, Mr. Madden. I see the room has already been paid for as well as all room service and the wet bar. I hope you enjoy your stay, Sir," he said to me but stared at Abigail.

"Thank you, Sir," I said, picking up the envelope with the key card in it and placed my hand on Abby's back and guided her to the elevator. A bellhop came by us with our luggage. He passed the elevator, and I watched him go by. I assumed there was a service elevator. We entered the elevator, and she pushed the button for the top floor.

"Well done," she said. "I'd like you to continue to do that if you don't mind."

"Do what?" I asked.

"Lead," she said.

"Sure, but why?"

"It allows me to watch the surrounding room and prep for any kind of attack. If I'm dealing with hotel clerks or waiters or whatever the case may be, I can't concentrate on the elements around me that I could pull power from," she explained.

It made sense to let her have as much control over her magic as possible. The elevator doors opened, and we approached the door with the 20 on it. It was the only door on the floor. The bellhop waited for us, and the luggage sat inside the room. She slipped him some cash. "*Merci*," he said, then slipped out of the room.

I expected a huge room, but actually, it was pretty small. Inside the room was only a small desk and chair, a bench at the end of the bed, and a king-sized bed which took up most of the room. There was also a small fridge and table. A doorway that opened to the bathroom. "It's small," I said.

"Yes. The venue is a short drive, but not too close. Plus, we didn't need anything else," she said. "Will you order food? I'm hungry. Then I need to set up my laptop and see who is in town."

"Sure," I said taking off my coat and laying it across the end of the bed. She walked over to the luggage, pulling out a laptop, then set it down on the small desk. She turned it on. While it booted up, she took a couple things out of the bag, disappearing into the bathroom. I just shook my head at her silence and went over to the phone next to the bed. Of course, the menu was in

French. I took out my phone and started translating the menu. A double glass door led out to a small balcony with a table and two chairs. I dialed the number for room service. I ordered what I hoped would be a couple of grilled chicken sandwiches and fries. I opened the doors to the patio and a cool breeze flowed through the room.

When Abby came out of the bathroom, she had on jeans and a t-shirt. Goodbye, little black dress. I watched her as she walked through the door. At first, I thought she was leaving, but she put her hand on it. She said several words and a golden light shimmered over it. She then put her hands on the wall next to the door and spoke more Latin. The whole room shimmered. She placed wards over the room to keep us safe, or at the very least provide a warning of attack. She walked over to the laptop and sat down. She started clicking away at emails. Her cell phone rang from the bathroom.

"Could you get that for me?" she asked politely. I walked into the bathroom. The black dress was on the floor tossed in a corner. I picked up the phone. Ashley's name flashed on the screen.

"It's Ashley," I said to her.

"Just answer it," she said as I walked back in the room.

"Hello," I said.

"Oh, hey Tadeas, did you guys make it okay?"

"Yes, we did," I said. I suppose it sounded dry because she picked up on it.

"Oh no, what's happened now?" I didn't respond to the question.

"She's on the laptop, and wanted me to answer the phone," I said.

"Oh, okay, you aren't going to tell me, because it will make it worse. I get it. Tell her the dress will be delivered this afternoon as well as your suit. I sent her all the emails on the intelligence of who has entered Paris in the last 48 hours. If you guys need anything, one of us is monitoring the phone constantly, okay?"

"Thanks, Ashley, anything else?" I asked.

"No, but please you two try to get along, okay?"

"Everything is fine Ash. See you soon," I said, then hung up the phone.

"Thanks," Abby said. I sat the phone down next to her, and she touched my hand. "Everything is fine."

"I know," I said walking over to the bed. I laid down on it, testing to see if it was comfortable. It was more comfortable than any other hotel bed I had ever slept in. I stared at the ceiling and waited on the food.

It wasn't long before it arrived. I set hers out for her on the desk next to her, and I took mine out to the table on the patio. As I sat down, she got up from the desk. She picked up the food and brought it to sit with me.

"You don't have to entertain me, Abby," I said. "I know you are working."

"We won't have many more opportunities in the future to sit and have a meal when we aren't in a fight, or on a job, or on the run. I'm going to take every opportunity we get because I never know when I'll get another chance to enjoy time with you."

That was the best reason I could imagine hearing from her. She started talking about the venue for the auction, and where the exits were. She went into full business mode. I let her talk and took it all in while we ate.

Someone knocked at the door. I got up to get it. She pulled a roll of Euros out of her pocket, slipping them to me as I passed. The bellhop stood there holding two garment bags. I gave him some cash and took the bags. I put them in a small nook just outside the bathroom with a pole for hanging clothes. I unzipped the one that felt like a suit. Inside I found a black Armani suit with black shirt and tie. I unzipped the other bag, and a beautiful pink dress flowed out of it.

"Wow," I said. She looked up from her food, and her eyes widened.

"I didn't expect that," she said.

"Expect what?"

"Pink. Technically its rose." She got up and walked over to it. She reached inside the suit and pulled out a wallet, handing it to me. "Oh, this is a Tony Ward. Very nice."

I opened the wallet, surprised at what I found inside. The identification inside had my picture and the name Carlos Madden. "Um, Abby," I said, handing it to her.

"Damn it, Ashley," she said, handing it back to me.

"Married?" I asked.

"Yes, married," she responded. "And apparently you took my name." I could tell it frustrated her. Ashley pushed a relationship on us again.

"She means well, Abby," I tried to calm her.

"I know she does, but it's not like we needed any added tension," she said.

"Is there tension between us?" That confused me because other than the comment about the dress, I thought everything was fine.

"Not that kind of tension," she said as sat back down at her food, but she didn't eat.

I went back over and sat down. "Hey, we are doing our job, right?"

"Yes," she said. "I just, we just——" She stopped and tried to gather her thoughts. "This auction thing is going to be rough, and we don't need the added distraction. But I figured we probably would have to have a very outwardly show of affection to each other while there to make sure you were connected to me and my reputation at these sorts of things. Or rather Annalise Madden's reputation."

"Like the deal," I said.

"Yes, but no deal, because I need to be free to act. I can't have one of us accidentally saying something that might cause us problems in a fight. Does that make sense?" she asked.

I thought about how hard it was just to talk to her without giving her an order. "Yes, I remember the party very well. You are right." I reached over and took her hand. "Abby, it's fine. We can do it. It won't be a problem." I realized then, she wasn't worried about me. She feared how she would act.

CHAPTER 48

ABIGAIL

*a*s much as I wanted to avoid the subject altogether, I knew that I had to tell him. I knew now was the right time to do it. "I think I'm done eating," I said.

"The food not good?" he asked.

"No, I'm just distracted. No appetite," I replied.

"Are you going to tell me what's bothering you?" he asked. "You don't have to, but if it will help, I'll listen." I sat there and tried to gather my thoughts. He got up, cleaning up all the plates before taking them to the room service tray.

"If you push it outside the door, they will come get it," I said. I heard him open the door and push the cart out. I got up and closed the patio doors. "*Bulla.*" My silence bubble consumed the room, and he turned to look at me with concern in his eyes.

"It warrants a bubble?" he asked.

"Yes," I replied, sitting down on the bed. I crossed my legs and leaned against the headboard. The whole room exemplified classic French decor. While small, it was luxurious and private. I enjoyed the closeness of it. It had a certain intimacy. As much as I hated the thought, I needed to get over my reservations. Tadeas and I were about to start hunting the evils in the world. We needed to be as close as possible, but not too close. There was a fine line there, and even I wasn't sure of where that line was for us. He turned the chair around at the desk, sitting down to face me. I closed my eyes and gathered my thoughts. "I don't know how you are handling what happened to you with Meredith. I want you to know if there is anything you need to get out of your system I want you to come to me. Let me be the one you lean on."

He bowed his head. "I think overall I'm handling it okay, but it's not like she accomplished her goal. I was upset last night. It's still a nagging pain, but I promise, if I need to talk about it, you are the one I'll come to. Is that what's bothering you?" he asked.

"Not entirely," I responded. "I know all too well what it's like to have something taken from you that you did not freely give."

He looked up at me and seemed puzzled at where I was going with this. I did not want to prolong any of this story. I just needed to get it out.

"What do you mean Abby? Someone did that to you?" he asked.

"Yes, sort of. Every story is different." I said quietly. I could see the anger welling up in his eyes, and his body became rigid.

"It is one thing that a woman that I once found attractive got desperate enough to drug me, but you are talking about something entirely different," he said.

"Not really."

"Yes, really." He stood up, moving to the end of the bed across from me. "But Abby you don't have to tell me this."

"I do have to. There are things you need to understand about me, and why I am the way I am. Why I act the way I do, and maybe, just maybe I can find a way to finally heal from it. To move forward and..." my voice drifted off. I rarely admitted that there was something wrong with me. I was powerful. I was beautiful. I was smart. But I was unequivocally broken. Tadeas waited patiently for me to speak. I didn't deserve him after the way I treated him the night before. Especially when I had been the victim of an assault myself. "I'll do the best I can to get it out if you will just listen."

"Whatever you need," he replied.

"In 1917, New York City had one of the most uncivilized mayoral elections that they've ever had. The Agency sent three of us to help Tammany Hall in an effort to stabilize the city. The machine that was Tammany ran the politics in the city and had heavy ties to the mob. A man by the name of Charlie Murphy ran Tammany, and somehow a second endorsement arose out of Tammany for mayor. It ended up that their two candidates were competing with each other and thus dividing the vote of their supporters.

"We went in to encourage Murphy to do some public appearance and newspaper interviews which he hated to do, to clear up Tammany's position on the race. Holding control in New York City was extremely important in those days. We could not jump on a computer and check the stocks. Everything traded there on the floor of the Exchange. The Agency had to have a stronghold there. My grandfather sent Jeremy Stafford, a man named Brian Trevant, and myself to deal with the issues there to assure Tammany that they had the Agency's full support.

"On top of all of that the United States had declared war on Germany in World War I. The country was in a state of turmoil. Murphy helped with the war effort, too. Especially recruiting in the districts that Tammany controlled. Murphy was different than most of Tammany's leaders. He pushed the politicians to avoid the dirty money of gambling halls and brothels. Tammany was not without corruption though." I paused. "Sorry for the history lesson."

"It's okay. Keep going. You are working yourself up to it. I'm listening," he said.

He understood me far more than I ever imagined he would this early in our partnership.

"Several of the controlling families, Italian families, were upset that the Agency involved ourselves in the mayoral problem. Ultimately all the things going on in New York at that time, combined with the war, eventually lead to the Great Depression. As a side note, on July 4th, 1917 both Roosevelt boys were in New York. Theodore Roosevelt gave a speech in Forest Hills. FDR visited New York City and sat next to Charlie Murphy cementing his ties to Tammany, and it would eventually get him the White House. He would be the one to lead the States out of the depression. I met them both while there. Interesting men to be sure. After the rally with FDR, I attended a banquet. Trevant, who posed as my husband, went back to our hotel to complete some reports to send back to the Agency. Everything had to be hand-written back then and relations took time. I attended the party on behalf of the Agency, and Stafford drove me back to the hotel afterward.

"I always rode with him in the front seat. I hated being chauffeured around when I didn't have to be. He and I were friends. He was the same flirt then as he is now. I was very young, so I enjoyed his company. That night after sitting in the car talking, things got serious, and he tried to kiss me. I told him no. He obliged but assured me that one day I would give into him. Looking back, it was an innocent exchange. He liked me. Hell, I liked him, too. I only worked with Lincoln part of the time, and Heaven knows, he wasn't romantic at all. Jay really was the only one that had ever shown that kind of interest in me.

"In fact, back then, Lincoln scared the crap out of me with what he could do. In turn, Lincoln despised my lack of maturity.

I went upstairs thinking about Stafford and what my feelings were toward him. I did not take the precautions I should have, because when I opened the door to the room, there were 5 men in the room that I did not know. Trevant laid bloody and dead on the floor. I panicked and tried to get out of the door. I put up a shield barrier, then tried to pull power. I suddenly realized one of the men in the room was a far more powerful wizard than I was at the time. I could not pull power, and my shield failed immediately. The four thugs with him were mobsters. They came to inform us that our interference in the elections would not be tolerated. One of them went to punch me. I avoided the punch and got a hit on him. When he hit the floor, the other three rushed me.

"The wizard sat back and laughed. Each one of them tried to subdue me, but even in an evening gown, I kicked their asses. Finally, the olive-skinned wizard with his dark almost black eyes stood and said, 'Enough.' The four men stopped trying to fight me. I tried to move, but his spell froze me in place. To this day, I do not know what kind of spell he used, but I could not move. 'Take her into the bedroom,' he told them. They all approached me slowly, and when they realized I couldn't move, they dragged me into the bedroom pawing things they shouldn't have been touching. They tied my hands together. Even then I didn't cry, I was constantly reaching out for power, trying to grasp it from anything. I had been taught not to pull power from humans. It was dark magic. Samara had actually shown me how to do it. He wanted me to know what it felt like so that I would resist using it. He didn't want me to stumble upon it and corrupt myself. However, I felt like I had no choice. The thugs who were part of the hustlers for the mob asked the wizard if they could take turns on me, and he granted it to them. When the first one," I stopped again. I had to breathe. I pulled my knees up and put my head on them.

"Abby, please don't tell anymore," he said. "I can't stand it. Please." He fidgeted and his eyes flared with hatred and concern.

"I have to," I said.

"No, you don't. You don't owe me any explanation or have to tell me this. I get the idea of what happened. What they did to you. I get it. You don't have to say it." He touched my arm lightly. His hands were warm, and I was getting too used to him touching me.

"It's not what they did to me. It's what I did to them," I replied. I resolved to continue and finish the story. "When the first one got on me, I reached out to the life inside the one holding my right leg down. I could feel his blood pumping through his veins. I looked at the wizard, and he laughed. He knew what I was doing and let me do it. He wanted me to corrupt myself. I pulled the life out of that man and used his power to kick the man who laid on me into the wall. I heard his neck snap.

"The other two men started to run out of the room, but the wizard shut the doors and windows, so they could not escape. He laughed. I realized what I had done. I felt the darkness welling up inside of me. No matter what they did to me, I refused to do it again. The wizard ordered one of the men to have his turn. The man begged him to let him go. The wizard assured him that I couldn't hurt him. I then tried to pull the life out of that thug, but the wizard had exerted more control over me and I couldn't. After that one finished, he made the other guy do it too. I watched as the dark wizard sucked the life out of the both of them like I had done. I saw his eyes gloss over black. He pulled a black bladed knife out of his coat and leaned into my ear, 'You should thank me, Miss Abigail. I avenged your rape. Unfortunately, my dear, we have rules. And the rules say, you cannot take the life force of another by magic and live. You are now an abomination to magic, and you must pay with your life.' I lost all control. I screamed, but no sound came out. I cried and tried to thrash around. Sheer panic set in, but he had me bound. I watched as he took that cold black knife, pulling it slowly across my neck. I felt the blood rushing out of my body and the life drained out of me. I had murdered two men, and now I would die for it.

"The world went dark, and I wandered in the darkness for I don't know how long. I later found out that my grandfather had put a soul binding spell on me, the mark everyone sees now, that kept my soul from leaving my body. I never made it to heaven, Valhalla or Elysium. I just wandered in darkness until they brought me back. When I came back, the darkness inside of me due to pulling the life out of that man consumed me. It drove me mad. The island and its supernatural properties helped steady me. You probably noticed how peaceful and calm it can be there. That's when Grandfather assigned Lincoln to me full time. He hated it. He had compassion for me and my plight, but he hated being confined to the island. Later on, when I was ready, Grandfather forced him to work with me. I realized that work helped to keep me sane. The one thing that I could focus on and really make amends for my past actions.

"Jay was the one that found my body. He came up to the room about an hour after we parted to apologize for being forward. He has never been the same. I give him slack for a lot of things. He blamed himself for putting me out of sorts, for not escorting me to the door, and for not being there to help. But the truth remained, if he had gone in that room with me, he would have died too. I…" my voice faltered then. I couldn't speak anymore. I got it out without crying. I looked up to him and tears rolled down his cheeks. Whoever said that real men didn't cry was a fool. He crawled up the bed, sitting next to me. I reached up and wiped his face.

"I don't know what to say," he whispered.

"I thought you should know everything. You should know there is darkness in me. That over the years, I've learned to control it. However, our enemies know that it is there. There may come a day that it consumes me, I need you to either bring me back or cut me down." He got the most horrified look on his face and shuddered.

"No, I won't do it," he said.

"You have to. It's why you are here. It is why I need a powerful partner with me all the time. Lincoln had the same task," I said.

He kept shaking his head. "I will just bring you back, no matter what."

"I believe in my heart that you are a guardian, not only to me but to all people. If there is a threat that comes along that needed to be neutralized, you would do everything in your power to stop it. One day that power might be me," I explained.

"No, I've seen you. You won't go there, and I won't let you," he said. I did not want to push this with him too much. But there was one other thing that needed to be said.

"That is why we cannot ever be together. No matter what tension or attraction or whatever there is between us. If we were in a relationship, I couldn't count on you to do what I needed you to do if I lost control. Our judgment would be clouded by our relationship," I said. He moved out of the bed quickly and went to the door.

"I need some air," he said.

"That's fine. I understand. Do you have your bracelet?" I asked. I had noticed he wasn't wearing it.

"I think Meredith took it. I haven't been able to find it since then," he said.

I put up my hand, calling another one to it. I had more than one in my vault. Jewelry was easy to replace. He looked at me, and I tossed it to him. He put it on.

"I'll be back in a little while. I promise," he said as he slipped out the door.

Then I cried. I did not know if he would come back. If he didn't, I would understand. Part of it would be that he couldn't fathom hurting me. I curled up on the bed and drifted away to sleep.

CHAPTER 49

TADEAS

*A*s soon as the elevator door opened, I bolted in and hit the button for the lobby. I had forgotten my key card, but I was not sure I would need it. Part of me wanted to run far away. I would be doing the very thing she accused me of yesterday, but this overwhelmed me. There is no way in the world I could end her life. It would be like Isabel all over again. Even if we weren't together, there was no way.

The doors opened and the small, opulent lobby smelled like cigar smoke. A small smoking room sat off to the side of the lobby. I considered stopping for something strong and dark to drink, but I decided against it, hitting the front door into the city. It was loud and bustling. I winced, trying to control my senses. I wasn't in a large city very often, because I did not like them. The sounds overloaded my animal senses. I started walking down the street in a mindless gaze. I did not know where to go, but I needed to breathe.

As I walked, turning down streets on a whim, I knew I would

be lost before I knew it. I felt lost before it started. I walked down one of the large boulevards and came to a huge building that favored a Grecian temple. It was a Catholic Church, L'église de la Madeleine. The building was impressive. It stood out on its own block in the city. I could hear music playing on the inside. Walking up the steps, I looked at the relief carved above the large pillars. Christ stood in the middle flanked by two angels, one was Gabriel and his horn. I thought back to Abby, and Gabriel coming to her giving her the warning. The angels put their faith in a woman who had murdered two men. Granted, they got what they deserved for what they were doing to her. If they weren't dead already, I would want to hunt them down myself. Standing in front of the church with murderous thoughts, I decided perhaps I should go in to visit the confessional. There were people seated in sparse collections in the pews. Several people were praying at the altars and lighting candles. It felt familiar. It had been a very long time since I stepped into a Catholic Church. I wanted nothing to do with them after the exorcism. I sat down in a pew and stared at the extravagance of the place. The statue of Mary Magdalene in the front of the church was enormous and imposing. I sat quietly thinking about Abigail opening up to me with her story. While I did not believe in the Church, I did believe in God. I bowed my head and said simply, "Help."

The first thing I noticed was a cool breeze blowing through the room, and it got utterly silent. I raised my head, looking around. I sat alone. The people were gone. I thought I had sat too long with my eyes closed that the place closed with me still inside. Then from the back of the room, I heard a shuffling noise. I turned to see an elderly man hunched over a cane. He started to stumble and fall. I jumped up to steady him.

"Why thank you, Son, I can barely get around these days," he said. He looked at me with kind eyes. They were the bluest blue I'd ever seen.

"I can help you to a seat if you'd like," I offered.

"Right here is fine," he said as he sat down in the pew I vacated. He left enough room for me to sit next to him. "Have a seat, Son. You look to have a heavy heart."

Mindlessly I sat down next to him. There was something about him that felt calming and comforting. "I do, Sir, but I won't bother you with such things."

"I think I may have lived on this earth a little longer than you, young man, perhaps my wisdom can help. We all have times in our lives where we question our purpose in this world. We get lost and try to find our way. You look lost, Son," he said.

I put my hands in my hair and said, "Yes, I am."

He smiled. "Well, then you are in the right place to be found."

"Forgive me, Sir, but I don't have much confidence in the Church. I just happened by here earlier. I took a walk trying to clear my mind. The place looked impressive, and I wanted to see inside. I've never seen anything like this before in my life," I explained.

"That's understandable. The place is impressive but ostentatious. Faith does not require such elaborate adornments. Faith is simple," he said.

"Doesn't seem simple sometimes," I replied.

"If it isn't simple, it's because you make it complicated. This world is full of people trying to prove things. They want concrete evidence that the world was created by evolution or by the hand of God. They want unequivocal proof, but I say, if we found proof of everything in this world, we wouldn't need faith. Faith is a driving and inspiring force. There are those who pervert faith and use it for evil. In contrast, there are those who use faith to fight evil. The whole of the world would suffer without faith," he explained. He focused on faith. The same thing that Abigail had tried to drive home for me.

"If there was proof of God, then everyone would believe it. We wouldn't need faith anymore," I said.

"Sure, we would. We still need have to have faith in our fellow man. God is absolute. Those who believe in Him find it simple because their faith is what He is to them. Having faith in our fellow man is much different. Man is flawed. We make mistakes. We do bad things, but faith allows us to not only forgive but to strive for redemption. I had a priest once tell me that God has already forgiven us of our sins. It made no sense to me, but then I realized the faith I needed was not in God, but in my gifts and my fellow man. This world would devolve into chaos without faith. Anyone can obtain redemption if they have faith and seek it out."

"I see what you mean," I replied not sure how this all tied to me or whether it was just an old man rambling.

"I don't think you do. Look within yourself, Son. Are you lost because you lost faith?"

Perhaps he wasn't a crazy old man. I looked him in the eye, and he smiled. He started to stand, and I raised to help him up. He turned to walk out, and he grabbed my arm very tightly. I looked up at his eyes, "No, Sir, I have not lost faith. I just forgot about it. Thank you for reminding me. May I ask your name? I'm Tadeas."

He smiled, patting my hand on his arm. "Tadeas, I am Gabriel, and now you must go back to her. I have faith in both of you."

I froze in place. I turned my eyes from his face. The young Catholic boy in me kicked in and I couldn't look at him. He talked with me as a human. I did not sense any supernatural vibe from him. He did not stand before me like he had to Abigail, but nonetheless, I was touching an archangel of God.

"Do not be afraid, but you must go. You must go quickly. They are here. They will kill you if they get the chance," he said, as a wind blew all around me. The people who were in the church before reappeared. Then I realized, we had been in the spirit world. He pulled me through to that plane. I looked around the room, and my eyes locked with a man in a cassock. I was stunned. I had not seen him in over 100 years, and there he stood in Paris in the same church as me. It was Father Sergio. His eyes locked with mine.

"Tadeas, is that you, Son?" he said. I trembled. He was supposed to be dead. I looked for other exits. I only saw the one I entered in the front of the church. He stood between it and me. "My dear boy, I have longed to find you once I heard you still lived. Please, let us talk." He started to approach me. I felt two other beings in the room turn their attention on me. I looked behind me to see a grey-headed man in an expensive suit. He did not approach. I felt the power within him. He was a wielder. Just behind him stood old Milt from the tavern in Boulder. My heart pounded as I looked back at Father Sergio.

"We mean you no harm. Please, come with me and let's talk. We know you have been in the employ of a very dangerous woman. If you come with me, I can help you get out of her grasp," he said.

"I do not want to be out of her grasp," I said.

He continued to walk toward me, speaking quietly and calmly. He held his hand out toward Milt and the wizard motioning for them to stay. I felt the wizard reaching for me with his power. I put my hand over the bracelet that Abby gave me. I concentrated on her and her power. I turned to look at him and said, "Stop that."

I felt his power retract from me. Sergio motioned again for them to back off. They moved to the front of the church, standing beneath one of the large carved statues on the sides of the building.

"Tadeas, my Son, I have missed you. Please, at least, sit down and let's talk for a bit."

"I can't. I have to go," I said. "I have plans for the evening."

"Plans with her?" he said.

"She is not here," I said. "She sent me here to monitor things." God help me, I was lying in a church.

"What things?" he asked.

"I work for the Agency now," I said. "There are supernatural beings descending on Paris. I was sent to investigate." I tried to make my story so they would not know she was here. It would blow our cover for the auction. It was bad enough they knew I was here.

"Who are you here with?" he asked.

"I'm here with my wife, Anna," I replied.

"Oh, delightful, I did not know you were married. Congratulations."

"Thank you, Father, but I must go. She is waiting on me," I replied, summoning the courage to walk past him toward the door.

As I passed him he said, "Do you think that is wise?"

"What?" I stopped and asked.

"Being married. Don't you think you will kill this one too?" he said quietly.

I felt the anger rise in me. I grabbed the bracelet again and focused on how Abby's peace spell made me feel. "I am not that man anymore."

"But you are, the beast inside you rages. Even past the protections, I put on you with my necklace. You have no control. It is only a matter of time, and you will kill your wife. The beast cannot be controlled. I beg you to come with me, so I can help you," he said. I reached up around my neck, jerking the necklace off. I let it slide through my fingers, hitting the marble floor of the church.

"I don't need your protection. I have faith in myself and my abilities. She has faith in me too. I have nothing to more to say to you, Father Sergio," I said, walking toward the door. I picked up my pace once I hit the doorway. I crossed over the street, looking behind me. The wizard followed me. I started to run. Heading back the way I thought I had come, I tried to recall the steps I had taken to get here. I could not stop and ask for directions. I moved faster than he did, but it seemed like he just followed me. Not actually trying to catch me. I cut up a different road. I knew I hadn't been on it before because there was a bakery that smelled wonderful. I would have remembered it. I ran past it, ducking around another corner into a smaller alley. I could see the adjacent street. I took off running. I had almost gotten to the end when I heard him turn the corner behind me. I turned back around, plowing into a woman with long brown hair and violet panicked eyes. She steadied me, looking over my shoulder to the man running down the alley.

"Abby," I breathed with relief.

"Hurry," she said, grabbing my hand. We both sprinted down the street. At an opening, she darted across the street into another alley. It had a dead end.

"Abby, dead end, we can't go this way," I said.

She turned, looking at me. "Shift planes. Quick."

I looked behind me and waited for no one to be passing the end of the alley.

"Now!" she yelled, and I tugged on the edge of the spirit world and pulled that cold blanket over us and the sounds of Paris faded away. Silence enveloped us. The only sounds were our hard breathing and her steady heartbeat.

"How did you know?" I asked.

"I felt you pull on the power of the bracelet," she said. Her eyes, still concerned, darted around us. "I got up and started running to where I could feel the power being pulled until I felt you. Then I just ran to you, but you were moving around. It made it harder to track you, but here we are."

"We need to get back to the room. Behind the wards, as soon as we can," I said.

"Okay, let's go," she took my hand, and we walked through

the back wall of the alley, through a restaurant and into the street beyond it. We walked through the next building which was a men's clothing store and into the next street. It was the street of our hotel. She ducked into another alley, then nodded at me. I pulled on reality, shifting us back into the cacophony that is Paris. She wrapped her arm around mine, leaning into me. We walked casually out of the alley and into the hotel. She smiled and waved at the clerk as we walked by. We took the elevator to our room. As she pulled the key card for the door, I put my hand at her waist and leaned into her, smelling her hair. I listened to her steady heartbeat. She opened the door for us, and we both went in. I let the door shut behind us, pulling her back to me. She turned, putting her arms around my neck. I could feel her tears on my skin.

"I was coming back. I swear I was," I said.

"I know," she said still holding on tight. She pulled back. "Who was it?"

"A wizard. And Old Milt was at the church I went into down the street. There was a priest too," I said. Her eyes grew alarmed.

"What priest?" she asked.

"It was Father Sergio from when I was younger. Abby, he should be long dead. They told me that he was dead," I said.

Her forehead wrinkled. "I have intel that the GEA has a priest on staff."

My former mentor worked for the GEA. They were here in Paris. They had come for the auction and the book. "*Madre de Dios*," I said and crossed myself. Instinctively I reached for my crucifix.

Abby watched me. "Where is it?" she asked.

"In the floor of the L'église de la Madeleine where I left it," I said.

"He gave it to you?"

"Yes. He tried to convince me to leave you," I said.

"What?" I sat down on the bed and told her everything about the church, Gabriel, Father Sergio, Milt and the wizard.

"Now you are talking to *my* angel?" she smirked. She always found a way to make fun of a serious thing.

"Hey, he talked to me. Not my fault," I said.

"It's amazing isn't it," she said.

"I'm still not sure it was real," I countered.

"Trust me, I understand that. I had hoped we could go out for dinner, but it looks like we should order in."

"Yes, we need to stay here in some semblance of safety until it's time to go to the auction," I agreed.

"You can spend the night having quality time with your wife, how nice," she grinned.

"I'd say that sounds like heaven to me," I replied. I got up and pulled her to me again. "Abby, I know why I am here. I accept that, but I swear to you, I have faith that I will never have to end your life. We will help each other, and we will do what we have to do to save this world."

She put her fingers on my face, tracing the line of my jaw. She smiled at me as I leaned into her. I wanted to kiss her again. Her heart skipped a beat, and she shuddered. I pulled myself back a little, then it pained me, but I kissed her cheek instead of her lips. I wanted to do more, but a small kiss on the cheek would have to do for now. Perhaps her reasons before she told me about the darkness inside her was just an excuse to hide another reason for us not being together. She had unresolved issues with Lukas Castille. Or maybe Lukas Castille and Lincoln were the reasons she never wanted to feel that way again. I decided it was probably a little of both.

LATER THAT EVENING, WE ORDERED FOOD. SHE MANAGED TO FIND a delivery place like the one in Boulder. We had takeout from an expensive French restaurant. We ate on the patio, discussing the possibilities of one or all of the men from the church being at the auction. Thankfully, they all would think that Abby was actually my wife, Anna. I was glad I had enough of my wits about me to pull that off. I hoped Gabriel and his boss would forgive me for lying in a church. She knew the auction would bring a lot of bad people to the forefront. Neither of us realized it would be people from my past, plus people from Boulder. All the puzzle pieces were revealing themselves. We just had to put them together to figure out the end game.

She made a call to Ashley, giving her all the information about my confrontation with the priest and the wizard. Ashley said that everything for the auction tomorrow was ready. Abby gave her the instructions to step up the evacuation of the compound. Abby feared that they would try to sabotage the facility. It would be a huge loss, but if we could save lives, that would make a huge difference in the recovery of that loss. Ashley informed her that all recruits and training staff had started their exit and that the team was trying to find them various modes of transport out of Boulder. She mentioned another secure facility, and Ashley said they already had a team there. It looked very much like Boulder was going to be a complete loss. At the end of the conversation, Abby told her that she and the team needed to leave as soon as possible too. Ashley protested, but Abby insisted. After the phone call, we got ready for bed. I laid down on the side closest to the patio door. She ducked into the bathroom. I heard her brushing her teeth and doing those things that women do at the end of the day. I knew that was a mystery that no man would ever understand. I turned on my side and tried to tune out the sounds of the city. "Hey, Abby," I called out to her.

"Huh?" her voice came back muffled from the bathroom.

"Can you put up a bubble? It's too loud outside," I asked. I heard a pause and running of water. She walked back into the room.

"*Bulla,*" she said as she crawled into the other side of the bed.

"That better?" she asked.

"Much. Thank you. I forgot how loud big cities can be. I've got to work on shutting out all the extra noises," I explained.

"I imagine you hear a lot more than the rest of us," she said.

I rolled over onto my back to look at her. She had dropped the glamour. "Oh, hello," I said smiling.

"I figured I could be myself for now," she said.

"The dark-haired woman, who is my wife, is quite beautiful in her own exotic way, but I prefer the real you," I said.

"You know, Tadeas Duarte, you say very sweet things sometimes," she said.

"Just sometimes?" I asked.

"Yes, the rest of the time I want to throat punch you," she smiled.

"I'm the best of both worlds," I said, stretching my arms above my head. The tense run through the city had made my muscles ache. I put my hands behind my head and closed my eyes.

"You are the best of everything," she said, then slid over next to me. She put her head on my chest and curled up next to me like it was the most natural thing in the world. She quickly went to sleep. For all the talk about her mind and having to quieten it down, she could fall asleep in a moment. It was almost unnatural. For a moment, I laid there not moving. Unsure of the line between okay and too far, I contemplated what to do. I knew if I stayed like this my arms would hurt more in the morning. I decided to live a little, wrapping my arms around her to hold her against me. I cannot describe how great it felt.

WHEN I WOKE UP, I REACHED OVER TO TOUCH HER AND REALIZED I laid in bed alone. I sat up quickly but noticed that she sat at the small desk clicking through emails. She had a chat bubble up on the side of her screen and talked to Ashley.

"Good morning," she said. "There is fruit and biscuits over there on the table. Compliments of the hotel."

I walked over to the table, picking up a piece of melon and took a bite. "What are you working on?"

"Just looking at the lists of people who have come into Paris," she said.

"Anything stand out?"

"Several actually. Fix yourself a plate, pull that chair up over here, and I'll show you these people. Give you a better idea of what we are up against."

I did as she instructed, watching her pan through the pictures. The profiles of the people we were up against was frightening. She told me who each person was plus what their supernatural abilities were. A pack of wolves from Philadelphia that had arrived concerned her. The Agency had never had any issues with this particular pack. Perhaps it was a coincidence, but we both agreed that there was no such thing anymore. The little box with Ashley's name on it, now in the background of the screen kept blinking. "You going to answer her," I asked.

"Maybe in a minute," she said.

"Were you talking to her about me?" I asked.

"Girl talk is none of your business," she said avoiding me. Her phone started to ring. "Hello, can't you wait a few minutes? Tadeas is up. I showed him the pictures. Wait, what?"

She went pale.

"What is it?" I asked. I could tell something was wrong.

"I'm putting it on speaker phone," she said and clicked the button. "Tell him."

"Tadeas, the authorities found Travis Reed's body in a seedy hotel off Hwy 119 this morning. The Agency claimed the body. Ichiro is working on a full autopsy. The early tests show that he was a son of Asmodeus. I'll let Abby tell you about that, but one of the psych's from the Agency came by to take a look at the body and said that his soul had been eaten."

"What the hell?" I said.

"Anything else Ashley? Have you found Sam?" Abby's voice quavered.

"No, but I thought you should know," she said.

"Thanks, Ash," Abby said, ending the call.

"I know what a son of Asmodeus is. I should have picked up on that from him. He had all those girls down there wanting him, but the soul thing. That's crazy."

"Necromancer," Abby said.

"In Boulder?"

"Seems so. Perhaps the person that destroyed my car and shot at us. A low-level Necromancer couldn't do much with us considering the power we both carry, but he or she wouldn't hesitate to put a bullet in us, especially if it was enchanted," she said. "Had we run up on John Mwenye or someone of his caliber, I would have known it. We would have been in deeper trouble then."

"Any Necromancers come through here for the auction?" I asked.

"No way to know, actually. They travel much like Chito does in shadows," she replied.

"Can you beat one? Like toe to toe," I asked.

"Yes, but it's not easy. There aren't many left in the world."

"Best prepare for one tonight," I replied.

WE SPENT THE REST OF THE DAY LOOKING AT PICTURES OF possible people at the auction. Abby pulled the database with known necromancer information. Time went by slowly. Around 5 p.m., she decided to get a shower and start getting ready.

I waited on her to tie my necktie when she stepped out of the bathroom in that dress. She wore the glamour as well, but she was mesmerizing. She fiddled with a bracelet on her right arm and looked up at me.

"Need help?" she asked.

"Yes, if you don't mind," I said.

"If you pay attention, I can show you how to do it yourself," she said.

"If I did that, what would I need you for?" I asked, as she jerked the knot so tight I choked. "I deserved that, I suppose."

"Yes, you did. You look very nice though, my husband," she smiled.

"If you were really my wife, I'd never let anyone see you in that dress," I told her.

"Oh, good grief, this one is practically harmless," she said as she pulled the split apart and strapped a dagger to the inside of her right thigh.

I coughed, "Harmless. Not the word I would have used."

"What word would you use?"

"Dangerous. Provocative. Ravishing."

She looked up with a light in her eye and a bit of a blush on her cheeks. "Those work too. Ready?" she asked.

"As I'll ever be, I guess," I said. I was a bundle of nerves, but part of me was ready for the fight.

We headed downstairs and out the door of the hotel where a cobalt blue Aston Martin Vanquish waited on the curb.

"You and your cars," I said as she dangled the keys for me to take from her. I helped her in and walked to the other side of the car to get in and drive this beauty. Both of them. She directed me to the venue, and we prepared ourselves for the fight of our lives.

CHAPTER 50

ABIGAIL

*A*s we approached the venue, I calmed my anxieties, focusing on the task at hand, my abilities, and my partner. It was time to put all the anxiety about Tadeas, the compound, Meredith, and Sam out of my mind. Our mission encompassed one thing, recon. However, it could take a turn for the worst very quickly. We needed to avoid a fight if possible. I did not worry about losing the book, because I owned the book which normally sat in my vault. I had no intention to buy it again. Our purpose here was to see who wanted it. The auction plan came to me several days ago and finally, we were here.

I began to doubt myself because it had been so long since I'd tried this sort of operation. It had been forever since I'd been in a foreign city with nothing but my partner to keep me safe. I searched over every detail in my head hoping that I hadn't missed anything and prepared for the unexpected.

"Abby?" he said, as he drove.

"Huh?" I asked.

"It's going to be fine. Stop worrying," he said.

"I just hope that I covered everything," I replied. "I've put us both in grave danger."

He released the gearshift long enough to put his hand over mine. "We can do this," he said with confidence. I didn't know that I'd ever be able to do without him from that point on in my life. I had been hard on him, but he had hung in there proving himself to me. I was damn lucky to find that in a partner again after I lost Lincoln.

Tadeas pulled the Aston Martin up to the curb and got out. A valet met him and he turned over the keys to the young man who looked eager to drive the machine. Tadeas opened my door, offering his hand to help me out. He looked fantastic. I wanted to slap myself for all the fronting about not being in a relationship. My resolve solidified because I knew we shouldn't. But when he looked at me like he did yesterday after running for our lives, I wanted to melt. If he had kissed me right then, I'm not sure I would have been able to deny him anything.

The venue was down in Bercy just off the Seine. Les Pavillons de Bercy housed several interesting venue spots. The one I procured was called Magic Mirror. It was one of the old magic mirror tents from Belgium. Basically, it was a portable dance hall built out of wood and fully restored to its original grandeur. These pop-up dance halls were all the rage in the 1920s. It was large enough for a dance floor but intimate enough to have privacy and hushed conversations. The party would go on for about an hour and those interested in buying the item up for auction would then take seats at the tables around the room while the auctioneer took bids. I fully intended to allow someone to take the book out of the building, then with a small casting, it would return to its spot in my vault.

"*You with me?*" he asked.

"*Mostly,*" I replied.

He turned to me. Concern filled his eyes. "*Mostly isn't good enough. I need you here. All of you. Focus, Abby. I've got your back while you do your thing.*"

"*I'm here,*" I assured him. He took my hand, and we entered the tent of magic mirrors.

The first person that came into view was Lukas Castille. I gritted my teeth.

"*Lukas? Why is he here?*" Tadeas asked.

"*That's a good damn question. I do not know why he is here,*" I said.

"*He's not alone,*" Tadeas said.

I decided to speak aloud. "I see that." Lukas was flanked by four beautiful women all wearing revealing red and black Asian style dresses with golden motifs. "Don't let their looks deceive you. They are Madam Quan's Kunoichi. They are assassins and spies and use their womanly wiles to accomplish their tasks. I suppose Lukas is on good terms with Madam Quan for her to allow him to take four of her girls to Paris."

"He was not on the list, I suppose," he said.

"No, he was not," I replied.

"That going to be a problem?" he asked.

"I hope not," I replied. I saw Lukas catch Tadeas' eye, nodding to him. Tadeas nodded back. He looked at me and cocked his head to the side then smiled. He knew my glamour because he had seen it before himself. I could not hide from him. I nodded at him, too. If Ashley thought we needed back-up, like there was a last-minute player to join the game, she would have called Lukas in to help. She knew that despite our differences, he would protect the interests of the Agency. I hoped that was what he was doing here.

"*He knows it's you. Will he compromise this?*"

"*Yes, he knows, and not if he wants to remain regent of the West Coast.*"

"*Ruthless.*"

"*You have no idea,*" I said, smiling at him.

We entered the main room where a small band played lively music similar to that of the calliope music you hear at fairs and circuses. Groups of people mingled around the room. Most of their faces I had seen as we went through the list of possible guests. Several werewolves, a vampire lord from Sweden, a couple of academic wizards—basically wizards who study magic, but rarely use it—and a few Fae littered the room, talking jovially to each other. On the far end of the circular room from us, I saw a beautiful red-headed young woman flanked by a raven-haired woman with dark haunting eyes. I felt like I had seen her before, but I knew the ginger. Her mother would be pissed to find her here. Her name was Cassidy, and she was Aunt Lianne's daughter. I suppose that made her a distant cousin. She was no more than 18 years old. As a miracle of the never-aging Fae, my Aunt Lianne produced a child very late in life. Cassidy spent half the year with her father and half the year with Aunt Lianne.

"*Which one are you intrigued by?*"

"*The ginger with the dark-haired woman in the back is Cassidy Theodoard. She is my cousin, and Aunt Lianne would level a city if she knew she was here,*" I said. "*Keep an eye on her. If things go bad, I do not want her hurt. We need to get her back to Lianne.*"

"*Like we needed something else to worry about,*" he said, grimacing. I turned and looked him in the eye.

"We can do anything, right?" I asked. He smiled at me, as he pulled my hand to his lips.

"Yes wife, we can," he said, kissing the back of my hand lightly. I did not need to get distracted by my handsome jaguar now.

Several people approached us throughout the night, and Tadeas took lead introducing me as his wife. A few of them I had met before and were interested to see how he managed to take my name when we got married. I let him roll with the story. He did great making up a believably elaborate reason to hide his true name and how his love for me was the only thing that mattered. I blushed and leaned into him in the right moments. We were doing great. It was strange how a group of absolutely evil beings could come together to have a bit of chit-chat.

The ones we expected to arrive did not. No Milt. No priest. No grey-haired wizard. As the time for the auction approached, Tadeas stepped away from me for a moment to grab a couple glasses of champagne. Lukas descended upon me like a hawk watching and waiting for a moment to strike on his prey.

He offered his hand to me and said, "Lukas Castille, business-man, philanthropist and incredible in bed."

More than one of those was most definitely true. I gave him my hand introducing myself. "Annalise Madden, married."

"Oh really? You two got married?" he asked letting go of my hand.

"Seriously, Lukas?" I chided him, "Why are you here?"

"Your assistant said you might need back up," he admitted. As I had suspected.

"Damn Ashley," I swore quietly. I could feel Tadeas approaching. He put his arm around my waist and handed me a glass.

"Carlos Madden, husband," he said.

"Lukas Castille, disappointed." I rolled my eyes. "You know if you are going to hide, you should learn not to roll your eyes and bite your lip."

"Heh," Tadeas smirked, and I elbowed him in the side. He just pulled me closer to him and leaned over my ear. He kissed me on the edge of it. Goosebumps erupted up and down my body and I shivered.

"*Good God Almighty, don't do that*," I said. He just laughed. Lukas tensed and leered at him. "Apparently my assistant back home invited Mr. Castille to the party for shits and giggles."

"Actually, that's not a bad idea, if we are on the same team," Tadeas admitted.

"I like him," Lukas said.

"Should I excuse myself and let the two of you have some alone time?" I asked.

"How about the three of us and the ladies go back to my place and have a good time," Lukas said. "Carlos, you would not believe the things those women can do."

"Actually Lukas, there is a young lady here you should meet," I said ignoring his innuendo because I knew Lukas. He meant none of it. I turned his attention toward the grouping where Cassidy stood with the black-haired woman.

"Who is she? She's young and hot!" Lukas asked.

"Lianne's daughter," I said.

"Never mind. What the fuck is she doing here?" Lukas said, knowing that the Fae were trouble, especially my aunt.

"I'm not sure, but if things go wrong, could you be sure to get her out of here for me?" I asked genuinely. "Lianne would burn Paris to the ground with all of us in it if something happens to her tonight."

"Yes, I'll make sure she gets out. Who is the raven-haired woman?" he asked.

"I'm not sure. I've never seen her before tonight. She's not on any of my lists."

"I'll go find out," he said.

"Please be careful," I advised.

"With looks like these, I don't have to be careful," he smirked.

"Let us know what you find out," Tadeas interjected.

"You take care of her," he said pointing to me.

Tadeas nodded at him, and we watched him work his way back around the room to introduce himself to Cassidy and her friend. Cassidy looked out of place here. She was too young to be in this setting. There were far too many predators who would devour her innocence. Perhaps we were too late depending on who her friend was and why she was here.

"You trust her with him?" Tadeas asked.

"Yes, because he knows Lianne would do to him what Gregory threatened to do to you, if he did something to hurt her," I said. "Lukas isn't all bad. I should keep my personal opinions of him out of the conversation. He was a good proxy, and he is an excellent regent. He knows the game and plays it well." It felt strange to praise him, but the truth can set you free.

We moved toward one of the darker areas of the tent, watching the scene as an attendant wheeled the book out into the center of the room. It sat inside a warded glass case. The interested parties approached it, no doubt to verify its authenticity. I had acquired the book thirty years ago, and it had been out of circulation in the world since then. It was one of the few evil books that I kept. It contained multiple spells on how to destroy the world.

I watched the book, and I watched Lukas working his magic across the room with the two women. The black-haired woman had attached herself to his arm while Cassidy looked unsure but gave him fawning looks. Tadeas watched me. I sat my glass down and looked at him. "You are supposed to be helping me watch these people."

"I'm sorry. I am watching you watch all of them. Studying how you operate," he said.

"Nothing special going on. I haven't even pulled any magic. I don't want to draw attention." Speaking of attention, the woman with Cassidy belted out a loud laugh, and Lukas laughed alongside her.

"Is it possible for you to talk to him like you do me?" he asked.

"It once was, but I doubt that I could connect to him now. I don't want to try. If he can, he will come back around and give us the information we need," I said.

I felt his body tense next to mine. I looked at a table where his focus locked on. I could see a grey-haired man seated at a table across the way, whom I had not noticed before now. He stared at us, then nodded. So, the GEA was here after all in the form of a Master Wizard. I could feel his power across the room, however, he had no intention of letting me feel it until that moment. He had to have been here a while watching us. I did not know whether to move, run, or stand still. I closed my eyes, and I felt Tadeas shift his position to block me from the man's sight.

"*Watch the room,*" I said.

"*I've got you,*" he replied. I reached out with my magical senses to pick up on each and every person in the room. Several people took notice of the magic flowing through the room, but most knew there were wielders here and went back to their conversations. I opened my eyes back up, and Tadeas guided me over to one of the small tables to sit down. He watched the room intently now.

"*He's the only one here that can match my skill. The black-haired woman is a necromancer, but not a strong one. Cassidy is in real danger. She is not tainted, yet.*"

"*Then we get her and get out of here. We have what we came to see, right?*"

"*Yes,*" I opened my eyes to try to find Lukas, but I didn't see him or the two women. I didn't see the four Kunoichi either. I froze as a tall dark form sat down at the table with us.

"I do hope the two of you weren't leaving," he spoke in a thick British accent.

"Actually, we were," Tadeas said, and he started to stand up.

"That would be a bad idea, Tadeas Duarte," he said. "If you want to live, and see another day, sit down." Tadeas looked down at me, and I nodded to him.

"Wonderful. Now perhaps we can have a real discussion. I dare say, Miss Davenport, I do not like this look on you. It's too dirty. The glamour is top notch. I can't even see through it, but I know good and well who you are," he said. He leaned back in the chair and motioned for one of the servers. "Three glasses of W.L. Weller."

"I'm sorry I did not catch your name," I said to him as the server walked away. Tadeas held my hand in order to keep physical contact with me at all times. I shifted my legs in the seat that way I could get to the dagger if I needed.

"I do apologize. I thought you knew me. I am Edgar Donovan," he offered to shake my hand. I just stared at him. He chuckled, retracting his offer. I wasn't shaking hands with a man who started the conversation off with threatening my partner.

"What can I do for you, Mr. Donovan?" I said.

"Well, the way I see it, Mr. Duarte here has my friend, the priest, all riled up, and he would like a private meeting with him. I suggested that I arrange the meeting, and he left this place to wait for your response. Then, you and I could have a talk wizard to wizard," he explained.

"I have no desire to speak to Father Sergio. You may tell him that for me, and I go nowhere without her," Tadeas replied, confidently.

"I will convey that message to the priest. I told him as much myself, but I promised him that I would try if I saw you here tonight. He has already left with a few of our colleagues to go back to the United States and continue our business." The server returned with the drinks. I pulled in power and waved my hand over Tadeas' glass and mine. If they had been tampered with the spell would have turned the liquid black. "You do not trust your own hired help. How very skeptical of you."

"He knows I set this up. I do not know what he wants, just be ready for anything," I said. "They are hired help. I always assume there is someone with deeper pockets than myself."

"Very smart of you. I knew you were quite savvy. I must say it is a pleasure to sit here and actually converse with you. You are a legend in your own right." He took a sip of the bourbon. "Oh, it's fantastic. Do taste it. I know you love bourbon."

"Mr. Donovan, I appreciate the bourbon, especially since I'm paying for all of it. I have business that I'm conducting here, and I assume you have a purpose or agenda. I do beg of you to go ahead with this purpose. I do not have time to dawdle with you," I said.

"Dawdle," Tadeas laughed. "That's a funny word. Yes, Mr. Donovan, please stop dawdling."

I could not help but smile at him. *"Would you stop before I start dying laughing?"*

"It is a funny word."

"That's very cute. The two of you are bonded," he said tilting his head side to side. I knew that he was looking at the bond like my grandfather had shown me. "It's a very unique bond that is for sure. You know a bond like that is very dangerous. If one of you dies, the other will either go mad or kill themselves. It would be a sad ending," Donovan said.

If he told the truth, and I read no falsehood in him, he just told me something I did not know about the bond with Tadeas. On cue, the jaguar leaned into me, kissing my cheek. He said, "That's fine with me. I can't live without her." Tadeas meant it.

Donovan's eyes turned cold for a moment, but he shook it off. I felt a cool breeze wrap around us. "I have no machinations for you tonight, Miss Davenport. I am here merely to see who would be interested in such a book. The TCA frowns on such items coming out into the open, but I see in your eyes that you do not intend on anyone taking the book today. My work here is done. However, you should know, I was ordered to kill you the next time I saw you. Good thing you are wearing that glamour. I can honestly say I never laid eyes on the blonde-haired beauty known as Abigail Davenport. Wonderful party. Thank you for the invite. I hope you find what you are looking for," he said as he rose from the table. He turned away from us to walk out the door.

I picked up the glass of Weller, downing it in one gulp. Tadeas' eyes widened at my rapid intake of alcohol. "I should have sipped it. It's really good. Donovan invoked the TCA. I wonder if the TCA and GEA have ties. Too many damn acronyms. More than likely the TCA has nothing to do with it. He did that for my benefit because he knows the TCA can't touch me."

He took a sip of his. "Hmm, that is nice. Do we have this at home?" He held his glass up to me offering the last of the nectar for me to drink.

"No, thanks. Weller is just a batch of Winkle that didn't make the cut. I have two bottles of Winkle at home," I said not thinking about the bourbon. I focused on the room.

"I'm ready to go home," he said.

"Me, too. Not much longer," I said, touching his face. He leaned in like he intended to kiss me as he did the day before, but the murmur of the party was shattered by the laugh of what seemed to be a drunk woman. Tearing my eyes away from Tadeas' smolder, the woman who had been with Cassidy caused the commotion. She walked into the center of the ring toward the book. Her hands were covered in blood. I flinched toward her, but Tadeas practically held me down in the chair.

"*No, don't rush in,*" he warned. I was thankful one of us had a cool head.

I frantically searched the room for Cassidy and Lukas. I saw neither one of them. The woman laughed, drawing all attention to herself. She put her bloodied hand on the glass holding the book, leaving a deep red hand mark on it. I could feel the souls inside her. The power of the souls consumed her like a drug. I knew she was new to the soul consumption. Necromancers can't just constantly take in souls without getting addicted. I'm not sure how many she had consumed, but the wildness in her eyes and her demeanor reeked of a full-fledged necromancer overdosed on souls.

"Good evening, ladies and gentleman, I regret to inform you that there will be no auction this evening. The book will be leaving with me. Would the seller of the book please step forward? I have it on good authority that the previous owner is here with us tonight," she said as she wobbled in the center of the room.

I shifted in my seat, trying to stand up.

"No. Not yet," Tadeas said physically holding me down in the chair. "Just wait. See what she is about first."

Pulling power from the world around me, I gathered as much of it as I could to myself. The rose gold cuff on my wrist started to glow. I had cast a spell on it earlier to hold stored magic in the case I started to run out. It was full now. Tadeas reached inside his coat, putting his hand on one of the Sig pistols from the vault. The other was strapped to his ankle along with his knife that he always kept there. Below the table I opened my hand, my four battle orbs floated above my palm. I closed my hand knowing they were close by, and my magic could call them in an instant.

"I know that I must look a sight with all this blood, but a girl has to eat," she chuckled. The people in the room slowly moved out to the edges. I felt a presence behind us. I tilted my head toward it and saw Lukas standing against one of the wooden columns. He had blood on his crisp white shirt. I tried to contain my alarm. His blue eyes were steady but concerned. Tadeas turned his head to him. He nodded to Tadeas, then slipped out of the tent through one of the loose canvases that were the walls of the tent.

"He has her."

"Good. One less thing to worry about."

"Please. I've always wanted to meet the famed Abigail Davenport. Sweetheart, I know you are here with your little pet. Please come out and play," she purred. "I won't hurt you, much."

I looked at Tadeas. *"Now, can we do this?"*

"I'm with you," he responded.

As we stood together, I walked toward the center of the venue so that Tadeas could shift into the spirit world without notice. Drawing all the attention in the room to me, I stepped into the light. I felt the cool breeze as he shifted into the spirit world to get behind her. As I walked into the light of the center of the room, she tilted her head to the side and looked puzzled.

"I didn't take you for a Tony Ward kind of girl," she said talking about the dress.

"No, generally I'm not. I prefer Mr. Murad, but alas he had nothing for me at such short notice," I replied.

"I also know that you are a ravishing blonde," she commented. "The glamour is quite impressive, Miss Davenport." Not only was she outing me, she was destroying the alias known as Annalise Madden.

As I let the glamour fall, a murmur filtered around the room. Most of these people only knew me as Annalise Madden. This was a charade I'd never be able to use again.

"I'm sorry I did not catch your name. Would you mind introducing yourself to the entire room? You seem to know quite a lot about me, but alas, I have no idea what insolent twat has decided to interrupt a perfectly good auction," I said.

She smiled, "Oh honey, you are going to talk dirty to me, and I won't be able to contain myself. Where is that beautiful man of yours? I do hope he isn't doing something unadvised. Or perhaps he had enough of you and moved on. I know a certain woman who would love a second shot at him."

Ignoring her banter, I raised my right hand to her, unleashing a small bit of force. "Your name!"

She stumbled back into the book display. It jostled but did not fall.

"Now that is not very nice. Do we not have rules of hospitality in this place?" she laughed.

"We do not. You are here at your own peril. I will not ask you again. What is your name?"

"My name, my sweet, beautiful Abigail, is Vanessa Vaughn. I have been the apprentice of Mr. John Mwenye for almost 50 years, but recently I decided to strike out on my own. It is liberating to get out from under the men who hold you down. But of course, you would not know what that is like since you still bear the mark of your grandfather, Gregory Theodoard. It's a shame." She sauntered toward me with her hands dripping in blood. I had no idea who she gutted, but she made a mess on the floor. The bill for this was going to skyrocket.

"*Focus*," I heard him say in my head. I smiled at my hidden protector. I rather liked him talking in my head. It gave me the confidence to face this wanna-be necromancer head-on.

I calmly said, "Miss Vaughn, I do believe Mr. Mwenye received the invitation to this event, not you. If you do not mind, I am asking politely that you leave on your own accord, or you will be removed forcibly."

"I'm not leaving, sweetheart. Not that anyone here could remove me. Come to me, little one," she said as she turned to her left, motioning into the darkness. Out of the crowd, a wiry, dark-haired young girl stepped into the light. My heart sank. Samantha Taylor stood there with a huge gash in her mid-section. Blood poured out of it. Several people screamed and people started moving to the exits. Curiosity of the morbid kind usually runs out when blood starts to flow. "I believe you know my little friend, Miss Taylor, correct?"

"Last warning, Miss Vaughn. I am going to kill you if you do not leave this place," I said. I knew in my heart Samantha was dead already. She was pale and barely standing. She hung her head down, and I could not see her eyes. She was simply a pawn to this woman's game.

"I'm sorry, Miss Davenport. I'm not done here. Samantha, go see your old bunkmate. I'm sure she misses you," Vanessa said.

Sam looked up at me with completely white eyes. I knew that this was the woman who had killed Travis and had tried to kill me in Boulder. She knew too much. I wasn't sure that she had gotten all of her information from Travis and Samantha but knowing that they both were involved with what Meredith did to Tadeas, I decided that she was definitely part of a larger scale attack on the Agency.

Samantha sauntered toward me as the necromancer controlled her body. I caught movement toward the outward edges of the light. Five more white-eyed hulking men formed a circle around us. These guys were much larger and would be more difficult to deal with than Samantha.

Behind them in the darkness, I could see the green eyes of my protector and partner. He had both Sigs poised and ready to pounce. I let Samantha walk toward me. I stepped back a little like I tried to get away from her. Vanessa laughed at the chase, which was good. I hoped to keep her focused on me, giving Tadeas plenty of time to act.

"She just wants to have a little sparring match like you used to in the compound," she said bouncing around like she was a boxer with her fists up. I wondered if she knew how stupid she looked, but I also knew that crazy was dangerous. "I think Sam felt quite betrayed when she found out you were far her superior. You let her offer to help you multiple times when actually you should have been helping her."

Samantha had spilled her guts to this woman, indicating that she knew her and trusted her. What a terrible miscalculation on her part. But the crazy woman was right. I should have tried harder to help the students in Tadeas' class. It was just a few days ago, she was alive and giddy for us in a tavern in Boulder. This was precisely why we needed to make the changes in the way we trained our crews.

"Abby, don't you dare listen to her. You focus on getting us out of here. Sam is gone. There is nothing we can do for her now. You take this woman out. I can handle the undead."

"I'm ready whenever you are. Hit them in the heart," I instructed.

"You make your move, and I'll follow," he said.

Sam stumbled into me, and I caught her body. It was cold and dead. She took a half-hearted swing at me, and I plunged my dagger into her heart. Her body sank to the floor at my feet covering me with her blood, and I lifted my eyes to the solid black eyes of Vanessa Vaughn. Calling my orbs to my hand, I swirled them around drawing all eyes to me.

Tadeas moved from the back of the room as the undead started to advance on my position. He picked two off immediately and then was blindsided by a wolf. I saw him shift to jaguar, burying his teeth in the wolf's neck as it tried to pin him. The wolf yelped then shifted to dead naked human. Zombie wolves. That was a new one for me.

Tadeas jumped to his feet shifting back to human. He took another shot at one of the undead on my left. I stood still and allowed him to work without worrying about hitting me. I kept my eyes on Vanessa who twirled around to each blow laughing and pointing at the action like a mad woman. She turned to me. "He really is sexy as hell. Please tell me you fucked him before I kill him. I would hate to take that opportunity away from you. Hell, maybe I can convince him to fuck us both."

Necromancer and sex. It was always the combination. I couldn't remember the number of times John Mwenye had propositioned me. He was a cool character. It was hard for me to believe that this lunatic was his apprentice. I worried that he might be nearby.

I forced the iron ball toward her like a bullet from a gun, *"Ecfundo."* She tried to dodge, but it struck her in the shoulder. Black blood dripped down her arm. She laughed as she hurled a dark black shadow at me.

I tapped the bracelet on my arm, and it cast a golden reinforced shield around me. The shadow surrounded me but then dissipated. One of the undead lunged at me but stopped short as Tadeas who was dealing with another wolf put a bullet between his eyes. I never took my attention off the necromancer. Tadeas had the wolves covered.

She pulled out a black knife. She ran it across her tongue. "Mmmm, I can almost taste you on this knife. You probably recognize it. Don't you?"

Chills ran down my spine. I did recognize it. It was the same knife that slit my throat. The one that the dark master wizard used to kill me. I cut my eyes to Tadeas.

"It's just a knife, Abby. Put her down or run! You decide. I've got this."

"I do recognize it, and as you probably noticed it didn't work," I said.

"Oh, but it holds many more souls than it once did. My mentor has been storing them up for you. He wanted to kill you with the same knife all over again. I took it from him because you needed to be dealt with now. Not later," she growled. So, she had left his teaching. I knew one thing for sure. If I didn't kill her, he would. John Mwenye didn't tolerate betrayal. Vanessa Vaughn was already dead.

I sensed there were very few people left in the room. There were several who looked like they intended to steal the book once we were done here. There were a couple where I wasn't sure what side they were on. I decided to address them all.

Behind me, I heard another gunshot followed by the wet chomp of fang to neck. I focused on Vanessa again as she waved the knife around. She did not look like a skilled fighter, but I did not want to underestimate her. Closing my hand, the rotating orbs vanished. I opened it again and whispered, *"Fulmen."* Just above my palm a ball of pure white lightning strobed in my hand, and I amplified my voice for the whole room. I could hear sirens in the distance.

"I am Abigail Davenport, descendant of Helios, son of Hyperion. I represent the Agency. Hear my voice." The sound echoed through the small room. I saw multiple figures starting to advance on the center area. A black jaguar bounded out of the darkness and brushed against my leg, curling his tail around it as he went. I had to smile at the show of loyalty. I felt his human body morph, and he stood back to back with me with the two Sigs ready to fire. He watched my back. "For too long the darkness has been allowed to creep back into our world. I will no longer stand by and allow any of you to destroy the lives that we hold dear. This is a warning that you can carry out of this place to every evil you know. You tell them I'm back. You tell them I have a deadly partner. You tell them we will hunt them all down." The lightning ball in my hand expanded and enveloped Tadeas and me in an orb of light with flashing streaks.

"*Impingo,*" I said, throwing my hand downward. The orb crashed down to the ground searing a perfect circle on the surrounding floor.

"*Oh, we are running,*" Tadeas said.

"*There are too many of them,*" I replied. He pressed closer to my back. I just had to bend down and empower the circle with my blood. I had used my knife on Samantha. I knew Tadeas had a knife strapped to his leg. The position we were in would not allow either of us to pull it without taking our eyes off the approaching enemies. Vanessa started cackling again.

"How cute, a girl and her kitty. Meow. That's hot. Are we all supposed to cower in fear that you are back in the game? I, for one, am so excited that you decided to come out of your hiding. It's time to rid this world of you once and for all," she said. I spoke in Tadeas' head telling him my plan.

"*Shit,*" I heard him respond as I dropped to my knee. I grabbed the knife from his ankle, slitting my finger in the process. As I lunged to empower the circle, she made her move. She was fast. I knew as a necromancer, she could shift to the spirit world and back. She bent space by pulling the veil open and shifting closer to me.

The knife plunged into the back of my left shoulder and a burning fire sensation ripped through my whole upper body. I grabbed her leg, speaking the word *"Discutio"* which would dispel or shatter any shield or personal protection she placed on herself. Tadeas spun, shooting twice. One in the chest, one in the head. In her madness, she must have considered herself invincible. She fell backward away from us, knocking the table with the book over. The book disappeared as part of the protections I had put on it.

Those remaining in the tent murmured at the disappearance of the book. I looked down at the black blade protruding from my shoulder just above my heart. Tendrils of inky blackness spread outward along my shoulder and chest. The world started to spin. I reached for the edge of the circle, touching it with my bloody finger. A wind flew up around us empowering the circle. I rolled over on my back. I could see the dark figures backing away from the empowered circle. Tadeas stood above me watching them. Both guns poised to shoot. He never looked down at me. I pulled the blue crystal out of my bra and focused on home. The darkness spread across my body and down my arm. I looked down at the crystal in my hand as the darkness spread across my veins. I couldn't move it anymore. The darkness spread faster than I thought it would. I had miscalculated the power of the knife. I found comfort in that Tadeas had a crystal to get back to the island because I knew I was breathing my last breath.

"Abby, the crystal. Use it now!" Tadeas yelled.

"You were amazing, Tadeas. I couldn't have asked for a better partner," I said.

"Don't you dare!"

I looked down at the end of the knife as the blade evaporated into dust, leaving a long black wound on my shoulder. The wound closed up on its own, but the tendrils of blackness continued to spread. I lost control of my hands, and the crystal tumbled on to the floor. I looked up to him. His beautiful green eyes. I wanted that to be the last thing I saw as I died. He dropped to a knee still holding one of the guns up in case someone tried to charge us. He picked up the crystal. I heard his voice in the distance. He spoke the word I taught him yesterday.

"Don't you dare do this to me, Abigail Davenport. You know I can't live without you. Don't die. Hang in there. I've got you. I promise. I've got you."

I felt a strong burst of wind, and the darkness consumed me.

CHAPTER 51

TADEAS

I felt the rush of wind taking us back to the island. Dropping the gun and the crystal, I bent down to her as her eyes rolled back in her head. The moment I saw the basement of Casa Del Sol I screamed, "George!"

He was already there waiting for us. I picked her up off the ground. The black lines extending from the knife wound had stopped moving, but they covered most of her upper body. They had crept up her neck, and I could see them on her thigh where the designer dress split open not covering her legs. She was dying in my arms, and suddenly I couldn't breathe either.

"Bring her. Hurry," George instructed as he hustled up the stairs, and I followed him. Her body felt heavier than it should as if the blackness spreading through her veins was lead or iron. I followed George into the dining room. "Lay her on the table," he said. The table glowed with a large circular symbol with strange words and patterns. I could feel the power flowing around it. He had a tray with a knife, scissors, a wet cloth and basin of water.

"Now what?" I asked, trying to remain calm. I could hear her heartbeat slowing down. "She's dying. Her heart is slowing down."

"I know, Son," he said, handing me the scissors. "Cut the dress away."

I started cutting the sheer upper part of the dress from around her neck down to the thicker fabric covering her breasts. I stopped there and tore away the sheer parts opening up the place where the wound had closed off. There was no blood. No real wound there. Just the darkest place on her body where the knife struck. Blood streaked down the once beautiful dress where Samantha's body slid down it. George was taking the cloth and cleaning Samantha's blood off of her hands. I heard the rumble of thunder in the distance.

"No time, Tadeas. Cut the dress off of her," he spouted.

I ran the scissors down the center of the dress, and he pulled the edge of it while I lifted her up. It made it easier to get it off her. The storm thundered loudly as if it had moved miles in just a few moments. The double doors in the adjacent sitting room swung open as did the set in the dining room. The wind swirled around the room. The night sky ignited in ripples of purple light. The lights flickered like they were candles. The circle on the table glared with a blinding golden light.

"Move the tray. Get the scissors," he said. I picked up the scissors but was mesmerized by the storm outside. It was as if it had moved into the room with us. George put his hands on my shoulders and started pushing me out of the room.

"No. I'm not leaving her. No, George let go of me," I cried. "She's dying. I promised I wouldn't leave her."

He was much stronger than I gave him credit. "Tadeas, he is coming. Back away."

A blinding white light filled the room, and the immediate report of resounding thunder shook the house. I fell to my knees knowing that this was an angel, and George turned his back on her lying on the table. He put his hands over my eyes. I wanted to see as the figure approached her on the table. I looked down and began to pray the same guardian angel prayer Abigail had used on me.

"*Ángel de Dios, mi querido guardián, a quien su amor me compromete aquí, siempre esta noche estar a mi lado, para iluminar y guardar, para gobernar y guiar. Amén.*"

"Amen," George echoed.

Opening my eyes, the blinding light was gone. My ears echoed with the silence. Silence without her heartbeat. I hadn't acted fast enough. She was gone. I gritted my teeth and wanted to scream. George put his hand on my shoulder, pulling me up off my knees. As I approached the table, I noticed the black tendrils that were up and down her body had disappeared. The bright circle's power faded, leaving the charred imprint of the sigil on the table. She laid there still and quiet. Dead.

George stood behind me, watching her intently. I would have given anything for her to cuss me or make fun of me. Her face illuminated in a strange way just as before when Gabriel visited her. He came to heal her, but I didn't get her here fast enough. A piece of her blonde hair laid across her mouth. Moving closer to her, I brushed it out of the way. When my finger barely touched her skin, she drew in a deep breath and lurched up from the table. She gasped for air like something was choking her.

"Abby!" I grabbed her, pulling her toward the edge of the table. She lunged forward again, causing us both to tumble to the floor. Her heart pounded extremely loud. So loud that it made my ears hurt, but it was a wonderful pain. Her body was rigid, and she lurched forward again. Black inky fluid poured from her mouth. I wrapped my arms around her waist from behind and held her up the best I could. George waited beside us with a white sheet. The blackness stopped surging out of her body after the third wave. The black mess covered the floor. When it was over, she leaned back into me.

I spoke to her the whole time. *"I've got you. Just get it out. I'm here. Just breathe. Breathe, Abby. Thank God, you are alive. Please breathe."* She breathed quietly now. Her body still felt cold. I looked over at George, and he wrapped her in the sheet. I got my legs under me, keeping my arms around her waist, and hoisted her up. She felt significantly lighter to me, and I carried her to her bedroom. George stopped at the door as I carried her in. I looked back at him.

"There are things in the bathroom and the closet to clean her up. Get her some clothes, too."

"You can't come in," I said realizing, that she told me the room was warded. I just didn't realize it kept George out, too.

"I trust you with her. I'll be right here if you need anything," he said. I knew that it pained him to be away from her. I should have taken her to my room where he could have entered, but it was too late. I wanted to get her cleaned up and in the bed.

Maneuvering her dead weight proved to be the biggest challenge in removing the blackness that had covered her body. I managed it the best that I could. I gently wiped her down as the warm spray of the shower soaked us both. She stared off into space, but her heart continued to beat loudly.

"Come back to me, Abby," I begged as I washed her body.

After the shower, I found a pair of flannel pajamas for her to wear even though it was the middle of summer. Her body felt cold which bothered me because she had always been so warm.

Laying her down on the bed, I tried to keep my wet clothes from soaking the mattress and sheets. As soon as she was down on the pillows, I stripped off the tie and shirt. I pulled the covers up around her on the bed. Grabbing the chair from across the room, I dragged it over to her bedside.

As I sat in the chair listening to her heartbeat, I could also hear George breathing outside the door. He murmured prayers of thanks for saving her life. I bent over her and whispered, "Rest, beautiful. I'm here with you, and I'm not leaving. I swear it on my life. Close your eyes and rest." When I pulled back, her eyes closed, and her body relaxed. Her heart settled into a normal rhythm. I couldn't hold my emotions back any longer. I sat in the dark, holding her hand as tears rolled down my cheeks.

I DON'T KNOW HOW IT WAS POSSIBLE, BUT I SLEPT SITTING UP IN the chair. As the sun started to creep into the room. I stood up and stretched. I moved the chair back to its original spot. George appeared in the door and startled me.

"Can I get you anything? She might sleep for a while," he said.

"No, George, I'm fine." I looked down at my bare chest. He smiled at me and held up a duffle bag. I swear he pulled it out of thin air. I took it from him. "Thanks, George."

"I'll be back with some food and drink," he said. I started to tell him no but telling him no was about as difficult as telling Abby no. I turned and looked at her. She still rested. I felt her heartbeat steady and getting stronger. I ducked into the bathroom, ripping the rest of the clothes off me. The pants were covered in blood from the kills I had made. With a quick look at her laying still in the bed, I jumped in the shower to wash off the battle from the night before. Looking down at my hands as the water ran over me, I realized that I used them to kill. Multiple times. They were all valid kills, but taking any life hurt me on the inside. I reminded myself that it was either them or us. Which in the end, they had taken Abigail from me. The deaths didn't weigh on me like when I had killed my Isabel. All I knew was that they were intent on harming Abby, and I didn't care who they were. I wasn't letting anyone touch her. A part of me knew that I had failed, but the other part reminded me that I took out most of the room while she battled the necromancer. I lowered my hands, watching as the left-over blood drained down into the center of the shower. I allowed it to wash away any regret I had about the deaths I had caused.

Shaking myself out of the introspection, I jumped out of the shower to dry off quickly. I'd been away from her longer than I wanted to be. If she woke up, I wanted to be right there beside her. I threw on the clothes that George had in the bag for me. I went back to the room and sat on the edge of the bed.

"*Abby, can you hear me? I'm still here. Please come back to me.*"

She didn't move, and I got no response. I thought about the last time I heard her in my head. She had said, "*Look I'm gonna do this. It's probably going to be painful. I trust you to get me out of here. She's going to come after me with that knife. I'm going to pull your knife, remove any shield or protection she has, and you shoot her. Put her down. Then I will activate the circle, and we get the hell out of here together.*" Before I could react, she had dropped to her knee to pull the knife from my ankle. I remember spinning to fire at Vanessa before she got to Abby because I knew she would take the opportunity. I just was not fast enough. She moved in a blur toward Abby, and Abby knew she would take the hit. She knew that one of us would have to do it. She had taken the knife so that I could get us out of there.

I clenched my fists angry at myself for not reacting faster. I was just thankful she was alive.

"Remember in Colorado, you took the bullet for her. This was the same," George said at the door as if he knew exactly what I was thinking. He held a plate with a sandwich, chips and a glass of milk. My stomach screamed out in sheer glee. I stepped outside the door and took the plate from him. On the table outside the door in the hallway, a cell phone started to ring. George answered it and handed it to me.

"Hello," I said as I devoured the sandwich.

"Tadeas! I've been trying to reach both of you. Are you okay?" It was Ashley, and she was frantic.

"I am okay, but she is..." I did not know how to explain it. "Look, Ash, something happened. I don't know how to explain it, but she is not conscious right now."

"Oh, no. I have the police reports from the scene. They found multiple bodies including Samantha's," she said.

"Yes, I know. Ash, I'm sorry, but I just can't talk about this right now. I need to be with her, okay?"

"Yeah sure, but Tadeas, just remember that she's my best friend. I can't come to her right now. So, I'm depending on you to tell me what's going on. Is she going to make it?" she asked crying.

"I think so. I hope so." I replied to her. "I'll call you if anything changes."

"Okay, bye."

I walked back into the room, juggling the plate, the glass of milk and the phone. I laid the phone on the table next to the bed. I downed half the glass of milk, setting it on the table as well. It only took me a few minutes to kill the sandwich, chips, and finish off the milk. I walked back out to the door. George was not there. I laid the cup and plate on the table in the hallway.

I went back to Abby. Hours crept by slowly. Her heartbeat thumped once again its normal steady rhythm by the time it started to get dark. I tried to speak to her out loud and in her head multiple times, hoping that she would respond. As it started to get darker, I laid down on the bed next to her, holding her hand. I could see George lurking at the door. I drifted off to sleep listening to her breathe.

I AWOKE ONCE IN THE DARKNESS. I SWORE I HEARD HER VOICE.

"I heard you, Abby. Are you there? Can you hear me?" There was no response. I moved closer to her and wrapped my arm around her waist. I closed my eyes again concentrating on her heartbeat.

THE SUN STARTED TO RISE ON WHAT I THOUGHT WAS WEDNESDAY, but I wasn't sure. I opened my eyes and those bright green eyes stared back at me.

"Hey," she said.

"Thank you, God," I said. I leaned down and lightly kissed her lips.

"Oh, my, well, okay," she spoke quietly and nervously.

I had my face buried next to her ear, holding her tightly to me. "Sorry, I just thought I lost you."

"It's okay. You are stuck with me, remember?" she said.

"Yes, I remember."

"George, you can come in," she said.

He stepped through the doorway with a forced smile.

"You scared us, child. Please don't do that again," he said.

"What he said," I followed.

"It worked out," she said unaware of what we had been through.

"It didn't actually, but we can talk about that later," I said. The frustration of her purposefully taking the hit to get us both out of there could wait until I knew she'd fully recovered.

"Abby, Gabriel had to come. There was no other way," George said.

She gritted her teeth and winced.

"What does that mean? How is he allowed to interfere?" I asked.

Abby looked at George and nodded to him. "She belongs to them because of the sword. They have the ability to protect their investment, so to speak. But if he has to interfere like this, he loses power. It's like he has to transfer part of himself to her. If he has to do it too much, he will be forced to retire." George's face grew dark. I knew then that George did not just suddenly retire his responsibilities. He saved someone multiple times, resulting in losing his power. Love like that had to be like a father to his child.

"No more mortal wounds for you," I said.

"Yeah, let's not do that again," she agreed. My frustrations evaporated now that she was alert and talking. "Can you help me sit up? And I'm hungry." George hustled out of the room.

I put my arms around her, lifting her up. She was still very weak. I could tell that for the lack of tension in her muscles. I propped a couple of pillows behind her.

"I could hear you calling to me," she said. "I didn't know what was happening. I just knew you were extremely upset. I just focused on your voice, but I couldn't respond. I was using every-thing I had to try to keep the darkness from spreading through me. Thank you for being there for me."

"I will always be here, Abby. From now until we both leave this earth, I'll be here," I said it, and I meant it. She smiled weakly.

George returned with a tray of food for both of us including bacon, eggs, toast, and juice. While we ate, she asked a ton of questions. She wanted to know what happened after she blacked out. I tried not to explain it in too much depth, but she wanted to know.

"You finally got my clothes off," she said.

"Deflecting," I said.

"I'm just sorry I wasn't conscious for it," she said, and I almost choked on my toast. "Serves you right 'deflecting'." She mocked my voice.

"Gosh, I'm not sure how I'd survive without this banter, Abby." I paused because I wanted her to understand that I wasn't joking anymore. "Please, don't ever do that to me again."

Her face turned serious. "I know you are upset because I pulled the knife knowing that I would go down. But I felt the power in that blade before she ever stabbed me with it. If it had hit you, I don't know that anyone much less an archangel could have brought you back. I don't know that it wouldn't have taken over your body before I could even get us back here. I had to fight it with everything I had to keep it from spreading through me. Healing the power in the fire elemental bullet was a minor task compared to the evil in that knife. I knew the only way we both survived was if I took the hit. Please don't be mad at me."

"I considered it actually, being very mad about it. But we agreed to trust each other completely, and if you thought that was the best option, then I will concede any frustration over that decision. I don't have to like it though. Seeing you go through that pain. Hearing your heart stop," I said, choking up. "Those things were excruciating for me. I don't want to ever do it again."

"Agreed."

"You need to call Ashley before she freaks out," I said, handing her the phone from the nightstand.

"She's probably already freaked out," she said. She pressed a few buttons along with the speakerphone, and I heard the phone ringing.

Ashley answered and her voice was worried and strained, "Tadeas Duarte, I said to call me. Tell me how she was doing. Damn it. I'm just sitting here not knowing."

Abby quirked a smile. "If you'd rather talk to him, I'll give him the phone."

"Abby, thank God. Are you okay?"

"A little weak, but I'm fine," Abby said.

"You guys should get back here when you can. Your little speech has set the world a buzz. People are even googling your name," Ashley said.

"Whatever for?" she asked.

"That's what people do when they want information," Ashley explained.

"Is that what you do?" Abby asked.

"Sometimes, but anyway, there have been movements with the GEA. Big ones. We need you to get back here. Get the rest of the stuff moved out of the compound. I had both of your apartments packed up and moved. Whatever you said at the auction has the magical world in an uproar. The TCA contacted Gregory, but he told them to fuck off."

"Yeah, my big speech ended in getting stabbed by a black blade and running for our lives," Abby said.

"I did all the work," I said.

"You did, indeed," she conceded.

"You don't get humility from her very often Tadeas, you better write that one down," Ashley said.

"Oh, get bent, Ash," Abby shot back. "One last thing. Cassidy was at the auction. I had Lukas take her out of there. She should be with him. We need to get her back to Lianne and find out why she was hanging out with a necromancer. I hate to admit it but having him there came in handy."

"You are welcome. I'm writing it down too. Humility twice in one phone call, check. I've talked to Lukas. So, I know about Cassidy. She's staying with him for the moment. Lianne and the other six have already moved from the compound. He will look after her until you give him instructions. You know he won't hurt her," Ashley explained.

"I know. See you soon, Ash," Abby said.

"Bye, girl. Love ya."

"Love you, too," Abby said, clicking off the phone. "It's a never-ending cycle now. The ball is rolling. I've got to get up and get things ready to go back to the compound. Gregory has got to talk to his brother about the entrance to the portal. See if he will move it. If not, I'll have to ward it extensively and jump to it as needed from wherever we end up."

"If you can rest a bit longer, I think that would be best," I told her.

"I know, but we can't," she said as she started to push out of the bed. "Thank you for everything, Tadeas. You exceeded all my expectations."

"No problem, but you do the heavy lifting next time."

CHAPTER 52

ABIGAIL

*A*fter a shower, I felt better, but still very weak. I wished that I could have talked to Gabriel. He should not have gone to such lengths. The world needed him far more than it needed me. I walked down into the sitting room, and Tadeas sat on the couch looking at emails from Ashley. Already in the game, working it like he belonged here.

He looked up at me and smiled. "Yeah, just going through a few emails. No big deal."

"I see. Anything important?"

"No, just the normal stuff. Ashley sent me pictures for our next outing. I get to pick out my own suit," he said plainly. I had to look back at him to see if he was joking. He had the biggest shit-eating grin on his face.

"You think you are joking. Before you know it, you'll be getting suit emails from her. If you are a good boy, she might let you pick out your own knickers," I teased him.

"I don't wear knickers," he dead-panned. It worked. My face

went blank, and my mind started running in all sorts of directions. He died laughing at me. "In America, we call them underwear."

"Sod off, Tadeas Duarte," I laughed at him.

"George is down in the vineyard in the back. He told me to ask you to come down there and join him. Said he had something he wanted to talk to you about," he said seriously.

"Did he say what about?"

"Nope, but he told me not to come."

"That's strange. Okay. Well, I'll go see him, and then as much as I hate it, we will go back to Boulder," I replied.

"I'll be here with my emails." He smiled at me.

I walked out into the daylight. It was warm, but not overly so. Walking through the corridor between the house and stables, I saw George sitting on a bench close to where the rows of vines started behind the house. I walked down and took a seat beside him. He had that far off look about him. I waited until he returned from wherever he had gone. He shook it off, placing his hand on mine.

"Abigail, I am thankful you survived that one," he said in that fatherly tone.

"Yes, it was not pleasant, but you remember the good old days when it was one thing after another. I just started this round off with a bang." I made light of it and smiled at him. He focused on a young woman tending to the vines. I looked at her. She stood a few inches shorter than me. She had the same golden hair. I looked more closely at her features. There was something very strange and familiar about her. I started to stand up and approach her.

"No, child, leave her be," he said with his hand on my leg keeping me on the bench next to him. She turned her head to us. She smiled at me with bright green eyes. She turned back to her work.

"What the hell?" I said. "George, who is she?"

"Her name is Sarah, and she is my daughter."

I turned to him shocked. "You can't have children. You are an angel or you were one."

He smiled sadly. "Abby, you know as well as I do, that there are ways around everything. A long time ago, I gave my grace to a man who desperately wanted to have a child with his wife. They had Sarah. She is as much my child as she was theirs."

I sat speechlessly. "Has she been here all along? Working in the fields?"

"She came here shortly after I came here," he said wincing.

I turned to him. There were tears in his eyes. "I had to save her too many times."

"You gave it up for her?" I asked.

"The love of a father is the strongest love that I know, Abby. Our Father loves us, as we love our children," he explained. "We love our children enough that when they find themselves in grave harm, there is no choice. We do what we have to do to save their lives."

My heart started to race. He held tightly to my hand. "No, it can't be. George, what are you saying?"

"All I am saying, child, is please take care of yourself. There will be a day when he cannot save you anymore."

I stood up, jerking my hand away from him. My body shook. "No, it isn't true."

He turned his bright blue eyes to me, and they were filled with tears. "You should have been told a long time ago. You have a human father and a Fae mother, but there is one who loves you more than either of them ever could."

I felt dizzy teetering with the gravity of what George had told me. I felt strong arms wrap me up from behind. I looked down to see Tadeas' strong arms holding me up. "*What is it? What's wrong?*"

I just shook my head. "No, George, no."

He stood up, looking at both of us. He walked to me and put

his hand on my face. "I love you like you are mine, but you aren't. I know how he feels. You are and have always been your father's greatest joy. He couldn't tell you. He's not allowed. I should have told you, but Gregory didn't want it. Well, I don't work for Gregory. I work for you. Forgive me for not telling you sooner, child."

Tadeas stood silently behind me. He held on tight. I turned away from George and buried my face in his chest. "George, what's wrong?" he asked as he embraced me tightly.

"Master Tadeas, sometimes the truth is shocking. She will be okay when she processes it all. I'm confident that she is in good hands now. I know you will take care of her," he told Tadeas.

I heard him start to walk down into the vines with Sarah. I turned and bolted toward him. I hugged him as hard as I could. "I love you, George."

He hugged me back and smiled. "Now, go. You have work to do."

My body still trembled. I turned back to Tadeas who looked confused and concerned. I walked to him, grabbing his hand. "Come on." He walked with me quietly. When we got to the corridor he stopped. He wasn't going to let it go until I told him everything, but that was what he was here for now. I could tell him everything and anything. He knew my darkest secret and still stood by me.

"Abby," he said. I turned to look at him. I wanted no secrets between us. I walked to him and touched my cheek to his. I whispered in his ear all the things George had just told me. I felt him shudder too, but he held me close while I told him. I leaned back to look into his eyes.

"What does that make me?" I asked him. He knew all my vulnerabilities about my lineage.

"I don't really know if there is a word for it, Abby. I just don't know," he said honestly.

"Abomination," I whispered. His grip tightened on me.

"No, not that. I know that for sure. It's not that. We've both been called that, and I know it's not true about either of us. Many people lied to us about that, used it to motivate us to their ideals. You are not that," he assured me but refused to repeat the word.

"You don't think you are now, but have you ever thought about it?" I asked.

"Of course, I have. But I had a beautiful and frustrating woman come into my life, and she convinced me that I was special. She believed in me. She was right, and I believe in her, too," he said as he wiped the tears from my cheeks.

"She sounds like a real pain," I said.

"She is when she's deflecting," he replied. We were in another of those moments when the tension between us was overwhelming. I wanted him more than anything right now. The alarms sounded in my head as I pushed my feelings down once again. I couldn't give in now. The stakes had been raised with George's revelation.

Actually, the stakes hadn't changed. I just knew better now what they were. He watched me intently. I knew he felt it too. I swear my heart skipped a beat if that is even possible. I tried to shake it off. He quirked a smile at me. His face was so close to mine that I could feel emotion rolling off him in waves.

"What?" I asked.

"*When you are ready, you let me know,*" he whispered in my mind, then led me back into the house, and we took the portal back to Boulder. I could never be ready. Especially now.

CHAPTER 53

TADEAS

*T*he compound was strangely quiet when we returned. We found the rest of the team in Ichiro's lab. Ashley plowed into Abby so hard when she hugged her that they both almost ended up on the floor. I shook hands with Ichiro, then Ashley turned around and hugged me, too.

"Thank you for keeping her safe," she said.

"Well, I got her home. I don't know about the safe part," I admitted. Abby rolled her eyes at me.

"Whatever it was, she's still alive," she said.

"What's the word, Ash?" Abby asked. "Pretty quiet in the building."

"Yes, Gregory left just a little while ago. Like in the last 5 minutes or so. You just missed him. He said he would meet you at the next point. We went ahead and assigned all the canvas groups that were in training. They are already with their proxies or on their way to them except, of course, Travis and Samantha. There are still a few instructors in the center removing essential equipment. We opened up the backup elevator shaft to help get some of that equipment out."

"We have eyes on that elevator?" Abby asked.

"Yes. It's being monitored. Tony and Tommy are still here watching everything. They intend to stay until the last person is gone. Vince is in the back, packing up the last of his boxes. Jay went to his apartment to get a few last-minute items. Both of yours are already packed and gone. I was elbow-deep in Tadeas' underwear drawer. Woo-hoo," Ashley teased.

"Knickers," Abby said.

"Underwear," I retorted with a blush. Ashley watched us with a lifted eyebrow. Nothing got past her.

Ichiro shook his head and gave me the "Sorry, dude," look. I just waved it off.

"Where are Aiden and Fayola?" Abby asked.

"They have already gone. Setting everything up in the new place," Ashley said.

"Where is the new place?" I asked. They kept talking about it, but no one would say where it was. They all looked at each other.

"Oh, good grief, the new place is actually an abandoned town that was sold at auction several years ago. It has a very old west feel to it, to say the least. The unknown buyers, ahem, have owned the place since 2005. It's a little town called Palisade, Nevada. No living underground for now. Two years ago, we started building homes and restoring the buildings. Tommy and Tony have been working on technology to secure the town. We are going there ahead of schedule. It's not completely ready. We will be spread out right now until security is set up completely," Abby explained.

"Why was that hard?" I asked.

"Because I have a hush order on it. They aren't allowed to talk about it. If you want to be upset about it, you may direct that toward me. Not keeping you out, just haven't got there yet. As far as that goes, guys, Tadeas is part of us now. If I know it, he's allowed to know it. Don't assume he knows everything. The learning curve is going to be steep," she said looking at me with raised eyebrows.

I nodded at her, accepting the explanation. I knew there were things I still didn't know. I could roll with it now. Two weeks ago, maybe not so much, but now, I was signed up for the long haul. Much more of my heart and emotions were tied into it now.

The doors to the lab opened, and Jay Stafford walked in. "Well, welcome back, you two," he said with a smile on his face. Everyone in the room tensed in silence. I could feel all of them holding their breath, except Abby, she just rolled her eyes. Jay walked up to me, and without a word between us, he shook my hand. I nodded at him, and the tension left the room. Then he walked over to Abby and hugged her tightly. She winced, pushing him away. I held back the urge to growl at him.

"Stop that, you goof," she said smiling.

"Glad you are still with us," he said quietly to her. She just nodded at him. He meant it. His feelings for her were real, and I understood why now. I understood how he could look at her with both love and pain. I knew that he would do anything for her, and that was good enough for me. He walked away, and I sat down on one of the couches, watching them all bustle about, discussing which equipment in that room needed to be moved. Abby would occasionally look at me and smile. I watched her several times drift from the conversations. I knew the information George gave her weighed heavily on her heart.

Frankly, none of it surprised me. I didn't understand from the beginning why an archangel would be directly involved in a person's life, and how she was chosen in the first place to carry the sword. All of it made perfect sense to me now. Even though neither of us could name what she was, she immediately thought the worst, an abomination. A child cursed because of the act of an angel of God. George told her that she had real parents. I didn't believe she was cursed. If anything, they blessed her with gifts beyond normal wielders. In return, the responsibility of the sword fell to her. All of these were assumptions on my part. Gabriel said he had faith in both of us. She had her responsibilities, and my responsibility involved taking care of her. The fact that he trusted me to do that was a tiny bit overwhelming.

She came over and sat down next to me. "What are you thinking about?"

"Just everything from Paris to George in the vineyard," I said.

"Conversations we can't have here," she said.

"Yeah, I know. As long as you are holding up okay, I'm fine. You need more rest. How much longer are we going to be here?" I asked.

"A day or two. Just got to start getting this equipment upstairs. You prepared to use your muscle?" she asked pinching my bicep.

"Which muscle?" I asked, watching her face turn from playful to embarrassed. I laughed. "I didn't mean *that* muscle, Abby. Damn, your head is in the gutter."

"No, that's not what I thought," she protested.

"The hell you didn't!" I said. "I saw it all over your face."

"Ashley, you got some boxes for Tadeas to take to the surface?" she asked.

"*Deflecting*," I said.

"Shut up," she said.

"Actually, I do, just paperwork and stuff. There is a van up there in the parking garage. Just put all of them in it. And try not to drop any of them. My filing system is going to be a mess to sort out," Ashley explained.

"I can help," Jay offered.

"Yeah, me too. I need some fresh air," Ichiro said.

We grabbed boxes and started out the door.

"*We can revisit that conversation when I get back,*" I teased.

"No, we can't," she shouted through the door. I just laughed. The guys looked at me and questioned. "Women!" I said.

"For real," Jay said.

"Tell me about it," Ichiro added in our male bonding moment.

Vince came out the door carrying two boxes and said, "What did I miss?" The three of us laughed. He looked puzzled.

We rode the elevator up in silence. When we got to the top, we walked through the abandoned building to the parking deck. I helped the guys load the boxes in, and we turned to go back toward the elevator. I stopped dead in my tracks. My body tensed. I searched the area for something off. Someone hiding. I couldn't place it.

"What's wrong, Tadeas?" Jay asked.

"Something is not right," I said. Then it hit me, the intense smell of lavender and sage. "No, it can't be. Did you all ever find Meredith?"

Ichiro said, "No, Tony and Tommy looked the compound up and down. They set trap spells throughout her apartment. In fact, her apartment hasn't been cleaned out. We just left everything. Why?"

"She's here or was here not very long ago." I stayed tense.

Jay walked back into the abandoned offices and out the front door of the building. "He's right. There is a car out here."

I ran toward him but didn't see the car. "What car?"

He waved his hand and the glamour on the car wobbled just enough for us to see it.

"Holy shit, she's here," I said.

Jay turned and sprinted to the elevator. "No Jay, don't use the elevator. They have to get out," I yelled. "I'll tell Abby, hang on." I concentrated on her. I could feel her much more strongly than I ever could before now. "*Abby, you and Ashley need to come to the surface right now. Meredith is here somewhere. We need to go right now. Something's wrong!*"

"*Tommy and Tony already have Ashley in the elevator, they are on their way to the surface. I'm going down to warn the crews downstairs. Someone cut the power. We activated the emergency generator for the elevator. We will come up the secondary elevator. Go there and wait on me. I'm fine.*"

"No!" I screamed gritting my teeth.

"What is it?" Ichiro said.

"Ashley, Tommy, and Tony are coming up in the elevator. The power is out in the facility. Abby went downstairs to get the people out of the training center. As soon as they get up here, I'm going down after her. You guys get in the van and head toward Boulder, okay?" I said giving them orders.

Vince was already running back to the van. I heard him crank it up.

"I'm going with you," Jay said.

"No, we already have one too many people down there. I'll go. You get them out of here, Jay. She would want you to," I said.

He shook his head no. I knew what was going through his head even if he wasn't aware that I knew their story. The doors to the elevator opened and as Ashley stepped out the ground started to shake beneath us. A low rumble. "What the fuck is that?" Jay said.

"Go! To the van now! Go!" I yelled.

Ichiro ran to Ashley, and they ran hand in hand to the van. Tommy and Tony were close behind. I watched them all get in. The shaking was very subtle. Ashley screamed back at me, "Don't you leave without her!"

"I won't," I said as I entered the elevator. The ground continued to rumble.

"*Abby, earthquake?*"

"*She's here. She's going to bring it all down.*"

"*I'm coming down the elevator, come to me. Let's go. This is one of those moments when we run. There is nothing to stay and fight for now,*" I tried to persuade her.

"*She's got Blake,*" she said.

"*Abby, Blake knows what he signed up for, you meet me at the elevator. What floor are you on?*"

"*One,*" she said.

"It had to be the fucking bottom!" I screamed to the elevator and punched the button for the training center floor. I reached down to my ankle and pulled out the Sig I'd carried with me since Paris. I checked it for ammo. I had reloaded it on the island. I looked at the counter for the elevator. The elevator stopped on four. Just a few more floors and I could get us both out of here. The earth started to shake harder, and the elevator stopped completely. It felt like one of the cables snapped. I grabbed the doors, forcing them to open.

Fortunately, I wasn't between floors, I pushed the outer doors open and stepped out in the hallway near Abby's office. I hit the stairwell, sprinting down steps until I got to the bottom. I busted through the bottom door screaming her name, "Abby? Where are you?" I could hear her heartbeat nearby. I ran down the hallway to the cafeteria. When I rushed through the doors, a large gaping hole widened in the center of the room. Meredith stood on the other side with her hand raised toward Blake who was pinned against the wall by her force. Abby stood right in front of me near the edge of the hole.

"Meredith, please let him go. He's not a part of this. You don't want to kill anyone," Abby said.

"Well, Tadeas, I'm glad you could join us. I've missed you. I came back here just for you and Abby. I knew we had some unfinished business," she said to me.

I walked up behind Abby and stood close to her. I didn't aim the gun at Meredith. I kept it down, but I had a bullet chambered and ready to go. "Let's just go. The elevator is broken. We need to take the portal," I said to her.

"Damn, Tadeas. That's heartless. Even Abby wants to try to save Blake. Some friend you are. All those classes he covered for you, so you could go around fucking your new girlfriend," she seethed anger. Blake looked terrified but resigned to his fate. I knew there were others down here with him. I did not know whether they had gotten out or had fallen into the hole.

I was determined to ignore Meredith. I put my hand on Abby's back and leaned into her ear, "Please Abby, this whole place is going to come down on top of us. Let's go."

"She doesn't want to go. She wants to know why I'm doing this," Meredith said as the earth shook harder. The emergency lights went out. Meredith immediately called to her hand an orb of light that illuminated the room.

"She has a way out or she wouldn't be here," Abby said.

"Yes, but we don't. So, let's go," I said, reaching to pull her out of there by force if I had to. The earth shook again, and the hole grew. I latched on to her and lunged back toward the door as the earth opened beneath us both. We scrambled closer to the door as the hole grew. I looked at her desperately. *"Please, let's go, Abby."*

She finally nodded, and I pulled her off the floor with me. I opened the cafeteria door, and we ran out. As we ran down the hallway, Meredith came through the cafeteria door and threw a wave of force at us. Abby latched onto my wrist on top of the bracelet that she made for me and murmured *"Resus."*

The wave ripped tiles and brick from the walls but blew past us. We remained unmoved. I raised the gun and pointed it at her. "No," Abby yelled, pushing it back down. She stood between Meredith and me.

"You would never forgive yourself. I won't let you kill her."

"How sweet, she doesn't want you to have to live with killing me. I assure you, Tadeas, your little gun wouldn't do anything to me. You see, I'm far more powerful than either of you know. You know how easy it is for me to pick out someone that's binding their magic? It's easy because I bound my own. *Diluvio.*"

Once she spoke the word, the water rushed into the hallway like the water pipes had burst. The whole floor started filling with water, while the ground shook harder. Abby started backing up toward me keeping her eye on Meredith. *"I'm watching her. Guide me to the door."*

"You know Tadeas, I've got a way out of here. You can come with me as long as you agree to leave her behind. I'm sure someone will come along to save her. Someone always does. She should have died long, long ago, and yet here she is. She is a plague. Everywhere she goes people die. It's her fault poor Blake fell in the hole back there. It's her fault that Travis and Samantha were killed by a sex-crazed necromancer. Who else has to die, Tadeas? You? You know she's pretty hard on partners."

"Almost there, keep backing up to me. Once we hit the door, you go up the steps as fast as you can, I'll follow."

"Tadeas, you won't be able to get out that way. I made sure the elevator was sabotaged. I'm actually thankful you made it down in it. I'm surprised you didn't plummet to your death coming after her. She will be the death of you. Or they will torture you like they did poor Lukas. Turned him into a monster just to punish her. He lives a life of torment because he loved her. Then she left him. She will do the same to you when you are no longer useful to her."

"Oh Meredith, shut the fuck up, we are leaving together, or we don't leave at all. I don't give a rip about your diatribe," I said. She reached her hand forward and pulled it back toward her like she was playing tug of war. The door behind me exploded forward, hitting me in the back of the head. I hit the water hard, and I felt blood running down my cheek. I stood up, but it was too late to stop Abby. She charged Meredith hitting her in the mid-section, and they both went sliding back down the hallway in the water. It rose up to our knees. The concrete walls started to crack as the earth rumbled. Meredith shoved Abby off of her and launched a fireball the size of a basketball at Abby.

Abby screamed, *"Murus."* She lifted her hands upward, and the water rose from the floor making a wall in front of her. The fireball fizzled out the moment it hit the wall. She looked back at me, and I waved her back to me. She started walking backward with her hand up guiding the wall of water back in front of her. Meredith jumped through the wall, tackling Abby back. She wrapped her hands around Abby's neck and held her head under the water. I rushed her, and as I hit her, I felt a stinging sensation in my side. I pulled away from Meredith, and she smiled at me as the dagger she had in her hand slowly retracted from my body. It hurt like hell, but it wasn't going to stop me. I turned to run back to Abby. She raised up out of the water after almost being drowned. I didn't stop my momentum, and she turned to run with me as I reached her. We almost got to the steps when a shadow figure coalesced between us and the stairs. We stopped and stared at Nalusa Chito.

"I do believe my partner, Miss Spence, isn't quite done with the two of you just yet," he said calmly as the ground shook and the water rose. Abby turned to face Meredith, and I kept my eyes on Chito.

"He's right. I was just getting to the good part when you rudely interrupted," Meredith said.

"*What do we do?*"

"*I don't know. I'm out of ideas. I can't fight them both,*" Abby said. I knew she was exhausted from the ordeal in Paris, but we couldn't give up now.

"*Don't give up. Just be patient. Wait for an opening.*" I heard the resignation in her voice in my head. We were pinned in an underground bunker that was about to come down on our heads. If it didn't, the water would rise and drown us. Or we could go with option three which was being blown to bits by a sorcerer and his partner, my ex-best friend. I felt her shudder.

"*If you shift planes, you can get out of here, and I will cover you,*" she said quietly.

"*I am not having this discussion with you right now,*" I replied.

"*I had to try,*" she said.

"Ah yes, the reality is sinking in. She is going to be responsible for the death of another partner. Another lover down. Because I assure you, Tadeas, she will live. They always find a way for her to live like her life is any more important than yours, or mine, or Lincoln's," she spouted.

I felt fiery anger well up in Abigail. "You have no right to speak his name. Don't you ever speak his name again," Abby screamed at her. She had nothing left she could do but lash out verbally. I nodded to Chito, turning my back on him. Something struck me that this wasn't his fight. He just observed. I put my arms around her waist. I could feel the power surging through her. She could probably strike Meredith down cleanly if she wanted to do so.

"I have every right to speak his name. He was my blood. Mine, not yours. You took him from me," Meredith screamed.

Abby gasped, backing into me. "No, you aren't."

"I am. He abandoned me for you," Meredith said.

I squeezed her tighter. *"I don't know what this is Abby, but you need to think of a way to get us out of here."* She did not respond to me.

"No, we looked for you," Abby said. "We looked everywhere for you."

"I didn't want you. I wanted him. He was my father. You had no right to him. You should have let him go. You should have let him find me," Meredith said.

"Madre de Dios," I said.

"That's right Tadeas. There was a time when Lincoln couldn't stand the sight of Abby. He fell in love with my mother. He abandoned us for *her.* I searched my whole life for him, but every time I found him, he was with this filthy bitch."

"We wanted to find you, Meredith. We wanted a family," Abby cried.

"She took him from me, Tadeas. She let him die. He gave up his only child to die, because he loved her," Meredith screamed with tears streaming down her face. "She will ruin you. She does not love you. She is using you for her own purposes."

"Meredith, we all need to get out of here. This isn't going to be solved right now," I tried to reason with her.

"No, Tadeas, you see, I came here and waited for 20 years for this shot. I'm taking it," she pulled out a pistol, firing it directly at Abby. Abby's steel orb appeared above her hand and turned to liquid metal. She waved her hand through the metal. It curled around her hand latching to it like a glove. She covered her heart with it as the bullet hit her steel-covered hand. It happened in slow motion. I looked up to Meredith, and before she could fire a second shot, a blur came around the corner behind her, slamming her into the concrete wall. She slumped down unmoving. I could hear her heart beating. I looked at Abby. She stood in shock. The metal glove thing must have been pure instinct and reaction. She dropped her hand to the side, and the spell released. The chunk of the bullet and liquid metal sank into the deepening water. I looked at the figure who hit Meredith. It was Jay Stafford.

"Get her, and let's go, Duarte," he screamed. I turned to look at Chito, but he turned to black smoke, reappearing next to Meredith. He hoisted her up in his arms, and they both faded to smoke.

I grabbed Abby by the waist and screamed in her ear. "Snap out of it. Let's go!" As I ran toward Jay, her legs moved with mine, but she still seemed dazed. We ran around the corner, and Jay held the door open to a back room. There wasn't as much water here as in the front hallway. As we entered the room, the backup elevator door was propped open with a chair. I started dragging Abby to it. Jay rushed ahead of me and grabbed the chair. He stepped into the elevator and held the door open for us.

"Hurry, it's all coming down," he yelled frantically. I started to toss Abby to him when the earth lurched, and we slipped and hit the floor. I struggled to find my footing.

"Damn it, Abby, get your fucking head out of the clouds. We

are going to die," I yelled trying to lift her off the floor. She looked up at me, and her eyes came into focus.

"You better be glad I like you. I wouldn't let just anyone cuss me like that," she smirked. For the love of God, she could switch in and out like it was nothing.

We turned toward the elevator, as Jay frantically waited for us. I heard the loud screeching of metal, and the top of the elevator buckled. I put on the brakes, grabbing Abby before she went into it. It crumpled in on itself and dirt and rock spilled out in the floor in front of us. The metal, rock, and dirt buried Jay Stafford.

"Jay!" Abby screamed and struggled to get away from me. "Jay!"

I grabbed her face and got very close to her. I looked her in the eye. She pushed against my chest to get away from me. "Abby, he's gone. I don't hear his heartbeat. We have to go. I can't carry you out of here if you fight me. We might not make it, but we have to try. Abby, we will mourn for him if we live. He wouldn't want you to die here because of him. Please, honey, come with me. I need you to come with me," I pleaded, but it felt like my heart was bleeding.

She nodded her head but didn't say anything. I ran back into the hallway with her on my heels, and we started up the back steps.

We got to the fourth-floor door. If we could get to her office, we could jump through the portal to the island. I got to the door and hit the armbar for it to open. The latch came open, but the door would not move. I pushed harder, and Abby joined me.

"The ceiling, wall, or something is collapsed behind it. Let me shift and see what's there. If it's safe, I'll come back and get you," I said.

"No, we shift together," she said.

"Okay," I pulled on the edge of the spirit world. I tried to walk through the door, but if it was solid earth behind it, I couldn't walk through it. We were underground, and I don't know if that affected it or not but we could not pass through the wall, the door, or whatever was behind it. I pulled us back to reality.

"Now what?" she asked.

"Up," I replied, and we kept climbing stairs. If we could get to the elevator shaft, maybe we could find a way to climb it or something. We raced up the stairs to the door that lead to the tenth floor which was the banquet room where we had had the party. We turned out of the stairwell to the elevator door bay. I pushed open the doors, and dirt and rocks cascaded down through it. We could not climb the walls with all the debris falling. I grabbed her arm, and we ran into the large banquet room. The memories flooded over me. The night she belonged to me.

"You want another dance," she said sadly.

"I do, but not here," I said, looking for any way out of the place. Suddenly, the floor shifted downward to the right. We turned running upward to our left. We had nowhere else to go. The compound collapsed and sank into the earth on the other side of the room. The floor continued to shift that way.

"Tadeas," she said. "This is it. She was right. You are going to die because of me."

I wanted us to get out of here alive. To prove that Meredith was wrong. I held onto a lamp fixture and to her keeping us both from slipping down the floor as it started to tilt harder. The ceiling on the other end of the huge room started to fall in. We were going to be buried alive.

"I only have one regret, Abby," I said.

"What's that?" she asked as she held onto me, then hoisted herself up using the lamp fixture.

I pulled her as close to me as I could. Gravity worked against me. She put her arm around my neck. "I should have kissed you again," I said.

She smiled, pulling her legs up around my waist as the floor started to crumble under our feet. Her lips met mine. I couldn't hold the lamp any longer, and I let go. We slid toward the falling ceiling and the crumbling room, but it didn't matter. Her lips were on mine, and I kissed her back like we were sliding into the depths of hell. My hand tangled up in her hair, and I was over-whelmed with the taste of honeysuckle.

CHAPTER 54

ABIGAIL

*H*is lips were warm and soft. The kiss wasn't eager or panicked even though we were as good as dead. We continued to slide when his feet caught on something. He groaned in pain releasing my lips. I had to hope that our deaths would happen quickly. The last thing I wanted was for him to suffer, because of me. I kept my face pressed next to his even though he had stopped kissing me. Darkness surrounded us, and I waited for the ceiling and earth to come crashing in on us. But the earth stopped shaking, and it got very still and quiet. I felt his heart pounding, and he clutched me harder to him. I was scared to speak or move.

"Are you hurt?" he asked.

"No, are you?"

"My right leg hit something pretty hard. I don't think it's broken, but it hurts like hell."

"If I can reach it, I can heal it," I said, sliding my hand down his leg. When I did the earth beside us started to shift.

"*No, no. It's okay. Don't move. Just be still and let me think,*" he said.

My heart pounded, and I couldn't breathe. The dirt and dust were choking us.

"*Jag, it's just a matter of time before the rest of this place gives in. Just hold on to me until it does,*" I said to him resigned to our fate.

"*Oh, hell no, I'm not giving up. You kissed me. There is no way I'm not living to tell that story,*" he teased. I tried not to laugh because I didn't want the debris to shift anymore. I closed my eyes and pulled power from the surrounding earth. If he wasn't going to give up, then neither would I.

"*Fulgo.*" The sun pendant containing a sunstone around my neck started to glow with the warm light of the sun. It was a gift from my Aunt Lianne, a symbol of my bloodline. It illuminated Tadeas' face which was covered in scrapes and bruises. "*What about the stab wound?*"

"*It's bleeding, but not too bad. I didn't really think about it, because of the adrenaline and running for our lives, you know?*"

"*Yes, my lips can make men forget things like mortal wounds,*" I teased. I might as well get as many shots in as I could.

"*If I could smack you right now, I would,*" he said.

"*No, you wouldn't.*"

"*Maybe I would.*" He smiled. The earth shifted above us again, and he pulled my head to his chest and tried to block anything that fell. It would have been a useless measure if something truly large fell on us, but it was his instinct.

"What the hell," he said looking over my shoulder.

I tried to turn and look. I could see just a tiny bit of daylight.

"Just don't move," he said. "Think about this. That is daylight. That means above this ceiling that is about to crash in on us is open air. We just got to get there, without falling further down or having the rest of this fall on us."

"Shift us to the spirit world again," I said.

"No, I'm not sure what that will do," he replied.

"Do you have any other options?" I asked.

"Well, I might think of something if you would just give me a second," he shot back at me. I shut up and waited. "Yeah, I got nothing."

"Thank you. Shift us and we move to the light, and whatever happens, happens," I said to him. He winced again.

"How bad is the leg?"

"I'll shut it out. It's better than being dead," he concluded.

"That's one way to look at it, I suppose. I'm ready whenever you are."

I felt the tug on the edge of the cold dark. He reached and pulled it over both of us. My necklace continued to glow which was interesting. Usually, my magic died out once we went into the spirit world. He looked at it and then me. I just shrugged. I had no idea. If we lived through this, I needed to make a call to my old master, Samara. I was sure he would know how to fix this lack of magic on the spirit side.

I let him move first. He found his footing and pushed himself up to a standing position. He helped me stand up, too. I looked down. He held my hand constantly, not letting go. We were standing on the slanted floor that we had just been laying on. He leaned on me a bit to take the pressure off his leg. I could see the blood that was running down his side from the stab wound. He moved us both toward the edge of the light peeking through. We walked through what was left of the ceiling, and the earth opened up above us to a hole where the building above used to be. He looked down at our feet. We seemed to be standing on a fairly stable large piece of concrete. "Here goes nothing," he said. He pulled on reality, and the sun assaulted us from above. I shaded my eyes. We were both covered in dirt and mud. We had been soaked from the flood on the first floor, then collected the dust and dirt along the way to the top floor.

"Now how do we get out of a hundred-yard-deep hole?" I asked.

"I don't know. You are the wizard. Do a levitation spell or something," he said.

"Ok. Sure, but if I do this, I can't hold it long. Be ready to lunge to the top depending on how long I can hold it," I said.

"Seriously, you are going to fly us out of here?" he said.

"Honey, didn't you know? I'm a badass wizard." I smirked at him.

"No, but I'm sure you will continue to remind me," he groaned.

"Damn straight. Hold on to me," I said.

"With pleasure," he grinned, and it was my turn to groan.

I put my hand on my necklace and my left arm around his neck. He wrapped his arms around my waist as I pulled power from the earth and my necklace. *"Praevolo."*

A wind came up beneath us and thrust us upward toward the sky. I felt the power quickly fading. If I couldn't hold it, it would hurt when we hit bottom. I wasn't sure that Tadeas would survive it considering the damage his body had already taken. I had the feeling he was hiding it for my benefit. I let the spell drain the power in my necklace, and it ceased to glow. I then allowed the spell to pull the power out of me. I tilted my head up to see how much longer.

"You've got it. I believe in you," he said

The power rushed through me again with his statement of faith, pushing us upward. I felt myself losing consciousness, but I held on. We were almost there. As we reached the edge, tried to shift the wind beneath us toward the closest edge.

"Almost, Abby. You've got it." I pushed a little harder for him. As we came up over the edge, I felt myself slipping. My arm loosened around his neck. I felt him try to throw me toward solid ground. With one last effort, I pushed us both that way. We hit the ground hard, and my vision faded with the pounding of a massive headache. I had pushed harder than I ever had to save us.

"Abby, get up. We gotta move," he yelled at me. I felt the earth shift under me. We had destabilized the edge, and it was about to fall in right back to where we once were. I drifted in and out. He hoisted me up the best he could. I tried to run, but my legs were like jelly. My survival instinct kicked in. I felt my legs stabilize, and we both moved as quickly as we could as the earth started to crumble behind us. I could see where the ground turned to more stone than dirt. If we could make it to it, then perhaps the collapsing would stop.

"The rock. Get to the rock," I managed to gasp out.

When I got close I lunged for it, but he didn't have the power in his leg to do it. But before my eyes, he shifted to a sleek beautiful black cat, bounding over my head. He hit the rock hard and rolled. As he rolled, he shifted back to human and cried out in pain. I crawled over to him. I tried pulling power to heal him, but I was tapped. He held up his wrist showing me the bracelet that I gave him. I wrapped my hand around it. It still held a bit of power. I thought the stab wound needed the attention. I lifted his shirt up and put my hand on it, pressing down. He winced in pain. "*Consano.*" The warmth of healing rushed through me to his side. He groaned with the heat that was transferred from me to him. I pulled my hand away, and the wound had closed. I had nothing left for his leg.

"I'm sorry. There's nothing left for your leg. I can't," I said as I fought to stay conscious.

He pulled me to the ground next to him. "It's fine. You are completely amazing. You flew us out of a massive hole in the ground and still had enough left to keep me from bleeding to death." He pushed my hair out of my face. "I dare say that qualifies as badass."

Everything that happened started rushing in on me. Meredith was Lincoln's daughter who we had spent half of our lives trying to find. It was a long sordid story, but I loved him. And no matter what happened, I wanted him to find his daughter. Jay Stafford had saved my life and died in a heap of rubble underneath the earth in Boulder, Colorado. He deserved better. My heart ached for him. I didn't know if Ashley, Ichiro, Vince or the twins had made it or not. To top it all off, in some weird cosmic confluence, the archangel Gabriel had a direct connection to my birth. I wanted to talk to George more about it if he could. Then it hit me, the portal. I started shaking. "No, no, no, George."

"George is fine. He's back on the island. When we get patched up, we will go home and rest, okay?" Tadeas said.

"We can't go home. The portal was in the building," I said.

"Gregory will get it rebuilt. In the meantime, we will set up a safe house somewhere near where the ferry takes the workers to the island every day, and we will just take the ferry. No crazy portal jetlag, right?" he tried to encourage me.

"We can't take the ferry, Tadeas," I said.

"Sure, we can. Are you afraid of boats?" he asked. He leaned over me as I laid on my back. He blocked the sun from hitting my face.

"I'm not afraid of boats, but we cannot ride the ferry without paying the ferryman," I said to him.

"The ferryman, like Charon, the boatman of the underworld?" he asked starting to realize what I was saying. "I don't understand, Abby." He looked up, and I could hear a vehicle approaching us. We had no weapons left, if they wanted to kill us, they could just go ahead.

He raised up and looked in the direction of the oncoming vehicle.

"Who is it?" I muttered. My heart ached. I did not care who approached. I could never go home again, not until my time on this earth ended.

"It's a black Hummer," he said shielding his eyes from the sun.

"Grandfather," I said.

"You think?" he tried to push himself up. His right leg hurt

ABOMINATION

him badly. He winced as he stood trying not to put pressure on it.
I just laid on the dirt looking up at him. "It's okay now. We can
go somewhere safe."

The Hummer pulled up, and he reached down to try to pull
me up off the ground. He just didn't have the power to do it. I
waved him away.

Grandfather actually got out of the vehicle and approached
us. "By the gods, you are both alive." He looked down at me, and
the happiness from seeing us alive covered his face. He looked
down at Tadeas' leg. He touched it, and I heard his leg snap back
into place. He must have dislocated it when we hit the concrete.
He tested it and reached down to pick me up. I wrapped my
arms around his neck.

"Let's get out of here, Sir," he said to Gregory.

Gregory opened the back door of the Hummer, and Tadeas
sat me up in the seat. He climbed up beside me and tried to put a
seat belt on me. "Fuck that," I said, curling up next to him.
Gregory got in on the other side.

"Boulder Municipal, and quickly please," he told the driver.

"Sir, the portal?" Tadeas asked for me. I couldn't think
straight. He seemed to know that I had nothing else in me to
give.

"It will take time to rebuild. And there will be a price to pay,
because my brother is a real son of a bitch, and yes, I know what
that makes my mother," he scoffed.

"What is the island?" he asked.

"We don't talk about what the island is actually, but you
deserve to know, Tadeas. The island is part of the Fortunate Isles.
It is part of Elysium. The workers there are those who lived a life
that was deemed pure and good. They find the greatest pleasure
in a hard day's work and a work that is well done. It's heaven to
them," he explained.

Tadeas did not ask anything else. He sat and processed it all
in his head. He held me tight, kissing my forehead. There were

567

many things he needed to know, and not enough time to tell them all to him. The world I had thrust him into was far larger than he knew. He was my protector, but I needed to protect him, too. Part of that protection included telling him all my secrets and all the secrets of the Agency. But not now. I couldn't even hold my eyes open. I did not have the energy to cry for what I lost in the collapse of the compound. I fell asleep listening to his heartbeat as we rode to the airport.

EPILOGUE

GEORGE

I sat in one of the large leather recliners and waited. I felt everything on the island. I felt the storm moving toward the island. Most importantly, I felt Abigail sleeping. She had exhausted herself with this endeavor, and it hadn't turned out like she had planned. My heart went out to her. I wanted to show her the way, but I knew she had to find it herself. It was difficult watching her make decisions that might get her killed, again. I could not see the future. My job was to advise. Occasionally, I got to comfort her. But I have lived for eons. I didn't need to see the future to know what would happen.

The jaguar impressed me. He withstood the insanity of the last couple of days, and he would return. He and his abilities were a perfect fit for her. Lincoln told me about Tadeas what seemed like ages ago. I felt Lincoln too. His wards surrounded the place. His remains rested on the far side of the island within reach, but out of sight. He knew all too well her impulsiveness. I remember laughing at him trying to resist her charm and getting angry when I would point out how his fondness for her grew. He never intended to love her. But like myself, or anyone else she let get close to her, he couldn't help but love her.

I saw those early signs in Tadeas, too. Before long, he would give into his feelings. I just hoped she would be ready for it. I had my doubts. She continued to blame herself for the things that evil did in the world.

Throughout history, humans pointed fingers at each other for the terrible acts that occurred in our world. They have always occurred. Humans changed and developed, but these hideous things still happened. The reason was that evil still lurked in the shadows. Evil was eternal. It built in silence and exploded in violence. There were those who are consumed by it. There were those who tried to make friends with it. Some even tried to wield it, but in the end, evil overpowered them. That's why people like Abigail and Tadeas existed. They fought the evil.

It wasn't long before the tall, blonde young man entered the room and sat in the recliner next to me. His face was solemn. Gabriel, like myself, spent eons watching the evil move through the world. There were times we affected the outcome of events, but those times came rarely. This was one of those times.

"Are you sure?" I asked him.

"Raguel, old friend, you know that this must be done," he replied.

"I don't know that it must be done. I cannot see like I once could," I reminded him.

"You know that I can see, and thus, you know it must be done," he said.

"I know that you love her. I know that feeling too well. I know that your judgment can be clouded by that love," I explained.

"This is what I want for her," he said.

"What about what she wants?" I asked.

He winced. He would no more take her free will away than God would allow him to. "She will still be able to choose, as will he. Each step they take will bring them closer together. The world depends upon it."

This, I knew, was true. Each person who had a hand in Abigail's birth had their own agenda, even Hyperion. Her ultimate purpose, I believed, got Gabriel involved. She was a means to an end for most of those involved, except Gabriel. I imagine she might have been at first for him, but once he looked into her face, his fatherly instincts kicked in. The truth remained that he could only help her so much.

"She will awaken soon. I will speak to her. Please call him and get him to come back," he requested.

"It won't be a problem. He's called multiple times already," I said smiling. "He is anxious to get back to her to resolve their issues. I don't think they need any help, Gabriel."

"I can't take that chance," he said sadly.

"This won't be the first trial they go through," I responded.

"I thought you couldn't see, my friend," he smiled at me.

"Experience, not premonition," I stated.

"It won't be the first trial. I know. They are already bonded simply by their status in the world. They are both guardians. They complement each other. All I am doing is strengthening them for the tribulation ahead. It will be a light along the path for them," he said in full confidence. He stood and walked to the door. "The storm is coming, George. We must be ready."

I got up and walked into the sitting room. I could feel her stirring. She would be up soon. I picked up my duster and contemplated the moves Gabriel intended to make. I did not fear because I knew he was right. Nothing he was doing would hurt either of them. It would only make the bond stronger. Humans had all sorts of bonds. The bonds between friends, lovers, spouses, parents, children, siblings, family and even pets. These bonds held the world together. When these bonds broke, grief and sadness crept in taking their places. Too many bonds in this world were breaking, but this bond would last forever.

AFTER SHE WOKE UP AND SHOWERED, I THOUGHT SHE SHOULD eat, but she was determined to go for a walk. I didn't know if Gabriel put that compulsion in her head or not. It did not matter. As soon as she left the house, I made the call to Master Duarte. As expected, he immediately agreed to return. I may or may not have implied that she was in danger. I played on his guardian senses.

My days as an angel were not spent guarding humans. It was not my duty until Sarah came along. I guarded her by choice. I knew that I would give my life for her, and I did. In a way, I knew how Tadeas felt. I knew how Gabriel felt. I knew how I felt about Abigail. In the end, I didn't save Sarah. I hoped things turned out better for Abigail.

I SENT TADEAS DOWN TO THE CHURCH TO GET HER. GABRIEL WAS almost done with their talk. When he returned with her, she had, as I suspected, walked too long. She hadn't eaten. She lost time by sleeping too long. Tadeas surprised me with how calmly he reacted. He worried about her, but he took steady care of her. I looked at her body as he laid it on the couch. I could see the bond already forming around her. I saw the remnants of Gabriel's glory on her face. He had touched her to start the bond. It had not spread to Tadeas yet, but it would. I retrieved a few things for when she would awaken, and we waited.

Once she awoke, she told us about the vision. Gabriel had not shared that part with me, but it helped me understand his urgency. She lifted her chin to show Tadeas where Gabriel touched her. He rubbed his finger over the mark. She shivered at his touch, and a purple spark jumped from her to him.

I watched as the bond spread around him, and as it weaved its way around his body, it pulsed with divine light. They were bonded now. There was no turning back.

With her story of the impending doom, I saw the bond around him pulse. He agreed right then to partner up with her. I hoped the decision was of his own doing and not prompted by the bond. I had to believe he decided to join her before he returned here. He was overly eager to return to her. Perhaps her charm had already done the job on him, and the bond acted as a reinforcement of his decision. Either way, it was done.

It didn't mean that they would become intimate or go beyond being partners. But, it did mean that they had Gabriel's blessing in all their endeavors. They could pull on his strength to fight any fight. They were better together than apart. They would not survive apart. While it strengthened them, it was also a beacon to evil. It would be drawn to them. They were bonded by an archangel. They would be a lofty target for someone who wanted to deal a blow to the Almighty.

I wasn't sure what the future held for them, but I knew that her time here was coming to a close. I knew she needed someone. Despite my concerns about the bond, I felt relief watching it swirl around them. I couldn't provide them with that kind of protection anymore, but I knew how important it would be for them. I knew how it would make the evil in the world cringe. That, in itself, made this retired angel smile.

ACKNOWLEDGMENTS

Above all, I have to thank my partner, my guardian, and my soul mate, Jeff. Every wife dreams of a husband who believes in her and supports her dreams as his own. You are my dream come true.

I have to thank my parents who have believed in me for 40 years no matter what endeavor I chose to undertake.

My wonderful friends Tabitha and Kristie, a new friend and an old friend. Your excitement for the story pushed me through to finish this book, and fully plan the entire series for Tadeas and Abigail. Thank you for loving my characters like I do.

Kimbra Swain began writing in her teens, and even submitted books for publishing in her college years. After many rejections, she decided to become a good reader.

Twenty years later, she wrote the book, Abomination, which started an addiction that has produced over twenty-five books in two years.

Kimbra focuses on Southern based Urban Fantasy, but enjoys delving into the realms of fantasy, suspense, and thrillers.

You can view Kimbra's publishing schedule and collection of works on her website.

https://www.kimbraswain.com

Follow Kimbra on Facebook, Twitter, Instagram, Pinterest, and GoodReads.

Made in the USA
Middletown, DE
23 December 2019